AUTHOR	CLASS
BENNETT, R	AFG

TITLE	The second prison

THE
SECOND PRISON

THE
SECOND PRISON

—

Ronan Bennett

HAMISH HAMILTON · LONDON

HAMISH HAMILTON LTD

Published by the Penguin Group
27 Wrights Lane, London W8 5TZ, England
Viking Penguin, a division of Penguin Books USA Inc.
375 Hudson Street, New York, New York 10014, USA
Penguin Books Australia Ltd, Ringwood, Victoria, Australia
Penguin Books Canada Ltd, 2801 John Street, Markham, Ontario, Canada L3R 1B4
Penguin Books (NZ) Ltd, 182–190 Wairau Road, Auckland 10, New Zealand

Penguin Books Ltd, Registered Offices: Harmondsworth, Middlesex, England

First published 1991
1 3 5 7 9 10 8 6 4 2

Copyright © Ronan Bennett, 1991
The moral right of the author has been asserted

Printed in Great Britain by Clays Ltd, St Ives plc

A CIP catalogue record for this book is available from the British Library

ISBN 0-241-13087-5

PART ONE

— I —

The hard men by the bar on the corner wore Wrangler jeans, bomber jackets and lace-up boots. All four were short and pale, and even from where I stood, a few yards away in the smoky shadows of the doorway, it was difficult to tell them apart. Seanie, red-headed, I recognized. He was no taller than the rest, but heavier, threatening. In one hand he held a rolled-up newspaper; the other hid a lighted cigarette from the wind. From time to time he took a drag and surveyed the rain-slick street and the low, bare hills that rose gloomily behind the terraces. He exchanged nods with the occasional passer-by.

To one he said, 'Frankie.'

'Seanie.' And that was that; the man continued on his way.

Seanie smoked and watched the street. Then he smiled, showing his broken teeth. He flicked his cigarette into the road and stuffed the newspaper into his back pocket. 'It's him,' he said. The men with him stiffened.

Maxi Maxwell approached the bar. He threw a calipered leg out slightly to the left and hobbled on. When he reached the corner, Maxi hailed the group. ''Bout ye, men.'

'Maxi, 'bout ye,' Seanie said.

Maxi grinned. He was thirty years old but still like a boy, pleased and always surprised to be in the company of men, and he was flattered that Seanie had addressed him by name in the presence of men. Emboldened, he said, 'You're looking fit, Seanie.'

Seanie grinned back. 'Maxi, straight to the point. Who said this? "We are come to ask an account of all the innocent blood that hath been shed"?'

3

Seanie said it evenly, and Maxi, who had known Seanie all his life, recognized the danger: it was the prelude to something unpleasant and Maxi tried hard to think. But all he could do was laugh nervously and say, in a whisper, 'What?' He looked at the men, from one to the next. They gave nothing away. I could feel Maxi tense.

Then Seanie grinned, the others relaxed, and Maxi eased. 'It's a joke?' Maxi said.

'Aye, it's a great big joke,' Seanie replied in his even tone; the grin faded.

Maxi was confused. He laughed. 'That's a good 'un, Seanie, so it is. Good joke.' He chuckled. He looked at each man in turn, smiling, trying to encourage them. 'Good joke.' But their faces had set like Seanie's. Maxi said, 'Seanie, what's this about, what's the crack?'

'Good question. What's your crack?'

'My crack?'

'Good to see you on form, Maxi. Good to see someone's still got a sense of humour. Something funny about innocent blood?'

Maxi's confusion rose; he hesitated.

'Is there?' Seanie pressed him.

'I don't know. Suppose not, no. Look Seanie, what's the score?'

'Who said, "We are come to ask an account"?'

'Don't know.'

'Oliver Cromwell.'

Maxi's bewilderment was complete, his voice a squeak. 'Cromwell?'

'That's right. And do you know what he said next? In full, he said, "We are come to ask an account of all the innocent blood that hath been shed, and to endeavour to bring to account a certain crippled bastard named Maxi Maxwell."'

No one moved. Maxi looked dumbly at his accuser. On the surface it looked calm, from where I stood it could have been any street encounter between friends – until Seanie lifted his fist and drove it into the side of Maxi's face. There

4

was a crunch, blood, Maxi moaned but did not fall down. Seanie hit him again, on the mouth. Maxi was transfixed, his senses scrambled. Slowly, like a condemned building, its foundations blasted away, he began his descent, slipping sideways until his head cracked the pavement.

'Get him up, Billy,' Seanie said.

Billy needed the help of one of the other men to pull Maxi to his feet. They supported him underneath the arms. Maxi's head lolled stupidly on his chest. Billy took a handful of Maxi's hair and raised his head. He said, admiringly, "Sake Seanie, look what you done to his teeth.' It was impossible to make out the line of Maxi's mouth. The lower part of his face was smashed and smeared with blood. Billy found something on Maxi's collar: a tooth. 'He might have been a cripple, but he did have nice teeth,' Billy said, holding out the tooth. Seanie took it and scrutinized it like a jeweller examining a stone.

'I hate people with nice teeth,' Seanie said. He dropped the tooth to the ground, raised his fist and slammed it again into Maxi's face. 'Don't like people with straight noses, either.'

Billy peered at Maxi's face. 'Well, you and Maxi should get on all right now.'

'Put him in the car.'

*

He looked and dressed like a failing roué, and I loathed him on sight. I loathed the humble manner and the in-gratiating eyes. Smiling too much, he stood at the threshold, waiting for a sign from me. Every part of him strained to please. He handed me a paper bag. I took it. He introduced himself, meekly, as Ralph. I made no reply, and he disengaged without fuss. He was a man used to rejection; the kind disliked by a company of strangers before he had even opened his mouth. He nodded, and was gone. The door pulled to behind him and the key turned in the lock.

It was a week before I saw him again, on exercise. He said brightly, 'Hello there.' I had already forgotten him

5

and would not have recognized him had it not been for the orphan-like look. 'Please like me,' it said, '*please* like me.' I said nothing and watched him walk away to resume his circuits of the yard. Rejected again, he looked dismal and avoided my eyes for the rest of the period. Why, I thought, why did you let that happen?

I looked at him as we came off exercise: grey-haired, stooped, trying hard not to let it get him down, struggling against disappointment. He had put a note in the paper bag he had given me on my first night in the prison. I found it along with the half-dozen teabags and twists of powdered milk and sugar. It said only 'Good luck'. How had he lasted here? How did he get through reception?

When first I had been through it, fifteen years before, the name 'reception' caused me to smile. Then I had confused it with welcomes, homecomings, weddings. It was the remembrance of my own naivety that made me loathe the man; for this reception was cold and stank of carbolic and soiled clothes. In this reception men were photographed, numbered, stripped, measured and weighed.

Here I had repeated my name, age and the date of my last release from prison. My clothes were taken from me and exchanged for regulation 'browns'. The shirt had been freshly starched and was a good fit. The trousers, patched and stained, were for a taller, thicker man. In the shoes the elastic sides had given out and only the grey woollen socks, still damp from sweat that would never wash out, kept them on my feet.

I had arrived at reception late and evening slop-out was already underway. As I passed along 'A' Wing I saw pale men filling jugs and emptying pisspots, and glimpsed through the occasional open door plastic mugs and buckets, and pornographic photographs glued to the walls. We got to the security unit – 'A' Seg – myself and my escort. Different, *apart*, from the main prison, the unit's compactness, neon lighting and muffled sounds evoked the atmosphere of a hospital ward. Then, standing there with my kit, waiting to be led to a cell, I saw a man hobbling towards me. Slopping-out, with fingers clamped round his pisspot and thumbs hooked round crutches, he dragged himself along, alternately heaving his bulk forward and swinging his leg after him. The knot in the leg of his dungarees swayed with the motion. I thought of Maxi Maxwell, but this was not him. This man glanced in my direction, and immediately looked away. He turned and I watched him disappear into the recess to empty his pot.

I was taken to the 'fours' and locked up. There was an iron bed cemented into the floor, a thin foam mattress, some grey army blankets, a wood and steel chair, and a small cupboard fixed to the wall. The previous occupant had kept it tidy: there were no cigarette ends, no dried orange peel, no semen-filled tissues. Half an hour later the door swung open and Ralph appeared bearing his gifts. I forgot him the instant the door closed. I lay on the bed and thought of Tempest.

Tempest the policeman. I thought of the morning of my arrest. I had been sitting in an armchair, my hands cuffed behind me while detectives moved around the flat, prodding floorboards, examining furniture, books, light fittings, curtains. One detective, bad-tempered, agitated, spoke into a walkie-talkie to confirm the van to take me to Paddington Green was in position. Then I saw Tempest for the first time. He was tall and thin-faced, with eyes so deep-set that from some angles they could hardly be seen at all. I was pulled from the chair to my feet and I heard him say, 'Get him some clothes.' By the time they fetched a shirt Tempest had gone. A uniformed policeman draped it over my shoulders, but the detective with the walkie-talkie snatched it away. 'Cunt,' he said. I was half pushed, half pulled through the door of the flat and down the stairs to the street.

A crowd had gathered, large enough but outnumbered by the police and their dogs. I was pushed towards a van and was being hoisted through the rear doors when Tempest reappeared. He said to me, 'Keep your head. You'll be fine.' There was no hint of threat or malice, but his voice was strange. It had control in it, but there was also an edginess. He put my shirt over my shoulders and watched as the doors closed. As the van pulled away I had a picture in my mind of Tempest standing there in the street. I had that image in my mind when he said to me, many hours later during the last round of questioning, 'I've lost my way.'

During our first interrogation at Paddington Green, Tempest said, 'Tell me why you came to England.'

'To work.'

He shook his head. 'No,' he said flatly. He took out a cigarette and lit up. He smoked in silence and, when the paper had shrivelled to the filter, stubbed the butt into an ashtray and shook the packet for another cigarette. 'There's no need for lies. This won't be an interrogation. This is a resolution.'

Again, the voice, its mixture of reason and tension, unnerved me.

'A resolution of what?'

'The past, your past – something that began with Michael Maxwell.'

*

The house was derelict and smelt of damp wallpaper and rotten wood and lino. I entered by the back, through the kitchen, where Dec was waiting for me. 'Upstairs,' he whispered.

In what had been the back bedroom Seanie stretched out, relaxed and comfortable-looking, in a plastic armchair whose foam innards were spilling out from long tears.

'How's the form?' Seanie said pleasantly.

'Where is he?' I replied.

'At the end of the landing. You'll see Billy outside.'

I motioned to Dec to stay with Seanie while I went to the landing. Billy was leaning against the wall, half hidden in an alcove. Silently he indicated a door. I opened it and went inside.

In the corner Maxi Maxwell, dressed in bloody rags, lay

inert and crumpled on the floor. His hands were tied to an iron bedstead and he rested his head on the metal frame. There was blood in his matted hair. I do not know if he heard me, for he did not look up. I crouched on the floorboards beside him and said, 'Maxi, it's me, Kane.' I took his head in my hands; it felt wet, and unpleasantly, frighteningly sticky. I turned his face towards me. His nose had been broken, both eyes blackened. His mouth was a bloody mess.

He mumbled something.

'What?' I said.

Maxi swallowed, the effort paining him, 'You're hurting me.' As gently as I could, I guided his head back to the metal frame. 'Feet,' he groaned.

My eye followed the line of his body from shoulders to waist and legs. I saw that Seanie had taken away his caliper. 'Feet,' he mumbled again. I moved down for a closer look. Both feet were badly bruised. There was blood between his toes, and the soles had been burned.

'Maxi, did you do it?'

In a hoarse whisper he said, 'No.'

In the other room Seanie was still sitting in the plastic armchair.

'Did he give you any trouble?' I asked him.

'No.' Seanie grinned, and pulled on the cigarette. 'He didn't give no trouble.'

'The four of you were able to handle him?'

Seanie's grin vanished. He said defensively, 'You were the one said pick him up. We picked him up. If you send people out to do something, the important thing is that it gets done. This got done. So Maxi got hisself knocked about a bit, a few scratches here and there, that's because he shouldn't have done what he done.'

'What has he said?' I asked Dec.

'Lies,' Seanie said firmly.

'Dec?'

'Like Seanie says, lies.'

'That means he hasn't admitted it?'

9

Dec did not reply. Uncomfortable, he glanced shiftily at Seanie, a silent and guilty appeal to get on with it, to tell me what they had decided in my absence. Seanie got to his feet, sluggishly, like it was an effort, but really because he was squaring up. Some men, when they are preparing for confrontation, move excitedly; they slash the air with their arms and jab fingers and talk quickly and loudly. They are nervous. Other men – Seanie was one – move slowly. They are practised. Long ago, on street corners and bars, they perfected a look of ominous and terrible uninterest that at once signalled contempt for their opponent and for themselves, for although they never betrayed any sign of doubting the outcome, neither did they care about losing; another scar, a split lip, a busted rib – that was nothing new, they could live with it.

Seanie dropped his cigarette to the floor, put both thumbs under his belt and moved them around his waistband. He drew out a Browning 9mm.

'Straight to the point, Kane. We do him tonight.'

The Silver BMW was parked opposite, windows down, glinting in the strong sun. The overheated driver was slumped against the door, his right hand supporting his sweating head, the fingers of the left spread listlessly on the rim of the wheel. In the passenger seat a man leaned back with arms folded, head on chest. Behind them was a third man, his back propped against a rear door, a leg stretching across the seat.

I first noticed them when I returned to the flat in Bayswater. Climbing the steps to the building's front door I saw the three heat-stupefied men cooped up in the BMW. The third man, the one in the back, watched me, apparently without interest, while the others dozed. I found the keys and let myself in. Turning to close the door behind me I glanced at the car. The third man had transferred his indifferent gaze to a pair of tanned, bare legs moving lazily past in a cotton skirt. His face had an arrogance that made me think he could only be a policeman.

The flat was on the fifth floor of the narrow building. I opened a window to let in whatever air there was. The BMW was still there. I went to the kitchen and found some milk; by the time I returned to the window the BMW was gone.

The letter I had been sent contained a name and an address in north London. I would go in the evening. I stripped and lay down and waited for the time to pass.

Surveying the street from the doorstep I found nothing unusual. No bored men, no BMW. I made my way to the address. It turned out to be a shabby house near Finsbury

Park. Dec answered my knock, and before his sense of surprise, or shock, or fear, became whole I said, 'Dec, how's the form?' I said it in a friendly way, to put him at his ease.

Dec had always had a sad face, the cast of a man permanently in retreat. With his mournful moustache and downward-slanting eyebrows I used to think some terrible sadness was poised to overtake him. Now, looking at him, it seemed that he had been overtaken; he seemed a man no longer in retreat, but on the very edge of defeat.

It took him a minute to assess things, and then he said, in a voice I knew to be genuine, 'There's not a day that I haven't thought of you.' He hugged me and patted my back. 'Come on in.'

'How are you keeping?'

'Tolerable. I knew I'd see you again one day, I just had that feeling.'

We passed into his dingy house. Dec put me in the front room with Tommy while he went to inspect the kitchen. Tommy affected not to remember me.

'You're on the pig's back,' Dec said. 'Grainne is just making the tea.' He went to the hall and shouted, 'Grainne, put on a couple more eggs and bacon for Kane.' To me Dec said, 'You look like you haven't eaten for about six months. Did you eat today at all?'

'Earlier, yes.'

'What, like about ten this morning? That's no way to treat yourself. Tommy,' Dec said. 'You know who this is, don't you?'

Tommy began to shake his head and did not stop until Dec said to me, 'He's a terrible over-actor.'

'Tommy hasn't seen me for over five years,' I reminded Dec.

'So he would have been two then. He remembers you rightly. Tommy, you know who this is. It's Kane. This is the man himself.' Dec looked at me and said, 'He's seen your picture. Son, come and say hello to Kane and don't be acting the lig.'

Tommy came over to the chair I had settled in and put

out his hand. 'I'm seven and a half now,' he announced. I shook his small and sticky hand.

'You look older,' I said seriously.

Tommy thought this over, then looked at is father. 'Am I older, da?'

'No son, but you'll soon be eight.'

Satisfied, Tommy went to wake up a mongrel dozing by the sofa.

'When did you get out?' Dec asked.

'In April.'

'Any plans? I didn't think you'd come to England.'

'I've no plans. Just thinking things through.'

'I know the score. Hey!' Dec shouted at Tommy, 'Don't grab the dog's tail.'

'Why not?'

'You wee torturer. Do you want a job in Castlereagh, you wee bastard? Leave the dog's tail!'

'Why?'

'Because it'll bite your hand off.'

'Would it make me cry?'

'You better believe it.'

'I wouldn't cry. I'm brave, so I am.'

'Come here, child.' Dec hauled Tommy to him and sat with the struggling and giggling youngster between his knees. 'I know you wouldn't cry. You're a brave boy.'

I had always admired Dec with his children: he was slapdash, indulgent and put-upon. Only occasionally did their demands and misdemeanours provoke a burst of temper from him; it was short-lived and no grudge was held on either side. Looking at him with Tommy I felt regret, not for the first time, at having come to England to find him.

Dec stroked Tommy's hair and repeated, 'You're a brave boy, but if the dog bites your hand off it'd make life very difficult.'

'Why?'

'Let me show you,' Dec pulled the sleeves of Tommy's scruffy blue cardigan over the boy's hands. 'Now, how do you like it without hands?'

13

'I do like it,' Tommy said defiantly.

'Oh you like it? Let me look at you.' Dec shoved Tommy's head back and peered up the boy's nose. 'Right, there's a good fat bogey in there. Can you feel it?'

Tommy tried to put his hand up.

'You've no hands, remember? Can you feel it?'

Tommy snorted and giggled, 'Yes.' He squirmed between his father's knees.

'Now, how are you going to get it out?'

'I don't want to.'

'Oh no? I thought it was your favourite pastime, picking bogeys.'

'So it is. He's disgusting,' Grainne, Dec's daughter, said. She had appeared at the door from the kitchen. She carried two plates, knives and forks, and had a Saxa salt carton tucked under her elbow. 'I'm nothing but a skivvy,' she said to me, with a smile. 'Hello, Kane. How long have you been out now?'

'A few weeks.'

'And are you staying out this time, or what?'

'I think I'll stay out.'

'Really? I thought there must be something you liked in the Kesh, the way you kept going back.'

'What age are you now, Grainne?' I asked.

'Thirteen,' she said, reddening.

'You're getting very cheeky for thirteen.'

'I'm not cheeky, just smart. I take after my da. Anyway,' Grainne said, 'you're just a wee lad yourself, Kane.'

'Kane hasn't been a wee lad since Moby Dick was a tadpole,' Dec said, with mock outrage. 'Listen, love, get us a couple of cans from the fridge.'

'See what I mean? Nothing but a skivvy.' Grainne disappeared into the kitchen.

'She's still got a powerful notion of you, you know.' Dec released Tommy as he arranged his plate on his lap. 'Go and watch the TV,' he told his son. Tommy settled in front of the television and tried to pick his nose.

'She's growing up to be lovely,' I said.

'No hands, remember!'

Tommy turned and gave Dec a gap-toothed grin.

'The notorious Ulster fry,' Dec said as he plunged a fork into a fat sausage.

'Where's Cappy?' I asked.

'How would I know? She's only my wife.'

'Where's your wife?'

'That's what I'm saying. I haven't a clue. She still lives here, I mean.' He glanced at me. 'Forget it. It's not a cheerful subject.' Dec called into the kitchen and Grainne reappeared with two cans of lager. We sat eating and drinking. After a time Dec got the children to agree to go to bed.

'Will you come up and sing to me, daddy?' Tommy asked.

'I will.' Dec blushed. He said to me, 'He thinks I'm a brilliant chanter.'

'He is too,' Tommy shouted.

'See? Frank Sinatra, me. Now go on up to bed. I'll be up in a minute. You too, Grainne.' Reluctantly they went. 'Grainne,' Dec shouted as she passed to the stairs, 'make sure he cleans his teeth, and give his face a wipe.'

Dec got another couple of cans from the kitchen.

'Do you think you'll stay in London long?' he asked.

'Not long.'

'By the way, how did you know where I was living?' Dec was guarded.

'Why? Is it a secret?' I said jokingly, to make it harder for Dec to press the point.

'Of course not, but, like, we haven't been in touch with anyone since we left, and that was a pile of years ago.'

'Five years,' I said.

'Would be about that.' Dec was getting uncomfortable. We finished the cans in silence. Dec asked if I wanted another and I asked for coffee instead.

'Coffee? You can't have coffee. Grainne has already gone to bed. There's no one to make it.'

'I'll make it.'

'Listen,' I said, when my coffee was finished, 'I'm going to leave in a minute. Are you doing anything on Wednesday night?'

'Nothing more than this,' he said, indicating his beer can. 'You fancy having a proper drink?'

'Yes.'

'Good! Look, I'll tell you what. Let's you and me get steaming and have some crack. What do you say?'

'Where?'

'There's a bar . . .'

'What about outdoors?'

'Al fresco? Like at home? There's a fine spot near here – a disused railway line. Wait there.' He slapped my back and got up. 'I'll just tuck the kids in. I won't be two minutes.' He left the room and I watched the television. A few moments later Grainne reappeared in an oversized dressing-gown, probably her mother's.

'My da forgot his drink,' she said, without looking at me. She snatched Dec's can and ran out of the room. I waited for about a quarter of an hour and, when Dec had not come down, I went up the stairs. From the landing I saw him kneeling at a double bed.

'Sing the one about the Thompson gun,' Tommy pleaded.

'Whisht! You'll wake Emmet. No, I'll sing "She moved through the fair", okay?'

And Dec sang.

> *'My young love said to me, "My mother won't mind,*
> *And my father won't slight you for your lack of kind."*
> *And she put her hand on me, and this she did say,*
> *"It will not be long, love, till next market day."'*

His voice was flat, but not unpleasant. I had heard it many times before and the memory of it made my heart ache. When Tommy at last succumbed, Dec kissed his forehead. He leaned across, kissed another sleeping infant and pulled the covers around them. As he came out of the room he was startled to see me.

'He thinks I'm the world's greatest singer,' he said, closing the door behind him. 'In fact, he thinks I'm great, full stop.' I watched him start down the stairs. 'Wait till he grows up.'

16

'Was that another child in the bed with him?'

'Emmet,' Dec said. 'You won't have seen him. He's only two. He's the image of wee Dec. Not just the way he looks, the way he gets on. Everything about him reminds me of wee Dec.'

Dec opened the front door for me and said, 'It's good to see you again.'

'Where's this disused line you were telling me about?'

Dec stepped out of the doorway and pointed to a bridge over the road. 'Just there,' he said. 'You get to it up the side of that bridge.'

I was about to go when he stopped me and said, 'You haven't mentioned the thing about wee Maxi.'

'What's the point? It's over a lot of years ago now. No one came out of it well.'

'You come out of it worst.'

'Maxi came out of it worst.'

'I swear to God if I could turn the clock back,' Dec said.

'Me too. But it happened and it's over.'

Dec regarded me sadly and nodded, as if in resignation. He looked away for a moment and then hung his head. He said quietly, 'You're not here to play a game on me, are you, Kane?'

I put my hand on his shoulder and said, 'No.' I wanted to say more to put him at ease, but could think of nothing to add, nothing I could say convincingly.

'See you on Wednesday,' I said as I left.

'Wednesday it is,' Dec replied, with forced cheerfulness.

I waited at a bus stop on the main road. I recognized Cappy's walk long before I made out her face. She had changed more than Dec: her hair was cropped and severe; there were bitter lines around her mouth, and her eyes seemed smaller, more confident, but also more suspicious. She stopped when she saw me, looked away for a moment to compose herself, and said, 'Hail the returning hero. I knew this would happen. I bet you planned this in your cell, sitting there wallowing in self-pity, how you would return. Am I in character for you? That's part of it, isn't it?

Rejection? But of course the hero takes it so stoically, giving nothing away of the hurt he feels so terribly inside. And then he wins them over with some heroic deed. What deed have you in mind, Kane? Some little murder? Another shooting in an entry? Another corpse thrown from a passing car?'

I had no reply for her. She bit her lip, and after a moment asked viciously, 'Is the bastard steaming?'

Cappy had two characters: one ironic and perceptive; the other the Belfast fishwife, weary of her husband's shiftlessness and refusal to make something of his life, shrilly resentful of his inability to provide for her, hating the streets she lived in and frightened of the world outside. There had been a time when she used to switch from one to the other to amuse us; now it was a declaration that she had outgrown us and seen through us.

'He's had a drink.'

'*A* drink?' she said. 'A *single* drink? Well, let's be thankful for small mercies.'

'Would you come for a drink with me?'

'Is this how the fantasy goes? We go for a drink and you, with your noble manner, start to win me over?'

I had first met Cappy thirteen years before, in Belfast. One night at a drinking club Dec and I were sitting at a long table, in company: there was Roisin, Hughie and Siobhan, and, in a corner, out of the flow of the conversation, Maxi Maxwell. Dec tugged my arm and pointed to another table, to a girl with long dark hair. She wore a shiny blue blouse and a tight black skirt; she was in high heels. 'Isn't she lovely? She's looked over here a couple of times.'

'What makes you think she's interested in you?' Hughie, who had overheard him, mocked.

Normally Dec would have risen to the banter, but not this time. He kept his eyes fixed on the girl and did not turn to Hughie. Siobhan raised a knowing eyebrow, and then her drink. Hughie made a face.

'I didn't think she was at first,' Dec said to me, 'but the last time she looked straight at me and smiled.'

This was not how Dec usually talked, and the company fell silent to take it in.

'What are you staring at?' he said, glancing sideways at us.

'I thought it was Declan Mulholland,' Hughie said, 'but it can't be. It's someone like him talking like a human being for a change.'

'Fuck you!'

'It is you after all!'

'Your man's in love,' wee Maxi smirked.

'Shut up, runt,' Hughie said.

Dec swallowed his drink and got to his feet. He ran a hand through his hair and smoothed the front of his shirt before walking to the girl's table. He bent down and whispered to her. She nodded, got up and walked with Dec to the dance floor. They did not dance well, but Dec at least was unselfconscious. When the band started a slow number Dec gently pulled the girl to him and, after a token resistance, she hung on to him. When the last dance was over Dec whispered to her. The girl smiled demurely, and Dec took her hand and brought her to our table.

'This,' he said, 'is Cappy McDonald. And this is Kane. His real name is Augustine, but for obvious reasons he prefers to be called Kane. This is Roisin, who goes with Kane, and who's very smart and clever. She's studying to be a lawyer.'

'Which is very handy, Cappy. She can get us all out of trouble,' Hughie said, leaning forward and beaming. 'I'm Hughie.'

'Do yous often get into trouble?' Cappy asked, surprised.

'Never,' Dec said glaring at Hughie. 'This is Hughie . . .'

'I already told her.'

'. . . Hughie, who isn't smart and clever, as you have probably already noticed. That's Siobhan, who's unlucky enough to be his wife, but who bears her cross with fortitude.'

Cappy took a seat next to Dec's.

'Can I get you a drink, Cappy? I said.

'I'm Michael Maxwell,' Maxi said, pushing himself forward.

'Oh yes,' Dec said. 'This is wee Maxi.'

'Hello, Maxi,' Cappy said pleasantly.

'Are you anything to the McDonalds from the Clonard?' Maxi asked. 'Jim McDonald is the one doing life for a Brit. You've got the same kind of nose as him.'

''Sake Maxi,' Hughie said, exasperated.

'Cappy, would you like a drink?' I repeated.

'A Babycham,' Cappy said.

From that night Dec and Cappy McDonald, seventeen years old and still at school, were inseparable. They went everywhere, did everything, together. In the streets they went arm in arm, and the kids on the corners used to taunt them, threatening to get a saw to saw them apart. Dec just smiled; he could not believe his luck. As a couple they were a contrast. Cappy had been shy at first, but she soon showed she was intelligent, quick-witted and firm in her dealings with other people. She compensated for Dec, who was lazy, generous and easy-going. They seemed always to be happy.

Two months after the dance Cappy was pregnant, four weeks later she and Dec were married. I was the best man.

At the reception, where the men wore Burton's suits and nylon shirts, everyone was drunk and happy. Hughie asked Dec, 'What made you get married, then?'

'Simple,' Cappy intervened. 'My da held a shotgun to his neck and asked him if he was going to disgrace me.'

'What'd you tell him?' Hughie asked Dec.

Dec said, 'I said to the aul' lad, "Just make it quick." '

'You're a bad man, Declan Mulholland,' Cappy said, and she kissed him.

Cappy and I got to a nearby bar just before closing time and Cappy bullied the barman into serving us. When we got to a table she said, 'He always drank too much, even back home.'

'We were all surprised when he came to live here. Why did he do that?'

'Do I not count? What is it with you people? Why do

you say, "him, him, him?" Have I nothing to do with it? Am I only a woman and I don't count? *He*,' she said savagely, 'came here because *I* told him to. What are *you* doing over here, anyway?'

'I won't be here long.'

'Not if the Branch get their hands on you. Do they know you're over here? Are you wanted?'

'I got out only a couple of weeks ago. I'm not wanted.'

Cappy swallowed her drink. 'Listen you to me,' she said. 'Dec is a very soft man. Being lifted and in the Crum, all that shattered him. He has never really been himself since. And then there was Hughie and Maxi, and,' her voice thickened, 'wee Dec. All that wrecked him. We needed to get away. I didn't want to come at first. You know I'd never been out of Belfast except to Donegal, remember? I didn't want to come, but I knew we couldn't stay.'

I did not want to hear any more. I finished my drink and got up. Cappy looked at me as if I had done something surprising, then she laughed.

'You just get up and walk away?' she said. She drained her own glass. 'Nothing new in that, I suppose. That was always your way. Prison hasn't changed you, Kane.'

'Prison doesn't change people,' I said. 'It just makes you more of what you were before you went in.'

'God help us then,' Cappy said quietly.

We went outside and I said goodnight.

Cappy said, 'You only get one chance at life, Kane. To have a chance we needed to get away, from the town and all the things that happened there. You being here is wrong.' She paused, perhaps to give me a chance to make some reply. When I said nothing she went on, 'Look, I'm sorry about what I said when I saw you. But it's not good for us.'

I said to Cappy, 'Don't be sorry. A lot of it, maybe all of it, was true. I won't be back.'

Cappy touched my arm in gratitude. But I had lied to her. Even as I looked at her standing in front of me, tears just behind her eyes, and with Tommy and Grainne and

Dec's sad singing still in mind, I lied to her. I was going to see Dec again, and I was going to kill him.

I took a taxi back to the flat. The BMW was parked in the street.

— 3 —

Access to the exercise yard for Category 'A' prisoners was through the gable end of 'A' Seg and down an iron staircase. The yard was small, but never crowded. The security unit contained about thirty remand prisoners, most of them armed robbers, who were exercised in two batches twice daily for half an hour. But the robbers preferred life and card games indoors, and even on the sunniest days there were rarely more than five or six men out at any one time.

The yard was fenced off by thick wire sheeting, but it was just possible to see where the ordinary prisoners walked, and see the path leading from reception to 'H' Wing, the prison hospital. One hot afternoon I watched three screws, one with a dog, escort an elderly prisoner towards the hospital. The man wore regulation 'browns' and clutched a pillowcase stuffed with his belongings. He walked awkwardly and stumbled more than once. The screws sniggered and jostled him. The dog-handler encouraged his animal to growl and snap. It was not until the party was close up that I realized the prisoner was blind. One of his escorts thrust out a foot, pitching him forward. The screws snorted. When they picked him up I could see that he had scuffed a temple. It was not the prisoner's only injury. His face and neck bore several violent marks, some old, some new. Behind me someone shouted to the screws, 'You heartless bastards!'

'He's a fucking nonce,' a screw replied matter-of-factly. 'Save your breath. He's been putting it up little boys.'

The blind prisoner was hauled to his feet and dragged towards 'H' Wing. His pillowcase lay on the ground, a reward for the black alsatian, which ripped and tossed it. By the time the dog was led away the shredded remains of the miserable possessions were scattered everywhere. The warm breeze picked up a letter and wrapped it against the wire.

'It's inhuman!' I turned to see Ralph staring after the blind prisoner.

'Fuck him. He's only a nonce,' a blond-haired man, a robber I had noticed in the yard exercising with two other men, replied. His friends laughed. One of them said, 'It was a *bit* wicked. His eyes didn't look too kosher.' They laughed again and resumed their circuits, occasionally glancing at Ralph as they would at a freak. Here, a show of concern for anyone who was not a close friend was taken as proof of simple-mindedness. Ralph stood staring at the pillowcase. This time, for the first time, I did not feel loathing or contempt. Harden your heart, I told him silently, harden your heart.

I left him standing at the wire and walked on. Ten minutes later a screw announced the end of exercise and summoned us into the unit. As we climbed the iron staircase I glanced back at the yard. Ralph was still there, but on his knees, plucking at the letter on the other side of the wire, hurrying to retrieve it as a screw shouted at him to get inside.

Later that day, as I passed along the landing of the 'fours', the blond-haired man called me into his cell. He had the manner of someone who expected his invitations to be accepted. Inside there were three men playing cards.

'I'm Dave,' the blond-haired man said. 'That's Ron, that's another Dave, and that's Terry.' A couple of the men nodded.

'So what you in for then? Paddy stuff?'

'What?'

'IRA, that sort of thing. Bombs.'

'No bombs. Conspiracy.'

'Yeah? Ron's on a conspiracy. They're a bit, what's the word, loose, aren't they? I mean, they got it all their own way with a charge like that. The pross can say you were going to do this or you were going to do that, and how can you prove you weren't going to do it?' Dave asked, indignant at the manifest injustice of it.

'You don't have to prove anything in court!' Ron rebuked him. 'Only the pross has got to prove something. That's the law.'

'But it ain't the facts. When you get in there, in the dock, it ain't the law that counts, it's the facts.'

'If I was you, Dave, I'd pin my hopes on the law. If the facts come out at your trial you'll be doing bird for the rest of your natural life.' It was a new voice. I turned to see the one-legged man leaning on his crutches in the doorway.

The other men greeted the new arrival warmly; he was evidently well liked. They called him Benny.

'Now's your chance, Dave. Ask Benny about that bird, the one with the chain,' Terry said.

'Listen,' Dave said to Benny. 'If a bird wears a chain on her ankle, what does that mean?'

'No idea,' Benny replied without interest.

Dave said, 'Me and Terry were at this party and there was a bird. She was *lovely*. She had on a little chain, gold, on her ankle. And that means, if a bird wears one of these gold chains, or it can be silver, on her ankle, it means she does oral.'

'Bollocks.'

'It's a fact, it is.'

They did not notice me leaving, except Benny, who gave a half-nod. I went on to my own cell. As I entered I glanced across the landing to the cell opposite. Through the open door I saw Ralph sitting on his bed and staring at the barred window. He held a letter in his hand.

A little later I was slopped-out, then locked up again. I paced the cell; time passed. I had no idea what hour it was when the night guard turned on the security light and bathed the cell in a warm red glow. I lay down to sleep.

At six o'clock the fluorescent light bounced off the walls. I made to shield my eyes. The door swung open. From my

25

bed I saw drowsy men carrying pisspots on their way to the recess. They padded along, hair uncombed, eyes bleary, faces stubbled. A radio played pop music. I got up to join the procession, emptied my pot, and picked up a plastic bowl and mug to queue for breakfast. I returned to the cell. The door closed and the key turned in the lock.

*

The interrogation room was painted in magnolia and lime green and was lit by a neon strip with a protective cover. There was a small, high window. Outside it was getting dark. Between us there was a table, its surface scored, its legs chipped, on which Tempest had placed a number of manila folders. Occasionally he would rise from his chair and silently circle the room. At intervals an officer would knock and enter and offer to bring coffee. Once, Tempest sent out for more cigarettes. But for most of the time we simply sat in silence. I stared at the wall, the window, the floor. It was six days after my arrest.

At length Tempest said, 'Michael Maxwell was a pathetic character from all accounts. Polio, cleft palate. He was a baby when his father deserted the family, mother an alcoholic. Maxwell himself drank heavily, probably also an alcoholic. Worked for a year as a butcher's boy when he was fifteen, after that permanently unemployed. Unmarried. Approved school, borstal, two jail terms for theft. Only stopped thieving when he joined the movement. Not much of a life.'

I shrugged.

'You people have such low expectations.' There was something in his tone, almost an accusation. 'Maxwell probably never complained,' he said.

'No. He never did.'

'Do you complain?'

'No.'

'Augustine Kane. Age thirty-two. 1973 interned, aged seventeen. In 1977 jailed for eight years on possession of a firearm, unloaded, under suspicious circumstances. Released January 1982, with remission. Out a year. Jailed for ten years on a charge of possession with intent to endanger life. Released, only six weeks ago, after serving five years, four months. Now facing more charges. Have you no complaints? Are your expectations so low?'

'I have no complaints.'

Tempest lit another cigarette and I watched him as he smoked. I had been interrogated many times before and, more than once, by violent policemen. I had never been afraid and I had never given away any information, nor made any kind of incriminating statement. I had always held out. Tempest did not appear violent, but I felt more uneasy with him than I had done with any other interrogator. The edge in his voice produced in me a sense of foreboding. There was nothing I could do except wait to see what would happen.

We sat in silence for another hour, perhaps longer; then we began to talk about Maxi.

*

I stood by one of the plastic bins at the end of the landing and scraped out of my bowl the remainder of a prison breakfast. Blond Dave joined me to toss away some of the food he had not found time to eat. As a robber Dave liked to maintain his standard of living in prison. He would not eat prison food, but was never short of supplies. Over the weeks I had become used to seeing the robbers prepare for visits with their girlfriends and wives. They showered and shaved and went off smelling of too much talc and lotion, and when they returned they bore enormous trays of cooked meats, tinned vegetables, chocolates, fruit and cigarettes, more than they could consume. They tended not to give anything away, for they believed that charity demeaned the recipient, and uneaten food they simply threw out.

'Can you believe it?' Benny said. He had dragged himself to the bin and was peering in at the discarded food. He shook his head. 'What a waste.' He called after Dave, 'There's a famine in Africa!'

'What do I care about a bunch of darkies,' Dave shouted back, without turning round.

Benny said, 'If someone like Hitler ever comes back the first place he can recruit is in here. Benny Morris.' He put out a hand. 'We ain't been properly introduced.'

Later, in the exercise yard, I was surprised to see Benny work his way in careful, slow stages down the iron staircase. It took some effort, and once or twice I thought he might give up. But, refusing the help proffered by the robbers, he succeeded in making it to the yard. He joined me on my circuits.

'I ain't been out since . . . when? December, come to think of it,' he said. 'I used to take exercise all the time during my last lot of bird. I just finished a ten eighteen months before I came in this time.'

He dragged himself along and said, thoughtfully, 'One thing I cannot get used to is the crap that's talked in here. I saw you that day in Dave's cell. You thought that was a lot of crap, didn't you? You don't hide that too well. To think we're going to have to listen to more of the same every day we're in here.'

We did a couple of laps before Benny said he needed to rest. We picked a corner in the sun and Benny, his back against the wire, slid carefully to the ground.

'I can do that no problem. It's getting up that kills me,' he said cheerfully.

'How did it happen?'

'A shotgun. I drove up to Birmingham, on my way to do the shopping. I park the car and what happens? I was outside the supermarket when this character with a sawn-off robs a security guard right in front of my car. Well, me being an upstanding citizen and all that, I said, "Now look here, my good fellow. Put down that firearm and give yourself up. Crime does not pay." And know what he did then?'

'What?'

'Bastard shot me. Left me lying in my own blood. You can imagine the scene. There's me lying on the pavement with a great big hole in my thigh. This geezer, he drops the sawn-off and legs it. Now the thing is so confused, happens so quick, that the security guard thinks I'm the thief. He rushes over and puts his foot on my neck. I'm lying there, claret all over the pavement, and he puts his foot on my neck and shouts for the police. They come and by that stage I'm too far gone to tell them that it wasn't me. So they arrest me.'

Benny continued, 'I ain't complaining really. But in my blacker moments I tend to think I've been a little hard done by. Instead of getting a medal for foiling a desperate robbery, I'm nicked.'

'Your previous probably counted against you.'

'True, but I done my time, paid my debt, and that should be the end of that. Instead, when I'm lying there in Birmingham, my leg hanging by a thread with some idiot stamping on my neck, the police get the wrong end of the stick. I'm going to write to the papers. I think it's important for the public to know that if they find themselves in the same situation like what I was in, on no account should they have a go. I did, and look what's happened. Instead of getting a George Medal, I'm banged up.'

'If I was you I'd try to get a better line of defence at your trial.'

'You think so? I was hoping to leave the court without a stain on my character. Didn't you believe it?'

'No.'

'I was looking forward to trying it out on you. Get an unbiased opinion, if you know what I mean. You really didn't believe it?'

'No.'

'I've held something back.'

'The car was stolen?'

'Borrowed, I like to think. There's something else.'

'Where were you living?'

'You spotted that? As it happens, I'm living in London and I'm doing my shopping in Birmingham.'

'Does seem a long way to go for your baked beans.'

'It wasn't baked beans. I'm one of these people that likes to buy the month's groceries in one go.'

'Bulk buying.'

'Bulk buying. Saves money in the long run.'

'You holding anything else back?'

'One more thing.'

'Fingerprints on the shotgun?'

'I can explain them. It's the shells in my pocket I'm having trouble with.'

'And you were hoping to leave the court without a stain on your character?'

'Help me up and we can do another lap.' I took him underneath the arms and made to hoist him up. He was heavy and for a moment I was afraid I'd drop him.

'I've really got to lose some weight,' he panted when he at last managed to get to his feet. 'I don't get enough exercise. I should come out more. I think I will.'

We had finished the lap by the time the screw called us in. It was a long, slow climb up the stairs for Benny. He was gasping for breath by the time he made it into the unit. On our way to the cells we saw Ralph. Benny said, 'He's back.'

'Where's he been?'

'You don't socialize enough, you disagreeable bastard. If you don't get about, you don't hear nothing. Old Ralph was down on the block.'

'What for?'

'You remember that blind nonce, the one our fearless prison officers bravely tackled in the yard? Well, old Ralph was a trifle miffed about it, got himself into a right state. He found a letter belonging to the nonce. So along he goes to the PO. Ralph gives him the letter and says it should be sent on. The PO ripped it up in front of him and said something like what does a blind nonce want with a letter anyway, which I thought was a fair enough point. Anyway, Ralph went potty. 'Course Dave and the others thought he was a mental case. Poor old geezer, he don't belong here.'

It was time for lock-up.

'See you tomorrow,' I said to Benny.

'Take care.'

During the night I thought about Ralph. Benny was

right, he did not belong here: he was too soft, too un-prepared for this kind of life. I did not care much one way or the other about him, I still would not have spoken to him, but next morning during slop-out I passed an open cell and heard the sound of a man sobbing. I backed up far enough to see inside. There was Ralph. He sat on the bed with his hands between his knees. His shoulders trembled with each wretched sob. Tears dripped from his nose and chin on to his thighs.

Unable to bring myself to go in, I left him. But that afternoon when exercise was called I made my way to his cell. He looked weak, but managed a smile. Dark, long lips spread across receded gums and capped teeth.

'We met the first night I came in,' I said. 'But I wasn't too aware of what was going on, so I didn't say much.'

'I know how it is, old boy. After all that time with the police, all the questions. When you get to your cell the last thing you want is people barging in on you. I should have left it to the morning, but I thought you might need a few odds and ends.'

'No problem. I was grateful. Thanks.'

'Don't mention it. My pleasure,' he replied formally.

After exchanging a few further polite words I asked if he wanted to go on exercise. 'I would be delighted,' he replied.

I wore a pair of prison-issue dungarees I had picked up from the screw who kept the kit; they were more comfort-able and more convenient than the 'browns'. The afternoon sun was warm and I had not bothered to put on a shirt. Ralph, however, was smartly dressed. He wore a light-brown shirt, a mauve cravat and a pair of keenly creased navy slacks. 'My loved one is coming to visit this afternoon,' he explained, indicating his slacks and polished shoes. I immediately thought up a grey-haired wife for him: worried and decent.

'How are you settling in?' he asked me.

'Tolerable.'

Slowly, our conversation became less stilted. We walked

31

and made prison-yard small talk. Ralph described the routine; he told me which screws were best avoided and which were approachable. He also pointed out one or two of the more famous robbers and made approving noises at the high sums they had stolen. Blond Dave, he recounted with undisguised admiration, had stolen more than half a million pounds from a security van. He and three other men had ambushed it in the Blackwall Tunnel while it was out of radio contact.

'They were able to take as long as they liked to get the thing open. They used chainsaws. The whole thing was terribly impressive,' Ralph concluded.

'What are you in for? Not robbery?' I asked.

'Lord no! Fraud. I'm just as crooked as everyone else in here. I'm just as much a thief as the robbers, but I couldn't use violence. I'm not judging those who do. We all have our skills, it's just that mine don't run in the direction of the pavement. I wouldn't feel right about using force.'

'Any particular reason?'

Ralph said, 'I think it probably has to do with being in the Air Force. I was in Korea. I didn't like what I saw.'

'What was that?'

'A long story, old boy.'

Ralph went silent, to suggest, I supposed, some experience that had had a profound impact on his life. If he was in for fraud he must be part conman; but for a conman he was not much of an actor. Still, he seemed decent so I consented to go along with his story.

'What are you doing in 'A' Seg? They don't normally put fraud cases in here.'

'Another long story, old boy. I'll talk to you about it, if ever we have an uninterrupted week together.'

A whistle blew. We finished our lap of the yard. At the foot of the stairs I was about to ask Ralph more about his charges when a small, black-haired boy, whom I had not noticed in the yard, brushed impatiently past. He turned to rebuke me for getting in his way, but instead of speech he made a strangled sound at the back of his throat and looked at me with violent eyes before hurrying up the stairs.

'That's Anthony,' Ralph said.
'What did he say?'
'Didn't you hear?' Ralph said. 'He said; "Fuck you."'

— 4 —

When I heard the knock my first thought was that it was the police; my second was to check for the BMW. It was nowhere in sight. There was a second knock. I went to the window and leaned out to take in the square. The silver car was not there and I relaxed. I opened the door to Penny – that was the name she gave. She was tall, taller than me, in her late twenties, with confident good looks. She pushed a strand of dark hair behind her ear and smiled.

'Hello,' she said, widening the smile. 'I'm from the flat above.' Her eyes were hazel and flirtatious, and her voice had an affected coolness. 'I was hoping to find you in. You see, my agent called today. Apparently he's found me some work, at last. Goneril, in *Lear*.' She added languidly, 'I'm an actress.'

'I see.'

'Only rep, of course, boring old rep.' Her voice quickened, 'I was wondering if I could leave my keys with you. You see, yesterday, before I knew about the part, I arranged for the plumber to come to see to my pipes. They've been giving me such horrible trouble. Frightful clanking noises. You can probably hear the clamour down here?'

'I hadn't noticed.'

'Oh good,' she said. The problem is that the plumber is coming tomorrow. I don't want to cancel because it's such a nuisance trying to get them to come out again. I thought if you were going to be in I could leave the keys with you, and get the plumber to call here for them. Would that be possible?'

'No problem. Leave the keys with me.'

She rewarded me with her brightest smile. 'It will save me the most horrendous trouble. Would you mind terribly watering my plants on Sunday? I'll be back the following weekend.' She pressed the keys into my hand. 'These are a spare set. Just pop them through the letterbox when you're done. And do help yourself to a drink while you're there. There's Irish whiskey. You are Irish? I thought I detected a certain lilting in your voice.'

'Only southerners lilt. We Belfast people speak from the back of the throat.'

She laughed, 'Not at all, it's a lovely accent.'

'I'm not sure I'll be here at the weekend. If I am I'll water your plants.'

'Oh, that's so kind. Don't worry if you're not here, they'll survive. They have often enough in the past. Are you going on holiday?'

'No. I think I'll be leaving the flat.'

'Really? You haven't been here long. At least, I'm sure I haven't seen you.'

'Three weeks,' I said.

'Are you moving somewhere else?'

'I don't know yet.'

'Very mysterious,' she said.

'Indecisive. I'll probably be gone by Sunday. But if I'm still here I'll water your plants.'

'Thanks *so* much. He'll probably come quite early,' she said, 'the plumber. He'll be here at the crack of dawn.'

'I get up early.'

'Are you sure? You really are kind.'

'No problem.'

'I hope I'll see you again.'

'I'll probably be gone by the time you get back.'

'Not if you're so indecisive. I'm sure I'll see you again.' She turned to go, looked at me sideways and said, 'Bye.'

That afternoon I sat at the window and watched the tourists go back and forth from their hotels in the square. I thought of Dec. Tomorrow night I would see him.

*

35

Dec came out of prison in March 1982. He had spent eighteen months on remand in Crumlin Road on charges of membership, murder, attempted murder, conspiracy and possession. Few people rated Dec's chances and most had already consigned him to the far reaches of their memories where they keep dead friends and brothers. The trial had been going on for more than two months when the prosecution case unexpectedly collapsed, and Dec, who on the day it ended woke at seven, showered, shaved and dressed and was in court by ten, found himself home at two in the afternoon. The night before, his lawyers had told his relatives that the next day's proceedings would be taken up with complicated legal arguments. Cappy and Dec's mother, for whom the trial was bearable only during the cross-examination of the police by the defence, did not turn up. Consequently, when Dec walked through his own back door that afternoon Cappy and his mother looked at him as if at a ghost. After the kisses and hugs and tears, Dec took his family to Donegal for a holiday. They were gone a fortnight. The day after their return Cappy invited Roisin and me to the house for a drink. That night I had to see Seanie. I told Roisin I would join her later.

'It'll be good to have Dec back,' I said to Seanie.

'That's if his bangers are still in one piece,' Seanie said. 'If he's still as good as he was he'll come in handy. It'll keep the Brits on the run, in our district anyway.'

'I don't see any sign of them running.'

'They're taking a hiding here. Two dead in the last five weeks, and a peeler. That's why they've brought in this so-called expert Branchman – to try to sort us out.' Seanie grinned. The Branchman's arrival a couple of weeks earlier, widely discussed and unanimously scorned in the district, he saw as a personal triumph, testimony to his prowess.

I made my way to Dec's house. Dec sat on the sofa cradling his infant son Tommy. Grainne went promiscuously from admirer to admirer. Hughie, Siobhan and Roisin sat drinking and talking. Dec stayed in his seat when I entered. He put out a hand and I took it.

'How are you?' I asked him.

'Sound.' He smiled, but sounded subdued.

Cappy brought me a drink and hugged me. She was trembling so much that her body against mine felt like feathers. She kissed me and said, 'I'm so happy.' But her voice sounded strained and anxious. I drew my head back and saw tears in her eyes.

There was a sharp knock on the door. 'Whisht!' Cappy hushed us. 'That'll be the tickman and I've nothing to give him.' There was a second knock; everyone was still. 'Mrs Mulholland! Mrs Mulholland!' a voice called. Cappy, eyes wide, a finger to her lips, turned to each of us. The tickman called again, but he had a forlorn tone; he had already accepted defeat. After a minute we heard his departing footsteps.

'Thank God for that.' Cappy flopped down beside Dec and lifted a drink. 'Kane, you want to do something about that man. He causes me more trouble than the Brits.' Cappy was exaggerating to amuse us. She was in her role of Belfast fishwife.

'I'll look into it,' I said.

'I thought you'd do more than that. If yous can keep the Brits out of here, how hard do you have to look into fixing a tickman?'

Dec said to me, 'I hear the Brits have been taking a pasting round here.'

'They have. And they're running around like crazy scooping practically everyone,' I said.

'Watch yourself, boy,' he said.

Siobhan said confidentially, repeating the rumour sweeping the district, 'They've called in some Branchman from England.'

'He'll have his work cut out for him,' Hughie laughed.

'Enough of all that,' Cappy said. She put on some music and tried to pull Dec to his feet to dance, but he shrugged her off. She was hurt but tried not to let it show.

'You know,' she said, 'I think they turned him queer in there. Since they let him go he hasn't laid a finger on me once.' Cappy glanced at the sullen Dec to see if he would respond to her banter. When he did not she continued, with a last effort. 'He hasn't, you know,' she said directly to me, 'been making any unusual approaches to you, has he? I mean, you two were always great friends.'

'Anything in that, Dec?' Hughie said.

Siobhan punched her husband hard in the arm. 'Stop you talking dirty in front of the child,' she said with a glance at Grainne.

'Grainne, go you upstairs to bed,' Cappy ordered the child.

'Let her alone,' Dec said wearily.

'It's half-past nine nearly. She should be in bed. These children need some discipline. That wee Dec runs about the streets like a wee hood.'

'Where's wee Dec now?' Siobhan asked.

'Out roaming the streets,' Cappy said. 'Go on, child,' she told Grainne, 'up the stairs.'

'Will you come up, daddy? To sing to me?' Grainne pleaded.

'I'll be up, darling. Do as your ma says.'

Grainne kissed Dec with a great show of affection, then Cappy.

'And what about Kane? Have you stopped kissing him?' Cappy teased. Grainne fled from the room. From the stairs she shouted to her mother, 'You're terrible, so you are!'

'Don't you talk to me like that, you wee scallywag! Get up those stairs!' Cappy said to me, 'She has a notion of you, you know. You better watch out, Roisin. She's a wee hussy.'

Dec said sharply, 'She's six years old. Give the wee girl a minute's peace.'

'I was only joking,' Cappy said, exasperated. 'You can say nothing to him.' She slapped Dec's thigh playfully, and when he pulled a pained and put-upon face she jumped on him and started to pull his hair.

38

'Now children!' Roisin said.

'Don't stop me, Roisin, this is as near as I've been able to get to him since he's got out.'

''Sake!' Dec said between his teeth.

Cappy, suddenly with a softness in her voice, said, 'I know darling, you're a great lover really.' She kissed him on the forehead.

Dec got to his feet. 'Time Thomas was in bed.' He lifted the sleeping child from the couch. 'Come on, you gorgeous wee thing.'

When he had gone Cappy said, 'He loves putting the kids to bed. He'd spend half the night up there tucking them in. Sometimes I go up after him and he's singing to them, or telling them stories. Wee Thomas can't even understand. And I say, get you down here and talk to me. He'd prefer to talk to them.'

'Cappy,' Hughie said lugubriously, 'have you ever asked yourself why that might be?' Siobhan punched her husband.

As everyone was leaving Maxi arrived. The night was still and warm but Maxi was dressed, as usual, in his brown woollen overcoat. Dec had given him the coat, a cast-off, three or four years before. Maxi had thanked him profusely for his kindness, asked him if he was sure he wanted to part with such a valuable item of clothing, and promised Dec he could have it back any time he changed his mind. Maxi had rarely been seen without it since. The coat was now grubby and frayed. It was many sizes too large and the sleeves covered Maxi's hands. Maxi limped to the door, greeted the company and, with a magician's flourish, produced from his sleeve a bottle of vodka.

'The party's over, Maxi,' Cappy said.

Maxi's face fell. Hughie said to him. 'There's a brave wind tonight, Maxi.'

'I don't notice it with Dec's coat,' Maxi answered innocently.

Hughie and Siobhan sniggered at him and went on their way. Maxi hobbled over to Cappy, pushed an uncombed lock out of his eyes and handed Cappy the bottle. 'Tell Dec I was asking for him.'

'I will,' Cappy replied. 'Thanks for the bottle.'

Maxi's brown eyes beamed. He rubbed his unshaven chin and grinned. 'I'm glad he's home.'

'So am I.'

As Cappy was about to close the door, wee Dec arrived. 'Well, look who it is,' she said, feigning surprise. 'Where have you been all this time? I was going mental worrying about you.'

The boy rubbed snot from his nose with his sleeve and grinned.

'There's no controlling him, Roisin,' Cappy said in a kind of appeal. She parted the boy's hair and swept the fringe out of his eyes.

'Wait'll you hear this, Kane.' She took her son by the shoulders and said, 'Tell Kane what they call you.'

The boy said proudly, 'Wee Dec Mulholland.'

'And what do they call your da?'

'Big Dec Mulholland.'

'You're a great boy.' Cappy kissed him and stroked his hair. 'Go on inside now.' The child rushed away. Cappy said, 'He's the image of Dec. Goodnight Maxi. Goodnight Roisin, Kane.'

Cappy closed the door. Maxi said to me, 'Kane, have you got any money? I spent my last pound note on that bottle.'

'I haven't anything,' I told him.

Roisin gave him £2. He thanked her. 'Roisin, you're an angel, so you are. You look after her, Kane, you know.'

On our way home Roisin said to me, 'What was that about Cappy saying Dec hadn't made love to her since he got out?'

'That's no one's business but theirs.'

'Dec might be sick, he might need help.'

'Dec is not sick. I would know if he was.'

She stopped. In a quiet voice she said, 'No, Kane, you'd be the last to know.'

We fell into a silence. Nearer home she said, 'Kane, I know you don't want to talk about it but I have to say it again.'

'I won't leave, Roisin,' I interrupted her. 'I will never leave.'

'You've never seriously thought about it.'

'I won't leave.'

'You take decisions by instinct. And once you've made your decision you pride yourself on it being final, as if there's something admirable about that. It's just an excuse for you not to think, it saves you having to justify your choices to me, and to yourself.'

'You're wrong,' I said. 'This is where we were born. This is where our people are. If we went away we'd be like gypsies.'

'I didn't feel like a gypsy when I was in London.'

'Then why did you come back?'

'You know why – to be with you.'

'Roisin, I belong here.'

'You don't belong, you're a prisoner here. Let's leave, let's get free.'

'You can't be free in a place you don't belong, with people you don't know.'

She shook her head slowly. 'I'll come back with you tonight. But you have to make a decision soon.'

During the night she kissed my face and said to me, 'You are the one. I felt that about you almost from the start. But you're so unrelenting. Sometimes I love you because of that; I'm fascinated by it. I'm frightened by it, too. All that time in prison, was that what changed you?'

'I am the way I am because of what I do. There's no other way.'

'You sound like that fanatic Seanie.'

'Seanie is no fanatic. He's taken a side and he understands what that means. There's no turning back, there's no stopping, there's just going on; and to do that you have to harden your heart.'

'That's as close to a definition of a fanatic as you can

41

get.' With that Roisin put her head on my shoulder and was quiet.

*

I was fed up watching the tourists and when I looked at my watch I realized it was later than I thought. I grabbed my leather jacket and rushed to the hardware shop on the main road, reaching it just before closing time. I bought a roll of Denso Tape, some light machine oil, a Tupperware box, a cheap pair of gardening gloves, and a gardening trowel. I paid the assistant, put the goods in a plastic bag, taking care over my prints, and crossed the road to the tube station. When I arrived at Finsbury Park I bought a newspaper, found a quiet bar and settled in to wait for the dark. At half nine I left the bar and made my way to the disused railway line. I chose a spot behind a chestnut tree, within sight of Dec's house. I put on the gloves, scraped away the earth using the trowel, and dug a shallow hole big enough to take the box, which I had wrapped in the Denso Tape. I covered it with about an inch of earth and twigs, collected the remaining bits and pieces, put them in the plastic bag and headed back for the street. I dropped the bag into a bin in someone's garden, removed the sticky gloves and dumped them too.

It was almost midnight by the time I got home. The night was still, there was hardly a sound. A car pulled up in the street below, a silver BMW. It sat for about ten minutes with the engine idling. Then a girl stepped out of the passenger seat. She bent and put her head back inside. I heard the sound of laughter and 'cheerios'. The car drove off. The girl might have been Penny. It was after two by the time I went to bed.

A sharp rap at the door woke me from a deep sleep. I pulled on a pair of jeans and lifted Penny's keys from the dresser. The rap came again. It was then that I felt something was wrong. I hesitated and stood motionless at the door. Then I opened it, though I knew for certain what was on the other side.

The force of their entry sent me flying against the wall. Before I could get to my feet a revolver was pressed into my throat. All context vanished. For a few seconds I did not know where I was; I did not see colour, shape or form. Slowly, as the shock subsided, my impressions began to come together. I noticed first the green eyes of the man who held the gun, the faded freckles on his face, his sandy hair. I noticed the blond hairs on his fingers, liver spots on his hands; broad, clean manicured nails.

I became aware of other shapes and movements in the room. I was hauled to my feet by two men while the man with the gun kept me covered. I was spun round and spreadeagled against the wall. Someone kicked my heels back, transferring my weight to my hands and immobilizing me. When the body search was over I was brought upright and my hands cuffed behind my back. I was led to the sitting-room and brought to the armchair. I felt a strand of hair brush against my shoulder. I turned.

'Hello, Goneril,' I said.

'Take a seat, Paddy,' Penny said. I could taste in my mouth the poison with which she spat the words out. She pushed me down into the chair and went off in the direction of the bedroom. Another group of detectives entered the living-room. That was when I first saw Tempest.

The boy walked round the yard with his hands stuffed in his pockets, head bowed. He could not have been more than five feet tall and his rib-cage poked through a tight, grubby white vest. He looked up and scowled when I passed him, and from the back of his throat came a strangled curse.

Benny said he needed to rest. 'Do you know who that is?' he asked when he had settled on the ground, nodding in the boy's direction.

'Ralph said his name was Anthony,' I answered.

'Donald Duck more like.'

'Do you call him that because of the way he talks?'

'Have you ever heard him talk?'

'We exchanged pleasantries.'

'Yeah? Well that must have been a miracle considering he's a dummy. We call him Donald Duck because he's got the same personality. You know, frustrated, always angry – a bit like you.'

'What's he in for?'

'Robbery. He tried to do a bank by himself. He's supposed to have gone in with a shotgun. Even if it was sawn-off it would still have been twice as big as him.'

Anthony may have sensed we were talking about him for he scowled as he passed. Benny smiled pleasantly at him.

'Friendly sort of kid,' I said.

'Only one he gets on with is Ralph. I suppose the old geezer must have taken a thorn out of his paw or something. Speaking of Ralph, he's been in "H" Wing, sick.'

'I didn't know,' I said, surprised.

'Course you didn't know. I told you you don't put yourself about enough. Dicky ticker, I heard.'

I changed the subject. 'How's the defence going?'

Benny seemed uninterested. 'Coming along,' he replied airily.

Benny, who had been taking exercise more regularly, was now able to get about better and could do a dozen circuits of the yard between rests. 'This is doing me a power of good,' he said. He nodded to Dave and Terry who were walking together. They nodded back.

'You married?' Benny asked me.

'No. What about you?'

He told me he had been married for more than twenty years, that during his last sentence his wife, Sheila, had refused to divorce him, although he had begged her to do so. She insisted on coming to visit him every month, and on bringing their daughter, Meg, now aged fourteen. In prisons where the regime was reasonably flexible the family could sit round a laminated table for an hour every month and he could hold hands with his wife and Meg. More often the visits were conducted through a glass partition and communication was by microphone. But Sheila was not put off. Every month she came, following him even when he was 'ghosted', moved without warning to another prison. She travelled hundreds of miles to find him, and to bring Meg to him.

'What happened when you got out?' I asked.

Benny was about to reply when from 'C' Wing someone shouted through the bars, 'Look at that silly bastard!'

'Who's that, Benny?' Dave asked. He had stopped and was looking over to 'C' Wing.

'Don't know.'

There was another shout. We stared at 'C' Wing, trying to identify the source of the shouting.

'You silly bastard! Benny Morris! Shot your own leg off. Next time aim it at your chopper.'

Dave and Terry began to shout back insults at the anonymous barracker.

'What a prick. Sounds like a coon,' Dave said to Benny.

Benny did not answer, but hauled himself up and hobbled across the yard to the stairs. The barracker poured out his abuse.

'You prick,' Dave screamed. 'What's your name?' I heard Dave say to Terry, 'You've been in "C" wing, Tel. What cell's that?'

The barracker came again, 'You prick, Morris, why don't you shoot your dick off next time!'

Terry said, 'I can find out.' He and Dave resumed their walk, shooting occasional sidelong glances at the now silent wing.

That afternoon I passed Benny's cell on the way back to my own. He called me in.

'You get some sick people in here,' I said. 'Do you know who it was?'

'Some mental case. Forget it,' he said quietly. He sighed heavily and continued, 'You get so tired going over the same ground. Every day we sit down and play cards and within five minutes we're talking about Parkhurst in '67 or Gartree in '74. Right old lags we are. I'm the worst, I think. I do love a good old gossip. I should have been a cabby, me. But it gets depressing. You realize you're nothing but a crook, with nothing to say except what a dog such and such a cozzer is, or what a slag such and such a grass is.'

Benny poured me a cup of tea from his plastic pot. 'How come you never got married? You're not that bad looking – bit thin. You got a girl?'

'I had one, Roisin. But she left me ten years ago when I was doing a sentence.'

'Didn't you go after her when you got out?' Benny asked.

'She came back, for a while, but it was never the same.'

'Why not?'

'I was angry with her for having left me. I never got round to forgiving her. She left again and I haven't seen her since.'

'"Forgiving her"?' Benny snorted. He shook his head. 'How much time have you done?'

'About eleven out of the last fifteen.'

Benny frowned. He stroked his stubbled chin and throat, and tapped his adam's apple. 'I didn't realize you done that much time. You don't look old enough.'

'It wasn't all in one stretch. The longest was just over five out of a ten-year sentence for possession of a gun. I got out in April.'

'And now you're in for conspiracy? You hardly had time to tie your laces, never mind getting involved in a conspiracy. Conspiracy to what?'

'To kill.'

'Who are you alleged to have been conspiring to kill?'

'It's complicated.'

*

Tempest sipped coffee and smoked. He drew deeply and exhaled until there was nothing of the cigarette to hold on to. He popped the butt into the near-empty polystyrene cup and swilled the cold liquid around until the ash was extinguished. It was dark outside. I supposed it was about two o'clock in the morning. Tempest paced the interrogation room, moody, edgy, unpredictable. From time to time he would stop long enough to stamp out one cigarette and light another.

'Do you want to go back to your cell?' he asked me.

'No.'

'How did it start?'

It was on the morning of Hughie's death. Roisin said to me, 'I've been offered a place in chambers in London.' We were in the kitchen of my house. I sipped my tea and said, 'I won't try to stop you.'

'Come with me.'

'I can't go to live in England.'

Roisin was suddenly on the floor, at my knees. She took my hand and kissed it gently. 'Come anywhere with me, then. It doesn't have to be England. Come away from here. Marry me.'

I kissed her. 'What would I do?'

47

'You could find work. I'd soon be earning enough for both of us.'

'In another country what would I do? I'd be nothing over there.'

'You mean you wouldn't feel important?'

'There's a difference between feeling you have value and feeling important.'

'I don't see the difference. I see you in clubs and bars, and men come up and whisper in your ear, and you nod or shake your head and they disappear. It flatters you, but I just think to myself, "Whose life just came to an end there?"'

I brushed her away from me and said bitterly, 'Go to England then.'

That afternoon, as arranged, I met Dec, Maxi and Hughie in a drinking club in the Markets. The club was dimly lit and smelled of stale beer, cigarette smoke and damp. Its grey- and red-squared lino had been pocked by cigarette ends and was stained with spilt liquor and street grime. Dec was hunched over a snooker table, cueing on the black. It was a tricky shot, but he managed it and got back into position for the next red. Maxi scoffed.

'What are you drinking, Kane?' asked Hughie, who had been watching the game.

'Coke,' I said.

'Hurry up and get this over with,' I said to Dec.

'Be right with you.'

'Now.'

'I said I'm coming.'

Dec miscued and the white ball veered into the pink.

'Foul stroke!' Maxi cried.

'That's the only way you'll score a point off me,' Dec said testily, throwing down his stick. Dec and I moved to a quiet table while Maxi gathered his overcoat.

'Calm down,' I told Dec.

'I was on a century break.'

'We have work to do,' I reminded him, but he looked away like a petulant child.

I watched Maxi hobble towards us, throwing his cali-pered leg out to the side and twisting his body to propel himself forward. Hughie joined us and brought my drink.

Hughie said, 'That's a bit of good news, Seanie getting out this morning.'

Seanie had been arrested a few days earlier. The details were hazy and for a while it was rumoured that he had been caught with a gun. Since he had been released that morning the rumour about the gun turned out to be false and it was assumed that he had been arrested for a routine screening in Castlereagh interrogation centre.

Dec said, 'Has anybody seen him? He'll have to be de-briefed.'

'Later. It doesn't change anything for tonight,' I said.

'Seanie knows about this operation,' Dec said.

Maxi was quick to defend Seanie. 'Seanie'll have told them nothing.'

Dec ignored Maxi and said, 'It's bad security. I reckon we'd be safer calling it off for tonight. Wait and talk to Seanie.'

'We're going ahead,' I said. 'Hughie, we'll need the M2 and the banana mag for tonight. Bring it to O'Heggerty's at nine. Dec, you go with him to pick up the weapon.'

'How can I go?' Dec was edgy. 'I'm the one has to square it with O'Heggerty. He won't let Hughie or you in the house without me being there to square it.'

'Hughie has to be watched and you're the other one who knows where the dump is,' I said.

'I'm telling you, Kane, if I'm not in O'Heggerty's to sweet-talk him you might as well call it off. I can't be in two places at one time.'

'All right. Dec, you go square it with O'Heggerty, I'll get the ·45. Maxi, you go with Hughie and keep watch.'

'Aye right, no problem,' Maxi said, pleased.

'What do you mean? I ain't taking him,' Hughie said, outraged.

'Why not?' Maxi protested.

'Because you're a fucking idiot,' Hughie shouted.

'Keep your voices down,' I said.

'Call it off,' Dec said. He was nervous, shaking. 'We're not ready. It's not good just after Seanie's been scooped.'

I said, as calmly as I could, 'We're going ahead. Dec is going to O'Heggerty's. I'm going to pick up the ·45. Hughie'll get the M2 and Maxi'll keep watch. Once you've lifted it bring the M2 to us at O'Heggerty's. Maxi, you can disappear then. We make the hit and bring Hughie back the weapons at O'Heggerty's. They might have to stay the night there. We can dump them tomorrow night. Right?'

'Will I be carrying?' Maxi asked.

'No need,' I said. Maxi was disappointed. I explained, 'You don't need to be armed. All you're to do is scout around and keep watch while Hughie lifts the M2. Hughie, when you've got the carbine bring it to O'Heggerty's. Be there at nine o'clock on the button.'

'Kane,' Hughie said, 'it's bad security, you know, wee Maxi coming with me. Means we'll have to change the dump. I'm the quartermaster and only me and Dec are supposed to know about this one.'

'Hughie, that's the way it is. We'll just have to change the dump after.'

I was crossing the street outside when Dec came up after me. He was agitated and stood nervously scratching his arm, avoiding my eyes. He said, 'Call this off. It's a mess.'

'We go ahead. Keep an eye on the others, keep you off the drink and keep them off the drink.'

Tempest ceased his restless pacing and sat down opposite me. He spread his fingers on the table. I noticed for the first time he wore a wedding ring. He fingered it and when he realized I was watching he said, 'It's over. I tried taking it off.' He turned the ring on his finger and shook his head. 'She was young. I'd always lived alone. When we got married she moved into my flat, and I remember looking at my bathroom the next morning – all I could see were bottles and tubes. It was like a forensic lab. I couldn't find my razor. I was a bit put out at first. I was just getting used to it when I came home one day and the bottles were gone.

She's divorcing me now, but I'm contesting it.' Tempest spoke quietly and slowly, and stopped from time to time to smile at some memory. He told me this in a half-joking way, but there was a brittleness in his voice.

I said, 'What's the point fighting the divorce? She's gone; contesting it won't get her back.'

'I know. But in these situations you become petty and spiteful. It's the other side of being sick with love. She wants to marry someone else, and I don't want her to. That's all there is to it. How does that sound to you?'

'Unrealistic.'

'True. It makes her hate me more, my behaviour over the divorce, but I find I can't help myself. You get locked into a pattern that leaves you no way out. You would understand that.'

He straightened and stood up. 'Why didn't you call it off?'

'To keep the pressure on the Brits.'

'You're sure Roisin wasn't right?'

'About what?'

'About making decisions, about not thinking them through.'

Roisin was always right.

*

Slop-out was normally between eight and nine in the evening. Prisoners were unlocked separately to empty piss-pots, refill water jugs and collect hot water for a cup of tea. If the screws on duty were reasonable they would let men swap newspapers and magazines with their friends, or exchange a few shouted words through the fortified doors.

I had already been slopped-out and was pacing the cell when I heard Benny's voice outside.

'Kane! Kane!'

I went to put my ear to the door.

'All right?' he said.

'Yes.'

'Listen, you miserable sod, why didn't you go after your girl?'

'I told you.'

'I'll tell you something. There's a bloke after my wife and there is nothing I can do. I have to wait for her to come to see me. Then I get fifteen minutes with her in a room filled with screws. I can't tell her lovey-dovey stuff without half a dozen of them pulling faces. What chance have I got? Now, the way I am, I can't even wallop the bastard. But I tell you, if I could go after her I would.'

'I can't go after Roisin now.'

'There could still be time.'

The truth was that our time had run out long ago. I had nothing more to add, and Benny, sensing this, changed tack. 'I bet you're a chess-player. Well?'

'I play, but I'm not that good.'

'Just as well for me. We'll play tomorrow. Got to go now, the screw's going mental.'

Next morning I was tipping the remains of my breakfast into the bin when I heard Benny approach.

'Morning,' he said when he got to the bin.

'Morning.'

'How do they make this stuff?' Benny was trying to scrape out uneaten porridge from his bowl. He had to balance on his crutches. 'What do they put in it, milk or super glue?'

Dave joined us and was about to tip out the contents of a tray he had brought back from a visit the day before.

'Dave, wait a minute,' Benny said. 'Are you throwing this out?'

'Yeah.'

'Well, instead of throwing it out why not just leave it here for us less fortunate souls to pick through.'

Dave looked uncomprehendingly from Benny to me and back to Benny. 'Benny, if you need anything just let me know. But this is rubbish.'

'There's fresh fruit in there.'

'It ain't fresh, I got it yesterday,' Dave said, emptying the tray into the porridge and teabag sludge at the bottom of the bin.

'Would you believe it?' Benny rolled his eyes.

'Benny, you going on exercise?' Dave asked, almost as an afterthought.

Benny dropped his head and concentrated on cleaning his bowl. 'No. I've got a letter to write.'

'I think you better get down all the same, know what I mean?' With that Dave ambled back down the landing.

'Will you be on exercise?' I asked Benny.

'When Dave invites you out for exercise you go. He might be a bit of a div about women and ankle chains, but otherwise he's someone to watch out for.'

The yard was empty when Benny and I got down. We did a couple of laps and Benny reminded me that I had promised to play him at chess. He told me he had some chess books in his cell.

'What I like in these books is the little histories of the players at the beginning. There's one bloke, Rubinstein. He was interesting, an old Jew, just like me. I'll let you have the book. You'll like it. You can learn a certain amount from books, but to be really good you need imagination. That's what I ain't got,' he said with a smile, 'else I wouldn't have been a robber. Robbers are just thieves with no skills. If I had imagination I'd do what the field marshal does.'

'Field marshal?'

'Field marshal, corporal, whatever he says he is. Ralph, the old boy. He was in the war, so he says. He's a bit of a dark horse. No one really knows him, but he's supposed to be in for a tasty little fraud. I don't know the full story, something to do with VAT is what I heard,' Benny said confidentially. 'When we get our collars felt it's a fifteen to twenty stretch straight off. Old Ralph, what'll he get? Throw himself on the mercy of the court, shove in the old mitigation, put on his war medals, letter from the general. What'll he get? Probably an invitation to tea with the judge. Two years at most in an open nick and parole after six months, and that's if he's unlucky. Hold up, here's Mutt and Jeff.'

Dave and Terry came down the stairs and joined us.

'Someone wants a word with you, Benny,' Dave said.

'Yeah? Who's that?'

'You'll see.' Dave winked and walked on with Terry.

'Loves a bit of mystery, does Dave.'

'What's he in for? Ralph said it was something very big.'

'Big, yeah – half a million from a security van in the Blackwall Tunnel. Lovely bit of work.'

'What happened to the money?'

'The cozzers got a few grand. It was tragic the way it came on top. Him and Terry went to Ireland to deposit the money – a lot of it was in foreign currency – in a bank, but the bank clerks chose that day to start a strike. So they packed the dough in suitcases and flew to Switzerland. They wedged the money in Swiss accounts and went to a bar where Dave tipped a waitress he fancied £500 for a vodka and coke. She told the manager, the manager told the police and the rest is history.'

From 'C' Wing there was a shout.

'Benny,' Dave called over, 'hark at this!'

'Mr Morris, sir. I didn't mean no offence yesterday, know what I mean?'

'I can't hear you, you fucking prick!' Dave bawled.

'I didn't mean no offence!'

'Who the fuck are you talking to?' Dave yelled.

'Mr Morris, sir, I didn't mean no offence. I'm sorry.'

'You're sorry, toe rag!' Dave was unrelenting.

'Yeah, I'm sorry, sir.'

'What are you?' There was no reply. 'I said, what are you?'

'I'm a toe rag. I'm sorry, Mr Morris.'

'That's enough, Dave. Thanks,' Benny said quietly. He was a little embarrassed, but I could see he was also pleased, not by the man's apology but by Dave's efforts on his behalf.

'Listen to me, you no-good slag,' Dave instructed the man in 'C' Wing. 'If you ever say another word to anyone in this yard I'll go over there and rip your fucking black heart out. Understand?'

There was no reply.

'Understand?'

'I think he's probably got the message, Dave,' Benny said.

'He's a coon. You've got to spell it out for them,' Dave explained patiently. He shouted over to 'C' Wing again, 'Understand?'

'Yes, sir.'

'All right! Now fuck off!'

'I never realized you had so much power in the prison.' Benny was flattered and amused.

'You know me better than that,' Dave winked. Then he and Terry, their business concluded, left the yard.

I looked at Benny. 'I'm going in now,' he said. 'If you want a game of chess, pop in the cell after exercise.'

I walked on, doing my circuits alone in the yard. I was wondering why Anthony was not out when a screw blew his whistle to announce the end of the exercise period. I remembered that Benny had said Ralph had been sick. As I passed Ralph's cell I saw the door was ajar. I knocked and pushed it open. The cell light was off and a blanket had been crudely hung to block the light from the window. I could just make out Anthony. He was sitting on a chair beside Ralph's bed. He looked at me menacingly and started to snarl. Then a gaunt figure raised his shoulders from the bed. It was Ralph. He put a pacifying hand on Anthony's arm.

'Kane,' he said, 'good of you to drop in.'

'You look like death,' I said.

— 6 —

'Do come in, old boy,' Ralph said, propping himself up in bed. He wore blue-striped pyjamas; they were something not often seen in prison. 'Take a pew and have some tea.'

'No tea, thanks.' I sat on the edge of the bed. 'You don't look so good. I heard you were in "H" Wing.'

'Nothing serious, old boy. Spot of bother with the breathing.' Ralph's voice was hoarse and weak. 'Are you sure you won't have some tea? Anthony was kind enough to make me some a minute ago. It's still hot. Anthony, would you be good enough to get Mr Kane a cup of tea? You've met Anthony?'

'Not exactly.'

'He's a trifle hard to get to know. He's deaf.'

'I thought he was dumb.'

'Oh no. There's nothing wrong with his vocal cords. The trouble's with his hearing. He's profoundly deaf and unfortunately no one took the trouble to teach him to talk. Isn't that right, Anthony?' Ralph shook Anthony's arm and said, deliberately and slowly, 'I was just telling Mr Kane that you are deaf. He didn't know.' Ralph accompanied his speech with sign language. Anthony gave me a hard look and decided I was not worth further attention. He picked up a book and leafed through the pages.

'Not the most open-hearted soul, I have to say, but good as gold. Anthony, would you get our visitor a cup of tea?'

Anthony scowled at me. 'I'll get it myself,' I said. The tea was in a large plastic mug on the cupboard. I poured myself a cup.

'There are some biscuits too. Do help yourself.'

'All the comforts of home.'

'Well, not quite. But some at least to make life a little more civilized. Could you pass me a biscuit?' I'm feeling rather peckish. My appetite's returned with a vengeance.'

'If he can't talk, how did he manage to rob a bank?' I asked. 'Did he write a note?'

'Oh no. Impossible. You see this boy can't read or write.' I took a closer look at the book on Anthony's lap. It was a travel book, on Turkey, and it was the big glossy pictures that absorbed him.

'Tell Mr Kane how you robbed the bank, Anthony. Listen to this, it's terribly funny.' For a moment I thought Anthony might swear again, or spit out his tea and biscuits. His scowl became fiercer. Then he launched into a string of guttural sounds which he accompanied with violent, sweeping gestures. For emphasis he twisted the muscles around his mouth and narrowed his eyes.

Ralph directed some more sign language at Anthony. It took some effort and, every now and then, a look of pain crossed his grey face, as if the movements were too much for him. But he continued, and Anthony responded with more of his vehement gestures.

'He says,' Ralph began, 'that when you go into a bank with a shotgun and point it at the cashier, no one thinks you're from Interflora.'

'He has a point,' I admitted.

We sat sipping our sweet tea and munching our biscuits. Ralph asked, 'Are you settling in all right?'

'I know my way round now.'

'Is your family over here or are they in Ireland?'

'I have no family to speak of.'

'You need family or friends outside to help you out with little things. Like a change of clothes or a bit of decent food. We're isolated enough as it is. Without people outside it's like being in a grave.'

I bridled at this well-meaning talk, and I was barely able to stop myself from swearing at him and getting up and walking out. I just managed to keep an even tone. 'I prefer not to have people outside. There's less pressure.'

'That's a bit harsh.'

'How long have you been in here?'

'Here? In "A" Seg? Only a little longer than you. They moved me in here a day or two before you arrived. I was in "A" Wing before that. I've been in about six weeks now.'

'Have you got a date for your trial?'

'Not yet. It will probably be another six months or so. I'm pleading: I have no choice. The trouble with fraud is that it tends to generate paperwork, invariably of an incriminating nature. If I was ten years younger I'd probably plead not guilty and drag the trial out for three months in the hope of boring the jury to death, or at least confusing them. But I haven't the stamina. If I plead guilty I stand a chance of a reasonably light sentence in an open prison. I can't do any more time. I've got a chance to make something of my life and for once I'm going to do my best not to mess it up. I owe it all to my loved one.' He pointed to a photograph on his cupboard.

I had heard Ralph refer to her before as 'my loved one'. It brought to my mind an English matron, a sturdy woman fond of gardening and bridge. I could not see him with one of the empty-headed blonde models the robbers liked to keep in tow.

'She's all I live for,' Ralph said. He motioned to me to take the photograph. I lifted it and examined the woman. She was in her late twenties and beautiful. She stood, a little self-consciously, against a background of green sea, one arm across her breast, the hand at her elbow. She had probably been stroking her arm waiting for the shutter to click. She wore a sleeveless burgundy dress.

'Her name's Ruth. It was taken on holiday, in Kas,' Ralph explained. I felt his eyes on me. I knew he had read my surprise at not finding the grey-haired matron.

'Kas?'

'Turkey. We went there on a kind of honeymoon.'

'You're married?'

'Well no, not yet. We plan to very soon. At the minute there's a little problem standing in the way – the usual one of an old spouse. It's all but resolved now.' He continued vaguely. 'The weather was beautiful. The sun shone all day. We were so happy.'

I looked again at the girl. She was lightly and evenly tanned, and she was smiling, except to me she did not look happy. I imagined Ralph urging her to face the camera, to strike a pose, and she giving in to please him. Her hair was dark brown and short, and the eyes, as far as I could tell, were blue-grey.

'She looks lovely,' I said, and she was. Ruth had a fresh and, for all the awkwardness of the pose, a natural beauty.

'She's all I live for.' I took another look at Ruth. I could easily imagine that she could be, literally, all Ralph lived for. Unlike the robbers' girlfriends there was nothing flighty of frivolous about her. There was something serious in her expression, something knowing. To a man in prison, a man like Ralph, she could be a lifeline, or the breaker of his heart. For a mad moment I wanted to walk out of the cell with the photograph in my hand. Instead I smiled at Ralph and gave Ruth back to him.

For some reason I felt embarrassed and guilty. To change the subject, I asked him how he had picked up sign language.

'My daughter, Natalie, was born mute.' He paused. 'I suppose I can see your point of view – about family ties, that is. I know they can be an intolerable strain in prison. My wife left me when I was in Long Lartin. I don't blame her, I didn't blame her then. She'd been more loyal to me than I deserved. She just couldn't take it any more. She met someone else. The usual story.'

Ralph was engrossed in the photograph. I took a sip of the sweet tea and from behind the mug I scrutinized him. His face was falling down, his eyes, murkier than I remembered, seemed to be shrinking into his head. The lines scored between the corners of his mouth and nose, which had given his face definition, were disappearing. His grey hair was dull. Everything about him conveyed an impression of impending collapse.

Ralph said, 'When I got out of Long Lartin, after my wife left me, I was on my uppers. Drinking too much, in a terrible state. And I was into a very stupid piece of fraud, getting more and more sucked in every day. Totally losing control over my life. My partner,' he emphasized the word to invest it with an unmistakable meaning, the opposite of what it is intended to convey, 'was a rogue. Not even a lovable one. You may have heard of him – Joe Varvakis? He's always in the papers.'

'No, I haven't heard of him.'

'Well, you'll hear more of him in the future. He's the proverbial bad penny. Anyway, there I was, enmeshed in a crazy scheme with Joe, drinking myself into oblivion, and then I was saved – by my loved one.' He glanced at Ruth's photograph, which was lying on the bed. My eyes followed his. Yes, I thought to myself, looking afresh at the girl's beauty, there is a magic there. If she returns only a fraction of your adoration it could still be enough to save you.

'I can't tell you what impact she has had on my life. She's given me a future.' He laughed. 'Listen to me, I sound like a schoolboy.'

'No you don't.' No schoolboy was in love like this. Ralph liked what I said; it encouraged him.

'I've told Ruth about you. You'd like her, Kane, you really would.'

In all, if the minutes were counted up, I had probably spent less than an hour with Ralph. Yet he had already told Ruth all about me. At first I was angry, then I felt touched. I heard myself say, 'You'll be very happy together.'

It delighted him. He said, with sudden enthusiasm, 'We will. We plan to marry when I get out. You must come to the wedding. Anthony'll be there too. I wasn't thinking of anything grand.' Joyfully he tapped my arm with the back of his hand.

'How will you arrange this with the law? I asked.

Perhaps Ralph picked up an edge in my voice. He became serious. He leaned towards me. 'We won't be in here for ever. One day this will end. We will get out of this awful, hopeless place. Things will work out; they have a way of doing that.' His tone changed. He was back to his fantasy. 'What we must do is arrange to have our visits at the same time so I can introduce you to Ruth.'

I was getting tired of Ralph's fantasy and his sentimentality. 'I don't have visits,' I said harshly.

Ralph had an optimism about him, a goodness. I think he was incapable of recognizing bitterness in those he liked. He looked at me earnestly. 'I'll ask Ruth to get one of her friends to visit you. We could have a visit with the four of us. It would be wonderful.'

Now the anger in me would not give way. 'No thanks,' I said sharply. I got up. I caught the look of hurt and concern on Ralph's face. Anthony did not bother to lift his gaze from the pictures of Turkey.

*

John Joe O'Heggerty, eighty-eight years old and with cancer of the throat, was a nervous man. He stood by his television set and trembled.

'Uncle John,' Dec said soothingly, 'sit yourself down and relax. There's a guy will be coming here in half an hour. He's going to bring us something and then we'll go. Nothing to worry about.'

O'Heggerty was unconvinced, but knew there was nothing he could say to get us out. 'I'll make some tea,' he wheezed. There was a rattling sound in his throat.

'I'll make the tea,' Dec corrected him. 'You sit down and watch the snooker.' To me, Dec said, 'We won't see that tea until Friday morning if John Joe goes to make it.' To O'Heggerty, Dec said, louder, mischievously, 'Tell Kane about your operations.'

O'Heggerty settled in an armchair. 'I'm very sick,' he said. 'The doctors say it's miracle I'm still alive. Six months, they gave me.'

'When was that?' I shouted.

He nodded vaguely, as if he had not heard. Then he said, '1965.'

There was nothing I could think of to say, so I tried to look impressed.

O'Heggerty had just finished telling me about his most recent operation when Dec appeared with three cups of tea.

'Can't drink tea,' O'Heggerty rattled.

'Oh yes, I forgot,' Dec said. 'How's the snooker?'

Dec turned up the sound on the television set and dropped on to the sofa. It was ten to nine. 'Hughie'll be here any minute,' he said. Dec, satisfied that O'Heggerty's attention was fixed on the television, asked in a whisper, 'Are you carrying?'

'I've got the ·45.'

'Have you got it on you?' I tapped the small of my back. Dec said playfully, 'If the Brits raid, John Joe can take responsibility.' Dec shook O'Heggerty. 'Can't you, Uncle John?' O'Heggerty looked blank, then nodded gravely. Dec said, 'I was just telling Kane that if you were lifted you'd refuse to recognize the court, like a good republican.'

'Aye,' O'Heggerty mumbled uncertainly.

'Good man!' Dec patted him on the back, and O'Heggerty, anxious to get out of this dangerous line of conversation, returned to the snooker.

'I shouldn't tease him, the poor fucker.'

Nine o'clock came and went. By half past, Hughie had still not arrived. Dec became fidgety and his growing tension communicated itself to O'Heggerty.

'Relax,' I said to Dec.

'I said not to send wee Maxi. He's too unreliable and he's not, you know, the stoutest of hearts.'

'There's probably an army patrol in the area. They're probably hanging about.'

'Someone would have come to tell us if there were Brits in the area.'

'Look, instead of yapping get out and see Gerry D. Tell him to get the Fianna out to scout around, find out what's going on.'

'It's cold out there.'

'Dec, I'm carrying the ·45 so just do it.'

'Do I tell Gerry D you're here if he has something to say?'

'Tell him, but no one else.'

Dec, moody, went. O'Heggerty, trembling in his chair, tried to concentrate on the snooker. Every now and then he stole a nervous glance at me and looked quickly away when his eyes met mine. He could sense things were going wrong and was desperate to get me out of his house.

It was not until nearly eleven that Dec reappeared. He was followed into the room by Gerry D.

Dec said, 'Uncle John, go on out to the kitchen and make us some tea, would you?'

O'Heggerty, shaking and aware that he was being got out of the way, left the room gladly enough. Dec waited until he had gone before flopping into a chair. He ran a finger back and forth across his forehead, then let his arm fall and his head rest against the back of the chair. He stared at the ceiling. It was bad news of course, but I was in no hurry to hear it, no more than Dec was to tell it. Gerry D, not twenty and knowing no difference between good and bad news – the important thing was that something was happening and that he was in the middle of it – said impatiently, with a near-contemptuous glance at Dec, 'Hughie's dead. He was shot by the Brits.'

I had known the minute Dec came into the room that Hughie was dead. I had been in his house, only a few months before, when he had come in and slumped into a chair without saying a word. Then, as now, he had stared in silence at the ceiling until Cappy wrung from him that their son, wee Dec, had been hit by a car and was dead.

Gerry D was becoming more impatient. Dec kept his gaze fixed on the ceiling when I asked him where Hughie had been shot.

'At the dump,' Gerry D told me when Dec would not answer. 'Looks like they were waiting on him. They got the M2. The place is swarming with Brits.'

'What about Maxi?'

'He ain't been seen,' Gerry D replied. 'He might have been scooped.'

'Gerry, get your lads out and ·have a look round for Maxi. If you find him bring him to me or Dec.'

When Gerry D left I said to Dec, 'Get Cappy to go and see Siobhan. I'll get Roisin to go and see her as well. I'm going to have to leave the ·45 here. You'll have to fix it with O'Heggerty.'

'Yes.'

'Wipe the dabs off it and put it under the bed or wherever.'

Dec stared at the wall and said drily and numbly, 'What about Maxi?'

*

I paced the cell, trying to work off the anger that Ralph had sparked in me. When it was dark, images of Roisin came to me. Oh Roisin, I thought, if I could only be with you. I remembered the lines of a poem Roisin liked. I had read them to her in bed one night. She was half asleep and dreamy, but I felt her slowly come awake. Her body stiffened against mine and she took hold of my hand.

> O would that a freezing, sleet-wing'd tempest did sweep.
> And I and my love were alone, far off on the deep;
> I'd ask not a ship, or a bark, or pinnace to save –
> With her hand round my waist, I'd fear not the wind or the wave.

She asked me to read them again. When I had finished, she whispered, 'I'd like to have that power over you, but I know I never will.'

When I went to Long Kesh to begin my ten-year sentence, Roisin said she would wait for me. 'I'll keep my arm round your waist for as long as you want. But I need a sign from you,' she said during a visit. 'I need that reassurance.'

Oh Roisin, I thought as she looked at me, hoping I would soften, waiting for me, how can I give you that sign? How can I, when I have no control, when I would be completely at your mercy?

'You don't need a sign from me,' I said stiffly, with stupid anger.

'Don't shut down on me like this.'

'I have no sign to make. You go your own way.'

She did not visit again for some time. When I saw her next she looked subdued.

She started slowly. 'I have to tell you this. I've met someone. We're going to go to England.'

'Why do you have to tell me?' I shouted at her. 'Why not just keep quiet?'

'I can't deal with it like that. I have to be honest. I can't be like you. You can make a decision and just move on to the next stage without a thought for other people. I can't do that. I have to explain. For my peace of mind.'

'Don't write to me again, ever. Don't ever visit me. I don't want to hear from you or see you. I don't want to hear your name.'

'I wanted us to talk about this.'

'I have nothing to say. You are dead to me now.'

'Oh Kane, please.'

Roisin, Roisin. I watched her go and she never looked back. And I let her go because I was too weak to call her back and wrap my arms around her and beg her never to leave me.

That night, in Brixton, five years later, I dreamed I was standing naked in a bombed-out street. It was dark and raining. At the top of the street there was a set of traffic lights bent at a forty-five degree angle. The lights, constantly changing, were the only colours in the debris-littered street. Suddenly a woman ran past me towards the lights. I followed, but could not catch her. I ran harder and harder. I fell. She stopped and looked around, expressionless, then vanished. It was a face I had seen before. As I struggled to remember, I noticed that my leg was bleeding. I rubbed it with my hand. A shadow came over me. It was Tempest, his face blue-pale, eyes dead. He pointed a skeletal finger at me. Before my eyes his finger transformed itself into a gun.

In prison you wait and wait. You wait for other people and for the days to pass. There is nothing else to do. On a cold morning I sat with Benny in his cell and played a desultory game of chess.

Benny was feeling low because the day before the judiciary had taken a heavy toll on 'A' Seg. Dave had been sentenced to twenty-seven years, Terry had received twenty-two. The sentences had depressed everyone in the unit; Benny, it seemed, more than most.

He was not concentrating on his game and I was well positioned and two pawns up. I was about to take a third when Ralph appeared.

'I hope I'm not interrupting anything,' he said.

'Come in,' Benny said, 'take a chair.' Benny, like the other robbers, was never fully at ease with Ralph, but, unlike them, was always polite, indulgent towards him, as towards the amiably fraudulent and harmless. 'There's some tea in the jug.'

Ralph helped himself and said, 'I've just had some good news and had to tell you. You probably won't remember that I told you that Ruth and I were planning to marry.'

'Of course I do,' I said. 'There was a problem. Something to do with a divorce?'

'That's right. Well, I've just this minute heard that it's all been sorted out. We are now free to get married.'

'Congratulations.' I put out my hand, which he took with both of his and shook enthusiastically. He had been ill for several weeks, but seemed to be getting better. His eyes looked brighter, though the bruised crescents beneath them were still as dark.

When Ralph let my hand go he turned to Benny who shook Ralph's hand briefly and said perfunctorily, 'Congratulations.'

'Thanks, Benny.'

'When will the wedding take place?' I asked Ralph.

'Well, I'm a bit stunned at the moment and I haven't collected my thoughts. But I think if I get a suspended sentence, unlikely as that seems, we'll get married straight away. If I get prison, we'll get permission to marry in jail.'

'So either way your days as a single man are drawing to a close,' I said in the manner expected when such announcements are made.

'What about your trial?' Benny asked. 'When's that listed for?'

'January or February.'

'How long do you think you'll get?'

'I'm hoping for three or below.'

Benny pondered a move and said, without taking his eyes from the board, 'I don't want to sound pessimistic, Ralph, but isn't that a bit on the low side for what you're in for?'

I had to look twice at Benny; his question was harsh and Ralph, sensitive to tone and mood in others, was unable to disguise his hurt. He replied shortly, but without much conviction, 'My solicitor says three will probably be the maximum.'

Benny did not let up. 'For a hundred-grand swindle? What was it you said when you first came in here, a hundred grand, two hundred?' The edge in Benny's voice had sharpened.

'It's hard to be exact, old boy. With fraud a lot of the money is on paper.' Ralph was defensive and looking for a way to disengage without being seen to retreat.

But Benny pressed him. 'How much did you actually get away with?'

Ralph gestured vaguely with his hand. He shrugged and

said with patient but fragile good humour, as if explaining to an overly inquisitive child, 'It's not like robbery. You don't go home and count up the takings. The money is dispersed in different accounts. Some of the takings aren't always converted into cash straight away. Well,' he said, clapping his hands together, 'I've got to go. I promised Anthony to teach him today. He's learning to read.'

'Good luck, Ralph,' I said. 'And congratulations.'

'Thanks, Kane. See you later. See you later, Benny.'

'Yeah.'

When Ralph had gone I asked Benny why he had been so cool. He inspected the chess-board and waited until he had made his move before replying. 'You didn't believe any of that, did you?'

'You obviously didn't.'

'It was bollocks. Ralph said he just heard. How did he just hear? It's half-past nine. The mail doesn't come in until eleven at the earliest. No visits have been called yet.'

'The PO might have told him.'

'Oh, very likely! I can see the PO knocking on his door to bring him the glad tidings. He didn't get a visit yesterday. Did you notice that?' I had. I had seen Ralph, dressed in his slacks and shiny shoes, anxiously checking his watch every two or three minutes. He would appear at the door of his cell and gaze at the security gate from where the visits were called. He took deep breaths, checked the time, ran his thumbs through his waistband, paced the landing, then disappeared into his cell only to re-emerge two minutes later.

Benny said, 'He didn't get a visit yesterday. His girl never showed. He's worried, thinks maybe she's run off. So he invents this fantasy about them getting married. But it isn't real unless he tells us. If he can convince us he can convince himself. That's the kind of man he is.'

Benny considered a move in reply to mine. He put his hand on his surviving rook and pronounced, 'He's a wrong 'un.'

'Ralph?'

'No one really knows him, no one trusts him.'

'What about Joe Varvakis? Ralph says he worked with him.'

'Maybe I'm wrong. Maybe it's jealousy. I'm losing my wife and he's finding his. But mind your step with him.'

Benny, normally so competitive, lost interest in the game and conceded before I could mate him.

*

Close up, Seanie's face was mottled and boiled, the legacy of acne scars and drink. His eyes were small and blue, and dully malevolent. He sipped his Guinness and watched the television set with no sign of interest.

Billy came in and sat next to him. He ordered himself a pint, another for Seanie and a coke for me. He said, 'I backed Tommy Gunn in this race.'

Seanie checked the runners in his paper and said scornfully, 'That's a beaten docket.'

'With a name like that how can it lose?' Billy replied.

Seanie shook his head and lifted his glass. He was a man of concentrated contempt.

Tommy Gunn did not show and Billy screwed up the betting slip and tossed it to the floor. He asked Seanie, 'Did you have an interest in that one?'

'The winner,' Seanie replied evenly. 'So, Kane, what's the score?'

Hughie had been buried that morning. I had watched as Siobhan, in a state of near-collapse, supported by Roisin on one side and by Dec on the other, looked on uncomprehendingly as the coffin was lowered and the first spadefuls of earth danced on the polished wood. Roisin and Dec led her away. As they passed me Siobhan stopped and took hold of my wrist. Her grip was hard and her fingers dug into my flesh. 'It is a beautiful day,' she said with force, as though trying to convince me of some outlandish proposition. But it was a beautiful day. The sky was a hard, wintry blue, the air tasted thin and fresh, and the sound of the motorway traffic mingled with the song of the birds to make a strangely comforting city melody. 'I haven't paid the milkman,'

Siobhan added with equal force. Her grip on my wrist tightened. Roisin dropped her head to hide a sob, and Dec, his eyes red and swollen, swallowed hard. He eased Siobhan's fingers off me and gently led her on. I tried to catch Roisin's eye, but she would not look at me. As they left me I began to feel envious of Roisin and Dec; their grief was so all-consuming. I felt sorry for Hughie, and for Siobhan, but I was not, I never had been, knocked down by grief. Already I was thinking about Maxi, calculating.

Maxi had been arrested immediately after the shooting. He had been held for two days before being released without charge. Later, he had turned up at Dec's house to explain what had happened. Dec came to find me and we met outside Hughie's house the night before the funeral.

'Maxi was about twenty yards from Hughie when the Brits opened up,' Dec told me. 'He was lifted and taken to Castlereagh.'

We stamped our feet against the cold and watched as neighbours filed into Hughie's house to pay their respects to the family and say goodbye to Hughie. The coffin stood in the parlour.

'Who saw him in Castlereagh? RUC?' I asked.

'Yes, and there was an English Branchman.'

'Not this expert they're talking about?'

'Who knows? Maxi says he told them he was walking across the waste ground on his way home when he bumped into Hughie, and that he didn't know anything about Hughie going to a dump to lift a weapon. He told them he heard a shot, Hughie fell down and he put up his hands and was taken in. That was the story he stuck to and they believed it.'

'Do you believe it?' I asked Dec.

'No,' he said quickly. 'I think Maxi touted.'

'You think he told the Brits about Hughie – arranged it so that they would be waiting for him?'

'More or less.'

'Then why lift him?'

'To make it look good.'

'I don't know,' I said.

'Maxi'll have to be talked to, after being lifted and interrogated by the Brits. It has to be done.'

'No one suggested doing that to Seanie. He was lifted before Hughie was shot and he knew all about the operation.'

Dec breathed out hard and said, with a hint of asperity, 'If you had to pick between Maxi and Seanie as a tout, who would it be?'

Seanie could not be an informer. He was hard and shrewd and he believed in what he did. Even to think he was capable of turning would have undermined my own beliefs. Maxi, on the other hand, was weak and malleable, the kind an experienced Branchman could corrupt.

'I'll get Seanie to pick Maxi up tomorrow and debrief him. You be there as well. You know the details and you can make sure Seanie doesn't go too far. I want Maxi questioned, not worked over.'

Dec nodded to the mourners as they passed. He looked tired and pale. I said, 'Siobhan told me you gave her some money.'

'She'll need some help,' he replied, almost guiltily.

'Four hundred pounds,' I said.

Dec pursed his lips and gave a half nod. 'I'm going in to see Hughie,' he said quietly. 'I'll see you at the funeral to-morrow.'

He walked to the house, hunched and small-looking. With all the speculation about informers I had forgotten that Dec and Hughie had been close friends, and that he had taken the death hard. I had reasons of my own for wanting to find out who was responsible for Hughie's killing, but they were not personal, not like Dec's. I went home. Roisin was not there, but during the night I woke to find her sitting on the bed.

'Come here,' I said.

'I don't think so, Kane,' she said. She traced the patterns on the quilt, her fingers making little circles and arcs. 'I've accepted the place in chambers. I'm going back to London,' she said at last.

71

'I knew you would.'

She nodded, but said nothing more. I felt an ache in my heart. Each second of silence made it worse, but I did not trust myself to speak. I thought, if she realized how I felt, how much I did not want to lose her again, she would reach for me and tell me she loved me and that she would never leave. But such words do not spring from a silence like the one between us then.

After some long minutes she said, 'After eight years you still don't know me. I used to be so intrigued by your distance; I could never understand how a person could be so solitary. Everyone else I know needs someone. Not you. And I was fascinated by that. There always seemed to be something that you were excluding me from. It transfixed me and caused me so much pain. It was a mystery to me until now. Now I realize it was no more than selfishness. Oh Kane, for eight years I've let that selfishness blind me. I see through you. It's you that doesn't know me, and you're too selfish to understand that, or to care.'

I watched her finger the quilt abstractedly. I listened to her breathing, and I thought: This is it, finally, it is the end between us. In a few moments more it would be all over and nothing I could say would make any difference. Roisin was the most loyal and honest person I knew. She had made her decision and there would be no going back.

She asked flatly, 'Will you be at the funeral tomorrow?'

'Of course.'

She got up and left. She went quickly and there was no sad glance from the door.

In the bar, the afternoon after Hughie's funeral, with Billy scrutinizing the list of runners, Seanie said, 'So, Kane, what's the score?'

'Dec has told Maxi to meet you here at the bar.' I checked my watch. 'He won't be long. Wait outside for him. You remember that house, the derelict one we were looking at the other day? Take him there. Find out what happened. I have to check with someone about what to do with him. When I've done that I'll be along to the house. It'll be sometime tonight.'

Seanie finished his drink, rolled up his newspaper and beckoned to Billy.

'I'll get a car and a couple of lads,' he said. 'We'll hang around outside until he shows up.'

'He won't give you any trouble,' I said. 'Question him, nothing more.'

Seanie grinned and tapped my arm with the paper. He and Billy went outside. I finished my coke and walked to the doorway. Ten minutes later Maxi hobbled into view.

*

Ralph, as always, gave me an enthusiastic reception. He was dressed in his visiting clothes and lifted the knees of his navy slacks before sitting down. Anthony, engrossed in a travel book, sat in his usual chair. He scowled when I sat down on the bed.

'I must apologize for his lack of courtesy,' Ralph said. He turned to Anthony and assumed the expression of a father who knows he is fighting a losing war where his son's behaviour is concerned, but goes through the motions anyway.

'Have you ever read your compatriot, Sean O'Casey?' Ralph asked me, handing me a mug of tea.

'Some of the plays. I liked them.'

'I prefer the autobiographies. O'Casey grew up in the Dublin slums at the turn of the century in terrible poverty and deprivation. There's one passage I recall, about the death of his brother. Do you know it?'

I shook my head. He went on, 'O'Casey's brother never left the slums and died while he was still quite young. O'Casey reflected that all the wonderful things in the world were unknown to his brother. The Nile and the Ganges were just blue lines on a map he saw at school, the Alps and the Rockies no more than brown patches.'

Ralph sipped his tea and indicated Anthony. 'Anthony is rather like O'Casey's brother. He's told me something of his earlier life and it is frightful – not that he complains, of course. He accepts it, as if that is all he was born for. I find that depressing. I'm trying to introduce him to the wider world. I wouldn't want him to end up like O'Casey's brother. What he needs is wider horizons. And money, of course. Money sets you free.'

'I don't believe that.'

'Then for the first time I have to say, Kane, that I think you are wrong. I want money. I am like the *conquistadores* Cortés wrote about. You know Cortés, the Spaniard who conquered Mexico? He wrote a letter once in which he said that he and his men suffered from a disease of the heart which can be cured only with gold.'

'How's your health?'

'I've got the disease, but I've also got the cure,' he said.

From the landing a screw called Ralph for a visit. He jumped up and went to the mirror. 'She's come,' he muttered absently. He shook Anthony and repeated slowly, 'She's come. Ruth is here.' Anthony rubbed Ralph's arm affectionately with a grubby hand. He had a slightly concerned look on his face. Ralph said to him. 'Don't worry.' Ralph turned to me. 'How do I look?'

'Fine,' I replied.

'Thanks,' he said warmly. He took a last look in the mirror and said, 'I knew she'd come.'

— 8 —

Everything was grey. The summer had gone and the skies now were low and overcast. And it was cold. The change in season was the only sign by which I could be sure that time had passed. There was nothing else to measure the days or weeks or months.

The bitter east wind drowned out Benny's voice and made my ears ache. We walked along, stiff, bending into the wind, hair flying. Benny shouted something I could not make out. I nodded vaguely, my thoughts elsewhere.

Before exercise a screw had tossed a letter into my cell, the first I had received since my arrest. I was shaving in a bowl on the cupboard and the letter landed behind me on the bed. The sight of it caused my heart to miss a beat. I wiped the soap from my face and dried my hands. The stamp had a London postmark, but the handwriting told me it was a voice from home. I sat down and stared at it. I fingered the jagged edge where the censor had broken the seal, but I did not take the letter out; it was a voice I had not expected and was not sure I wanted to hear.

Benny appeared. 'Good news?' he asked, pointing to the letter.

'I haven't read it.'

'You miserable sod,' he admonished me. 'Read it!'

'Letters here never bring good news.' Never. Only a line from girlfriends or wives to say they can take it no longer and want out; or anguished family letters, pages filled with sorrow and pain.

'You misery. You can't keep the world out for ever.

75

Well, if you ain't going to read it, come down on exercise.
I've got something very important to discuss.'

When we were in the yard Benny shouted above the
wind, 'I've got to get a not guilty. I can't go the way Dave
and Terry went.' He added in a serious tone, 'It'd kill me.'

I believed him, but his lack of realism made me feel sad.
'Your best course would be to plead guilty, do your best to
sound contrite.' I added, though with some hesitation, for
Benny was a proud man, 'And use your leg.'

Benny said, 'No. Even if I put my hands up and throw
myself on the mercy of the court I can't get less than
fifteen. That's a mite longer than I want to stay in this
admirable institution. I want to get out in the New Year.'

'The case against you is conclusive,' I reminded him.

'What sort of friend are you?' he cried.

'The kind that tells you what most other people are too
polite to tell you.'

'If there is a way out I'll find it,' he said. 'I have a lot of
experience with court cases.'

'Have you ever been acquitted?'

'No,' he conceded, although in no way put down. 'But it's
time to break the habit of a lifetime. I'm owed a not guilty by
the law of averages. Trouble is, the trial's not far off and I need
a solicitor. I sacked the last one because he was taking it for
granted that I'd plead guilty. Do you know a good solicitor?'

'What?'

'This wind!' He shouted, 'I said, do you know a good solicitor?'

'No,' I shouted back.

'I've got a lot of thinking to do if I'm going to get out of
this.' I nodded absently. Benny picked up on my lack of
interest and said tartly, 'You should be taking a bit more
interest in your own case, Kane – in your own life, come to
that. You could start by reading that letter.'

Without another word he turned and made for the stairs.
The wind dropped momentarily and Benny called over to
me, 'Pop into the cell later!' He began his laborious climb.
The wind whipped up again, screaming through the wire.

There were two mugs of tea sitting on Benny's cupboard. Benny fought for space on the bed with depositions, papers and files. When he had cleared enough of them away he dropped down, propped himself up and said, 'Did Ralph ever tell you he was in the Army?'

'Yes, I think he did. It was some time ago. When I first got here.'

'What? Did he say the *Army*?'

'Yes. No. No, it was the Air Force.'

'You sure?'

'Not really. I think he said he'd been in the Air Force in Korea. Why?'

'He told me just this morning, he was in the *Army* and won – can you believe this? – a medal.'

'Probably a campaign medal. They're two a penny.'

'It was a Distinguished Service Medal, so he says. He claims he was a marine. They don't go in planes, do they, marines? They go in little boats, I thought.' Benny frowned and sipped his tea. 'He's a wrong 'un,' he said at last.

'He seems harmless,' I countered.

'Well, maybe. Anyway, down to business. What I've done here is made out a list of things that look black for me, and another list of the things that look promising.'

He handed me a sheet of paper. I read its contents, a confection of scrawls, misspellings and, the result of the vocabulary-building exercises common in prison, high-flown and redundant words. I said, 'There seems to be an imbalance here. Under "Black" you've listed eleven items, under "Promising" you have one. Doesn't that tell you something? Like you should plead guilty?'

'Son, where is your optimism? I asked you in for your brains. Now are you going to help me get out of this or not?'

'Sure.'

'Well, let's get started. Number one: "Alleged fingerprints allegedly detected on shotgun." They'll definitely try to use that against me.'

'You think so? What's your answer to that one?'

'Simple. While I'm lying wounded on the pavement I'm

naturally thrashing about. It's the pain. So I touch the gun. I touched a whole lot of things that weren't mine; the gun just happened to be one of them.'

'I suppose that's as good a defence on that point as you'll ever invent.'

'Who's talking about inventing? This is the truth. Listen, if you want to get off, you've got to think like an innocent man. You've got to psyche yourself up so you can look at the evidence with an innocent man's eyes. Makes the answers more convincing.' Benny winked. He closed his eyes and gently massaged his temples. He repeated, under his breath, 'I am innocent, I am innocent, innocent.' He opened his eyes and said, 'Self-hypnosis. I read a book on it, *Reader's Digest*. Right, number two: "The alleged detection and discovery of cartridges in the pocket of one coat alleged to have belonged to the said defendant, Benjamin Morris."'

'And the answer to that?'

'No problem. I wasn't actually wearing the coat. I had it sort of draped over my shoulder to hide the shotgun. Now, when the shot goes off I obviously fall to the ground – I'm in shock, and what's left of my leg is hanging by a thread. It's the pain, you see. Anyway, while this security guard is stamping on my neck there happens to be a nurse who comes running up and gets this mental case off my windpipe. She puts the coat over me – it's all in her deposition – for the shock. And when I'm nicked the coat is nicked with me. Are you getting my drift?'

'Yes. The coat wasn't yours. Like the shotgun, it was abandoned by the real robber and it was used by the nurse to wrap you up.'

'Son, you're learning. Keep this up and you can be my counsel.'

'And the next one, please!'

'Number three . . .'

When he had concluded his defence, Benny said, 'What do you think?'

'Maybe.'

'Well,' he said, sounding satisfied, 'coming from you that amounts to saying I'm going to get off.'

'Not quite.'

'That's because we haven't looked at the "Promising" list.'

'That won't take long, there's only one item. It says, and I'm not sure I'm reading this right, "My honesty."'

Benny launched into a prepared speech of valediction. 'Whatever anyone says about me they have to admit I'm as honest as the day is long. When I've been before the courts in the past I've always put my hands up when I was guilty. This time I'm innocent and I'm saying I'm not guilty. "Members of the jury, I ain't trying to pull the wool over your eyes. I ain't saying I've always been an upstanding citizen. I have done prison before. I don't have to tell you that. The rule is that I don't have to put in my previous in front of the court. But because I'm an honest bloke I feel that for you to come to the proper verdict in this case, which is definitely not guilty, you must be in full possession of all the relevant facts. And the fact is that I, in the past, have been in prison. Even though it goes against me, I think you ought to know that."

'That's the speech I'm going to make at the end of the trial. What do you think?'

'If I was on the jury I would go not guilty.'

'See!' He slapped me on the shoulder. 'And if I can convince you, a jury'll be no problem.'

A screw poked his head in to announce lock-up. Back in my cell the letter was still waiting for me on the bed. I left it where it was.

That night I looked at the cool handwriting on the envelope a hundred times. The voice within I knew to be calm and clear, and part of me desperately wanted to read the letter, to find reassurance in its calmness. But another part was in an exultation of rage; it was white-knuckled and furious. I paced the cell. I walked and walked, and when my anger would not let go I punched the walls until my hands bled. I banged my head on the door. I sat down and punched my thighs. I cursed myself.

In the end I struggled into a sleep of sorts.

I dreamed again about the girl in the derelict street. I ran and ran after her, over the litter, over the broken bricks and glass. I wanted to catch her so badly that I was oblivious to the pain in my bare feet. Only when she disappeared at the traffic lights did I become aware of the bleeding. I sat down and although I could not see him I was aware of Tempest's presence. He was all around.

*

Seanie balanced the Browning 9mm in his hand and said flatly, 'Maxi picked the side he wanted. I'm not saying it was the wrong side. I don't make those kinds of judgements. I don't know if it was the right side or the wrong side. But it wasn't our side.'

The smell of damp and rot in the house was sickening. The cream-coloured wallpaper, stained brown and curling at the bottom, seemed like corrupted skin falling away from a stinking corpse. The decay made me think of death, of Hughie in his grave.

Dec was nervous. He wanted to get it over with and said so. I said, 'We have no proof either way. Maxi denies it.'

Dec crossed the room and threw his hands up. 'Wouldn't you deny it?' he half shouted. 'Wouldn't you deny it if you were faced with getting nutted?'

'The two of you tortured him and he still says he didn't do it. Does that tell you anything?'

'I never laid a finger on him,' Dec said with a glance at Seanie.

Seanie said simply, 'Maxi set Hughie up for the Brits. The Brits killed Hughie, now we kill Maxi.'

'I'm the one'll decide that,' I said.

Seanie said, 'Did you see Brigade this afternoon?'

'Yes.' After leaving the bar I had gone to find a man to give him details of what had happened, and I had outlined to him several options, one of which was to kill Maxi. The man had told me to do as I saw fit. I said to Dec and Seanie, 'Brigade says that I'm the one who makes the decision about anything that

80

happens here. If you don't like that then you can complain later. But tonight nothing happens without me ordering it.'

Seanie and Dec exchanged a brief glance. Seanie looked down at the gun he held in his hand. He said to me, slowly, evenly, in his most threatening way, without raising his head, 'Are you carrying, Kane? Because I am.'

There are some people who are afraid of guns, who are never comfortable with them, and who, when they have to carry them, feel full of dread. There are others who like the weight in their hands and revel in the feeling of power that guns confer. Seanie was like that. When he was seventeen Seanie had shot and killed a well-known republican during a feud. The man sat in his car with his bride of five weeks and was about to drive off when Seanie strolled up and fired through the windscreen. It was the first man he had killed and Seanie was surprised at how easy it had been; he had simply walked up to this man, shot him in the head and walked away again. He had felt neither fear beforehand nor regret afterwards, merely a momentary quickening of the pulse, a slight blurring of vision for an instant before the kill. Later he reflected on how little he had felt. He could recall hardly anything of the detail, was uncertain, even, about how many shots he had fired, and was aware that what he had experienced most strongly was a sensation of having been distanced from the scene about him. His footfalls, the explosions, the breaking glass, the woman's screams, he thought, had all sounded muffled to him, as if he had had cotton-wool stuffed in his ears. Everyone, including the man he had killed, had moved so slowly; it seemed only he had had the power of normal movement. Seventeen-year-old Sean Smith, four hours after the shooting, sat down on a bar stool and turned these things over in his mind; he was mildly puzzled.

But it was not in his nature to ponder these things long. Two days later he killed another man, and, as he pulled the trigger, a similar set of feelings overtook him. Afterwards, though, Seanie did not bother to question them; he could not see the point.

81

He was twenty-one and in prison facing four murder charges when I first met him. During his remand he did not seem remotely concerned about his fate; his conversation never turned on the outcome of his cases. He made no plans, he never speculated, and I never once, in the ten years I knew him, heard him use the future tense in relation to himself.

Nor did he speak of his own past. Certain things were known about him. But, unusually, for Belfast is a small town, details were lacking. He had never married, that much was certain; before he was sixteen he had fathered a son, that was known, although the boy's identity was not.

It was not that Seanie was secretive or furtive. He seemed too bored by everything, by himself as much as by anyone or anything else, to want to talk. Except about history, for Seanie had read widely in prison. He knew a lot about Irish history; but he was no sentimental Gael. He said during one of many political discussions we had in prison that the figure he admired most in Irish history was Oliver Cromwell. Some of his listeners were shocked, but Seanie maintained that 'Cromwell recognized the logic'. This earned him his jail nickname, 'the Logic', and in the yard men would say, 'Here comes the Logic' when Seanie crossed their paths. When there were arguments among us over how to proceed, Seanie would say drily, 'Straight to the point . . .', and men would nod because the Logic had spoken.

Seanie said to me as we stood in the bedroom of the derelict house, with the smell of rot all around us, with Maxi bleeding and crying in the bedroom, 'We kill him, that's it.'

That was Seanie's attitude. It was why he lived as long as he did. Seanie believed that to win a war you had to follow the simple logic of war. It puzzled him how many men, even those with experience, those who had been in prison, those who had faced similar decisions before, paused before deciding to kill their enemy. It was a weakness, he thought, and it was bad luck for them. Often enough in the past while his enemies were wasting time deliberating Seanie had appeared with his gun. He killed them while they were still making up their minds about whether to kill him. That way he stayed ahead. To him it was a mystery why a man who had taken up the gun in the first place had to think each time before he used it. Once I had answered that that was the difference between soldiers and revolutionaries. He replied that it was the difference between winning and losing, between life and death.

One time during a feud, in the early hours of the morning, Seanie was picked up by his enemies. He was bundled into a car and taken to an empty drinking club where he was beaten until, apparently unconscious, his teeth smashed, his nose broken, his attackers decided to pause for refreshment. They poured themselves generous measures of vodka and whiskey and drank to Seanie's demise. Every now and then one would go over to where Seanie lay in his own blood and kick him. It was like kicking a sack of potatoes. Seanie lay crumpled and motionless. But he was not unconscious. He waited until he heard the sound of an automatic pistol being cocked before springing to his feet, laying the man out and vaulting over the tables to get to the door and away.

Most men would have been happy just to have escaped, to go to hospital to have their wounds treated and bound and then to lie low. That is what the men in the club thought. They gave desultory and drunken chase and then shrugged, decided to cut their losses and return to the bar; they would find him tomorrow. Meanwhile, they thought, they might as well relax and have another drink.

Within the hour Seanie had returned. The men, sitting round a bottle-strewn table, did not at first register either surprise or alarm when he entered; they simply could not believe it was him. But it was him, and he was armed this time with a ·38 Smith and Wesson and a Browning 9mm. All three men were hit, but, though badly wounded, they survived. When someone later attributed Seanie's poor performance that night to his wounds, Seanie was indignant.

They lived through it, he maintained, only because the ammunition was faulty.

And that night in the derelict house, when Seanie produced the gun, I understood that his logic meant Maxi's life would soon come to an end. It was hopeless to try to change Seanie's mind; dangerous to stand in his way. Still I said, 'Not until he confesses.'

*

I did not go out on exercise that morning. Instead I lay on my bed.

'Kane!' It was Benny who, though often animated and enthusiastic, this morning had the exuberance of an excited ten-year-old. He bumped into the door, the chair, the cupboard, knocked a cup to the floor; and did not notice a thing. He said gleefully, 'I'm going to get out of this. Get down on exercise and I'll tell you what else I've thought up.' He paused and took a hard look at me. 'Are you all right? You don't look too perky.'

'Bad dreams.'

'Did you read the letter?' he said.

'No.'

'You ought to read it. I'll be in the yard this morning, or pop in the cell this afternoon. See you later.'

When he had gone I reached for the envelope and drew out the letter. It read:

Kane, a stór,

Forgive me for writing to you. You once told me that I was dead to you. You have an ability I've never seen in anyone else to cut people out of your life with such terrible finality. It always frightened me and that's why I've hesitated to write.

I wouldn't be writing now had I not been talking to a colleague, a barrister. He was at Lambeth Magistrates' Court when you appeared for your weekly remand. He told me that you were not legally represented.

This is undoubtedly none of my business. You may have a good reason for not wanting a solicitor, but I suspect I know why and I think you're making a mistake.

84

Oh, I know you hate being preached at. But can't you just this once take my advice. I know a good solicitor and have already asked her if she would act for you. She said she would, but needs a letter of instruction from you. Please write to her. Her name is Harriet Cockburn and her office is in Borough High Street. If you see her, don't be fooled by her diffidence. People tend to get the wrong impression, but those with any wit soon realize there is a powerful intelligence at work. If anyone can help you, she can.

I'll leave you now. I won't write again and I ask your forgiveness for writing now.

If I can do anything for you, you know I will.

My love to you,
Roisin

That afternoon I went to see Benny.

'Well, come in,' he said happily. 'It's good to see you with a smile on your face. Did you read that letter?'

'I did. And I've got good news for you.'

'For me?'

'I've got you a solicitor.' I showed him the letter. He read it. 'What's this "*a stór*"?' he asked.

'It's Gaelic, it means . . . It's a term of affection.'

'What? Like "darling" or "sweetheart"?'

'Something like that.'

'So you do have a girl!' Benny was gloating.

'Once, not now.'

'Can't you read? It says "darling".'

'Back to business. If Roisin says this Harriet Cockburn is good, she's got to be brilliant,' I said.

Benny was excited. He rubbed his hands together. 'Things are going to work out. Boy, we're going to get out of this awful place. But I'm only going to write to this Harriet Cockburn if you do the same.'

'I don't know.'

'Are you going to deprive me of my only chance? Are you that selfish? Come on!'

'Okay.'

'Right! Let's get cracking. Give me that notebook.'

Benny tore out a sheet and started to compose his letter to Harriet Cockburn. It featured prominently and repetitively the words 'innocent', 'tragedy', 'mistake', 'error' and 'miscarriage of justice'.

When he finished, he gave me a sheet of paper and I wrote and asked Harriet Cockburn to come to see me.

'We are getting out of this,' Benny crowed. 'And to celebrate I'm going to whop you at chess. This is for the world championship!'

We set up the pieces. Benny won, as usual. He rearranged the chessmen and analysed the final moves of the game we had just played, admiring his handiwork.

'You missed a mate back here,' he said. He showed me an elegant combination I had overlooked. 'You missed it and lost the game.' He swept the pieces into their box and said, as if remembering something, 'You know, getting out of here is only the first step. It's getting out of the second prison – that's the real challenge. Everyone gets a chance, one chance, to escape from the second prison. Trouble is, hardly anyone takes it.'

— 9 —

The note read: 'The pleasure of your company is requested at a farewell party for Mr Anthony Boggi esq. Immediately after afternoon exercise. Wine and cakes will be served. RSVP Ralph Wilson, cell seven (threes).'

'Did you get one of these?' I asked Benny as we stood beside the bins emptying our breakfast bowls.

'Yeah. You going?'

'Why not?'

The previous afternoon the PO had notified Anthony that his trial was listed for two days' time. Anthony had been unimpressed and received the news with his habitual scowl.

Anthony was pleading guilty and would be going to Wandsworth to begin his sentence if the judge decided to dispose of the case then and there, or on judge's remand to await disposition if the judge wanted time to consider reports. Either way he would not be back, and the morning Benny and I stood by the bins discussing Ralph's invitation was the beginning of Anthony's last day in Brixton.

'He is putting his hands up, isn't he?' Benny queried.

'He'd better,' I said, 'for his own sake. Caught with the shotgun – remind you of anyone? Perhaps others should take heed.'

'No need for sarcasm. It's obvious to any intelligent observer that Anthony has a hopeless case. He was caught in the jug with a gun and the whole thing was captured for posterity on video. My case, on the other hand, is full of possibilities. I expect to be vindicated. Truth will out.'

'Let's hope not.'

'You're not looking at it the way I told you to, with an innocent man's eyes. Try harder. Harriet Cockburn is already trying harder than you. I got a letter from her yesterday. She's coming on Friday.'

'She must be going to see us one after the other. My letter said she would be coming Friday as well.'

'If you get called first, don't take all day. I've got a lot to discuss with her.'

'Don't I know.'

'What do they put in this porridge?' Benny prised the leaden remains of his breakfast from his bowl. It fell with a dull, heavy thud into the bin. Benny stared after it and sighed.

Anthony glared maliciously when I got down to the yard that morning. There was no point in trying to approach him. We walked, the way we had walked for the last six months, separate and silent. The chill wind howled through the wire, fierce and high-pitched, whipping up the litter; discarded matchsticks and cigarette ends sailed in fits and starts across the concrete to gather in sheltered corners.

Benny made one of his rare appearances in the yard that morning. Since the onset of winter he came out only when the ground was frost- or ice-free. He had, he said, an exaggerated fear of falling.

'My leg doesn't feel right when there's ice down,' he said. 'Have you ever driven in the snow and you go to turn right and the car turns left? Well, that's how it feels for me when it's slippery. The thought of falling down brings me out in a cold sweat.'

Benny hailed Anthony. 'Morning, Donald!' he shouted. We caught Anthony's eye; he scowled back at us.

'Sheila's coming up later,' Benny said. 'I'm going to have to turn on all my charm. I've been practising in the mirror – that's why I was late for exercise.'

When anxious, self-mockery became his refuge. Benny's wife was on the point of leaving him. During his last long sentence he had asked her to divorce him, to build a life for herself, and she had refused. Now the positions were reversed: she was interested in another man and had asked for a divorce. The effort to find a way out of his case derived its special urgency from his collapsing relationship.

'You'll have no problem with her,' I assured him. 'And none with the jury. Harriet Cockburn's brains will see you through.'

'Harriet Cockburn's brains, and my charm.'

*

Tempest listened, but I began to realize he knew many of the details already. Occasionally, at the mention of a name or a place or a date, he would frown, but from the dark hollows of his eyes there was never any sign of surprise. He was listening to a piece of music he had heard before; perhaps in a different key, but still the same piece of music.

He knew the piece about Seanie's death, he knew that very well: the time and place, the calibre of the gun. 'Anyone could have predicted it,' he said. 'Sean Smith's death was inevitable.'

It happened five months earlier, in January. I was still in prison, preparing for release, preparing, in my mind, to journey to England to find Dec. I heard a radio announcer say a man had been shot and killed, and before Seanie's name was read out I knew it was him. As Tempest said, it *was* inevitable: he had killed too many people – soldiers, police and other enemies – to live long. I believe he was thirty-four when he died.

The funeral, I learned later, had been small. An elderly uncle, who had flown in from America and who had given permission for Seanie to be buried in the family plot, was the sole relative present. Some people from the street joined the procession, but, by Belfast standards, it was pitifully small. At the graveside, as the coffin was about to be lowered, a woman, about twenty years old, with two children in tow, went up to the American uncle and asked him where her husband was. The uncle, unused to Belfast people and the mocking cadences of their speech, politely replied that he did not know her husband. The woman, who had never been out of Belfast, mistook his formal politeness for

89

an insult. She asked again for her husband, this time with an unmistakable menace in her voice. The uncle grew anxious. He was more than sixty years old and had left Belfast as a child. He had been under the impression that he was returning for a hero's funeral; the scene he now encountered in no way accorded with the sentimentalized picture he had instantaneously constructed on being informed of the death of the nephew he had never met. The woman prodded him sharply with her fingers and he grew frightened: no one was coming to his aid; the straggling mourners, embarrassed, eyes fixed on their shoes, were leaving him, a stranger, to fend for himself. To placate the woman he began, in his best voice, 'And who is your husband?' These words merely enraged her. She swore at him and pushed him out of the way with such force that he fell backwards on top of the coffin. The gravediggers only just succeeded in keeping him upright and the coffin from tumbling prematurely into the grave. The woman began beating on the casket lid. She screamed abuse at the corpse of the man inside, the murderer of her husband she said, and, as she was dragged away, she spat at the American uncle. The woman and her children screeched. Their howls could still be heard after they had been led away to the cemetery gates, and they hung over the priest's prayers like a mockery.

Seanie had lived his life according to one simple, rigid rule of war. He had died because he had neglected a second rule: to keep his own people with him. Killing first had prolonged his life, but it could not guarantee survival, as Seanie had so often maintained – though he was too intelligent ever to have believed his own words. Survival could not be guaranteed, but death could: death was certain if the second rule was violated. Seanie's scorn for keeping his own people with him led to his death. In a way I had liked him, in spite of his cruelty, for he was brave and determined, and I admired that. A story later found its way into the jail. It was said that on the day of his death Seanie had driven to a bar he liked. He stopped the car, turned off the engine, removed the key from the ignition, opened the door and got out. He gruffly hailed a couple of men lounging by the bar when a boy, very young, walked up to him and, making no effort to conceal what he was doing from the bystanders, pulled out an automatic and said smoothly, 'You know what's going to happen now, don't you?' Seanie, so one version of the story went, recognized something in the boy's manner, a calmness, a confidence, something he knew he had himself – perhaps he would have described it simply as understanding the logic. He looked the gun over, so the story went, and said, without a trace of fear, 'Yes, I know.' And then he added, in his even tone, 'I like ·45s myself. When you hit someone with a ·45 they go down and they stay down.'

Seanie's flesh was blown apart by eight ·45-calibre copper-jacketed bullets. In the jail men whistled when they heard that: '*Eight* rounds. One in the breech and seven in the mag. That's what I call taking precautions.'

One version of the story had it that Seanie had been shot by his teenage son.

There was one final, grotesque twist in Seanie's story. The American uncle outlived his nephew by only a few weeks; he died in April, shortly before I was released. On his deathbed he requested he be buried in Belfast, in the family plot. He also repented his sins and, terrified or disgusted by the thought of lying side by side with his notorious nephew, stipulated that Seanie's body be disinterred before his own was laid to rest. At ten o'clock on the night of my release a young man, squat but with big, hard bones and curly pale red hair cropped short, came to my door and asked me, as someone who had known Seanie, to come with him to see the coffin moved. I asked him who he was and he said he was a relative. I suppose then I knew who he was. I agreed to go with him. We exchanged fewer than a dozen words on the way to the cemetery, where we found a priest, four gravediggers and some kind of official waiting for us.

I watched as the grave was dug up. The clay smelt of

worms and sickening damp, and the official put a handker-
chief to his mouth and nose. When they had raised the
coffin, the gravediggers lifted it on to a metal trolley and
moved off, one of them beckoning us to follow. We
moved in silence to a far corner of the cemetery, near the
motorway, where there were few headstones and the ground
was boggy. The graves here were poor and sad, marked by
small, plastic-covered portraits of saints, pinned to simple
crosses. There were jam-jars filled with yellow-green water
and wilted daffodils and daisies.

We gathered round a freshly opened grave while the
priest bowed his head and the official signalled to the
diggers. As they lifted the rotting box from the trolley a side
panel gave out, then the bottom, and the contents spilled
on to the ground like the butchered guts of a farmyard
animal. There was the cadaver of Sean Smith. I pulled
away, but not before seeing the blood-brown hair slapped
stickily to his skull, and the flesh of his face falling, it seemed,
in black lumps away from his broken mouth and nose.

'Jesus!' a gravedigger whispered.

'It's the cheap boxes,' I heard another say.

When we reached the cemetery gates the young man
held out his big bony hand and I took it.

'I have to catch a plane,' he said.

'Do you want me to arrange a stone?' I asked him.

He considered for a moment, and then shook his head.
'It's better unmarked. Too many people hated him.'

He squeezed my hand, turned and walked away.

Before leaving for England I returned to the cemetery
and to Seanie's grave. I do not know why I went. I stood
there and tried to trace in my mind, in some kind of ordered
way, the events that had brought us to where we were:
Hughie dead, Maxi dead, Seanie dead, Dec in England,
Roisin gone from me. I looked for a thread, some link,
some connection, something to explain the past and to
show me how things would turn out.

'Who was he?' Tempest asked me. 'The boy who came to
your house that night? Did you ever find out who he was?'

92

'Not for certain.'

'What was your impression of him?'

'Hard.'

'Like his father,' Tempest said, and I nodded and looked at the daylight coming in through the high window.

*

The wind screamed through the wire; gusts flapped and shook the cage. The day was blue and clear, and very cold. After half an hour, the shivering screws called me in. I went to Ralph's cell on the 'threes'.

'Come in, old boy. Jolly good of you to show up. Anthony's leaving us tomorrow morning and this farewell party is in his honour.' Ralph beamed at me and did a half-turn, arm elaborately outstretched, to introduce the guest of honour himself: a skinny, deaf boy with splayed tufts of spiky black hair, and, on his face, newsprint-like smudges and an ugly snarl.

'A pleasure to be here,' I replied formally. Ralph held out a large white plastic mug. Instead of the usual tea it contained red wine. 'My loved one sent it in. Beaujolais. I've saved the last few days' allowance so we can all get a little bit merry.'

Benny followed on my heels and Ralph went through his routine a second time. Anthony glared at us and then took a long swig from a mug he held tightly in his small and dirty hands. Red wine trickled from his mouth to his chin, to the collar of his prison shirt. Then he did something I had never seen before. His lips rolled back to display small, irregular and discoloured teeth. It was his attempt at a smile. I smiled back and he gurgled in a way that reminded me of babies.

Ralph noticed our exchange and said, 'Anthony's got rather a head start on you.'

Anthony made his joyous gurgling sound again while Benny and I found ourselves seats on the bed.

'Will Anthony be pleading guilty?' Benny asked Ralph.

'No question. The whole thing was caught on video, rather restricting the scope for an inventive defence.'

Anthony, who was scrutinizing Ralph as he spoke, became suddenly animated. He moved his hands furiously to express what I thought looked like an angry rebuke. The gurgles gave way to grunts and growls. Ralph said to Anthony, patiently, 'Be sensible.' Then he turned and said to us, 'He says that he has no defence except to tell the judge to fuck off.'

'Very shrewd, kid,' Benny said.

'I've tried to persuade him to adopt a more reasonable approach. But he won't listen.'

I faced Anthony and said as distinctly as I could, 'Do you have any previous?' He smiled again. I saw the rotten teeth and the unhealthy gums. From six feet I could smell his wine-soured breath. He grunted and moved his hands.

'Plenty,' Ralph translated. 'Robbery, burglary, theft and TDA, and' – Ralph's tone became like that of a father to a fanciful child – 'he says he once stole a Rolls-Royce.'

Anthony grunted to get Ralph's attention. 'Apparently,' Ralph began, 'he crashed it, the Rolls-Royce, into a telephone box in Bond Street. He didn't know how to drive. What age were you? Thirteen? Really.'

'How much time have you done inside?' I asked Anthony.

'Fourteen years,' interpreted Ralph, 'including approved school.'

'What age are you?'

'Twenty-two.'

'Not much of a life,' I said. It provoked Anthony's hands.

'He says he's had a short but happy life. He says if he died tomorrow he wouldn't give a fuck. At least he's always done what he wanted and he's never taken orders from anyone.'

'What kind of sentence will he get?' I said to Ralph.

'That's anybody's guess, really. The last one was four years. I can't see how he could get less for this one, especially as he had a shotgun. Probably six or eight plus.'

'This is just what I need,' Benny said, peering at his mug of wine.

'Drink up, old boy,' Ralph said. 'There's plenty more.'

Anthony grunted, and while Ralph was distracted I asked Benny how his visit had gone.

'Marriage over,' he announced softly.

'You'll get out at your trial,' I said. 'Then you can get her back.'

Benny smiled and dug me in the ribs with his elbow. 'Drink up, Kane. We're going to get out of this.'

'Gentlemen, your attention please,' Ralph was on his feet. 'I won't detain you long. But I feel I would be failing in my duty were I not to say a few words in appreciation of Mr Anthony Boggi and his remarkable contribution to the social life of "A" Seg.

'As you know, tomorrow Anthony goes to venture his fate before the enemy. There, they will undoubtedly have some harsh things to say about our young friend. But those of us who know him count ourselves privileged to have him as a friend. Gentlemen, will you please charge your glasses to toast Mr Anthony Boggi and wish him the best of luck. Good luck, Anthony!'

'Good luck!' Benny and I chorused.

''Ud lu',' Anthony grunted enthusiastically and I discerned the attempt at spoken words. We drank from our plastic mugs. Anthony held his out to be refilled; his greed was innocent and touching. He poured the wine down his throat, tossed the mug to the floor and snatched the bottle from Ralph's hand. Ralph tried to take it back, but Anthony had clamped the bottle to his lips. Ralph gave up trying to prise the fingers from the bottle and sat down beside me.

'The drink's gone to his head, the little devil,' he said.

When Anthony finished his slurping, he wiped his mouth with his hand, leaned back and belched. Then he laughed; it was like a simpleton's manic guffaw.

Anthony got unsteadily to his feet, waved his empty mug and fell face down on to the bed.

95

'Can't hold his drink,' Benny said. 'We'd better get him back to his cell before lock-up. If he's found in that state he'll spend tonight on the block.'

I checked the landing to see if there were any screws about.

Ralph and I supported the giggling Anthony and started for his cell. Benny dragged himself along behind. We had only gone a few yards when the PO and two screws appeared.

'What's going on here?' the PO demanded.

Benny came forward and said pleasantly, 'It's his trial tomorrow. He's a little tired and emotional, what with all the strain.'

'He's been drinking,' the PO said, incredulous. He put his nose to Anthony's open mouth. 'This man is drunk.' He sniffed Anthony's breath to confirm it. When the PO's nose was a fraction from his mouth Anthony breathed heavily. The PO jerked back. 'He's on report,' he said. Unable to believe it, strangely fascinated by the sight before him, the PO again lowered his nose. This time Anthony clamped his black teeth around it. The PO roared. A screw took out his stick and truncheoned Anthony to the ground.

'You shitbag!' Benny shouted. 'Leave the kid alone.' The PO turned and shoved Benny back. He stumbled awkwardly and screamed as he hit the floor. I swung at the PO. The first punch was a wild, hopeful loop and succeeded only in grazing his forehead; the second connected and put him down.

10

The punishment block was an annexe off 'B' Wing. It was on the 'ones' and had sixteen cells, eight either side of a dark corridor. There was a recess with a cold-water tap and a toilet, and, opposite, an office for the screws. The punishment cells contained no furniture of any kind: at eight o'clock at night the door was unlocked and a bed and mattress placed inside. At six in the morning the bed was taken out. That left a plastic pisspot, a bucket, a jug of water and a mug. There was nothing else: no chairs, no books, no magazines, no radio. Meals, three a day, arrived cold on a stainless-steel tray. They were brought by an orderly who did not speak: the door would suddenly swing open, the orderly would place the tray on the floor, the door would bang shut. A quarter of an hour later the orderly returned to collect the tray. Exercise was for one hour a day, alone. I walked round and round a small yard under the gaze of three screws. Lights went out at nine, but it made little difference whether they were on or off. The boredom of the block was crushing.

And so, like all prisoners in the block, I searched for a comforting dream, a memory to lose myself in. I had few, I realized: mistakes, embarrassments, defeats, they crowded unrelentingly in on me. It was harder to find a soothing memory. In the end I did, although it left me feeling disturbed and anxious.

I thought about my release from prison in 1982. It was in early January and I had spent four years inside, a short spell by local standards, but on coming out I had never felt more alone. Dec was in custody, facing trial, and no one counted on seeing him for the next ten to twenty years. Roisin was living in England; we no longer wrote to each other. Somewhere in my mind I had a mad hope that she would be there to meet me at the gate, but she was not. I put her out of my mind. Had she turned up, what would I have done? Gathered her up and kissed her and told her I loved her. But that was a fantasy. I was too tense and angry. I had no right to expect to see her that day, but still I felt disappointed and bitter at her absence. My anger at her started to spread. I felt angry with everyone at the gate, the wives and mothers and brothers milling around waiting for visiting time to start. Roisin had said to me once, teasing me in her ironic way, 'Don't be so disagreeable. Don't be so angry with everyone all the time.'

I got a bus back to Belfast and made my way home.

I spent most of the day clearing up my house. I bought some milk and bread, I bought some beer. And that night as I stayed indoors, getting drunker, I thought: If Roisin were to turn up now. Of all the things in the world I could think to ask for, that was what I wanted. I sat in my armchair and sipped beer from cans, letting the empties drop on to the floor at my feet. I dozed off; I dreamed furious dreams. I dreamed I was hitting people, that I was punching a hole in a wall; I dreamed I jumped naked through a plate-glass window on to a street: people gathered around to offer help and I shouted at them to go away; blood dripped from splits and gashes all over my body.

I woke with a start: the beer was leaking on to my lap. I turned the can upright and was about to put it to my lips when I felt a presence behind me. It was Roisin.

'You've lost more weight, Kane,' she said. 'But you don't look bad considering.'

She knelt at my feet and took hold of my hands and kissed them lightly. For me it was the thing she did that touched me most, the most tender and the most erotic thing she did.

'You've come back,' I said drunkenly. 'Have you come back?'

Roisin kissed my hands again. She stood up and tugged me to my feet. I hugged her. I said to her, 'Roisin, I hate you.' She said nothing but stroked the back of my neck. I could feel tears welling in my eyes. I wanted to hit her and hurt her, to punch the walls and smash my hands and jump through the window. Roisin held on to me tightly until my anger subsided. When she thought it was safe, she pulled back and said, 'Come with me.' I followed her outside. She put me into a car and we drove off into the rain.

She made for the motorway and within minutes we had disentangled ourselves from the city and its dirty rain. We passed the lights of Long Kesh on our right as we drove west. We passed through Omagh and Enniskillen, and on a country road I saw a horse standing, powerful and watchful, by the gate of a meadow.

By first light we were in Sligo. We went along the narrow roads, through low-lying mist that clung to the ground, waiting to be melted by the warming sun. We did not speak. I stared at the hills smudged with dark and light and at the wind-ribbed lakes. We reached Galway: stone walls and clear blue sky.

Roisin found a café and ordered breakfast. 'Tired?' she asked me.

'No. Where are we going?'

'Nowhere. I flew over yesterday and hired this car.' She put down her coffee cup and took hold of my hand. 'Let's go to Dublin,' she said excitedly. 'We'll be there by lunchtime.'

'Can we go to the coast?'

'We can go wherever you want.'

She found a hotel in Skerries. The room was small and stuffy and Roisin opened the window. She drew the curtains to shut out the afternoon light, and leaned against the wall and whispered, 'Let's get some sleep.' I watched as she pulled off her sweater. She wore a short-sleeved cream-coloured blouse whose buttons, most of them, had come undone. She wore nothing underneath. She unbuckled her belt and pulled down the zip of her jeans. At the top of her

99

panties, trapped in the elastic, there were dark, springy hairs struggling towards her belly. She looked, in the half-light, so careless, her clothes disordered, hair a mess. She put her palms against the wall and breathed heavily. The curtain flapped in the wind. Roisin looked away from me and undid the last couple of buttons of her blouse. Her breasts were large and heavy and veined, like a nursing mother's, and the nipples were dark and puckered. She pushed her hands inside the top of her jeans and slithered them over her hips.

The bed was narrow and soft. She moved under me and her hips found me out. I did not want to move. She waited for me to go on. I wanted to lie there and be loved by her.

When I awoke the light had gone, Roisin was asleep and I was still inside her. The room was cold. I raised my chest to look at her. She did not wake up. I rested on her and went back to sleep.

At some point in the night she rose and was gone for an hour or more. I was disturbed, but too tired to get out of bed to look for her. When next I awoke she was in bed beside me. It was daylight. I got up as quietly as I could and left the hotel.

I walked along the rocky shoreline. There were three seals in the water and they followed me, their heads bobbing in the waves, curious black eyes watching me. When I headed back to the hotel they started to follow me, but after a while they lost interest. They ducked their heads under the water and were gone.

When I entered the hotel room Roisin was on the telephone and she was startled to see me. I had only to hear the inflexion in her voice and see the emotion muddying her eyes to know there was a man on the other end of the line, and that he had caught her surprise and had asked if she was all right. She said yes, that she had to go, and goodbye. I said nothing about it.

Roisin got up and kissed me. She regarded me for a moment and said, 'You're not handsome, you know. You're too dangerous-looking to be handsome.'

'I want to thank you for all this,' I said.

'*A stór,*' she said. She seemed to be about to say something more, but changed her mind and brushed past me to the door. 'Breakfast?'

We spent two days in Dublin. We went to the pictures three or four times, we ate Chinese food. We drove to the Wicklow mountains and tramped the hills. She held my hand and we walked for hours in the cold rain. We slept in the narrow bed.

One night Roisin said, 'What makes you so hard, Kane?' She was lying on her side, a hand tucked under her face. Her voice was dreamy.

'You think I'm hard?'

'You're the most unrelenting, remorseless person I've met.'

'I was just born that way.'

'I know you weren't. I talked to your mother.'

'And she told you what a nasty little tyke I was as a kid.'

'No. That was what I had expected – this little streetwise kid always getting into fights, being tough, hard. But you weren't, according to your mother.'

'Mothers are not the most reliable witnesses about their sons, dying mothers particularly.'

'She got it wrong, then? Like when she was working for a pittance and you went to see if you could find your father?'

'That's only normal. You run out of money, you go to someone who's got some.'

'A thirteen-year-old boy goes off to school in the morning. His mother thinks he'll be back at tea-time. Instead, he travels from Belfast to London to find his father, who he hasn't seen for years, to a city he has never been in, and comes home a week later with a couple of hundred pounds. When your mother told me that, I wasn't at all surprised. When I was thirteen I hardly thought about crossing the road to the sweet shop without my parents' permission. But I thought, that's exactly what Kane would do.'

'He missed on the maintenance payments.'

'How did you get the money for the ferry?'

'I stole it.'

Roisin laughed and kissed my cheek. 'You little vaga-bond. Your mother didn't tell me that.'

'She never knew.'

'Didn't she ask where you got the money to get you to London?'

'No. She knew not to ask me those things.'

'You little tyrant. Where did you steal it from?'

'From a cash register in a corner shop – about eleven pounds. I knew I had to get the money, so I went into this shop and bought a pint of milk. It was an old doll behind the counter and when she had opened the till I asked for a box of matches. She turned to get them, I grabbed the money and ran.'

'I thought you didn't rob from the poor.'

'I have no such scruples. When I got back from London I took the eleven quid out of the money my father had given me and went back to the shop to give it to the old doll.'

'What happened?'

'I was just going to leave it on the counter and not say anything. But the old doll spied me in the street, coming towards the shop, and she picked up a broom and flew out into the street after me like an old witch. She chased me all over the place. I was lucky to escape with my life. I con-sidered spending the money on drink just to spite her, but in the end I told Dec to bring it back to her.'

'Dec! Did he bring it to her? I bet he didn't.'

'He said he did.'

'Did you believe him?'

'Yes. Of course, it was the time he bought himself a new watch.'

'You're so honourable.' I swore at her. She ruffled my hair and kissed my forehead and nose. 'You don't like it when I admire you.'

'Oh, I do. What I don't like is the smugness I feel after-wards.'

'It's not smugness. You shouldn't feel bad about it – relax for once, let me admire you.'

'I can't live up to it.'

She raised herself up and leaned over me. Her breasts fell on my chest, exciting me, and my heart beat fast. She kissed me.

One morning Roisin made a telephone call from the hotel. She was on the phone for more than an hour. She said she had to return to London and would catch a flight from Aldergrove.

On our way back to Belfast, Roisin asked me, 'What happened when you found your father in London?'

I rarely thought about that time. My father had turned out to be a shell of a man. Although I had expected nothing I had nevertheless felt an angry disappointment. 'Not much,' I answered.

My father had left us when I was very young, two or three I think, so I never knew him and I never missed him. All Dec's father did was beat him and his mother, order them both about and come home drunk. From time to time my mother would ask my brother and me if we were sure we were happy with her, without a father. We always replied, truthfully, that yes, we were happy. The last time she asked that question was when I was ten years old. I was playing in the street with my brother when a man, tall, dark-haired, came up to us. He was well dressed. He wore a blazer with brass buttons, sunglasses and a tie. He did not look Belfast. When he spoke it was with an English accent. He asked for my mother. My brother was about to tell him, but I stopped him because I knew who he was and I did not want him in our house. Our father took off his sunglasses and said, 'I bet you don't know who I am.' He was enjoying it: the man, made mysterious by years of absence, returning to his past. I answered him, 'No. I don't know. Who are you?' He smiled indulgently. He was suntanned and healthy-looking, carefree. So he said, 'I'm your father.'

My mother came out; she had seen him from the kitchen window. She said quietly, in a voice brittle with emotion, 'Come with me.' My father followed her into the house. About half an hour later he came out, smiling broadly. He said how proud he was of us, that we were growing up into fine, strong men. Then he went away.

My brother and I went inside and we saw that our mother had been crying. She went to her bedroom while we sat in the kitchen. We did not say anything because we felt so miserable. After a while my mother came out and she said for us to get our coats because we were going out to the pictures. We saw 'Mutiny on the Bounty'. Next door to the picture-house was a chip shop and my mother bought us pastie and chips, and we walked along eating out of the greasy paper bags. When we had finished we walked all the way home holding hands. Just before we reached the house she asked us if we were happy in spite of not having a father, and we both said we were very happy.

Roisin asked, 'When you went to see your father in London, was that the last time you saw him?'

'No. He came to see me in the Kesh two years ago.'

'He visited you in jail? You never told me.'

'I didn't see you for four years until a few days ago. I didn't have time to tell you.'

Roisin said nothing for a while. I watched the scenery of the Newry countryside. The sky was dark blue-grey and the air smelt of damp forests.

After a time Roisin said, 'What happened on the visit?'

'I hardly recognized him. He was still tanned, but it was like someone had taken a corpse and painted it brown. He was nothing by then, a drunk. He was drunk when he came to see me, it was about half nine in the morning.'

'What did he want?' Roisin asked.

'He said he was my father and he had a responsibility for my life. He wanted to know what I thought I was playing at, in and out of jail, guns, bombs. I couldn't get angry because he was just a drunk.'

'Where was he living? Did he have a job?'

'He told me he was a journalist working for the BBC in London and was doing a very important programme.'

'You never told me any of this.'

'I'm telling you now.'

'Did he work for the BBC?'

'I thought he was lying. You see, he had failed at everything. He had been a brilliant scholar at Queen's and he went to Oxford to do his Ph.D.'

'You're kidding?'

'No. I have his books in the house. My mother kept them when he left. He was studying the metaphysical poets of the seventeenth century. But he just couldn't make it, and so one day he stopped. He left his family, left the country and wandered abroad for years like a gypsy. Occasionally we got letters, a page and a half of him telling us how important he was. It was all lies. So when he came to see me on the visit, with his shabby clothes and his sunken cheeks, I thought he was lying again. I stopped the visit early.'

'Were you upset?'

'No. I just didn't want to go on with it. I wanted to stop it, to cancel him out.'

'That's your way of dealing with feeling upset. I've seen you do it a hundred times.'

'I wasn't upset. I just didn't see any point. He said he'd write. He never got the chance. Two or three days later I was on the block on punishment when in came the chaplain to say he was dead. The chaplain didn't know any details, so I asked him to find out. What happened was that my father was drunk one night in his flat and he fried himself a steak, which he then choked to death on. The body wasn't found for four days. They missed him at work. He did work for the BBC, it turned out.'

'Really? So he wasn't lying to you?'

'He was a porter.'

'He sounds a sad case.'

'No. He was nothing, he's not worth a single thought.'

It was just after midday when we reached Belfast. There was a flight to London at half past. I asked Roisin to catch a later one and to come back to my house. She said she couldn't. She kissed me and told me she would come back soon, and a week later she did, only to leave again a year later after Hughie was killed.

I would pace the cell: sometimes I lost myself so completely in the memory of that time that I would come to standing still, unable to remember when I had stopped walking. The daytime passed painlessly enough, but I hated the night. At three, at four in the morning, fully awake but dazed with exhaustion, senses dishevelled, I felt violent, wanting to lash out and punch until my hands bled. These nights on the block left me feeling, when I was woken, like hiding away in some dark hole, never to be seen again.

*

I watched the sunlight advance across the wall until it conquered the door and began to creep on to our table. At last it reached us and touched my bare arm like a warm hand.

Tempest said, 'It will be another fine day.' He closed his eyes and let the sun warm his face. 'Did you know that I saw Roisin recently?' He spoke in that peculiar tone of his, off-key, unpredictable, just short of threatening.

He continued, 'It was in court, purely professional. She was appearing in a case I had some connection with. I didn't speak to her, except to say hello. She impressed me. She struck me as someone with integrity.'

And honest, incapable of deceit. Roisin had a goodness about her.

'How long is it since you last saw her?' Tempest asked me.

'A long time. I saw her at Hughie's funeral, but we didn't speak. I saw her again a couple of days after that – she spoke then. She called me a murderer.'

'Because of Maxwell?'

'Yes. Then she went away.'

'Didn't you think she'd come back? She'd left before.'

'It was different, it was the end between us.'

I thought of Maxi, of how Roisin had protected him, how sad it was that Maxi had needed her protection, from us, his friends. I remembered that once she had scolded us sharply when we had been making fun of him. She had said, 'Leave him alone, he's not some freak to be tormented.' And someone had replied, 'Well, if he can't take the slagging . . .' That had made Roisin angrier. 'Can't take the slagging? Is it some sort of badge of pride that you can take insults from your friends?' Maxi, close to tears, was embarrassed at Roisin having to defend him; he was sorry that he had been the cause of an argument between her and the company of men around him.

Roisin was not there to defend Maxi the night he needed her most.

Maxi stiffened when he heard me enter.

'I can save you if you'll let me,' I said to him.

'Kane, I never done it.' He sobbed. 'Seanie said I set Hughie up, but I swear on my mother's life I never.'

'This won't save you,' I hissed at Maxi, angry, only just keeping myself from punching him. 'You're making it impossible for me. You're not saying the right things.'

Maxi groaned in despair. 'What can I say? I'm telling you the truth.'

I said, 'It's this way. You're a tout. We know you set him up. If you don't admit that, you're dead – there's nothing I can do.'

'I swear . . .'

'Don't! You're a tout, but I can help you if you make a promise.'

Maxi, whose bloodied head he had kept turned away, chanced a look at me. Promises, he recognized, were for the future; perhaps, the thought struck him for the first time, he had a future. But then, I knew what he was thinking, he remembered Seanie and at once his hopes were extinguished. I said quickly, to divert him, 'Don't worry about Seanie. I am your only chance. If I say the word you are dead. You know that, don't you?'

He nodded, 'You're the OC.'

'I'm the OC, and Seanie does what I tell him.'

'You're the OC,' he repeated with a grimace of pain from the effort of speaking.

'No matter what you've done you can live, if you make me a promise.'

'I will,' he cried.

'You tell me you're a tout, you set Hughie up.'

Maxi blinked. He said, 'What if I say yes?'

'Fuck you! No questions. You want to live? Then do as I say.'

Maxi, the tears streaking his swollen face, whispered, 'I am a tout and I set Hughie up for the Brits.'

I pulled back and told him, 'You're getting shot.'

'Oh Jesus, Kane, oh Jesus. You said.'

'Listen to me. There's no way you can't get shot. But you'll get it in the leg. Are you listening?' I shook him.

He cringed with pain. 'Yes.'

'You'll be dumped near the Royal. When you get there you tell the doctors you were hit from a passing car. They won't believe you, neither will the police, but you stick to that story. There's nothing they can do. When you get out of hospital, you go straight to the docks and buy a one-way ticket to England. You stay there and you never come back. Understand?'

Maxi, through his tears, nodded once. I left him.

Seanie was back in his chair. He began to say something, but before he got his first word out I interrupted him.

'Are you carrying?' I asked Dec.

'All right! Now we're talking. I've got a ·22, Seanie's carrying a Browning 9mm.'

'Dec, you and Seanie get Maxi and bring him to the car. Put him in the back. I'll drive. When we get to the corner of Springfield Road put Maxi out of the car. You, Dec, use the ·22.'

Dec was puzzled, sensing something awry. 'I'll do him, no sweat,' he said. 'But it'd be better with the 9mm. I'd need about fifty rounds of this deuce of twos to stiff anyone, even Maxi.'

'One shot – in the thigh.'

'What!' Dec shouted. Seanie was on his feet, also protesting.

'No arguments. Don't hit the bone, just nick him in the fatty part. Put it in his good leg. If you shoot him in the other one you might as well take a saw and saw it off.'

108

Seanie said, 'You're letting a tout live? Whose side are you on? You think about that.'

'No,' I said, furious. 'You better think about what that side is about, why we do what we do. The two of you, you and Dec, are acting like gangsters here.' I had started towards the hall when Dec smacked his open hand against the wall to block my path.

'What did he say to you in there?' I had never before seen Dec like this: violent, murderous. I pushed his hand aside.

'Bring him to the car,' I said.

*

The door was opened and a screw waved me out. I was escorted along the 'C' Wing passage to a row of glass-fronted rooms reserved for Category 'A' legal visits. A woman sat alone at a table, leafing through some files. She was, I guessed, about forty, with thick brown straight hair. When she looked up I saw a long, pale face with cheekbones so high there was almost something Eurasian about her. She had blue eyes, which at first looked unfocused, and a long, straight nose. When she spoke it was with a small voice, a little like someone coming out of a bad cold.

'Mr Kane, I'm Harriet Cockburn.' She put out a slender hand which was cold, although the centrally-heated room was warm, even stuffy. She trailed it delicately away and I had the impression of something slipping through my fingers, vaguely of losing something. She gave me a formal smile and looked back to her files. I sat down opposite her.

'Thank you for your letter,' she said. 'I've seen Mr Morris just now and he told me that you, both of you, had some trouble with the authorities. If you want me to write to the governor I'll be happy to do so. I can also get a doctor in to see you if you feel you need one.'

'No, but thanks all the same. How was Benny?'

'Jolly good in the circumstances.' She gave me another formal smile. 'Have you already instructed a solicitor?'

She avoided my eyes and stared off into the middle distance. I was a little disconcerted, and wondered if I had made the right decision in contacting her, but then I remembered what Roisin had written about her intelligence and her manner.

'No. I would like to instruct you.'

'That would be fine,' she said with a shy smile and a glance in my direction; then it was back to the middle distance. 'As I understand it, you haven't been sent for trial yet?'

'No.'

'And you've been in custody for six months.'

'Nearly seven.'

'I *am* sorry. I've got a lot of catching up to do. So that would mean you were arrested in June?'

'June the fifth.'

'And have the prosecution indicated when they will be ready to present their case for committal? Did they say anything during any of your remand hearings?'

'Not that I remember.'

'I see. Have they served any papers on you so far?'

'No.'

'Who's the officer in charge of your case, do you know?'

'His name is Tempest.'

'Henry Tempest?'

'I don't know his first name. Do you know him?'

'Yes. At least I've acted in cases he's been in charge of. What did you think of him?'

'Strange.'

'Did he assault you, or try to intimidate you?'

'No. But I had the impression that he was fighting to keep himself under control. I don't think it would have taken much to spark his rage.'

Harriet seemed deep in thought, remembering something. Her eyes swept over my face for an instant and then were away again.

She said, 'There was a case, I seem to remember, involving allegations of violence against him. It wasn't one of my clients – a colleague's. I'm sure I recall something about Tempest having a breakdown.'

Unable to bring any further details to mind, Harriet jerked herself back to her files. She took out a blue notebook and lifted a pen. 'The charge against you is of conspiracy to murder.'

'Yes.'

'Who do the police allege you were going to murder?'

'They haven't said.'

'Is there anyone else named as a co-conspirator?'

'No.'

'So, essentially it's conspiring with persons unknown to commit murder of a person or persons unknown?'

'Yes.'

'Can I tell you what I want from you next time I visit? I'd like to take a statement about your "antecedents", as the police call them – you know what I mean by that? – and then an account of your arrest and interrogation. Would it be possible for you to give them some thought? Try to remember as much as possible about your interrogation, what was said, the sequence of the interviews and so forth. In the meantime I shall write to the Crown Prosecution Service to ask that the papers be sent to you, and also to complain about the delay in the committals. I'll arrange another legal visit with the prison authorities soon. We'd better make it all day. I'll write and let you know when it's been set for.'

'Fine.'

'Is there anything you want to ask, anything I can be doing for you in the meantime?'

'No.'

She got up to her feet and collected her papers and files. We shook hands. Again, when she withdrew, I had the sense of losing something valuable.

I watched her as she went, liking the way she walked – slowly and deliberately, but with a little trip of the feet that made me smile when I thought of her serious and beautiful face.

11

'Good to see you, old boy!' Ralph said. 'Back to the land of the living at long last. How would you like a nice cup of tea?'

It had been a month since I had seen Ralph. He looked a great deal more tired and grey. His shoulders were round and his eyes dull. He moved slowly and there was a slight tremor in his hands.

I sat on a chair while Ralph poured two mugs of tea.

'How have you been?' I asked him. He told me he had spent two weeks in the prison hospital. '"H" Wing is a hideous place, old boy. Absolutely hideous.'

'What was the problem?'

'Nothing serious.' He lifted in his artless hands two mugs of the inevitable tea and handed me one. The contents slopped carelessly over the side as he passed it to me. Ralph had a ponderous, unwieldy body, the kind that suburban wives would shoo from their living-rooms and china. The tea was pale and lukewarm. 'It's awfully good to see you again. You must have had a terrible time on the block.'

'Monotonous more than anything else.'

'I don't know how you stood it for a month. I spent ten days on the block and I nearly lost my mind.'

The blind prisoner. I had forgotten.

'I had one break when I was down there,' I said. 'My new solicitor, Harriet Cockburn, came to see me.'

'Good! How's the case shaping up?'

It was a normal question and he asked it in the same tone as he had asked me about the block – one of genuine interest, some concern, nothing pushy. But I did not like it and told him so. He flushed and shrank back a little. 'I didn't mean to pry, old boy. I understand of course that you don't want to talk about it. I'm terribly sorry.' He handed me my tea and I thanked him. He went on, 'I'm glad you're back. I'm off to the Old Bailey next week. I've had a couple of last-minute postponements, but this time it's the real thing.'

Ralph sipped his tea and I found myself a seat. I could see he was getting ready to say something but was not sure how I would respond. At last he said, in a different voice, precise like an accountant's, 'There's something I wanted to ask you. It's rather delicate. It has to do with money.'

'If you need money, Ralph, I'm the wrong person to come to. I haven't a penny to my name. I have a house in Belfast. I got it when my mother died. It's worth about £3,000 and that's it.'

Ralph chuckled. 'Old man, I wasn't going to tap you. But you've answered my question.' Suddenly, he remembered something. He slapped his mug on to the cupboard and clapped his hands together. I watched the tea trickle down the side of the mug. 'Of course!' he shouted. 'You wouldn't have heard. Anthony! Wait just a moment.' He searched among a file of papers on his cupboard. Retrieving a newspaper clipping, he said, 'Are you sitting comfortably? Then I shall begin. "Mercy for hungover robber" is the headline.' He read:

A 22-year-old north London man was given 'a second chance' by an Old Bailey judge yesterday after pleading guilty to an attempted bank robbery.

Deaf-mute Anthony Boggi was asked through a signer if he had anything to add before sentence. Boggi complained of a 'hangover' and said he 'didn't care' what sentence he received.

The judge, Mr Justice Hale, said that Boggi had a 'truly terrible record' and had behaved immaturely in court, but that after listening to mitigation he was prepared to give him a 'second chance to try to make something of his life'. Boggi was given two years' imprisonment suspended for two years and three years' probation.

The court heard that Boggi, armed with a sawn-off shotgun, had entered the Bow Road branch of Barclays Bank in March last year and held up staff and customers. Boggi's plans were thwarted, however, by Mrs Wendy Marchant, a local housewife, who snatched the gun away and quickly overpowered the robber.

Mrs Marchant, who has three children, said Boggi was 'no bigger than my eldest and I've had to give him a slap more than once'. She was commended for her bravery by the judge and awarded £50 from public funds.

The court was told that Boggi had spent almost a year on remand in Brixton prison, and the judge said he had taken this into account. The court also heard that the gun was manufactured before the First World War and was in 'poor condition'. It was unloaded.

Ralph folded the paper and smiled. 'What a result, eh?'

'Probation!' I could hardly believe it.

'I wonder who his barrister was,' Ralph mused. 'He must be pretty good at the old mitigation if he was able to melt the stony heart of an Old Bailey judge.'

'I think I'll brief him.' It was Benny's voice from the door.

'Benny!' I shouted. He bustled in and I hugged him. 'When did you get out?'

'Just now. I got a month like you. Weren't it dull? Do you know a sarky screw opened my door for slop-out and said every morning, "And what have you got planned for today, then?" I felt like doing for him and all, but I thought, hold up, what you need is to get back into the wing to get your case ready. See your brainy old mate.'

I saw that Ralph was feeling left out. He was standing awkwardly, like a deserted party guest. I said to him, 'Read the clipping again for Benny.' Ralph obliged, enjoying his role as bearer of good news.

'What a result!' Benny shook his head in disbelief.

'Ralph's for the Old Bailey next week,' I said.

'Well, good luck,' Benny said.

We three sat and drank tea. We speculated on what Anthony would be doing.

'I want to hook up with him when I get out,' Ralph said. 'If someone doesn't take the boy in hand, he'll end up back in here in no time.'

Ralph seemed suddenly gloomy about his forthcoming trial. It was something I had noticed many times in prison. Men welcomed news of acquittals or low sentences. It was confirmation that escape was possible, that this need not be the end of their lives. But prisoners, always superstitious and jealous, also looked on such results as presaging bad news for themselves: there was a finite number of acquittals, the unspoken theory ran, and each one taken up by a friend left one less in the barrel when it came to their turn at the lucky dip. Ralph's delight about Anthony was genuine, but it was tinged with a kind of perverse resentment: Anthony had jeopardized his chances of walking away from his own case.

We sat and talked until a screw announced lock-up. I said I would see Ralph the next day and I made my way back to my cell with Benny dragging himself alongside me.

He said, 'What did you think of Harriet Cockburn?'

'I trust her.'

'She's good, boy. I'm telling you she's very good. In just a couple of hours she found things in my favour that I hadn't noticed after a year of looking.'

'I think she is good,' I agreed. 'She isn't seedy the way so many solicitors are, and she isn't one of these young pretty things full of good intentions and sympathy but knowing nothing about the law.'

'I think she's marvellous,' Benny said. 'What about your own case? How's it going?'

'I want to talk to you about that.' Since I had seen Harriet I was desperate to talk to Benny.

'Son,' he said exaggeratedly. 'I thought you'd never ask. I thought maybe you thought I was a grass, or a tout –

whatever it is you funny people call them. Tomorrow we'll have a natter.'

When I lay down to sleep that night I dreamed of the broken street that on earlier nights I had wandered through, naked and bloody. But this time I was flying above the street. I winged over the collapsing roofs, swooping like a bird, diving into the street and soaring up again. I had a feeling of freedom and excitement and power. I flew high up and away. Then, from a great height, I started to dive to the ground. I would swoop up at the last minute, I thought, and clear the street. But as my velocity increased I began to feel out of control, doubting my power to stay aloft. I was falling, crashing towards the earth. My pulse raced, my heart thumped. I woke at the moment of impact and I am sure I cried out. There was no one to hear, and I fell back into my sleep, and dreamed more of the street, the lights and a naked woman who dashed past me, and whose face was tantalizingly shadowed.

*

I had told Billy to disappear. He had been disappointed, not liking to miss the climax, and he received the dismissal curtly, with a contemptuous glance at me. You don't have the stomach for it, he was thinking, so why don't you let me go, someone who will do it and gladly. I watched him make his way down the stairs and, when he had gone, motioned Seanie and Dec to the bedroom.

Maxi, seeing the three of us together, froze. I had once, when I was very young, seen a man knocked down by a car. I had been playing in the street with my brother and heard a screech of brakes. I looked up and saw the man, a few feet in front of me, a second before he was hit. His face seemed to consist only of eyes – they were so round and big: the only thing I have ever seen that resembled the look of terror on his face were jungle animals photographed at the moment of the predator's strike. Maxi had that look then, and it made me feel sick.

'Remember what I told you, Maxi,' I said to try to give him

some kind of reassurance. 'You know what to tell the police.' I do not know if he believed me, that I was not going to kill him, but I thought he relaxed a little. 'Seanie and Dec will take you to the car,' I continued. 'Don't give them any trouble, don't make a noise. We'll be going for a short drive. When I stop the car, they'll get you out. That's when it'll happen. You'll be right next to the hospital, so you don't have to worry.'

Maxi nodded uncertainly. I told Dec to untie him while I went to the car.

There was no one in the street. I got in behind the wheel, unlocked the back doors and waited, checking the rear-view mirror every few seconds. After ten minutes I began to get agitated. Perhaps they had shot Maxi in the house. Would I have heard the shot? Preoccupied with these fears I had given up looking in the mirror when suddenly there was a noise behind me of someone coming into the car. I turned to see Dec push Maxi in one door and Seanie climb in the other.

'What kept you?' I said.

Seanie replied in his even and most threatening tone, 'We were just underlining a few points you'd made yourself. I wanted to make sure there was no misunderstanding.'

Maxi, an inert bundle, was between them. He was barely able to hold his head up. I wondered how much he could see through his blackened and swollen eyes. I said to him, 'It's going to be all right.' I saw a faint smile come to his lips. It was for me alone. Maxi did not want to Seanie or Dec to see it; their rage was too unpredictable to tolerate a smile from him.

I started the car. The night was cold and rainy and our breathing misted the windows. It was now about one-thirty in the morning. There was no one about. The odd black taxi passed us; apart from that there was nothing else moving in the streets.

It was a short drive, six, seven minutes. When we rounded the bend and the junction came in view I slowed down.

'Maxi,' I said, 'we're here. Remember, you've nothing to worry about as long as you do what I told you.'

'I will,' he said with force, as much as he could muster. He added. 'Thank you, Kane.'

'Fuck you, you touting bastard,' Seanie spat at him.

About three hundred yards from the traffic lights I came to a halt by the park railings. My attention was distracted by the lights; they had been twisted during a recent riot and now were bent almost in half. The lights, which were still functioning, winked through their sequence in a horizontal row. I said, 'Take him out.' Dec got out on the pavement side, took Maxi underneath the arms and dragged him to the railings. Maxi, shoeless, bloody, slumped against the railings. He was breathing hard, but he seemed calm. I suppose it was resignation. Then he looked straight at me. You saved me, he was saying. You saved me, Kane, as I knew you would. His injuries made his doglike gaze harder to endure. Looking at him and reading his thoughts, I let a slimy feeling of pride creep over me: oh, I am just; feel the power I have. I felt so in control.

A car went past; the traffic lights, bent at their eerie angle, changed their colours. Maxi waited patiently for the end to his punishment, one last humiliation. Then I became aware of Seanie getting out of the car, slowly, not in a hurry, sure of himself. He raised his gun. Maxi's expression changed, he glanced at me, then away. I turned to see Dec take aim. Maxi's knee did an involuntary jerk. His head went forward and twitched. The second shot threw him sideways. There were more shots. Seanie jumped into the car. Dec fired a last careful round to explode Maxi's head and got in the back.

'Get going!' Dec shouted. 'Get this fucking thing moving!'

'What the fuck have you done?' I screamed at them. I reached back and grabbed Dec by the hair.

'Kane! Get going for Christ's sake,' Seanie was shouting.

Dec pulled out of my reach. We glared at each other. In

my mind's eye I saw Maxi's face, his fear, as he realized what was happening.

'Move this fucking thing,' Seanie shouted.

I put the car in gear and turned left at the junction. We travelled no more than a couple of hundred yards before the image of Maxi became so overpowering that I wanted to kill, to revenge him, and blot out the memory of the smugness I had felt. I took my hands off the wheel and thumped the side window. The car lurched.

'You fucking heartless bastard!' I screamed at Dec.

'He was a fucking tout!'

I put one hand back on the wheel and turned to hit Dec on the head. He grabbed me by the throat. I pulled his hair. I heard Seanie say, 'Jesus.' There were more shouts and screams. I did not care now, I took both hands from the wheel and fought Dec.

We swerved, hit the kerb, and bounced back on to the road.

'Jesus Christ!' Seanie was leaning over me and trying to take the wheel. Dec, his hands clasped around my throat, had almost pulled me into the back seat when the car went completely out of control, mounted the kerb, glanced against the wall and flipped upside down to come to rest in the middle of the road.

*

Just before morning exercise a screw came into my cell and told me I had a visitor.

'A legal visitor, you mean?'

'No, an ordinary visit.'

I had had no visits during my time in Brixton, and I was not expecting one. The screw's news made me feel uneasy. I asked the screw if he was sure the visit was for me. He was patient. He looked at the visiting order and read, 'Kane, Augustine, B19617. That's you?'

'Yes.'

'You got a visit.'

I was taken through the security doors that separated 'A'

Seg from the rest of the prison, down three flights of stairs to the 'A' Wing 'ones', through 'B' Wing, right at the end and into 'C' corridor. We passed the legal visits and entered a small anteroom where I was stripped and searched. At the other end of the room a door was unlocked and I stepped, for the first time, into the Category 'A' visiting area. It was, I suppose, about the size of an average sitting-room and had four formica-covered tables surrounded by chairs. At one end of the room sat a screw behind a desk. I was busy taking this in and did not at first notice Ralph.

'Kane. By God, this is a pleasant surprise! I wasn't expecting to see you down here.' He was on his feet, excited like a child.

Ralph's visitor entered. It was Ruth, I had not forgotten her from the photograph I had seen in Ralph's cell months before. She was like her photograph, just as beautiful, except that her carefully cut hair, dark brown, almost black, was longer. She had lost her tan; now her face was white. She was wearing a grey sweater and black ski pants. As Ralph fussed about her, I saw her take me in with a level gaze. I saw a little roughness on the skin around her mouth and chin, a patch of bad skin that her make-up could not quite obliterate. She and Ralph took their seats. He was talking fondly to her, enthusiastically, and she seemed almost overwhelmed by it. She lit a cigarette to give herself space and as she looked around for an ashtray she glanced at me again. Her eyes were between blue and grey and gave her an air of self-possession.

Overpoweringly aware of Ruth's nearness, I had forgotten that I was waiting for a visitor of my own until Dec came in. Under my breath I swore and when he reached the table I said harshly, 'What are you doing here?'

Dec, looking as sad as I had ever seen him, said, 'I have something to say.'

'I'm not interested.'

'I know your committals are coming up and I hear there's a chance you'll beat your case.'

'Say what you are going to say.'

'I know why you came to London. I knew the minute I opened the door to you. If you had tried to kill me then I would probably have let you. I'm still not that bothered, I suppose. But that doesn't mean I want to die; I don't.'

I looked over at Ralph. He was holding Ruth's hands, gazing at her fixedly as he spoke.

'Don't think I called the police after you left,' Dec continued. 'You probably thought it was me, but it wasn't.'

'What is it you want to say?'

'I am saying I am not going to let you kill me.'

Dec's eyes were wide, and there was a catch in his voice. I stared at him and I realized how weak he had become. He continued, a tremor in his voice, 'I'm sorry for what happened. I am sick about it, but you are not some avenging angel and I am not some dog to get knocked on the head. This thing has to stop.'

Dec wiped a tear from his eye. 'I want to get on with my life. There's no point in this craziness.'

I said nothing and the silence hung over us oppressively. At last he looked straight at me and said quietly, 'I should have known not to try to change your mind. I shouldn't have come.'

'You're right.'

Dec got to his feet. He said, barely audibly, 'I have a life.' Then he turned and went to the visitors' exit and through to the other side.

When he had gone Ralph came over to me. He had noticed nothing of what had passed between Dec and me. He said, 'Kane, let me introduce you to Ruth. I've been dying for you to meet her.' He put a proprietorial hand on my shoulder and led me to his table.

'Darling, this is Kane, about whom I've talked endlessly.'

'It's nice to meet you at last,' she said in a clear and soft voice.

It took me a moment to reply. Even then all I could say

was 'And you,' and immediately I felt foolish. She was so unlike anything you see in jail, so fresh-looking. I wondered how I appeared to her. I became intensely aware of my pallor. I felt grimy, soiled, dried up. I felt the short scar at the side of my face and wondered if it was noticeable. I wanted a bath, I wanted to scrub and scrub until I was clean. My head began to itch, my scars began to itch. Ralph was called by a screw to check some detail about clothes that had been left in for him. I had a vague sense that Ruth shared the feeling of opportunity that his absence had provided. She was not comfortable with me, nor I with her, and she fidgeted with a dead matchstick. The erotic distraction of her nearness tied up my tongue. In the end she said, 'Ralph's very fond of you. I hope that it won't be too long before we can meet outside.'

'I hope so too.'

'When will you be coming up for trial?'

'I haven't had a committal yet.'

'I hope it comes right for you,' she said. I could say nothing back. She looked to see where Ralph was, but, it seemed, it was not mentally to hurry him back, but to check if there was time to establish something more with me. In the end she decided not and we stood awkwardly in silence.

Ralph came up. I thought for a moment he caught the silence between us, more compromising than any exchange he could have interrupted. But any suspicions he had must have been fleeting and easily dashed. He said cheerily, 'I knew you two would get on. One day when this is all over we can meet up outside.'

The screw announced the end of the visit.

'Darling!' Ralph gathered her up. She kept her eyes open while he kissed her. When they had parted she gave me her hand. 'I hope we'll see you again soon.' I nodded, and waited until she took her hand and her eyes away. After a pause she said, 'I hope your visit was all right.' Unlike Ralph, she had noticed.

Going back through the anteroom Ralph said to me, 'Ruth likes you, I knew she would.'

'You must be very happy with her.'

'I am,' he said. 'Sometimes, in my cell, I look at the door and I think to myself: I don't care what they do to me. I have Ruth, nothing else counts. As long as I have Ruth I have a life. I have a future.'

That afternoon I went into Benny's cell. He greeted me cheerfully and asked, 'Who came to see you?'

'The man I was going to kill.'

Benny's mouth dropped. He hobbled quickly past me and pushed the door to. 'Are you out of your tiny little mind? These walls have ears,' he said, as if addressing a stupid child. 'If you're going to start talking dirty we got to get out on exercise.'

It took five minutes or more to get out into the yard. Benny seemed to be becoming less expert in negotiating the staircase. The day was blustery and cold and my ears ached. I buttoned up the thin canvas jacket, but it could not keep out the cutting wind. Benny hobbled beside me and shot me a scolding glance.

'You ought to know better than that, talking in there. Anyway, here we are. Spit it out.'

'It's complicated. About ten, eleven years ago, in Belfast, I was part of a unit.'

'Hey, before you go any further are you sure you want to tell me this? Don't tell me if you think you're going to wake up tonight and regret it, thinking maybe I'm a grass.'

'You're no grass.'

'But I tell you this, I don't approve of what's happening in Ireland. I don't like to see our lads getting killed. I don't think they should be there, but at the same time, I don't like to think of them getting shot. I am English, remember, and proud of it.'

I began again. 'I was in a unit, successful for a time. We carried out a series of operations in our area. Some soldiers and some cops were killed.'

'Was this before or after you'd been inside?'

'After. I first went to Long Kesh in 1973. I was seventeen. I got out after a bit less than two years. I was arrested again in 1977 and got eight years – out after four and a bit. Just after I got out, a friend, Dec, also got out. He was on separate charges, a whole pile of things, murder, robbery, membership, possession of explosives. The charges against him were suddenly dropped. I got out in January 1982, he got out in March. We re-formed and went back to work. For a time we were very successful, so successful that some kind of counter-terrorism expert, a Branchman, was brought over from England to sort us out. It wasn't long before the expert chalked up his first victim, a guy called Hughie. The way it happened it was certain the Brits had been tipped off. So people, me included, naturally started thinking about a tout. We suspected that this Branchman had turned someone.'

'What happened to this alleged expert? Who was he?'

'We never knew who he was. But it was found out later that he got shot. He survived, but it was the end of his career in Belfast.'

'So how much damage did he do before he got shot?'

'Lots. The first thing was paranoia. Everyone started looking for touts. There was an obvious candidate, a poor cripple who had never done anyone any harm in his life. His name was Maxi Maxwell.' Saying it brought Maxi freshly and disturbingly to mind and I had to pause to bring myself under control.

'So?' Benny said impatiently.

'Maxi was lifted, on my orders. He was worked over but denied he had informed and I was pretty certain that he wasn't the tout. I wanted to let him go, but by that stage, the men I was with, things had got so far.'

'Was Dec one of these men?'

'Yes.'

'And he wanted Maxi killed?'

'That's right.'

Benny understood. He nodded his head before asking, 'Maxi got killed.'

'Yes.'

'Was he the informer?'

'At the time I didn't think he was. Now I know for certain he wasn't. I got captured the night Maxi was killed and got ten years. Not for the murder, there was no evidence. I got done for a gun.'

'The gun that killed Maxi?'

'No. This was something else. I had been in a house belonging to Dec's uncle a couple of nights before and had to leave a gun behind. I told Dec to wipe the prints off it, but he didn't. The house was raided by the Brits and they found the gun with my prints on it.'

'So you blamed Dec. And when you got out you came over here to give him one for Maxi, and for the ten spot, right?'

'More or less.'

'Sounds like bollocks to me. If you want my advice, you concentrate on getting out of this case, forget Maxi, forget Dec and start living a life. You, my friend, have got to bust out of the second prison.'

Benny's words angered me. I stopped and said sharply, 'If I beat this case I can't walk away from Dec. If I do that then I repudiate everything I was part of, because this thing has to be resolved. If I walk away from Dec I'm turning my back on the rules I have lived my life by.'

Benny said calmly, 'These rules, they mean that you have to kill this friend of yours?'

'Yes.'

'Bollocks. What sort of game are you playing with yourself?'

'What would you know about it.'

'You're right. I don't know nothing about it. So why don't you tell me. What are they, these rules? These rules that you live your life by, that mean you're going to kill Dec?'

'Loyalty to your own people, taking a side and sticking with it – something a thief wouldn't understand.'

Shaking with anger I strode away from him to the stairs. When I got to my cell I pulled the door behind me and locked myself in.

— 12 —

'As I said, it's delicate.' Ralph looked sheepish.

'If it's about money . . .' I said.

'It is. But it's not what you think. Do you have a moment?'

I said I did and we went together to the yard. The day was grim and grey, the air so damp it was hard to tell whether it was raining or not. We walked a couple of laps before Ralph continued. 'I'm going to the Old Bailey the day after tomorrow. I'm pleading guilty, as you know. I don't expect to get long, a year or two at most.'

'You don't think that's a little optimistic?'

'No. I have a few things going in my favour. I'm pretty confident. I may even get a suspended sentence, who knows?'

Benny had warned me several times that Ralph was not to be trusted. I thought Benny had got it wrong, but Ralph's confidence about the outcome of his case was beginning to make me wary.

'Good luck,' I said flatly. 'Have you got anything planned for when you get out?'

'Well, Ruth and I will be getting married, of course. We want to tie the knot as soon as possible. Then it'll be a holiday-stroke-honeymoon. What about you? What have you got planned?'

'I have to get out of this first.'

'I understand your committals are coming up,' Ralph said. 'You stand a good chance of beating your case, don't you?'

'That's tempting fate. I haven't heard anything from my

solicitor for several weeks.' I had seen Harriet once, during the time I spent on the block. She had been up two or three times since to visit Benny and she had passed on through him a couple of friendly but meaningless messages.

Ralph said, 'You said you had no money.'

'It's true. I've never had any.'

'Don't you miss that? Don't you miss the opportunities money brings?'

'I've never had money. My family never had any and it was never expected that any of us ever would. You don't miss what you never had.'

'That's terrible. I like money. It makes you free. You can travel, you don't have to work. You can lie in bed all day and then in the evening you can get up and say to yourself, "I'm going to fly to Florida or Hong Kong." And you get on the phone and you book a flight leaving that night. Have you ever been able to do that?'

'Ralph, I have never been certain that I would have enough money to be able to pay my bus fare across town.'

'How much time have you done inside?'

'More than eleven years now.'

'How old are you?'

'I've just turned thirty-three.'

'Don't you think it's time you starting thinking about yourself, about making some money?'

The penny dropped. This pitch is something heard a thousand times a day inside prisons. Two men, they did not know each other before they came into prison, start doing their exercise together, talk a little, play cards or chess. They get friendly; they swap the stories of their miserable lives; they trade intimacies; they tell each other of their fears and hopes. Their friendship grows; they become prison comrades. Hard men, they show each other little kindnesses, like lending shampoo or toothpaste, and these exchanges help bind their sentimental friendship. Inevitably, they speculate on the future. They wish each other good luck at trial; and then the thought strikes them, wouldn't it be a good idea to meet up outside? From there it is only a short step before they start planning robberies together. Each of them knows of an easy piece of work, money there just for the taking. All it needs is two men with their proud courage. The money, the plans, the courage and the friendship are prison illusions; they are like mirages of oases in the desert, dangerous to follow; the friendship most of all. And so this was where Ralph was going.

I said, 'Now I get it.'

He said, 'If you want, I can point you to money.'

Barely keeping my temper under control, I said, 'I am not interested in money. I don't have that disease of the heart you and the *conquistadores* suffer from.'

With that I left him. I turned and walked to the iron staircase. As I entered the unit I caught sight of Ralph, standing where I had left him, forlorn and defeated. I felt no pity for him, although he deserved pity for his pathetic fantasies. I felt a resurgence of the loathing I had experienced when I had first seen him. Why, I wondered, had I let myself be befriended by him?

*

Tempest had also spoken about money. On our last day in Paddington Green, in the interrogation room, he said in a voice bitter with a hurt acutely remembered, still taking its toll on him, 'My wife was a child when she married me, eighteen. She grew up very fast, but she stayed greedy like a child. She would see a ring or a necklace, something bright and sparkling, and she would become very quiet. I always knew when she had seen something she desperately wanted. And when I bought it for her she was like a child at Christmas, utterly, deliriously, selfishly happy.'

'Is that why she left? Because of money?'

'No, not really, although money was important to her – and she went to live with a man who had lots of it. I think she'll always be like that; she'll keep moving on to men she thinks can offer her more.'

'More money?'

'No. Just *more*. She will always resent that part of herself, her admission of dependence. Because she needs men.' He drew deeply on his cigarette and twisted his wedding ring. 'She was the most passionate woman I have ever met.'

'She sounds calculating.'

'The two aren't incompatible. Passionate and calculating. It's a bit like you: recklessness and shrewdness in equal parts. There's nothing inconsistent about that. People are neither all one thing nor all the other. But that mix of opposites often makes people unhappy. It made her unhappy. Her passion made her miserable. You see, she did not want to end up recording her life as a series of anecdotes, going from man to man, finding temporary shelter, taking what she could get before moving on. She wanted more control, but, instead of establishing control, the older she got – she's only twenty-seven now – the more her life seemed to be turning into what she feared most, and it made her unhappy.'

He crushed the butt into the metal tray and gazed at the high window. He said in a bitter tone, 'I should have joined the robbery squad. My brother officers in the squad are very interested in money. Perhaps if I'd made more money, who knows?'

'Why did you become a policeman?'

He looked at me quizzically. 'I thought it was to do the right thing, uphold the law. Now I couldn't care less about the law. Somewhere I lost my way. Do you understand that?'

Listening to him, I was thinking of the morning of my arrest, of the arrival of Penny's plumbers. What was it had struck me then about Tempest? His separateness from the men around him? I thought of him standing in the crowded street as the van taking me to Paddington Green pulled away. My mind's eye cleared the street of other shapes and forms until only Tempest remained.

'Yes,' I said. 'It happens when things don't turn out as expected.'

'Important things. I lost my way, but each job I do I try to see things clearly and through to the end. I don't know why I do it any more, but that doesn't seem to matter. It's my job and I do it well.'

'What about the power, has that got anything to do with why you do what you do?'

'Yes. I'm like a juggler. I have to keep so many balls in the air. I have my targets; you're one of them. I have my informers. I have the courts demanding evidence. I have defence lawyers. I have my superiors. I have the men who work under me, and I have to keep the whole thing going until I can wrap it all up. And what I like best is when I have six balls in the air and I'm thrown another one, and another, and another.'

Tempest lit another cigarette. He said, 'We only have another hour or so. I'll finish it from here. The police files are quite detailed. This is the summary.'

He began to read:

Michael Gerard Maxwell was murdered by Augustine Kane, Declan Patrick Mulholland, William Anthony Cross and Sean Mary Smith, all of Belfast, in the early hours of the morning of 13 January 1983. Maxwell had been picked up by Smith, Cross and two other men whose names are not known, outside a bar in west Belfast at about 3.15 p.m. the previous day. He was taken by Cross and Smith by car, a brown Ford Cortina, to a derelict house in the Clonard area. Mulholland arrived at the house at about 5 p.m. Maxwell was severely beaten by Smith, Mulholland and Cross.

Shortly before 10 p.m. Kane arrived at the house and a discussion took place as to what to do with Maxwell.

At 1.20 a.m. Cross was seen leaving the house through a back door. He was followed a few minutes later by Kane who went to the Ford Cortina parked in a nearby street. Approximately fifteen minutes later Maxwell was taken by Smith and Mulholland from the house to the car. The car was driven to the Falls Road and came to a stop a few hundred yards from the junction with Springfield Road. Maxwell was pushed out of the car and shot repeatedly by Smith and Mulholland. The car drove off at speed, turning left at the lights and continuing down Grosvenor Road until it went out of control and crashed. Three men were seen to climb out of the wreckage. Two of them appeared relatively uninjured and were able to escape on foot. The third man, the driver, sustained injuries to the face, head and hands and was seen to stagger to a nearby house. By the time a joint RUC–Army mobile patrol arrived at the scene a hostile crowd had gathered. There was a confrontation between the crowd and the members of the patrol which resulted in localized rioting. During the disturbances a number of vehicles were set alight, including the crashed car.

During a follow-up search of the area several men were arrested, one of them Augustine Kane. He had visible injuries and was in some pain. He was admitted, under guard, to the Royal Victoria Hospital for emergency treatment and was later removed to the Musgrave Park Military Hospital where he was placed under arrest.

Kane was interviewed by RUC officers on three occasions about the murder of Michael Maxwell but he denied any involvement. Since the car had been destroyed by fire it was not possible to obtain any forensic evidence directly linking the car with Kane or Maxwell. Nor was there any other usable evidence, except of a broadly circumstantial nature, to connect Kane with the murder. Accordingly, on the instructions of the DPP's office, the charge of murder against Kane was not proceeded with.

Acting on information received, police raided a nearby house belonging to Mr John Joseph O'Heggerty and recovered a ·45 1911A1 Colt automatic pistol. Forensic examination showed that the firearm had not been recently discharged. However, subsequent tests revealed it to have Kane's fingerprints. Kane was charged with possession under suspicious circumstances and with intent to endanger life. At Belfast City Commission in December 1983 he received a ten-year sentence.

Smith, Mulholland and Cross were at a later stage arrested and interviewed separately about Maxwell's murder. All three denied involvement. No further evidence linking them to the crime was uncovered and they were released. Smith was subsequently killed (in 1988) in an unrelated incident. Cross is currently serving a 23-year sentence for terrorist offences. Mulholland left Belfast shortly after the Maxwell killing and settled in London where he now lives with his family.

Maxwell's death was ordered because he was believed by the others to have been an informer and of having been responsible for the shooting by the security forces of Hugh Gallagher, on 10 January 1983.

Much of the background information relating to Maxwell's murder came from an informant in place and could not be used in legal proceedings without jeopardizing the informant's life and continued usefulness.

Tempest flipped the file's cover closed. He said, 'One final point: how did you find out where Mulholland was living?'

'An anonymous note.' A few days after my release in April I had received a letter, hand-delivered. It contained Dec's name and address, nothing more.

Tempest stood up. He began to pace. From time to time he stopped to draw deeply on a cigarette; the ash he flicked to the floor, the smoke he blew upwards, head tilted back. He watched and waited for the cloud to dissolve before resuming his circuits.

After a time he stopped. He stubbed out his cigarette and collected his files. 'In a few minutes you will be formally charged with conspiracy to murder. This file and everything we've talked about will be part of the case against you. If convicted you can, with your record, expect a sentence of around twenty years.'

He left the room without another word, and I did not see him again while I was at Paddington Green. I remained alone in the interrogation room sitting by the table until two plainclothes detectives came to fetch me. One of them noisily turned gum over in his mouth. He had a practised sneer. He said to me, 'You know me, cock, don't you?'

'You were in the BMW that day,' I said.

'That's right. Now you tell me, you spotted us. I know you did, so I radioed in. I told Tempest, he's on to us, shall we pull him in now? Tempest said, "No, hang on, he'll stay right there." Now, why didn't you make a run for it?'

I did not reply. They shepherded me into the charge room, where another detective formally cautioned me before reading aloud from a typed sheet the charge of conspiracy to murder. When he had finished he asked if I had anything to say and I shook my head. He gave me a copy of the charge sheet, I was taken to the cells and locked up. An hour later I was in Brixton's carbolic-cold reception.

*

There was a letter on my bed waiting for me when I returned from exercise and the argument with Ralph. It was from Harriet: four lines to say that she had at last received from the Crown Prosecution Service a copy of the depositions in my case, that a committal date had been set for two weeks' time and that she would be up to see me the following day. It was brisk: no trouble, no fuss; it was just like Harriet.

I sat on the bed and re-read the letter. Ralph appeared. He stood tentatively before me in a way that reminded me of our first meeting. Somehow I had let Ralph grow on me during the months I had spent in the unit. We shared nothing in common. I disliked much about him: the outmoded and, for one of his age, incongruous raffishness of his dress; the lumbering limbs and artless hands; the affectation of his speech; his humble demeanour. I loathed his pathetic fantasies. There was something cautious about him and I hated that. I despised men who worried about money, or their health; men who thought about security in old age. But there was also something in Ralph I admired: goodness, I suppose. It irritated me, his unwillingness to think bad of people. He was also generous. Initially, I had believed it was bank-account generosity, common in prison, each act recorded in an invisible ledger, the interest payable building up out of sight. Later I changed my mind. I watched him befriend Anthony, buy things for him, spend hours trying to teach him to read. He had been kind to me, and had made no demands of any sort. My attitude towards him had softened, and, until he came to me with his money fantasy, I had grown to like him.

As he stood in my door I felt regret at the way I had treated him on exercise. I slapped my thigh and said, 'Ralph, I bet you wouldn't say no to a cup of tea.'

He brightened straight away. 'Jolly good! If it's not too much trouble, old man.'

I motioned him to the chair and he settled down. I made two mugs of tea. He said, 'I've come to apologize. I think because I have Cortés's disease of the heart I assume everyone else must have. That's the logic of greed, you want to think everyone shares it. I am sorry.'

'I was just about to go to your cell to apologize,' I lied.

He was pleased by this, but modestly insisted that it had all been his fault. I grunted and let it drop. He said, 'This is my last day. Bailey tomorrow.'

I had forgotten. 'You'll be fine,' I told him.

'I hope so. I've done everything I can.'

A screw poked his head in. 'Five minutes to lock-up, lads.'

'I wanted to apologize,' Ralph said, 'because I realized I had insulted you. You're not interested in money. You have other, more important things, and stupidly and thoughtlessly I forgot that.'

'Put it out of your mind. No problem, no sweat.'

We finished our tea. The screw reappeared to announce lock-up. Ralph got to his feet and extended his hand. 'Good luck for tomorrow,' I said.

'Good luck to you. If I don't see you again, take care.' The door closed behind him and I was left wishing I had treated him better.

Ralph was on my mind when I woke up the next morning. I was wishing even more that I had treated him better, for in the night I had dreamed I was back in the street, and this time I had the speed and power of a horse. I raced along the debris-strewn street, my bare soles glancing effortlessly off the ground, and when the woman appeared in the distance she was no match for me. I caught her easily. She wore a dark-blue cloak which I ripped from her naked shoulders. She held the torn remains to her breast and glared angrily at me. I felt very strong, unstoppable. I brushed her arms aside and pulled the cloak away. Her body was slim and fine, but her breasts and hips were large.

I pushed myself against her, I slipped a hand behind her, followed the curve of her spine and hips, felt the hair between her legs, and pressed my fingers into her. I drew her to me. She stood on tiptoes, the muscles in her thighs taut, and gave me wet kisses on my ears and neck. I took hold of her hair and roughly pulled her head back. I knew it was her, I knew it was Ruth. I kissed her deeply and was lost in it until I heard a madman's laugh from behind. It was Tempest.

By the time we were unlocked for slop-out Ralph was gone. I passed his open cell on the way to the recess. An orderly was cleaning it out in preparation for the next arrival. A kind of sadness came over me when I thought of the times we had sat talking together in the cell, of the endless cups of tea, of Anthony and his picture-books. I pushed the door open and the orderly stopped sweeping. He looked at me nervously, as if caught committing a crime. Then he said, 'I found this.' He took something out of his pocket and handed it to me like a small boy surrendering something he knows he should not have. It was Ruth's photograph. He seemed to accept that I had a right to it.

Shortly after breakfast the door was unlocked and I was summoned to the legal visits. Harriet smiled her small smile and, looking off into the middle distance, said quietly, 'I don't see a case.'

We sat facing each other across the laminated table. Confusion rising, I could say nothing; I could only wait for her to continue. I rubbed my thumb over my fingertips to keep my trembling hands under control. Outside two bored screws patrolled. Before us was a thin file of papers at which, every now and then, Harriet peered absently. After a time she jerked herself out of her preoccupations and collected her wits. She pinched the corner of a page and gently pushed it over. She turned another page and scanned it, then another.

She said, 'These are the depositions forwarded by the Crown Prosecution Service. There are, to be exact, twenty-three pages, the statements of eleven witnesses, all of them police officers. The charge, as you know, is one of conspiracy to murder a person or persons unknown in London and elsewhere between 11 April 1988 and 5 June 1988.'

She paused and checked to see that I was following. 'What these statements make clear is that the police had you under observation for some time before your arrest. They also suggest that you rented a flat in Bayswater under a false name and that you probably travelled to England under a false name.'

Again a pause. Her eyes were unfocused, she had a vague look about her. In a more decisive voice she said, 'What the papers also make clear is that no gun was discovered, no explosives, no timing devices, no "death list". At its baldest, there is no case against you.'

'What about interviews during police custody? Is there anything there?'

She let her gaze wander and said carefully, 'No. According to the depositions there were two brief interviews.'

I asked, 'What about the interview with Tempest?'

'There is a statement from Tempest,' Harriet said, flicking through the file, 'but it's very brief. One page. It deals with your arrest in a couple of sentences and there's a couple more to cover your interview with him.'

I had talked to Tempest for hours. I thought of the interrogation room, the lime green paintwork, the light outside the high window, the change from day to night and back to day. I thought of Tempest pacing the room, smoking, drinking coffee; of his long, dark silences, and his changes of mood. I remembered him saying, 'I've lost my way.'

I said, 'There must be more than that.'

Harriet flipped over the pages until she found what she wanted. Pointing a long finger at a line of typescript, she read: '"On 11 June 1988, together with Detective Sergeant McMichael and Detective Constable Prosser, I went to interview Augustine Kane at Paddington Green Police Station at 7.44 p.m. Kane refused to answer any questions and the interview terminated at 8.03 p.m. D S McMichael and I left the interview room. Kane remained in the room with D C Prosser. I returned to the interview room at 8.29 p.m. and spoke to Kane again. D C Prosser was not present. He had left the room. I believe he was going off-duty. I invited Kane to make a statement but he refused. He refused to say anything or answer any of my questions. This interview terminated at 8.45 p.m."'

It was not true.

Harriet had a vague and dreamy manner: everything about her, her unfocused eyes, the small voice, the languor of her movements, all seemed to say, 'I'm hardly here, you need never know. Don't mind me, I come and I go.' It made me feel uneasy, as if I was losing touch with reality. My thoughts wandered, I was only remotely conscious of her. Suddenly the previous night's dream came to mind and Ruth's presence seemed all around. I could feel her in my hands.

Harriet's voice became more insistent and it pulled me back to my senses. 'The committals are set for Tuesday week. I have briefed a barrister, Malcolm Turridge, to appear. We are going to apply to have the charges dismissed. On what they have supplied here,' she indicated the depositions, 'they have no case.'

'Can they introduce additional evidence at the committal?' I asked.

'Yes. In fact, I spoke to the CPS yesterday. They say there may be additional evidence, from Tempest. They have just one problem. Tempest has gone off on leave of absence. Apparently he's trekking around Spain and they haven't been able to get hold of him.'

Harriet gathered her papers and rose. 'If this is all they've got,' she said firmly, 'we have a very good chance of having the charges dismissed. On the other hand, if Tempest comes back and it turns out he has something, we could well be in trouble. Did you get a chance to write out notes on your background and arrest? We'll need them for the hearing.'

— 13 —

The afternoon before I was due in court for committal Benny came to my cell and brought his chessmen with him. We sat on the bed and set them out. Benny, with the white pieces, made the first move. He said, 'You take yourself too seriously, Kane. You sulk like a woman.'

We had not spoken since our argument in the exercise yard a week before. It was not that I held a grudge against Benny. I had avoided him because I did not want to think about what he had said. Part of me had agreed with him. I was afraid he would try to pursue the subject, but he did not. He concentrated on the game and we said almost nothing to each other.

We were in the middle game when a screw appeared and handed me a letter.

'For a man who claims to have no friends,' Benny said, 'you seem to be getting a lot of letters.'

'In nearly ten months,' I reminded him, 'I have had three: one from Roisin and two from Harriet Cockburn. This is my fourth.'

'I hope you're going to do the decent thing and make your move before you start reading it,' he said.

My black bishop put his rook under threat. Benny had overlooked the move and frowned with annoyance. He looked for a way to save his piece, but, I could tell, was distracted by the letter. He was hard pressed to keep his curiosity under control.

The letter was from Ralph. It read:

Dear Kane,

I've had the most ghastly time, a nightmare truly. The day my trial was due to start I got to the Old Bailey at about 7.30 a.m. and was locked up in the cells below the court – dungeons really, no air, full of cigarette smoke. There was no sign of my solicitor or my barrister and I was getting rather alarmed.

By 11 a.m. I was beginning to climb the walls. Just when I thought I would go completely out of my mind my solicitor and counsel, looking very grave, show up. They tell me not to expect too much, the judge is notoriously mean – a lot of flannel. After they had gone I fell into the most miserable mood.

It was not until after lunch that my case was called. I pleaded guilty and the facts of the case were presented for the judge to consider. The prosecution did their worst, making me sound like Ghengis Khan. I wanted to say, for God's sake I'm a conman, not a mass murderer. My lot did their best, trying to make me sound like St Francis of Assisi. Of course the judge would have none of it and remanded me to Wandsworth. I had expected to be out that morning. The disappointment was terrible. Wandsworth is an awful place.

I spent five days there, the worst of my life. I was taken back to the Old Bailey for sentencing. By then I was in pretty bad shape.

It was all over in a few minutes. I got eighteen months suspended for three years.

That was yesterday. I am a free man. Ruth is here with me. We have airplane tickets in our hands and in a moment we'll be flying off to the sun. Do you remember I told you it would all turn out all right? I know I doubted it myself – but it turned out all right for me, and it will for you.

Good luck,
Ralph

Benny abandoned his rook as lost and advanced his queen's pawn. I took his piece with a greedy smile; it did not seem to bother him. He pushed his pawn ahead and asked who the letter was from.

'Ralph,' I said.

'Well, come on!'

'What?'

'Don't mess about, what happened to him?'

'He got eighteen months suspended.'

Benny considered the news. After a minute's silence he said, 'Funny they let the letter in. They don't normally allow ex-cons to write into jail.'

'The censor was probably too lazy to read it.'

Benny made a show of being exasperated. 'You know you can be very naive at times. Ralph was a wrong 'un. That's why they let the letter in, he's working for them.'

'Before he left for the Bailey,' I said, 'he started to talk about money.'

'Don't tell me. And he was going to show you how to get your hands on lots of it.' I did not answer and Benny continued, 'There was no money. He liked to pretend he was in for big-time stuff. The man was a cheque-book merchant, fifty quids' worth of cassettes from Woolworth's – that was his scene.'

'Maybe, I don't know.'

We returned to the game, which I now realized I was losing. Benny won in another couple of moves, as usual; of the many games we had played I could remember taking only one from him – it had been on the day Benny learned of Dave and Terry's sentences.

Benny examined the final position and said, 'You always seem to lose the thread. This time you got greedy and went for material and it lost you the game.'

'I've told you, I don't have the imagination it takes.'

'Do you remember that old Jewish player I told you about? Rubinstein?'

'Yes.'

'He was one of the world's greatest players before the First World War. He was almost impossible to beat. But his nerves got wrecked during the war, and afterwards, when he started playing again, everyone noticed it was a different kind of chess. His games were so fine they were like music, they were magical. But the thing was he wasn't invincible any more. He lost more than he won, even though the chess he was playing was better than ever before. He entered this big tournament in Marienbad with all the other chess hot shots. In the early rounds he played a blinder and beat all comers. He was on the road to victory and had just one more game to win. It was all eyes on him and his opponent. They sat down and Rubinstein moved first. All the books say it was one of the greatest, most beautiful, subtle games of chess ever played.'

'What happened?'

'It lasted five hours. Rubinstein went for the ending a pawn up. But he lost. Afterwards it was pointed out that he had missed a combination that would have given him a forced win.'

'What happened to Rubinstein?'

'That was the end of him – as a player and a man. He died in a mental asylum. He missed his one chance, after that it was kaput. It's an important story. It shows that it's important not to fuck up because you don't get another chance. It also teaches you about material advantage. He was a pawn up, but it didn't help him. He was greedy, like you.'

'Not like you.'

'I ain't greedy, but you are.'

'You've come to this conclusion on the basis of me taking your rook?'

'Not just that,' he said. 'From the way you mentioned Ralph and his alleged money. You're interested, aren't you?'

'That's rich coming from – a man who's dedicated his life to robbing money.'

By now there was an edge in both our voices. We fell into a silence and avoided looking at each other.

'I made a mistake in my life,' Benny said after a while. 'Early on I took a wrong turn, now it's too late – things are over for me. My wife's gone, leg's gone, probably soon the next fifteen years of my life. If I had my life to live again I'd say you can take all the money in the world and pile it up in a big heap, put a match to it and burn the whole lot. Money, material things, they ruin people's lives. The funny thing is that I, a man who has been a thief all his life, have more sympathy for what you believe in than for what I used to believe in.'

'I thought you said you didn't approve of what's going on in Ireland.'

'I don't. What I mean is I respect people who have an ideal, who aren't out for themselves, who are trying to make a corner of the world a little less of a shithole to live in. But now you start talking like some sort of demented gangster who, when he's not going on about money, says he has to kill his friend, which as far as I can see has got nothing to do with any ideal.'

'I never said I believed in any ideal.'

'You're going to start sulking again if we keep on talking about this. Want another game?'

We played until lock-up. As Benny was leaving for his cell he said, 'How long will your committals last?'

'Harriet thinks two days, maybe three.'

'I'll see you tomorrow then. If you get a chance tomorrow night after court, give me a shout through the door and let me know how it went.'

When Benny left the cell I felt sad, not so much at having argued again, but because he seemed to be saying he no longer respected me. There had been a lack of warmth in our final exchanges, and I resolved to talk to him, to try to patch things up, when I got back from court.

At reception the next morning my own clothes were returned to me. After the baggy dungarees I had been used to wearing they felt tight and uncomfortable. The sneering detective I had seen in the silver BMW was waiting for me with another detective and three uniformed officers. The reception PO signed a form which he handed to them. They appended signatures, the PO tore away carbon copies, and, the formalities completed, I was transferred to police custody for production in court. I was handcuffed to one of the detectives, led to the courtyard and hauled into a waiting armoured van. The engine started up and we moved off through the gates into Jebb Avenue, where we were joined by a convoy of police cars, and on to Brixton Hill.

The detective chewed gum and beat a tattoo with his fingers against the metal seat. 'I bet you're feeling sick,' he said with evident pleasure. I said nothing and we remained silent for the rest of the journey.

We reached Lambeth Magistrates' Court after about twenty minutes. The armoured van came to a halt in a small courtyard and I was hurried out of the van and into the back of the building. On the roof I had caught a glimpse of police marksmen, binoculars dangling from their necks, wearing dark-blue, medieval-looking quilted jackets. I was delivered into the custody of the jailer and stowed in one of the cells.

I waited about an hour, pacing the cell and trying to imagine what would happen in court. I began to speculate about Tempest, about the possible reasons for his disappearance, but nothing seemed to make any sense to me. The more I thought about it the more nervously excited I became. I felt weak and began to wish I had eaten something at breakfast.

I heard Harriet's voice in the corridor. The jailer unlocked the door and Harriet entered, followed by a tall blond man with a fleshy face and wearing a double-breasted grey suit. She introduced the man as Malcolm Turridge, my barrister. We shook hands. He was friendly, in a formal way.

Harriet outlined the shape the proceedings were likely to take. 'The point of the exercise is for the magistrate to decide whether there is sufficient evidence to send you for trial. The onus is on the Crown Prosecution Service to show it has a case. They will be calling witnesses who will be sworn and taken through their evidence. When they've finished Malcolm will, if it's appropriate, cross-examine them. Once all the witnesses have been heard the prosecution will apply to have you committed for trial.'

Turridge broke in. His voice was powerful and confident. He fixed his gaze at a point on the wall behind me; he was a man used to addressing audiences. Occasionally his eyes would fall on my face in a lazy kind of way, as if they had landed there by accident, then it was back to his audience.

'We will argue that there is insufficient evidence to send you for trial and that the case against you be dismissed. The paucity of the police evidence is only too clear, unless they pull something out of the bag. Now,' he said with a glance at Harriet, 'as I understand it, there may be something in the bag?'

'Sorry?' I said.

'There's something about an interview with the officer in charge of the case. Detective Inspector Tempest?' he said.

Harriet opened a file and said, 'There is some inconsistency in the accounts of the interview times.'

Turridge was keen to summarize the position. 'As I understand it, there may be additional evidence from Mr Tempest relating to an interview at Paddington Green which, if it is put forward, may complicate matters for the defence.'

'What about Tempest? Is he here?' I asked.

'I haven't seen him,' Harriet answered. 'From what I hear he has been on sick leave for several months. I don't know if he has come back, and the prosecution may try to have the case adjourned if Tempest is not here.'

Turridge interrupted. 'They would have a hard time justifying it. You've been in custody for more than nine months, absolutely monstrous, and the case really should have been committed long before now. It's an indictment of the entire remand system.'

I had heard this kind of lawyer's speech many times in the past. Perhaps they meant it, but I was not interested in hearing their distress at my ill-treatment. I saw Harriet drop her head and I suspected she was embarrassed by Turridge's remarks. It made me like her all the more.

'Well,' Turridge said to me, 'we shall get off now and see you in court.'

He called for the jailer, who unlocked the door. On her way out Harriet said to me, almost in a whisper, 'On the face of it you have an excellent chance, but try not to build up your hopes. The prosecution look very smug.'

The courtroom was small and had a temporary feel to it; at first glance it seemed like a school assembly or a church hall pressed into service to cope with a sudden overflow of judicial business. But a closer look showed it had been purpose-built. All the standard courtroom interiors were there. The dock was at one end, opposite the magistrate and his clerk. The witness box was to the magistrate's right. In front, the lawyers sat at dark wooden tables, and to the left the police witnesses occupied two rows of benches. I recognized several of them: there was the sneering detective from the BMW, and the detective who, on the morning of my arrest, had pulled my shirt from me. Penny was there, with her hair carefully swept back from her model's high cheekbones and wide forehead. The only woman among the police witnesses, she was the centre of her colleagues' attention. There was no sign of Tempest.

As I stepped into the dock the prosecution lawyer turned to look at me, a glance to see who and what he was dealing with that morning. It did not take long and he looked disdainfully away. Harriet was right: he looked pleased with himself. I disliked him, of course. He seemed like every prosecution lawyer I had ever seen: a smug professional who probably dined out on his work, shocking his companions with tales of the sordid doings and miserable, broken lives of people they would never otherwise come into contact with. I thought, I wish I had you in the yard: you would not last five minutes.

On the magistrate's entrance we rose, and the usher called the court to order. I was told to identify myself, which I did, and the prosecution lawyer got to his feet, introduced himself as Justin Tudor-Birch, and proceeded to outline his case.

'Kane is a convicted terrorist,' he began, 'who was released from HMP Maze at the beginning of April 1988 after finishing, with remission, a ten-year sentence for possession of a firearm with intent to endanger life. Shortly after his release, using an alias, he came to England and rented a flat in west London, also under a false name. Kane was placed under observation by C13, the Anti-Terrorist Squad, and was followed by officers from the squad to several locations.

'His actions led officers to believe he was preparing the commission of a terrorist act and they obtained a warrant for his arrest. Kane was apprehended and an application was sought from the Home Secretary, and duly granted, for his detention in accordance with the provisions of the Prevention of Terrorism Act. Kane was interviewed about the terrorist acts while at Paddington Green police station between 5 and 12 June.

'The charge is one of conspiring with other persons unknown to commit murder in London and elsewhere between 11 April and 5 June 1988. Much of the evidence is circumstantial, though no less compelling for that. It falls into two parts; first, the Crown will seek to adduce evidence of Kane's terrorist past and continuing connections with extremist organizations; second, there is the evidence of suspicious behaviour, the false names and so forth – the Crown asks, what reasonable, law-abiding person going about his ordinary, lawful occasions would behave in such a manifestly suspicious manner?

'Sir, the Crown's case does not rest on this alone, although the Crown submits that it establishes a prima facie case against Kane and would be more than sufficient to convince a jury to convict. However, there is a third plank to support the Crown – the statements from Kane, made freely during interviews with police officers at Paddington Green, which the Crown maintains amount to a confession.'

Turridge, who was sprawled across his chair, threw me an uneasy glance. The magistrate removed his half-moon glasses and said, 'You'll have to help me here, Mr Tudor-Birch. I have a copy of the papers forwarded by your office. Can you point me to the relevant statements?'

Tudor-Birch smiled and made a half-bow. 'We will be calling additional evidence. It has not, I regret to say, been possible to supply your honour or my learned colleague, with copies of the new statement. But the witness will be appearing today.'

On cue a tall, thin, bearded man entered from the back

of the court and walked to the witnesses' benches. It was Tempest. His deep tan and uncut hair gave him a wild look. As he took his seat the other police officers shifted to make room for him. There was something in the way they watched him from the corners of their eyes that gave me the impression they did not know how to take him. I thought I saw a flash of uncertainty cross Tudor-Birch's face when he turned to look at his witness.

Turridge was on his feet. 'Your honour, it comes as a total surprise to the defence to hear of the existence of this additional evidence. Unless the prosecution has some very good reason for holding it back to this late date, and may I remind your honour that Mr Kane has been in custody for more than nine months, we submit that the additional evidence should not be heard.'

The magistrate broke in. 'Perhaps Mr Tudor-Birch can enlighten us as to the reason for holding back the additonal evidence.'

Tudor-Birch was on his feet. 'I am only too happy to oblige,' he said courteously. 'The evidence in question comes from the officer in charge of the case, Detective Inspector Henry Tempest. Inspector Tempest has, since June of last year, been on extended sick leave to recuperate from wounds received some years ago, but which required recent surgery. I have a letter from the police surgeon and from Inspector Tempest's consultant to this effect. Inspector Tempest went abroad to convalesce, and I am sure the court will understand why it was not possible to obtain his additional statement in those circumstances.'

Accepting the futility of further objections, Turridge sat down.

'Very well, Mr Tudor-Birch,' the magistrate announced, 'I will allow the additional evidence of Inspector Tempest.'

Harriet had left her table and come to the dock. She whispered to me, 'It doesn't look good. Can you think of anything we can use on Tempest?'

I shook my head, and, after a moment's thought, she returned to her seat beside Turridge.

Tudor-Birch bowed and said, 'May it please your honour, I propose first to call Detective Sergeant Prosser.'

Prosser's sneer was not something he wore solely for the benefit of prisoners in his charge; he could no more hide it than he could the colour of his eyes. He sneered when he held the Bible up, he sneered when he took the oath, and he sneered when he turned to face Tudor-Birch.

'You are Kenneth David Prosser and you are a detective constable in Scotland Yard's C13, or as it is more commonly known, the Anti-Terrorist Squad?'

'Yes, sir.'

'Would you tell the court how you first came to see Augustine Kane?'

'Acting on information received, myself and two other officers from C13 went to an address in west London where Kane was believed to be living. We concealed ourselves and put the address under observation. I first saw Kane on the afternoon of 2 June 1988 at about three o'clock in the afternoon as he returned to the address.'

Prosser described waiting in the car outside the flat, of following me to different places, among them a hardware shop in Queensway and the house of Declan Mulholland in Finsbury Park. He also spoke of having been present during a brief interview at Paddington Green.

Turridge rose. 'Detective Constable, I won't keep you long. There is just one matter I would like you to help me with. With regard to the first interview with my client, on 11 June, you were present with Detective Inspector Tempest and Detective Sergeant McMichael. Is that right?'

'Yes, sir.'

'And the interview, according to your original statement and that of Sergeant McMichael, began at 7.44 p.m. and terminated at 8.03 p.m.?'

'Yes, sir.'

'During that time Mr Kane refused to answer all questions?'

'Yes, sir.'

'In other words, he made no admission of any kind?'

'During that interview he did not.'

'Thank you.'

Turridge asked no further questions and Harriet came to the dock to whisper that Prosser's evidence was not damaging. She said, 'Standard stuff. Obviously it's Tempest they're relying on.'

Another officer, George McMichael, was called. He had also been in the BMW. His testimony was almost a repeat of Prosser's, word for word, and there was no cross-examination. Penny was called. She told the court that it had been her task to impersonate a neighbour and to lead me to expect that when the police arrived to carry out the search it would be the plumber. The point of this exercise had been to minimize the danger to the police should I have been armed. By one o'clock the first ten witnesses had all been taken through their statements and signed their depositions. Only Tempest's evidence was outstanding and the magistrate proposed to wait until after lunch to hear it. The lawyers began to collect their papers and the jailers pulled me to my feet. The court rose and I was taken back to the cell. I was joined by Harriet, who had the look of a doctor about to break some bad news to a patient.

Harriet said that the witnesses heard that morning had not provided the prosecution with the evidence it needed. 'It all hinges on Tempest,' she said.

We chatted for a few minutes about the earlier witnesses, but lurking in our thoughts was Tempest. My chest tightened at the mention of his name and the hopes that had sprung unbidden into my mind were being driven pitilessly out.

Turridge was let into the cell by the jailer.

'I've just had a word with Justin,' he said in his great booming voice. 'He told me something of interest. It seems that Tempest's little holiday in Spain was not entirely for the purposes of recovering from surgery.'

Harriet looked at him with interest and we waited for him to continue.

'It appears,' he began languidly, 'that Mr Tempest has a history of mental instability. It began when his wife left him a year or two ago. He did have surgery, very minor, in June last year, but the reason for his extended sick leave was an alleged suicide attempt.'

Harriet, I could see, was calculating something, frowning with concentration.

'By all accounts it wasn't his first attempt,' Turridge went on. 'So,' he said, with a rare look directly at me, 'even if he says in evidence that you made some sort of admission we are in a useful position to discredit his testimony.'

'Why did the prosecution tell you this?' I asked him.

'It's not something they could very well hide. Some lawyers might have tried, but Justin is actually quite fair-minded, all appearances to the contrary. Well, I must get off and let you have your lunch. Harriet, are you coming?'

Harriet said she would follow him shortly. After Turridge had been let out, she said to me, 'Please don't build up your hopes.'

'But it's good news about Tempest.'

'Yes. I should have remembered before. I think I told you that I knew of a case he had been involved in.'

'Yes.'

'I remember now. There was something about a suicide attempt in that as well. I don't know the details, and this is all terribly second-hand, but I think Tempest was supposed to have cut his wrists during the interrogation.'

It seemed incredible until I cast my mind back over my time with Tempest. I recalled his dark silences, his moodi-ness, and above all the strange tone in his voice, half rational, half on the precipice.

Harriet said, 'It may be that the magistrate will accept Tempest's evidence. If so, we'll have a better chance to discredit him in front of a jury.'

'Okay.'

'Is there anything I can get for you?' Harriet asked on her way out. I said no.

I spent an hour in the cell waiting for the court to reconvene. When the jailer unlocked the door I was burst-ing with nerves.

The usher called Tempest to the witness box. He gave his name as Henry Alexander Tempest, his occupation as detective inspector in the Anti-Terrorist Squad and his religion as none; he would not be sworn and affirmed instead. When he spoke it was slowly, gravely, and with his eyes fixed firmly on the magistrate.

Tudor-Birch was on his feet. 'Inspector Tempest,' he said, 'when did you make your first statement in relation to this case?'

'It was on 14 June, two days after Kane was charged.'

'May the witness be shown his original statement.' Tudor-Birch handed a sheet to the usher who gave it to Tempest. 'Can you confirm that this is the statement you made on 14 June 1988?'

'It is.'

'Will you please read that statement out aloud to the court.'

The statement was brief – a few lines dealing with my arrest and interrogation. When he had finished the usher retrieved the statement and returned it to Tudor-Birch, who said, 'Now, Inspector, does that statement contain a full account of your involvement with this case?'

'No. I left out some matters.'

'Pause there. Before going on to the other matters, will you tell the court why it was that you were unable to give a full account in your first statement.'

'For health reasons.'

'You were wounded, were you not, while on duty some years ago in Northern Ireland?'

Harriet, who had been busy recording the exchanges, gave a slight start and stopped to take Tempest in. She turned to see if I had caught the answer.

'Yes. I received gunshot wounds to the neck and back. Although this was a number of years ago I have had to undergo further medical treatment.'

'If it please your honour,' Tudor-Birch said, 'I have here copies of two letters, one from the police surgeon and one from Inspector Tempest's consultant, which I now make available to the court and to my learned colleague, Mr Turridge.'

The copies were passed over. I saw Harriet lean over Turridge to scan them. The magistrate looked at the letters, and, after checking to see whether there were any defence objections, gave Tudor-Birch a signal to continue.

'Inspector, as the doctors' letters make clear, you were in need of medical treatment in June of last year. Did you in fact receive treatment?'

'I did .'

'Of what did it consist?'

'Surgery to my neck to remove fragments of a bullet threatening the artery.'

'A very serious business. There was some degree of risk, was there not, of permanent paralysis should the operation have been unsuccessful?'

'So I understand.'

'What did you do after the operation?'

'I was on sick leave until yesterday. I went on an extended touring holiday in Europe and Turkey.'

'Were you contactable during that time?'

'Only with great difficulty.'

'But word eventually reached you about today's proceedings.'

'It did.'

'And you returned with all speed.'

'As fast as I could.'

'You referred earlier to some additional matters not in your original statement of 14 June. Why did you not put those matters in your statement?'

'Because of my health. By mid June last year my doctors were advising surgery, followed by immediate rest.'

'I see. Now if there is no objection from my learned colleague . . .' Here Tudor-Birch paused to look at Turridge. Turridge exchanged a few whispers with Harriet and then shook his head. Tudor-Birch continued, addressing the bench. 'If there is no objection, the Crown proposes to examine Inspector Tempest on the additional matters referred to earlier.'

'Please proceed, Mr Tudor-Birch,' the magistrate said.

'Inspector, you have referred in your statement to two brief interrogations conducted on 11 June with the prisoner Augustine Kane.'

'Yes.'

'Is it right to say that Kane made no answers of any significance, that is to say, he neither confirmed nor denied the charge against him?'

'That is correct.'

'Were those two interviews the only ones that took place?'

'No. There was another interview.'

By now I had become reconciled to going back to prison. Once Benny had chided me for not appearing more interested in my case. He had been right, for during most of the time I spent on remand I had not resisted, I had let things take their course. I remembered the first time I had gone into prison; I had been seventeen and very frightened. But once I had overcome my fear and shock, I fought back. The next time I felt less like fighting back. I just did my time and waited for the days to pass. During this remand I hardly felt like caring. I had come to accept prison as inevitable. But over the last few weeks – I could not pinpoint when the change occurred – I had started to care. I began again to think that there was a future outside, although I had only an attenuated sense of its pattern and no idea of its shape or form. It was hope I had discovered, a quiet hope, and its destruction by Tempest left me numb and cold. I felt I was shrinking, and would soon disappear into nothing.

Tudor-Birch, his right hand in the pocket of his double-breasted suit, puffed out his chest.

'There was a third interview?'

'Yes,' Tempest replied firmly.

Harriet, head bowed, was writing as fast as she could. Turridge, with an air of studied indifference, found something of interest in the ceiling.

'What date did that interview take place?'

'It was the eleventh. I believe it was after nine o'clock.'

The lawyers picked something up in this reply. Harriet stopped writing and Turridge, his head still back, his mouth slightly open, flicked his eyes over to Tudor-Birch. The prosecutor himself had a momentary inkling of something not quite right. It was the way Tempest had said 'I believe'. All his answers so far had been definite; about this reply Tempest had hinted at doubt. Tudor-Birch covered any doubts of his own quickly, but everyone in the court was on alert.

'Can you be more precise about the time?'

'No.' Tempest replied flatly.

The hint was now a statement, and disquiet spread over Tudor-Birch's face. He took his hand from his pocket and lifted up a sheaf of papers from the table in front of him. 'Did you have a conversation with the prisoner on the eleventh at about nine o'clock in the evening?'

'Yes.'

Tudor-Birch liked that, a firm reply, but there was still something tentative about his manner.

'What did you say to him?'

Tempest turned to face me. He said, 'I told him that he would be charged with conspiracy to murder.'

'What reply, if any, did Kane make?'

'None.'

The worst had happened. Tudor-Birch whispered hurriedly to his instructing solicitors. Turridge folded his arms and continued to inspect the ceiling. Tudor-Birch said, 'Inspector, during the course of the third interview did Kane make a statement?'

'No, he did not.'

'I'm sorry,' Tudor-Birch said.

'I said he did not make a statement, no.'

The detectives in the witnesses' benches exchanged angry but knowing looks. Prosser stopped chewing his gum and looked intently at Tempest, his sneer, for once, almost gone. Tudor-Birch looked blankly at his solicitor.

'Inspector, we are talking about the third interview, are we not?'

'Yes sir, we are.'

'Kane confessed to you that he was guilty as charged, did he not?'

'He did not. He said nothing that could be construed as an admission, or for that matter as a denial.'

Tudor-Birch did not know what to say. Turridge yawned loudly, his eyes still fixed on the ceiling. After a few moments the magistrate intervened.

'Mr Tudor-Birch, might I suggest a half-hour adjournment to enable you to take further instructions?'

Tudor-Birch agreed. Once more I was led back to the cells. By now it was shortly after four o'clock. There was no sign of either Harriet or Turridge. I went over in my mind the times I had waited on verdicts and on sentences. The time had seemed unreal. I remembered the quickness of my breathing, the tightness around my chest, a certain light-headedness. It seemed to me that on those occasions my senses were at their sharpest – my hearing, my vision, my sense of smell were razor sharp, yet at the same time I seemed unable to take in what was going on around me. I could not describe what I thought or saw or heard during that waiting time.

After three-quarters of an hour the door opened and three uniformed officers escorted me back to the dock. When I entered, Tudor-Birch was already on his feet. Harriet and Turridge did not look up. Tudor-Birch waited until I was seated before saying, 'Your honour, I have received new instructions.'

The magistrate nodded. 'Very well.'

'My instructions are that there is insufficient evidence to proceed with the case against Kane. The Crown asks that the charge remain on file.'

'Very well. Are there any outstanding warrants against Mr Kane?'

'No, your honour,' Tudor-Birch replied.

'In that case Mr Kane is free to go. If the officers will please take him to collect his property.'

On the way out from the dock Tempest gave me a look I did not understand. There seemed to be a smile on his lips, but it was not friendly; if anything it seemed mad.

It was dark and cold and damp, and the streets around the Elephant and Castle were crowded with men and women intent on getting home. Unused to the bustle, unused to weaving in and out of crowds, I bumped into people several times. Harriet took my arm and guided me to a neon-lit café with white-tiled walls and red plastic tables. The chairs were also of plastic and attached to the tables by metal tubing. We found a free table and Harriet went to get coffees.

She said to me when she came back, 'I have no idea what was going on there. Clearly the Crown expected Tempest to give evidence of a confession. That's what their case was built around. For some reason, Tempest failed to come up with the goods. Have you any ideas?'

I could think of nothing and shook my head.

We sipped the coffee and I watched the people hurry past on their way to catch buses and trains. I had always liked winter in the city. I was thinking: This is the best time to be released, in the dark, in winter. I thought, I will get on a bus and sit down beside a man who has just left an office or a factory and will know nothing of where I have come from. All he will be thinking about is how miserable the weather is and how he wishes he could be home, and I will be sitting there beside him and I will not care about the rain or the wind.

Harriet said, 'What will you do?'

'I haven't thought about it. I might stay in London, find a job.'

'Can you wait here for ten minutes? I just have to get something, I won't be long.'

I said I would stay. I watched as she went out into the rainy street and tripped past the window. I drank my coffee and thought about sitting beside the man on the bus. How I loved nights like this.

Harriet returned. She handed me an envelope. 'This is my address and my home and office numbers. Call me any time.'

'Thanks,' I said.

She said, 'Can I give you a lift anywhere? My car's parked just around the corner.'

'No thanks. I want to get the bus.'

She smiled vaguely and got up. 'Take care,' she said.

'Thanks for everything.'

As she was on her way out I suddenly remembered something. I called to her and she came back.

'Do you have those doctors' letters?'

'Yes,' she said.

'Can I see them?'

She put her briefcase on the table and rummaged through it. After a minute or so she found the letters. The first one did not have the information I wanted. I handed it back to her. The second one did.

'Did you know Tempest had served in Northern Ireland?' Harriet asked me.

'No.' I re-read the letter for the information I wanted. There it was: Tempest had been serving in Belfast when he was shot. The date of the shooting was February 1983, a month after Maxi was killed. I returned the letter to Harriet, who gave me a concerned look. She said goodbye and left.

When she had gone I opened the envelope she had given me. There was a sheet with addresses and telephone numbers, home and work, and two hundred pounds in twenty-pound notes. Her generosity deeply touched me, but I could not concentrate on it. How slow I had been. Tempest, I now understood, had been the expert brought in to break up the unit. He had been the one who had interrogated Maxi.

PART TWO

—

14

It was the noise of breaking glass that forced me to my feet. I pulled the grey army blanket that served as a curtain back from the window. Across the road a van marked 'Harrison's Aluminium Shop Fronts' straddled the pavement. Zhutu's window was being cheerfully smashed by the Harrison men while Zhutu, in his stained brown trousers and soiled green cardigan, watched, arms folded, his son by his side.

I dodged the morning rush-hour traffic and got safely across the road.

'What's happening?' I asked Zhutu.

'Expand,' he replied, with a careless wave of the hand.

'Expanding?'

'Yes, yes. You want milk? Bread?'

I counted the change in my hand. 'Just milk.'

'Okay. I can get you. But not tomorrow. Tomorrow no bread, no milk.'

'No? Why not?'

'Expanding! We expanding!' He said, irritated by my failure to comprehend this straightforward fact. 'To make money, more money.'

I went next door and bought a newspaper, but back in the flat I saw it contained nothing that I had not heard the night before on the radio, and I cursed myself for wasting the money instead of buying bread. There was no food in the flat, and what I had left would not buy anything. It was not even enough to get me a bus ride to work. I heard the jingle for the eight o'clock news and gathered my jacket. As I left, two of the Harrison men were drilling into the brickwork below the window, and two more, on ladders, were removing the sun-faded, flaking Zhutu Bros Groceries sign.

It took almost an hour to get to the lorry park. It was near King's Cross, a rectangle of open ground fenced in and guarded by alsatian dogs and men in overalls sitting on crates or sofas rescued from skips and playing cards with oily hands. I rattled the gate and the dogs bounded up. One of the men looked over suspiciously; he knew who I was and what I was there for. I had been working as a driver for eight weeks. The suspicion was part of his hard-man look. With a nod, he ordered another card-player, an older man with wavy grey hair and a ginger moustache, to call the dogs off and unlock the gate.

I was conscious of their eyes on me as I made my way to the lorry. The atmosphere in Brixton had been friendlier than this, I thought. I got into the cab and changed the tacograph while the grey-haired man moved a lorry from my path. I had to reverse out, and as no one wanted to help I had to get out of the cab twice to make sure I was not going to hit anything. The card-players watched with amusement.

I drove north to Tottenham to pick up my mate, a black kid called Viv.

'You're late,' he said when he got into the cab.

'You worried?'

'Couldn't give a fuck.'

We drove to the A1 and headed for St Albans. Viv fiddled with the radio, but gave up after a while.

'Useless thing,' he said. 'Tomorrow I'll bring some music. We'll have a good time. How do you like the job?'

'It's all right.'

'What did you do before?'

'Same sort of thing,' I said.

'I don't like it,' Viv said mournfully. 'Driving around all day to pick up so-called antique furniture. What a life.'

'What sort of life do you want?'

'Not like this. Ask yourself, man, can you handle this for the next forty years? Every day? There's got to be more to it.'

'More to what?'

'Living, man. To live you need money, and we ain't getting any like this.'

It was almost dark by the time I got home. The Harrison men were sweeping up the putty, glass and wood-splinters from the pavement in front of Zhutu's aluminium-fronted shop. I let myself in and climbed the lino-covered stairs to the first floor. The house smelled of dust and faintly of cats. I drank the remaining milk and went to the window to see the van pull away. The baggy-trousered Zhutu appeared at the door of his shop, relieved to see the back of it all. He produced a cloth and proceeded to wipe his new window. His son, a tall, square-shouldered, good-looking boy with straight black hair, came out to look at the redesigned shopfront. Inside I could see Zhutu's wife, a stumpy woman in a dark headscarf, rearranging the window's contents. She took away cans of baked beans and ravioli, boxes of washing powder and loaves of sliced white bread in polythene wrapping. Zhutu marched across the road and took up a position directly opposite his shop. He lifted his arm and let it fall in a signal. An extravagant, baby-blue plastic sign flickered as the neon warmed up, then burst into its full luminescent glory. The boy darted from the doorway across the road to join his father. The immigrant shopowner put an arm on his son's shoulder, and the two gazed at the sign that announced the conversion of their corner grocery shop into 'Zhutu & Son, International Automotive Associates.'

They gazed longingly at their establishment until beckoned impatiently by the woman. Then, reluctantly, they re-crossed the road, pausing for one last admiring look. Oblivious to everything else, they blocked the pavement, and a passer-by, a hard-looking man in a donkey jacket and woollen hat, roughly shouldered past them. The boy did not like it, and he stared resentfully after the man as he turned the corner at the green. Zhutu put a hand on his son's back, and gently guided him into the shop.

I picked up a book and lay down on the bed to read. It was a nineteenth-century French novel and I was three-quarters of the way through; the bookmark I used was the photograph of Ruth I had retrieved from the cleaner in Ralph's cell. I found myself gazing at it and thinking about her, of the time we met when Dec came to visit me. My thoughts wandered to Dec and away again. Like some memory too painful to contemplate for even a fleeting moment, I pushed him out of my thoughts.

I fell asleep and when I woke it was with a dry mouth and sore throat. I got to my feet, groggy, moaning and complaining out loud. I stretched and yawned. My watch said it was half-past ten. Then I remembered the man in the donkey jacket and the woollen hat. There had been something familiar about him. I had seen his face before. A feeling of unease crept over me; there were goose pimples on the nape of my neck.

I went to the window and looked across the road at the shop, picturing the scene when the man had pushed impatiently past Zhutu's boy. I was trying to place the face when the doorbell rang. I had been living in the flat for two months, having found it a couple of days after getting out of Brixton. It was sparsely furnished and had no phone. During that time I had had no visitors. The bell rang again. I thought of Penny, of Tempest. The bell rang again, an urgent sound. My heart was pounding as I made my way down the stairs to the front door.

'I have to talk to you.' It was Roisin. When I had first met her, Roisin had been twenty years old. Then she was a striking-looking young woman with large, trusting pale-blue eyes. She was tall and athletic, with strong arms and legs. She did most things in a rush; she talked and walked fast; she knocked things over and she was always critical of herself, of her haste and her clumsiness. Years later, during the time we spent in Dublin, I noticed how she had changed, how handsome she had become, more sure of herself, though not over-confident. When she had been younger she had not been pretty; there had been something too strong about her body to make her seem pretty to men. Now she was beautiful.

'How did you find me?' I asked her. I was not interested, but it was all I could think of to say.

'Harriet.'

'Are you going to come in?'

'No,' she said sadly. 'I want to talk to you outside.'

'I'll get my coat.'

Roisin had always liked going for walks around the streets whenever she had something important she wanted to discuss. It was the one time she would walk slowly, barely lifting her feet, walking and thinking and talking. We turned off the main road and wandered through a series of side-streets. It had rained earlier, and the streets were so shiny they seemed to have been freshly tarmacked.

'What is it?' I asked her after we had walked in silence for a while.

'Dec came to see me. Twice. The first time was the day after you got out.'

'How's he keeping?'

'Agitated. He wanted to know if I knew where you were. I didn't at that time. He came again this morning asking the same question, so I went to see Harriet.'

'What did he want?'

'He was practically hysterical, and he wouldn't or couldn't come right to the point. I had to drag it out of him. Even so, I think I probably got less than ten per cent of the story.'

'What story?'

'Dec seems to think someone's out to kill him. Apparently there was someone hanging around outside his house. It frightened him.'

'Who did he think it was?'

'As I said, he was almost hysterical, and it was difficult to get much sense out of him. But the impression I got was that he thought the person out to kill him was you. Were you the one outside his house?'

'No.'

'Tell me the truth, Kane.'

'It wasn't me.'

'But you're after him?'

I did not answer, and we walked on without speaking. Roisin looked at the houses we passed, at cars parked on the street; but she would not look directly at me. I let her get a pace or two ahead and from behind I admired her. I was thinking with satisfaction that with all her mature beauty, her nice clothes and unobtrusive jewellery, she still did not quite seem elegant or stylish; she was too natural for that.

'Are you with anyone now?' I asked her. The question came to me from nowhere. I had not formed it in my mind, and I felt as if I had been taken by surprise.

Roisin answered quietly, 'Yes. I'm married – to a barrister. We've been married four years. I have a son.'

Although I had suspected something like this I felt a great sadness come over me; a piece of me sank down inside. I found myself wondering what she looked like now without clothes. I would have liked to put my hand on her breast and kiss her. I tried to remember the feel of her. But it was so long ago. I did not trust myself to speak, so we lapsed into another silence.

'Do you have a job?' she said at last.

'Yes. I drive a lorry for an antique dealer.'

'Have you enough money?'

'Yes. It's well paid.' In fact, it was badly paid, the hours were long and the rent for the miserable flat was high, but I did not want to say so to Roisin. I knew she would have insisted I take money from her.

'Are you going to kill Dec?'

We came to a yellow street-light and stopped. A car hissed through a pool of water on the road. In front of us a bored man was being led along by an indiscriminately curious puppy.

She took my silence as meaning yes. She said, in a tone of barely suppressed anger, 'He has a wife and three children.

You remember them? Are you going to kill Grainne's father? Cappy's husband? Are you going to destroy their lives?'

I said calmly, 'If I killed Dec it would be no more than he deserves.'

Roisin turned abruptly away and it made me angry. If she was here to plead for a man's life she might as well know something about him. My voice rose insistently, 'He killed Maxi. I don't mean he was indirectly responsible for Maxi getting killed. I mean he pulled the trigger, him and Seanie.'

Roisin did not like this; she was getting impatient with me, about to say it was all over and done. My tone became harsher still. I continued, 'And before he pulled the trigger on Maxi he beat the shit out of him, out of a cripple, someone who couldn't defend himself against a six-year-old. He beat him until he was crying, until there was blood coming out of his ears and mouth and nose.'

Roisin started to walk away, but I followed her and I shouted, 'He took Maxi's caliper off him and beat him over the head with it. He stubbed out cigarettes on the soles of his feet.'

'Stop it!' she cried.

'Just take all that into account when you start talking of Declan Mulholland, the family man.'

Roisin glared at me and pushed past my shoulder. I snatched at her arm and drew her back. 'There's more, not as important, to you anyway, but more all the same. Dec got me ten years. He left a gun in his uncle's house, which I had touched and told him to wipe clean. He didn't do it and I got ten years.'

She tried to pull away, a defiant look in her eyes. I held on to her and she said, 'So revenge is what this is all about?'

I let go of her arm. 'No,' I said slowly, 'it's about loyalty.'

'This is rich.'

'It's difficult to explain. We were all part of something

once – me, Seanie, Hughie, Maxi and Dec. We belonged to something we believed in. It gave us a direction. Dec lost his way. And Maxi's dead because of that. Don't you see, Roisin, this thing has to be resolved. If I don't do it, I'm turning my back on everything I ever believed in.'

'You can't shoot the past by shooting Dec.'

'I can't betray it either.'

'That's why you hang around outside Dec's house, waiting to shoot him down, because of "loyalty"?'

'That wasn't me. I don't know anything about it.'

Roisin turned and strode ahead. I ran to catch up with her. I tried to get her to speak but she would not. We walked for another quarter of an hour. By then I did not know where I was. It had started to drizzle and I was beginning to feel cold. I put my hand on Roisin's shoulder. She was shivering.

She said, 'I'm glad you're out, Kane.'

Her tone was soft and I squeezed her shoulder. I thought for a moment that she was leaning lightly against me and I made to pull her closer. She did not like it and stiffened. She said, 'Have you wondered why Tempest turned funny in the witness box? Harriet told me about it.'

'Did you know he was the Branchman in Belfast that time, the one brought in to deal with us?'

'Yes.'

'I only found out at the committals.'

She looked at me, astonished. 'You mean you didn't know?'

'Not before the committals.'

'I thought you would have known. He told me all about it. I met him one time. He came up to me in a magistrates' court one day.'

'When was this?'

'Last year.'

'Before I was arrested.'

'I think so. Yes, but not long before.'

'How long? Days?'

'Longer. A couple of months.'

'What did he say?'

'He talked about you, at great length. He knew all about you. You were just about to get out from Long Kesh, he said.'

'So it was about February or March last year?'

'Yes. He admired you. He was scary, though. That quiet, reasonable voice – but those eyes. He's psychotic.'

Why was Tempest asking Roisin about me before I had even been released from prison?

In her next sentence Roisin answered my unspoken question. 'You know why he's doing all this, don't you? – he wants to finish what he started in Belfast. He wants total victory.'

'Why didn't he try harder at my committals?'

Roisin smiled and shook her head. 'Haven't you caught on yet? He doesn't want you in prison. He wants you dead.'

She let me have time to digest what she was saying. We walked aimlessly along for another ten minutes or so, neither of us speaking.

We found ourselves on a main road and made for a junction where Roisin looked around for a taxi. While we were waiting, she said, 'You look all right, everything considered. Still too thin, though.' She put her hand in my hair, and took hold of it and let out a small affectionate laugh. She looked me up and down and said, 'How long have you had that leather jacket?'

'Nearly ten years.'

'I knew it was the same one.' She laughed again, and I looked at her face with regret for something I knew was gone now. She had come back once before, but this time was different; there would be no night-time drive in the rain to Galway and Dublin.

She said in a serious voice, 'Kane, what are you going to do with the rest of your life?'

I did not like the question and I tried to joke my way out of it, but she cut me off with a hard look that told me not to be childish.

'I don't know. I'm used to seeing just getting out of prison as the main objective. It's hard to focus on anything else.'

'What about Dec? The truth.'

'The truth is I don't know. He killed Maxi, but he loved Hughie like a brother. You remember how hard he took his death?'

Roisin bit her lip and nodded.

'He gave Siobhan what money he had. That was just like Dec – he would give you anything he had if you were a friend of his, and if he didn't have what you needed he would borrow it from someone else.'

'Cappy hated him for that.' A fond memory had spread a little lightness in Roisin.

'So I understand his anger about Hughie, even though Maxi was no tout. If Dec thought he was, I suppose you can see his motive for doing what he did.'

'Let it drop, Kane. Just let Hughie and Maxi and Seanie alone now. Let Dec alone. You don't have to be driven. Don't mess your life up for that.'

The last woman to plead with me for Dec had been Cappy, although she had only suspected my intentions, and she had said something similar: that you only got one chance at life and it was a sin to mess it up. It made me think of Benny. He would have a lot to say if he could have heard this.

Eventually, a taxi responded to Roisin's waves and pulled over. We parted with strained smiles and I watched the taxi go until the driver flicked on an indicator and it turned out of view.

I had to ask directions several times to find my way back to the flat. I had a heavy heart. I would have preferred to remember Roisin in a different world, when she was mine, when she belonged in my house with me. The last time I had seen her had been at Hughie's funeral and that was where I wanted to remember her: in a place I knew, not here in London with a husband and a child. I realized how far she had left me behind.

There was a drizzle that felt like cold pinpricks on the skin, but it did not bother me. I tried to decide what to do about Dec. I had bided my time since the committal hearing, in a way waiting for a clue, something to show me what was right. I had been so sure I would kill Dec, but, I reflected that night, recently I had been spending more time thinking about money and the second prison.

15

It was well past midnight by the time I found my way back to the flat. The rain made the hallway smell worse, of mildew and mice, and my shoes made a gritty sound on the lino. I turned on the light at the foot of the stairs and saw two letters lying among the fluff and dust on the grimy lino. Both had been hand-delivered.

As I climbed the stairs I tore open the first. It was from Harriet. I let myself into the flat and flopped on to the bed before reading it. She was writing, she said, to let me know that Benny had come up for trial at the beginning of the previous week. The evidence against him had fallen into three main categories: there had been the welter of circumstantial evidence – his presence outside the supermarket at the time of the robbery, the gunshot wound, the stolen car; then there was the testimony of the security guard who claimed it had been Benny who had attempted to rob him; finally, there was a verbal confession, hotly contested by the defence, allegedly made by Benny to police during his interrogation. Harriet described the evidence as 'difficult' and said she had not rated Benny's chances highly. She had briefed Malcolm Turridge, who had worked wonders with the jury, although the judge was rather less impressed and had on more than one occasion rebuked him for 'excessive zeal' on his client's behalf. Benny had given evidence from the witness box and had been very impressive. He came across, according to Harriet, if not as an honest man, at least as one with enormous courage and dignity. The jurors, some of them at least, had taken to him. However, in spite of Turridge's best efforts and Benny's performance in the box, they could not bring themselves to acquit; nor could they find heart enough to convict, and the result was a split, six-six. A sullen judge discharged the jury and ordered a retrial to begin in two days' time, on the fifteenth.

I sat on the bed gazing absently into space, thinking how lucky Benny had been, when I at last remembered the second envelope. The handwriting, large and old-fashioned in its fussiness, I recognized, or at least I had seen it before – shortly after my last release from prison. There was no name I could put to the script, for the letter I had received then had not been signed: it had been a single sheet and had contained nothing more than the name Declan Mulholland and his address in London.

I ripped open the seal and withdrew three sheets of paper. They were formal legal documents, typewritten statements of witnesses. The first statement took up two pages; the second a single page. At the top of each was a date: the first was 11 March 1982; the second was 21 January 1983. At the top of the first document were two names: Tempest's, which caused me no surprise, and Dec's, which should have surprised me, but did not. Tempest's signature also appeared on the second statement, together with a third name that I would never have dreamed of seeing.

The doorbell rang. I looked at my watch: it was after one o'clock. I put the documents away and went down the stairs and into the hall to open up. It was Ralph, and beside him Ruth. Ralph grinned uncertainly and said, 'How do you do, old boy? Long time no see.'

I made them tea and asked them if they would mind having it black. Ralph said, 'Sorry to call on you at this hour. We were here earlier but there was no one in. So we went to have a meal and on the way back I saw your lights were on.' Ralph looked around the room. 'I must say it looks to me much the same as your cell in Brixton.'

'Well, the mugs at least are different, they're not plastic.'

Ralph said to Ruth, 'Kane had a certain monkish quality when in Brixton. His cell was that of a Spartan.'

Ruth smiled at him, then at me. Ralph continued talking,

but I did not hear what he was saying for I was too busy looking at Ruth. She was browsing through the few paperbacks I had collected and I was suddenly reminded of Roisin. When Ruth looked up I thought at first her eyes were like Roisin's; but no, they were very different. Roisin had candour in her eyes, and a gentle yearning. Ruth had secrets in hers; they were astute and watchful.

Ralph was saying something about having been in Spain, a holiday, sunshine, wine, money. He showed no sign of having derived any benefit from his holiday. He looked grey, vacant and neglected, a small, disappointed man in spite of size and bulk. There was a certain bravado in his voice, a boastfulness of the kind employed by old school-friends when they accidentally meet years later and tell each other how well they are doing. His talk was of money and success, but his effort at sounding confident was hope-lessly undermined by the lost look of desperation on his face. His confidence was like water in a sink, liable to drain away with one pull of the plug.

Ralph came to the end of his holiday story. He said, 'You don't look as if you're rolling in it, old boy. Have you a job?'

Ruth regarded him coldly. If she had spoken, it would have been a rebuke, a sharp calling of his name. She did not need to say anything, for Ralph picked up her meaning and laughed. 'Don't be so English, darling. Kane doesn't take offence at questions like that. You don't mind, do you, Kane?' He gave me a ragged smile.

'No. I drive a lorry. I've been working there for a few weeks now.'

'Is this a squat?' Ralph asked.

'Really, Ralph,' Ruth protested. Ralph laughed shallowly.

I interrupted. 'It's all right, Ruth.' She smiled shyly and turned away, and I savoured the sound of her name on my lips. I said to Ralph, 'I rent it.'

'It's pretty grim, old man.'

'What about yourselves? What have you been doing since the holiday?'

174

Ralph started to tell me, but I took in only the occasional word. The more Ralph talked the more I realized we had never had anything in common, beyond the misery and boredom of imprisonment. On he rambled. Occasionally, Ruth would interrupt to cut short one of Ralph's tortuous anecdotes, and she would glance at me to see how I was reacting.

Ralph eventually came to a stop. Some silent time passed. Ralph and Ruth exchanged a private look. I thought at first it was the kind couples swap when they are preparing to leave the house of a friend. But it was not: they were preparing something else. I could sense there had been a purpose behind their visit, more than just looking up an acquaintance.

At last, when the time had come either to speak or go, Ralph said, 'Do you remember just before I left Brixton I spoke to you about money?'

I had suspected this turn. I answered evenly, 'Do you remember what my reply was?'

Ralph started to say something, but Ruth cut him short. She said to me, 'Will you please listen? At least listen?'

I looked at her, into her blue-grey eyes, until she turned away. I said to Ralph, 'Go on.'

'I won't beat about the bush. Two, nearly three, years ago I met a man called Joe Varvakis. He's a crook, but a very clever crook, very successful. He started out his criminal life as a robber, but was arrested. They couldn't convict him; he was much too wily for that. He made a career move, into fraud, where the risks are lower and the rewards, believe me, are a lot higher.'

Ralph glanced sideways at Ruth, who silently told him to get to the point quickly.

Ralph continued, 'When I met Joe I had been thinking about a little number. It involved VAT and gold. I didn't have the resources needed to pull it off and, to be blunt, I didn't have the initiative.' He shrugged in a way that touched me and said, 'I had lost my initiative; it happens. So I explained my plan to Joe, who liked it. We set up as

175

partners. It was quite a big operation, and we made a tidy little profit.'

'How much?' I asked.

'Kane, you would not believe the money involved. I couldn't even attempt to put a final figure on it, hundreds of thousands at least in cash, more in other assets.'

'Did you get any of this money?'

'That's the whole point.' His thin purple lips became thinner and he said with a tinge of bitterness, 'Very little. Pocket money really, no more than that.' He licked his lips nervously. He was coming to the point. 'But. We had an office, Joe and I. One day I found a box file. Inside was an envelope with more than a hundred and fifty thousand pounds, mostly in fifty-pound notes.'

'You took it?'

'Yes. Like I said, I hadn't received more than a couple of thousand from my partner, so I took it.'

'So, you've got a lot of money waiting for you?'

'No. I had second thoughts, prompted, I have to say, by fears for my safety. I knew that when Joe found out he would kill me. I'm not exaggerating.'

He paused. 'I tried to take the money back to the office but it was too late. One of Joe's cronies was there, and I couldn't put it back without him noticing. By this stage I was in total panic, thinking about what Joe would do to me when he found out. I put the envelope into a leather bag, like a camera case, and took it to Joe's house. He lives in Highgate, very ostentatiously. When I arrived Joe said nothing about the money and I realized he didn't know it was gone. That night Joe was in a very good mood, very happy. He even tolerated me. There were a few of his cronies and we all sat around drinking; me, of course, feeling more and more nervous.'

'Why didn't you just get up and go, wait until the next day to put it back?'

Ralph said, 'If you only knew Joe. I couldn't risk letting him find out first.' Ralph hung his head. He said quietly, 'If I had had the balls to stand up to him . . . but I didn't. I just didn't have what it takes. And Ruth was away that night.'

Ruth looked at the floor almost guiltily, as if her absence had been responsible for the mess Ralph had got into. Ralph put a hand on her arm; it was a gesture normally meant to convey reassurance, but I had the impression here that he was seeking something from her.

'Go on,' I said.

'About midnight Joe's henchman, the one in the office, burst into the house. The box file had gone, he said. Joe, of course, not a man to suffer the loss of his money gladly, went completely crazy. He stumped around the room swearing death to the thief. Kane, my blood ran cold. Fortunately, there were about six or seven of Joe's men who had access to the office, and some of them knew about the money in the file. It was in transit, it had only been there a couple of hours and was apparently due to be moved the next day.'

'You didn't know about it?'

'No, that's what saved me. Joe never told me about money, ever. Anyway, Joe started picking on his cronies, accusing everyone in turn, though funnily enough not me, of having taken it. He decided he was going to search their houses. I knew he would get around to mine in the end, even though I wasn't the number one suspect.'

'What did you do?'

'I hid the money where Joe wouldn't think to look for it – in his own house.'

'Then what?'

'A couple of days of sweating, waiting for the inevitable, waiting for Joe to pick on me. I panicked. I made a run for it.'

'Where were you?' I asked Ruth.

She said coolly, 'I had to see someone.' From the way she said it, and from Ralph's reaction, I knew there had been something in that episode that Ralph and she had had to reconcile.

'I panicked,' Ralph said quickly. 'I had to get away before Joe fixed on me. I had no money, so, very stupidly, I used some cheques that didn't belong to me. I was caught, they put me in Brixton, you know the rest.'

'The money,' Ruth said, 'is still there.'

'You can have half if you'll help us get it.' Ralph at last spelt out the reason for their visit.

When Ralph had spoken to me in Brixton I had not believed him, and had turned him down. But now the details of the story, and Ruth's support for it, convinced me the money was real. Part of me was interested, a selfish part that recently had seemed to be pressing its case more insistently. It was saying to me now: Forget your past and take the money.

Ralph and Ruth eyed me expectantly, Ralph with the look of a man hanging on the word of a doctor about to tell him the result of a test for some fatal disease. Desperation stood by his shoulder waiting to knock him down.

I got to my feet and put my hands in my pockets. I said, 'No.'

Ralph leapt up. 'Kane, you're our only hope! You can have half. That's seventy, nearly eighty thousand pounds. My God! That's more than you'll earn in the next ten years! Look at this.' He opened his arms and took in the shabby room.

Ruth got up and took him by the arm. She said gently, 'He said no, darling.' Ralph hung his head; he would have dropped on to her breast had I not been there. She kissed his cheek, but I could feel the total absence of meaning in it.

I said, more to Ruth than to Ralph, 'I'm not interested. I'm sorry.' I was truly sorry because of what it meant to Ralph, and because of what it meant to Ruth.

Ralph, defeated, nodded. He seemed to be crying, crying without tears. Ruth started to lead him to the door, but he suddenly straightened up and broke free. Some trace of his hollow confidence returned. He said stiffly, without sarcasm, 'Thank you, Kane. Thank you for hearing me out.' He turned on his heels and left. I heard the gritty sound of his shoes on the lino.

At the door of the flat Ruth stopped. She was no more than a few inches from me and I was uneasy at her nearness. She said, 'Where did you get my picture?'

I was too slow. By the time I had formed the first word in my mind she was already gone.

The first statement read:

STATEMENT OF WITNESS.

NAME: Henry Alexander Tempest.
OCCUPATION: Detective Inspector.
AGE: Over 21.
ADDRESS: Headquarters, Crime Squad, Knock, Belfast.
DATE: 11 March 1982.
INTERVIEW: Declan Patrick Mulholland.

I am a Detective Inspector presently attached to the Royal Ulster Constabulary, Headquarters, Crime Squad, Knock, Belfast. At 8.30 p.m. on 3.3.82 I received a telephone call from a senior police officer of the Royal Ulster Constabulary asking me to go to HMP Belfast, Crumlin Road, the following morning to interview Declan Patrick Mulholland who was being held there on remand for terrorist offences.

Mulholland was known to me as I had been attached to a special task force investigating a series of terrorist offences in the Lower Falls area of Belfast where Mulholland lived. There was evidence to connect Mulholland with some of these incidents and there was reason to believe that he occupied a fairly senior position in the command structure of the organization responsible for them. I had reason to believe he knew the nature and structure of the organization as well as the identities of many of its active members.

Mulholland was currently on trial having been indicted for several offences including murder, attempted murder and unlawful possession of explosives and firearms.

As a result of the telephone conversation I went the following morning at 5.00 a.m. (4.3.82) by unmarked police car to HMP Belfast, Crumlin Road. I was accompanied by D/Sergeant David Meeke.

We were taken by prison officers, who had earlier been warned

179

of our arrival, to a room in part of the prison known as the Annexe. Mulholland was brought to the room and was formally cautioned by D/Sergeant Meeke. The interview commenced at 5.25 a.m. D/Sergeant Meeke was present throughout.

During the course of the interview Mulholland confessed to being a member of the organization and claimed to know its most senior members. He indicated a willingness to provide information about their activities. He said he would be prepared to do this if the charges against him were dropped and he were granted immunity for earlier offences.

D/Sergeant Meeke and I questioned Mulholland about offences in the area he came from going back nearly ten years. Although Mulholland would only speak about these matters in the most general terms I was satisfied that Mulholland's claims about the extent of his knowledge were genuine. I told Mulholland that we did not have authority to accede to his requests but that we would pass on what he had said to the appropriate authorities. Mulholland was anxious that a decision be reached quickly and we told him we would do everything possible to expedite matters. The interview terminated at 6.30 a.m. and Mulholland was returned to his cell.

The following afternoon (5.3.82) I spoke to the senior RUC officer and outlined what Mulholland had said during the interview. I recommended that we agree to drop the charges against Mulholland since I was convinced of his willingness and ability to pass on high-grade intelligence.

Two days later (7.3.82) I was informed by the same officer that the Northern Ireland Office had sanctioned the deal and that the charges against Mulholland would be dropped.

I declare this statement is true.

It was signed, Henry Tempest. The second statement was shorter. It read:

STATEMENT OF WITNESS.

NAME: Henry Alexander Tempest.
OCCUPATION: Detective Inspector.
ADDRESS: Headquarters, Crime Squad, Knock, Belfast.
AGE: Over 21.

DATE: 21 January 1983.
INTERVIEW: Sean Mary Smith.

I am a Detective Inspector presently attached to the Royal Ulster Constabulary, Headquarters, Crime Squad, Knock, Belfast. At 10.25 p.m. on 8.1.83 I was present at Castlereagh Police Office with D/Sergeant David Meeke and D/Constable Samuel Masterson where we saw Sean Mary Smith in interview room BF4. It was not a formal interview and Smith, who was being questioned by police about several serious terrorist crimes including possession of a firearm, was not cautioned by us.

As the result of a conversation D/Sergeant Meeke and D/Constable Masterson left the room. Smith indicated a willingness to provide information in return for his release. I told him I could not promise anything but would forward his request to the appropriate authorities. The interview terminated at 11.15 p.m.

As the result of a conversation with a superior officer I returned to see Smith at Castlereagh Police Office the following day (9.1.83) and told him I was not satisfied that he would provide the information I wanted. He appeared to be angry. I asked him for a sign of his good faith and after some consideration he gave me information to the effect that the following night (10.1.83) an attempt would be made by terrorists to murder members of the security forces. He gave me details of where the ambush would take place, what weapons would be involved and the identities of the gunmen. I subsequently arranged for Smith to be released and the charges against him to be left on file.

I declare that this statement is true.

Again it was signed by Tempest.

My watch said it was now half-past three. I was exhausted – by Roisin, Ralph and Ruth, and the statements left me feeling burnt out. Somewhere at the back of my mind I had already marked Dec down as a possible informer and so the first statement did not shock me. But Seanie, that was something else, as if a reference point on a map I was depending on to bring me to safety had turned out to lead to an infested swamp.

I felt crowded and unable to think straight. It was not until I had undressed and got into bed that I remembered Roisin had warned me that Tempest wanted me dead. I thought it was funny how it was possible to overlook news of that sort. Perhaps I had not really believed it when she told me. Reading the statements changed my mind.

16

I was awoken at half seven the next morning. I searched clumsily, sleep-blinded, for the alarm clock, desperate to shut off its insistent bell. I found it and fiddled with the switch, but the ringing persisted. Looking vacantly at the clock, I at last remembered that I had set it for eight. The ringing continued: it had another source, the doorbell. I made my way to the hall and the front door, and found Ruth.

When she spoke her voice was mild and deliberate. I must have appeared dishevelled, clearly woken before my time, but she did not apologize. She said, 'Can you come with me? I need to talk to you.'

In the back of my mind there was a thought of work, of meeting Viv at the lorry park, and somewhere there was a memory of orders to collect goods from different places. But I knew at once I would forget work. There was a sadness and worry in Ruth's eyes that made my excuse seem feeble; it would have been like hurrying past an accident victim because your favourite television programme was about to begin. I nodded and beckoned her in. 'I need to wash,' I told her.

Ruth stood by the window and gazed into the street while I washed and shaved in the sink. I did not take long; three or four minutes. I dried my face and pulled on a shirt. I said, 'I have nothing in the house, I can't get you tea.'

She smiled and said it did not matter; she would take me for breakfast if I would listen to what she had to tell me. I agreed, although not without a thought for Viv who would be waiting at the lorry park for me. I gathered the statements and put them in my jacket pocket. We left the flat and went to her car, an ordinary-looking dark-green saloon, which she had parked in a side-street opposite the flat. She started the engine and turned right into the main road.

'Do you know this area?' I asked her.

'Fairly well. There's a little Turkish café not far from here. They do good breakfasts.'

I sat back and waited for her to start talking. She did not get round to it while we were in the car, and my thoughts turned to the statements I had read the night before. Dec had been an informer: it was the explanation for his sudden release in 1982 when all the charges were dropped. It explained his subsequent behaviour. I remembered the night at his house when he, Cappy and the children had returned from Donegal: Dec had been silent, morose, and Cappy had teased him about not making love to her. A picture of that night came into my mind and a sadness entered my heart, but quickly made way for a searing bitterness: for the statement made me understand why Dec had been so keen to have Maxi killed. He had wanted to divert attention from himself. I felt like kicking myself for the excuses I had made the night before to Roisin. I wanted to shout out, 'Roisin, listen to this when you plead for the life of Declan Mulholland. He tortured and killed a cripple not because he loved Hughie, but to shield himself.' And the money Dec had given Hughie's widow? It was conscience money, probably provided by Tempest for information received.

Dec was a weak man, the kind that could be turned under pressure. But Seanie: that undermined me, for Seanie had been the embodiment of the fighter who rejected compromise as a concept. Such men do turn, I reminded myself, history was littered with them: fear, cynicism, exhaustion, greed – something leads them to betrayal. I began to chuckle, for a bizarre thought had struck me: Seanie and Dec had both been eager to have Maxi killed to divert attention from themselves, but neither would have known the other was an informer. What would they have done had they found out?

Ruth looked sideways at me and asked if I was all right.

'Yes,' I said. 'I've just seen the funny side of something.'

'What?'

I shook my head. Another thought struck me: the sender was Tempest, of course it was. He had sent me Dec's address when I got out of Long Kesh so that I would not forget. Now I understood: he wanted me to come to England and kill Dec. Roisin was right; he was finishing what he had started in Belfast. He had used Dec, and Seanie, to destroy the unit: now he was using me to destroy Dec. What other motive did he have for sending me Dec's statement? It was a reminder, in case I was forgetting my duty. And Seanie's statement? That was him showing contempt for Seanie, for me, for all of us: it was his way of showing that we were all in his power; that he could juggle all the balls and keep them in the air as long as he wanted; that he could let them fall to the ground at any time.

And me? What did he have in mind for me? If Roisin was right, it could only be my death. How would he arrange it? As I stood over Dec's corpse?

I was hardly aware of Ruth or the car. I suddenly felt miserable, utterly and hopelessly depressed.

The car came to a stop outside the Turkish café. We went inside. The walls and ceiling were billowing sheets embroidered with gold and silver lace. There were only two other customers, two young businessmen, engrossed in a conversation about interest rates and money. They both paused to admire Ruth as we took our places. I noticed that Ruth was aware of their attention. She ordered two coffees and some toast. She had her coffee black and strong. I put hot milk into mine, but it still tasted bitter. She noticed something was wrong.

'What's the matter?'

'It's the coffee. It's too strong.'

'It's Turkish. That's the way they like it.'

'I prefer pale instant myself.'

She asked if I wanted her to order a cup of instant coffee. I said no.

'What age are you?' she asked me.

It surprised me. I laughed weakly and replied, 'Thirty-three.'

'How long have you been inside?'

'Altogether?'

'You mean there was more than once?' She seemed mildly surprised.

I drew in my breath. 'Yes,' I said. 'Altogether about twelve years.'

She regarded me coolly, then turned to the waiter and said, 'Could we have a cup of instant coffee please, weak?' The waiter nodded and went to the bar. Ruth said with a smile, 'You deserve the coffee you like.'

'Where's Ralph?' I asked.

Her smile went. 'He's gone away for a couple of days.' There was an edge in her voice.

'Where?'

She hesitated before answering. 'He's gone to see Natalie, his daughter. He hasn't seen her since before he was arrested. His ex-wife's second marriage didn't work out and he wanted to go to see her, be a friend to her.'

'Do you mind?'

She gave me a tight smile and said, 'A little.'

'What is it you want?' I asked.

'You can probably guess – to try to persuade you to change your mind, and help us.'

'Why doesn't Ralph just go in and get the money?'

'He can't. It needs someone who knows what he's doing. Ralph can't do it, but you could.'

The waiter brought me my coffee and Ruth smiled at him. He gave her a flirtatious look. When he had gone I said, 'You're wrong, it's not something I can do.'

She took out a packet of cigarettes. For all the composure in her voice I noticed that when she lit up her hand was trembling.

'We need the money,' she said, again a slight edge in her voice. 'We need it to get away.'

'Get away where?'

She pursed her lips and blew out the smoke. 'Ralph did two very stupid things. He stole money from Joe. Joe is after him, and will kill him if he catches him. He did something else very stupid – there's another man after him.'

'Who?'

She shook her head emphatically and expelled a thin jet of smoke. 'I can't say.'

'Who?'

'Please.'

Her self-assurance was still there, but it was bruised and I did not want to inflict further damage just to have my question answered.

After a pause she continued, 'That's why we desperately need the money. It was my idea to come to you last night. Ralph told me that he had already mentioned the money to you in prison and that you refused absolutely to have anything to do with it. He didn't want to try again.'

'Why are you with him?' I asked.

'Where did you get my photograph?' she said, ignoring my question.

'Ralph left it behind when he went for trial. He had quite a few of you. He probably overlooked it. A cleaner found it in his cell and I took it from him.'

She nodded, and I knew she understood not just why I had taken it from the cleaner, but why I had kept it. I was not sorry it had come out this way, for, without any particular reason, I felt confident about her and I wanted her to know. I had been glad she had leafed through the book and found her photograph marking a page.

I said to her, 'Listen, I have to make a phone call. Can you hold on? I'll only be a few minutes.'

'I have as much time as you need.'

The café owner indicated a wall phone and I found a coin. I rang Harriet's office number. The tone sounded twice before she picked up the receiver. I thanked her for the letter telling me about Benny's trial.

She said, 'Benny has been asking for you. I'm glad you've called. I'll be able to tell him you are well. You are well?'

'Yes. Wish him the best from me. I'll try to get down to the court to see the trial.'

'He would appreciate that.'

'There's something I want to know if you can help me with.'

'Of course, if I can.'

'Do you have anything with Tempest's handwriting on it?'

She was silent for a few moments. 'As a matter of fact, yes. I had a letter from him this morning, hand-written and hand-delivered.'

'Is he a regular correspondent?'

Harriet laughed. 'I want to make it clear that I do not normally receive letters from policemen. No, he's not a regular correspondent. The letter was quite odd; I couldn't see why he had written it.'

'I'd like to see the letter. I don't mean read it, just look at the handwriting.'

'I don't see why not.'

'Can I call in at the office?'

'You'll have to be quick. I'm going to Brixton in about an hour – to see Benny.'

I rejoined Ruth at the table and explained that I had to get to London Bridge. She said she would take me. I had to let her pay for the breakfast. I did not have enough money myself. My empty pockets reminded me of Viv and the lorry. When we got into the car I asked Ruth if it was possible to go via King's Cross.

'We're ten or fifteen minutes at most from King's Cross.'

'Good.'

'What's going on?' she asked.

'I have to check something with my solicitor, but before I do, I have to see someone.'

Viv was lounging against the wire gate while a frustrated

alsatian snapped and barked at him from the other side. He did not recognize me at first when we pulled up beside him. I could see he was interested in the driver and was trying to steal a better look. I said to him, 'Sorry about this, but I'm not going to be able to drive today. Can you go back to the warehouse and tell them I'm sick?'

The alsatian, watched by the card-players on their skip-salvaged settee, redoubled its efforts to get at Viv. He turned to it and shouted, 'Fuck off or I'll bite your balls!' The dog sprang at the wire. Viv remained untroubled. 'Going to have a day of love?' he said, with a glance over my shoulder at the car.

'No. Something more important.'

'Nothing more important than love. What's she doing with you, then?'

'She's giving me a lift.'

'Why don't you take the car and I'll take the girl if all you want's a lift?'

'I didn't say that was all I wanted.'

He laughed and said, 'I didn't think so.'

'Can you tell them at the warehouse?'

'Yes. No problem.'

'Something else. Can you lend me some money?'

'How much do you want?'

'Twenty quid?'

'You must be joking. This is Tuesday.'

He searched his pockets and took out a ten-pound note. 'You are coming back to work, aren't you?'

'Yes. Thanks.'

When I got into the car Viv came over and leaned into the passenger window. Ostensibly it was to tell me that he hoped I would get better soon; really it was to have a look at Ruth.

Harriet's office was cramped. The little space available was filled with files, folders and books. Harriet was wearing a long summer raincoat, unbuttoned, and was stepping over an eighteen-inch-high stack of depositions when I entered. She looked up and giggled girlishly to excuse the chaos around her. She said in her smallest voice, slightly harassed, 'I was just trying to find Tempest's letter.' She stopped to pick something up from her desk, abandoned it, and moved to a filing cabinet on top of which was a precariously piled bundle of papers. 'I had it just a minute ago. I can't think . . .' There were long pauses between each word. 'I'm madly late,' she explained. She rejected the possibilities offered by the papers on the filing cabinet and looked around the room. She raised a long finger to her lips and said vaguely, 'Oh yes.'

She retrieved Tempest's letter from the bin under her desk. 'I threw it away after reading it. It seemed so odd. Here you are.'

I looked it over while she gathered her files and got ready to leave. I knew at once that I had what I wanted but I pulled out the envelopes containing the statements and compared the handwriting: Harriet's letter and mine were written by the same person.

'I've no idea why he would write to me, the letter says absolutely nothing. Have a look.'

I unfolded a single sheet of paper. It read:

Dear Mrs Cockburn,

It was good to see you and Mr Turridge in court during the Kane case. A very interesting affair. I thought you both did very well.

I hope you are keeping well.

Yours sincerely,
Henry Tempest

I said to Harriet, 'The letter wasn't for you, it was for me.' It was a nonsense letter and there was no other reason for having sent it: Tempest wanted me to see it; he wanted me to know who had put the statements through my letter-box.

A worried look crossed Harriet's face. 'What do you mean?'

I shook my head. 'Nothing.' He is goading me, I thought.

'Are you working?' she asked me.

I paused. 'No. I left.'

'When?'

'Thirty minutes ago.'

The look of concern of her face deepened, and to calm her I said, 'It's no problem. I've just had a better offer. More money.'

'Can I give you a lift anywhere?'

'No, it's okay. I have a car waiting.'

We left the office together and I pointed to where Ruth sat waiting for me across the road. As I was about to leave her, Harriet said, 'Does that letter have anything to do with Tempest's suspension?'

'What suspension?'

'I thought you might have heard. It was in the papers. Tempest was suspended, on full pay, the way they always are, shortly after your hearing.'

'I don't know anything about it.'

'It might be connected. I haven't been able to find out why he was suspended, but it was probably something to do with your case.'

'What reasons were given?'

'Publicly, medical – his old war wounds playing up. But I think the problem is psychological. At the committal he seemed barely able to hold himself together. He might blame you. Be careful.'

'Don't worry,' I said. 'He's not going to shoot me down in the street.'

Harriet grimaced before rushing away. I looked across at Ruth in the car, and felt my heart beat faster.

'Did you get what you wanted?' Ruth asked me once I was back in the car.

'Yes.'

'Where do you want to go?' she asked quietly.

'Drop me anywhere. I can make my way home.'

She nodded and drove north over London Bridge and into the City.

She said, 'Have you thought about the money?'

I looked closely at her. She wore a dark-blue short-sleeved top and a black skirt. Her face was pale and lightly made up. It looked nice with her dark hair. Her chin jutted out just slightly, giving her a determined appearance. There were one or two freckles on her bare arms, a small silver watch. Her hands were fine, her fingernails were painted red. She wore a simple ring with a small green stone; it looked expensive.

'Did you and Ralph get married?'

She did not reply straight away, and when she did she said no. I could not work out what her tone conveyed – anger, weariness, sorrow, regret? – one of these, perhaps all of them, but I could not fathom it. Once, when I was a boy, I came into our kitchen at home and found my mother talking to her sister. I heard my father mentioned and there was something in my mother's voice that made me feel shut out and unhappy because I could not understand what was going on. I knew something was going on, some pain was being suppressed, some anger being tied down, but the women would not let me in to find out what it was. I had gone away feeling sad and resentful. A similar feeling started to come over me then with Ruth. I managed to catch it, though, and suffocate it. Sometimes, I thought, she was quite obvious, in ways that I liked; when she ordered me instant coffee – she had been showing off. But at other times the secrets in her eyes confused my reading of her; I could not get past them.

I remembered what Benny had said the day Ralph announced his wedding plans. Perhaps, after all, he was right to have been so cynical. Then I had hoped it would work out for Ralph; now, with Ruth's answer in my ears, I felt a rush of excitement, and unfocused possibilities insinuated themselves into my thoughts. Ruth said unexpectedly, 'My husband wouldn't agree to the divorce.'

I was taken aback. 'You?'

'Sorry?'

'I thought it was Ralph who was having the problem with the divorce.'

'No,' she said. 'Ralph's been divorced for years. I have the problem. I married very young, a possessive, jealous man. When I left him he swore he would never agree to a divorce and he never did. He's making it very difficult. He's that kind of man, obsessive.'

'Is getting married important to you?'

'Ralph wants it.' We were in north London now, five minutes or so from where I lived. I did not want the journey to end. I had to say something that would capture her, but with each passing second it became harder to muster my courage, and instead I remained silent.

Ruth said, 'Ralph wanted us to be married so badly that he did something very foolish.'

'According to you, Ralph seems to have done a lot of foolish things.'

'He did them under pressure. He tried to do a deal with my husband. To get a divorce. That was part of the deal. My husband was in a position to help him. I told Ralph to forget it, but he wouldn't listen.'

'What did your husband do for him?'

'He fixed things.'

'Is your husband the other man, the other one after Ralph?'

She nodded slowly, an admission she did not want to put into words, that she had not intended to make, but could not avoid.

I did not press for a fuller explanation; it was clear she would go no further. By the time we pulled up outside Zhutu's shop I had accepted that I could not capture her. She felt too remote from me and I had no words to say that would bring her closer.

As I got out of the car she said suddenly, 'Don't leave me.' For all her composure she looked so young. I kissed her gently on the mouth. 'Child,' I said.

She turned her head away from me, put the car in gear and let out the clutch. We sped away. I put my hand on her neck and kissed her hair. After a few minutes I realized she was driving nowhere in particular.

'Turn back,' I said to her. 'We'll go home.'

17

Ruth stayed with me two days and a single night. When she had gone I could remember my time with her only as snapshots, isolated moments, not joined together in any sequence. Before another night had passed I found myself able to remember what seemed only moments of it. What went on, what we said or did in between, I could not recall. I had no memory of how we came to go to bed together.

When I tried to put it into sequence the first memory was of gripping the bedstead with both hands as she arched under me. She put her fingers in my hair and kissed my ear. I tensed and flexed; I kept with her rhythm. She turned her head and bit the muscle in my arm. 'I don't know where I am,' she said, without opening her eyes.

She slept heavily, and I took the chance to add to my impressions of her. Her head rested on my chest and when numbness forced me to shift I felt with my hand the wetness on my shoulder where she had dribbled on to me. I stroked the side of her head and kissed her hair. I felt the stretch marks at the sides of her breasts and on her hips. I traced my fingers across them. By turning my head I could just make out the tiny white lines they made. I stroked the plumpness of her belly. I did this until I felt the coldness of her shoulders. I pulled up the covers, the last thing I remember before falling asleep.

Once when I woke up in the night I saw that she slept with her head under the covers. I pulled them back and kissed her, and, like a child disturbed in its heavy sleep, she complained without waking up.

In the night she came to me, eyes still closed. She rubbed

coarse, sticky hairs against my thigh. 'Oh my love,' she said, kissing me. As gently as I could, uncertain whether she was asleep, afraid to break the spell with a rough movement, I turned her on to her back. 'You are my love,' I told her. All my awkwardness and nervousness had gone, dispelled by the words she spoke to me then. Nothing about her, not her beauty, not her smells, not her voice, affected me so deeply as those words: they robbed me of all my strength and almost made me cry.

In the morning I watched her scrutinize herself, naked, in the mirror, palming her belly and her hips, turning sideways and stretching on tiptoes.

'I'm losing my definitions,' she said to the mirror.

'What are definitions?'

She turned to me and laughed. 'It's something my husband used to say. Definitions are the lines on your body, like yours, on your stomach and sides where your muscles are. I'm losing mine.' She left the mirror as if it had offended her.

With a towel wrapped round me, I stood in the kitchen to make her coffee. She came up behind me, put her arms around me and kissed me between the shoulderblades. I had to close my eyes and swallow, to get myself under control. She let me go and went back to bed without a word. When she had gone I leaned against the stove and hung my head.

At twilight the heath was deserted. We sat on a bench at the top of a grassy incline. 'In the dark,' she said quietly, 'the shapes seem to come to life.' She pointed to a shadow.

'What do you think it is?' I asked her.

She considered carefully. 'It's a dog running and running up the hill.' She added with a chuckle, 'But he's not getting anywhere.'

Further on we watched some ducks settle on the grass. I felt a little giddy from lack of sleep, lack of food, too much coffee and too much time in bed. My hand shook when I put it on her shoulder. She turned to kiss me. Like all her kisses it was light and uncertain, the kind that reminded me, vaguely, of tentative teenage kisses. 'It's going to thunder,' she said.

There was thunder; it was far off and soft. We walked through the grass. There were raindrops, large and heavy, but few. I put my arm round her waist and pulled her to me. She kissed me and put her arms around my neck. I leaned into her and slowly we got to the ground. I put my hand on her thigh and brought it up between her legs. She kissed me harder.

The rain had become heavier. We set off back to the car. She was silent now; for a moment I thought she was angry with me for having made love to her in the grass.

In the car I put my hand on her neck while she drove. Every now and then she turned to smile at me, but she did not speak. We did not say anything more. The wipers pushed the rain upwards and aside, the tyres zipped through the pools on the road. The journey took almost an hour. I can only remember the heat of her neck, the headlights and the rain, and the smell that car interiors have on stormy nights.

When she stopped outside Zhutu's shop I waited to see if she would turn off the engine, but she did not. It was over, I realized. I looked once at the rain outside. Then I leaned over to kiss her. Her cheek was cold, her hands stayed on the wheel. We had not spoken for an hour. To break the silence now was impossible. I let my fingers trail across her neck and left without a word. I watched the car lights until they blurred into the traffic. I could not remember what our last words had been.

I found myself thinking about her all the time. Walking along the street, sitting in a café, on a bus, her face and body flashed into my mind. But there was no comfort in it. Once, walking by some shops, I glanced up to see myself reflected in a window. I saw I had a hollow, haunted look, accentuated by the shadows of the glass. Thinking of her brought only pain, and as I stood before the window I saw that pain everywhere in my face, even in the way I stood. I fought down the images, and went on my way.

The images would not leave me. Instead they became stronger. They were strongest when I was passive, sitting down. They were vivid. It was not just that I saw her in my mind's eye, saw her flick her hair from under her collar after she had finished dressing, saw her regard herself in the mirror before a final stroke of lipstick, saw the tan marks on her hips. I saw all these, but I also heard her voice, her laugh. And I could feel her. I remembered the delicate stretch-mark scars on her breasts. Once I found myself standing still in the middle of a busy street: I was tracing my thumb over the fingertips of my right hand, feeling for the gentle lines I remembered. And her smell, moist and dark; the beads of sweat on her neck, under the line of her jaw, on her throat and under her breasts; and her hair, sweet with perfume and sweat, hot in my hands as I kissed her.

She had rarely called me by name; I could remember only two or three occasions, and these I recalled time and time again. It occurred to me that she might not have liked my name, and that was why she never used it; or that she did not like me. Thoughts such as these tumbled one after the other through my mind, always leaving me gloomy. At times like these I felt out of control in a way I had never experienced. My breathing quickened and my hands trembled. It was hard to think clearly.

I gained a victory over her, in my mind. It was small and it was painful, masochistic. It was an incident, an exchange of words, that evening on the heath. I did not remember it at first, when the images of her were crowding in on me. It came to mind some days later, after there had been no word from her, and my memory provided the revenge my heart demanded. She had told me about a holiday in Turkey. She had said, 'I met this man. He was nice, at least he seemed so. He suggested we drive to a beach he knew. He said it was very beautiful. It was about a hundred and fifty kilometres from the town I was staying in. He was right. It was very, very beautiful, near a little fishing village. It was almost dark by the time we arrived and we were both very tired, so there was no problem that night.'

I had already begun not to like the story, the direction it, and she, were taking, so I did not immediately ask what she was waiting for me to ask. But then I did.

'What was the problem?'

'Oh! Well, the next night, after we'd spent the day on the beach, he came into my bed and announced he was going to sleep with me.' She gave a half-laugh, which seemed to me to affect some surprise. I waited for her to make her point. She glanced sideways at me and I realized she had already made it. In fury I grabbed her by the wrists and pulled her to me.

'That's so pathetic. You're flattered by that?' She broke free and started to walk on. 'Most men,' I said to her back, 'most men will fuck anything that moves. You're more than just anything.' I wanted to say more, but could only ask, 'Why did you tell me that?' She was angry and would not answer. I let it drop, so did she, and for several days I blocked it out of my mind. Perhaps, I thought later, the mistake was mine: perhaps the serious-looking woman I had fallen in love with was no different from the robbers' flighty girlfriends. As time went by, before she contacted me again, that was what I tried to make myself believe.

I played this incident over in my mind, over and over, until, like a favourite piece of music heard too often, it had nothing more to say.

There had been another exchange, one that left me equally disturbed, but for different reasons. In the morning she said cautiously, 'Have you thought about the money?' I lay on my back, her head on my chest, and stroked her hair.

'Yes,' I replied.

She lifted her head to look at me, recognizing a change. 'You'll do it?'

'Yes.'

She kissed my chest and said, 'What made you change your mind?'

'A letter.'

'What?'

'The night you and Ralph came, someone put a letter through the door. It was a trick letter; a man I know was trying to provoke me into doing something.'

'Doing what?'

'He wants me to kill a man and then he wants to kill me.'

I felt Ruth tense. She brought her head up and kissed me. She traced a finger over my ear and on to my neck and chest. She moved her leg across me, and as we kissed, as our breathing deepened, she rubbed herself against my hip. I said, 'Come here.'

Later she said, 'Tell me about this man, the one you're supposed to kill.'

I told her. 'His name is Dec. I knew him in Belfast – we were brought up next door to each other. Things happened. He got married, I went to jail. When I got out he went to jail. By the time he was released I was back inside. We just kept missing each other. I still took it for granted that we knew each other, but we didn't. Anyway, he had a choice to make and he made the wrong one.'

'You'll have to explain,' she said.

'Dec was on trial. This was in 1982, March. If he had been convicted he would have got life with a minimum recommendation of twenty or thirty years.'

'But he didn't?'

'No. He went free. It was very sudden. It turns out he made a deal with a policeman to become an informer.'

'You didn't know?'

'No. Later, a man was killed, a member of our unit called Hugh Gallagher, and we suspected there was an informer at work. Suspicion fell on a man named Maxi. I told Dec and another man, Seanie, to pick Maxi up and ask him a few questions. Instead they killed him, and I got ten years.'

'You want to kill Dec out of revenge?'

'Revenge has no part in it. I was going to kill him because we had all believed in something once and he betrayed it. It's something I can't, or couldn't, let go of.

When I got out of Long Kesh last year it was the single thing on my mind. It was always there, driving me on, it wouldn't leave me alone. Nothing mattered except killing Dec.'

'And now?'

'Now? Now I don't know any more. There's a cop playing games with me. He sent me these documents that show Dec was an informer – he wants me to kill Dec.'

Ruth had not moved since I had begun telling her the story. Now I felt her tighten against me. She said, 'Who is the policeman?'

'His name is Tempest.'

Ruth turned on her side, out of my arms; it was as if she had fallen away from me. I felt suddenly lonely and hugged her from behind. She said, 'Go on.'

I smoothed her hair and rested my chin on her head. 'Tempest is English. He was in the Special Branch, although now he's in the Anti-Terrorist Squad. He served in Belfast. His brief was to deal with our unit. But he didn't get round to finishing the job, he got shot. Now he wants to wrap everything up. Me and Dec are the last ones alive, and he wants us dead.'

'Do you think he'll try to kill you?'

'Yes. It won't be obvious. He might use someone else; that's his way.'

'What about the other man, Seanie?' she asked. Her voice was quiet; she seemed far off.

'Seanie? Dead. He was shot last year just before I got out of Long Kesh. No one knows why. Maybe Tempest was behind it. Tempest was in control of Seanie's life; he may have been in control of his death.'

'What do you mean?'

'Seanie was an informer. I didn't know until the night you and Ralph came round. The documents Tempest sent also show that Seanie made a deal. Tempest wants me to know.'

'Why?'

'He's trying to rub my face in it and tell me in his own

200

perverse way that I have been deluding myself for years, that my loyalties and the time I spent in jail are worth nothing.'

'Has he been successful?'

'I don't know any more. Everything's got mixed up. I don't seem to know where I am, what I'm doing.' I squeezed her and kissed her hair.

She turned quickly to face me and said urgently, 'You can escape. You don't have to do any of it. You can escape.'

'With the money?'

'With the money.'

18

It was a court in the new part of the building and its green leather-covered seats and pinewood panelling lent it a deceptively relaxed air. People spoke slowly and made long pauses during which the microphones picked up paper-shuffling sounds. Spectators at criminal trials are almost always disappointed by the lack of visible drama; unless, of course, someone they know is on trial. Then, every speech rivets them, for a life could hang on a single word, and the pauses become moments of excruciating tension.

The prosecutor was on his feet examining a police witness when I entered the spectators' gallery. The witness, a detective constable, spoke slowly and deliberately, allowing time for the judge to write down his answers. Civilian witnesses are not usually so considerate: they blurt out their answers, they run on from point to point and back again, and try too hard to please. Sometimes they defeat even the most disciplined trial lawyers, who are unable to recapture them or distil from their ramblings a single piece of useful information. The detective constable was the model of a good witness. He gave his answers calmly, one by one, and from time to time glanced at the bench to make sure the judge was keeping up with him.

I sat at the front of the gallery. There were none of the usual tourists that crowd the Old Bailey during the summer.

Benny, who had not noticed me come in, leaned forward in his seat. He wore a blue shirt open at the collar, and wide dark trousers. His crutches were stacked against the rail of the dock, facing the jury box; every time the jurors sneaked a glance at the man on trial they would see his crutches – it was something I was sure Benny had arranged deliberately.

The detective constable's testimony was damaging. He claimed that during one interview Benny had made a verbal confession. If the jury believed this, Benny would be convicted. Benny listened, and let the jury know, with an occasional slight tightening of the muscles around his mouth and a subtle drop of the eyelids, that this was a lie and that he resented his integrity being questioned. If there was a single romantic in the jury, Benny would have an ally. The detective constable continued his testimony, slowly and with precision; he was an experienced court hand. Benny continued to listen, with signals aimed just below the jury's subconscious; he too was experienced.

Harriet was in court. She sat behind Turridge, her head down, concentrating on getting the detective constable's evidence down in her notebook. When he paused, she would look up, brush a strand of brown hair from her eyes to study the witness. At one point she peered vacantly up at the spectators' gallery. I immediately stiffened and sat forward, but she gave no sign of having seen me.

The prosecutor asked, 'Were you alone when you saw Morris on the second occasion, that is to say in the interview room, on the seventeenth?'

'No, my lord. I was accompanied by Detective Inspector Lloyd.'

'Did you keep a contemporaneous note of the interview?'

'No, my lord.'

'Did Detective Inspector Lloyd?'

'No, my lord.'

'When were the notes made up?'

'Immediately subsequent to the interview, my lord. Within, I would say, fifteen minutes of its having terminated.'

'Where were they made up?'

'In the police canteen, my lord.'

'Thank you. I want now to turn to the interview itself. Was Morris cautioned?'

'He was, my lord, by Inspector Lloyd.'

'Did Morris make any reply?'

The detective constable turned to face the bench and, with a hint of supplication in his voice, just enough to suggest the proper degree of respect, said, 'May I refresh my memory from my notebook, my lord?'

'You say the notes were made up at the earliest opportunity subsequent to the interview?'

'They were, my lord.'

'Very well. You may refer to your notes.'

The detective constable gave a half-bow and retrieved his notebook from his jacket pocket.

'Now that you have your notes, are you able to tell us, officer, what reply, if any, Morris made after being cautioned?'

'He said, "You know my form, I never talk to cozzers."'

Benny dropped his head a fraction, his signal that the policeman was telling lies. The prosecutor waited to make sure the jury had taken in the answer. He addressed the judge. 'My lord, since Morris has chosen to attack the character of earlier police witnesses and has thus made an issue of his own character, I propose now, with your leave and assuming there is no objection from my learned friend, to explore the matter of Morris's character with this witness.'

'Are there any objections, Mr Turridge?'

Turridge, who had been sitting, arms folded, his protuberant eyes fixed arrogantly on the ceiling, lazily rose to his feet. He said in his powerful voice, bordering just on the safe side of contemptuous, 'My instructions are that Mr Morris is emphatic in his wish to have the whole truth placed before the jury. The defence therefore has no objection to Mr Morris's character being laid before the jury.'

He sat down abruptly to a scowl from the judge, who said coldly, 'A simple yes or no, Mr Turridge, would have sufficed. You can save your rhetoric for when you open the defence case.'

Turridge gave no sign of having heard the rebuke; his eyes

were back on the ceiling. Benny was pleased at the exchange, though he was careful not to let the jury think he was smirking.

The prosecutor resumed his questioning. 'What did you take to mean by "form"?'

'I understood it to signify that Morris was known to the police, and had prior convictions.'

'Were you aware at the time of the interview, before Morris's answer, that Morris did indeed have prior convictions?'

'I was, my lord. I did not know all the details but I was aware he had previous convictions for robbery and theft.'

'After he mentioned his "form", what was said next?'

'I said, "You've had some grief. Is there anything we can get you?".'

'What reply, if any, did Morris make?'

'Morris replied, "I'm going to fight this, you know. Don't think you've got me bang to rights."'

'Please continue.'

'Inspector Lloyd then said, "You're pulling our legs, aren't you? You can't get out of this one." Morris replied, "I've been thinking in the hospital. I think there's a way out of this." I said, "If you plead guilty the court will go lighter on you."'

The detective paused while his answers were taken down by the judge.

The prosecutor said, 'What did Morris say to that?'

'Morris replied, "Sod the court."'

The prosecutor put his hand up to stop the witness. He wanted the jury to savour this reply and did not want its impact diluted by anything the detective might add.

'Pause there. What did you take to mean by the exchange which had taken place up to Morris's remark, "Sod the court"?'

The detective realized he was being fed a line and came up with the rejoinder expected of him.

'I understood Morris to mean that although he knew the evidence against him was conclusive, he was going to chance his arm, so to speak.'

'Very well.' The prosecutor, having got precisely what he had hoped for, looked pleased. 'Was anything else said?'

'Morris continued, "You don't think the court is going to look favourably on me. I just come out of a ten stretch and I'm at it again, out there with a shotgun copping for a security guard. The court ain't going to do me no favours so I might as well have a go, see if I can get a result."'

Benny dropped his head, in grief it seemed, for that was what a wronged man would feel. My grief was genuine: Benny was going to be convicted. I had to look away, away from the awful scene that was unfolding below.

And there she was, coming towards me. All the anger I had felt for her, that had echoed throughout the days since she had gone away, was dissolved. She came towards me with a tentative look in her eyes that instantly told me that she loved me.

We sat in a nearby café used by visitors to the Old Bailey, and ordered coffee. I could not taste it; I do not think I was aware of very much apart from Ruth. There was a terrible tightness in my chest and my vision seemed defective, as if I had stepped from a dark room into blinding sunlight.

Ruth said, 'I tried looking for you at the lorry park at King's Cross, but they said you didn't work there any more.'

'I never went back to work after you and I went there on our way to London Bridge.'

'What are you doing for money?'

'I was paid in arrears so I had a week's wages coming to me.'

She nodded and lit a cigarette. She gazed out of the window and I had to hold myself back from taking her hand and kissing her. I said, 'You didn't come to the flat.' It came out harsher, with more disappointment, than I had intended.

'Oh, I'm sorry,' she said, as if she had used the same words a thousand times before to soothe infatuated lovers. I felt a mixture of anger and sorrow. It was not the first time I had been unable to fathom her. There had been a couple of occasions when she had seemed almost like a spoilt and heartless teenager, accustomed to having her own way with her sad and distracted lover. But she was more often loving, passionate and defenceless.

'How is Benny's trial going?' Ruth asked, to break the silence.

'I missed the first couple of days, but from what I've seen I think he has problems.'

'Do you think he'll be acquitted?'

'No,' I said. 'No, I do not.'

I noticed that the hand holding the cigarette trembled slightly, and this comforted me. It made me think her feelings for me were real.

'I couldn't get away to see you.' She said it with such calmness that for a moment I felt my anger return. I quickly suppressed it.

'Did Ralph come back?' Again, more disappointment than I had intended.

She nodded.

'Did Ralph tell you about Benny?' I asked her.

She seemed confused for a second – perhaps she had been expecting a different question – then said, 'Yes. He's someone you both knew in Brixton. Ralph liked him.'

'Did Ralph ever tell you about another man, Anthony?'

'Oh yes. He often mentioned him.'

'Anthony got a suspended sentence – he's out. Did he and Ralph ever meet?'

'No. Ralph couldn't find him.'

'Why did he want to find him?'

'I don't know. They were friends. Is that unusual?'

'Ralph wasn't going to pop him the question?' By now my voice was rising. There was no way out of this feeling of anger.

She said defensively, 'What question?'

I stared at her until she said, 'Why are you looking at me like that? What have I done?'

I said quickly, 'The question: will you help me get the money from Joe Varvakis? Did Ralph ask Anthony that question? Did Anthony say no? So Ralph thought he would get him to change his mind by sending you around to sleep with him.'

She froze. I hated having said it, but the thought that Ruth was using me had been torturing me. It was the source of my anger.

Ruth looked away. Her gaze followed a car passing the window until it turned the sharp bend. A man with nothing better to do than stand in the warm sun with his hands in his pockets stared moodily around him. A policeman on duty at the Old Bailey, hands behind his straight, stiff back, joked with a colleague. For a moment I began to feel easier, as if by watching these ordinary things I could enter them with Ruth and be part of them with her.

But I had deluded myself. Ruth got up suddenly, fury in her eyes, which for an instant I could not understand. My thoughts had become peaceable and I had forgotten what I had said. She brushed past me. There was the sound of cups rattling in their saucers. She walked quickly to the door and out into the street.

I paid the bill and ran out after her. She would not stop, she would not answer my calls to speak to me. Eventually, I took her by the arm. She pulled it viciously away and said through her teeth, 'Don't do that!' I held on, but she became so agitated that I gave in and let go. 'I hate that,' she said bitterly. 'I hate it when men use their physical strength to stop me. You have no idea what it feels like, how humiliating, how powerless it makes me feel.'

Like being under arrest, I thought. I apologized. 'I never thought of it like that,' I said. 'I'm sorry.'

She was calmer, still angry, breathing deeply.

'Let's walk,' I said.

I hesitated to touch her, but I could see her anger was giving way to upset, and I immediately regretted not only my words but the doubts I had had.

We walked towards the viaduct, weaving in and out of

the lunchtime office workers carrying their paper bags of sandwiches and polystyrene cups of coffee. We leaned against the ironwork and watched the traffic pass below.

She said, 'It would never have occurred to you about holding my arm. Some men, yes, they would have known, but not you.'

'What do you mean?'

'Did you say you've been in prison for twelve years?'

'Not twelve years in a row. There were gaps.'

'What does prison do to people?'

'Different things,' I said vaguely.

'Does it change them?'

'No.'

'You sound certain.'

'It doesn't change people. It just makes them more of what they already were. If they were weak when they went in, they come out weaker. If they were strong, they come out stronger.'

'I thought you would say something like that.'

I was annoyed. 'What are you saying?'

'You are thirty-three. You've been in situations that most of us have never been in, would be frightened to death just to imagine. You have such . . . experience. But emotionally, what do you know? When did that part of you stop growing?'

I could not answer. I watched the cars and buses. Slowly I became aware that Ruth was crying, silently. I took her and kissed her hair, and pressed her head to my shoulder. She trembled against me.

She sobbed and said, 'I would do anything for you. Ralph didn't send me. Believe me. I would do anything for you.'

'I remember when I first saw you,' I said. 'I remember what you were wearing, the way you looked.'

She hugged me, still crying, 'Oh, I remember so much,' she said. 'You'd be surprised at what I remember.'

I did not know what to think, or do, or say. She was in my arms, crying. It was only her tears I trusted, all else could be lies, but not her sad tears.

Across the road a man was watching me. I had seen him before: outside my flat the night Zhutu and his son were fussing around their new shopfront; outside the café next to the Old Bailey a few minutes before. Our gaze met and a look of strained disappointment came over him. He turned and vanished among the office workers. But I had recognized him; I knew who he was now.

I envied her her peaceful, deep sleep; her head on my shoulder, mouth slightly open, regular, untroubled breathing. It was only when she was asleep that I felt in command of myself and of what was going on between us. It was, of course, a false sense of control, for when she eventually woke what I would feel most would be alarm and uncertainty.

For a man who had spent a third of his life behind bars I nevertheless, until recently, continued to believe that I had control over my life. It was not something I had analysed or thought seriously about; it was like the undefined sense of wellbeing that springs up out of nowhere from time to time, inexplicable and faintly troubling if you stopped to think about its source.

Roisin had said I never thought about things, that I made my mind up and that my decisions were final, irrevocable. When I lay there with Ruth I realized that she had been right. I had never had real control – I had an illusion which came from having been in control of certain episodes in the past. I had confused this with a general feeling that somehow I was master of my own life.

How had I tricked myself into thinking this way? One night, I remembered, Hughie and I had ambushed a patrol. We had broken into a shop and taken up position in a first-floor room with windows overlooking the main road. I carried an Armalite AR15, black and light. I checked the magazine, pulled the slide back and let it spring forward to push a round into the breech. Hughie cocked his weapon and we settled down to wait.

An hour passed, another hour, and another. During that

time I felt tense, but not frightened. I put my hand to the back of my neck and felt the hard knots of muscle; massaging did no good. A police Land-Rover went by; we let it pass; we were waiting for a foot patrol. A couple of drunks staggered along the street, every fatuous word audible to us. They swayed to a stop to piss against an unlucky car, then moved unsteadily on.

When the patrol arrived I moved my rifle up to the window and took aim. All my tension had gone. I felt the muscle in my neck ease as if it were a knot in a shoelace unravelled by a simple tug.

The shooting, when it started, deafened me, and the next sounds I heard were of Hughie's heavy boots thumping on the bare floorboards towards the staircase. I fired another few rounds and followed him to the stairs. I burst through the shop's back entrance and into an alley.

We had arranged that a car would be waiting for us at the end of the alley, but it was not there. Hughie looked wildly about and cursed. He glanced at me and I saw his panic. Hughie's courage was never doubted by those who knew him, and I did not think then, or later, that his panic was a sign of cowardice or lack of bravery. But at the same time I knew I felt neither fear nor panic. In that instant I realized I was harder, for I truly did not care whether I lived or died. Later, when the unit's OC was killed and a new commander was to be appointed, I was chosen, and I knew that Hughie did not resent it; he was aware of what I had seen in that moment.

That night, the night of the ambush, Hughie fled away, dropping his rifle in the street. I picked it up and started to run in the direction of a house whose family I knew would let me hide. The rifles encumbered me and I was slow, so slow that, taking back alleys and climbing walls whose tops were crowned with green fangs of broken bottle glass, soldiers were already combing the streets.

My hands bleeding, my knees bruised, I crawled along behind a low concrete wall. On the garden side the householder had tried to encourage a hedge. His efforts had produced only a handful of anaemic and spindly branches with stunted leaves, providing little in the way of cover. Across the road was the house I wanted to get to. I lay under the thin hedge and waited.

Behind me the householder and his family had on a noisy television programme, and I watched the lights thrown by the set change shape and shade. The night was moonlit and very beautiful. Two soldiers weaved their way, dancing, crouching and twisting for cover behind cars and lamp-posts. They continued down the street and took up position on the opposite side of the wall, so close that I could hear their nervous breathing. I was nineteen years old and I was never so in control of my life. I felt no fear, I was almost without a pulse, without a heartbeat. Slowly, I relinquished my hold on Hughie's rifle and gathered my own to be ready to fire. I did not think that I was going to die, I could not believe it was possible, and I had no terror. I prepared to kill the two men on the other side of the hedge and trusted that I would make my escape.

I did not have to kill them. After twenty minutes they moved forward, weaving and dancing, until they and the cruising Land-Rovers disappeared in the night.

I had taken that episode as amounting to control of my life, in the same way that I saw wiping out all memory of Roisin as control. When she came to see me in prison to tell me that she was leaving I saw a tentativeness in the way she stood, and in her eyes, and it told me that if I pressed her, if I begged her, she would not go, for she was loyal and she loved me. But that would not have been on my terms; I would not have been in control, and so I told her to go. And when she had gone I made her dead to me. I dug a grave for her and I lowered her into it; I shovelled the dirt on top of her and trampled it down. Gone! and buried with her my love for her and my hate for her.

I had thought of that as control in a way that involved no thinking; Roisin was right, in her quiet, gentle, firm way. I had not thought about it. And with Ruth there, my arm aching from her weight and my heart from her sad tears, I realized that I had never had control of any sort. I had been pushed and pulled with nothing more than the pathetic illusion of freedom. For the last six years Tempest had been in control of my life, directing me here and there, to do this and that. He shared my absurd illusion. What he did not realize was how groundless our notions of independence are; how easily they can be undermined.

Ruth slept on, but now with a worried frown. I wished she would sleep for ever with me. Looking at her and wanting always to be with her, I decided I would take the money away from Ralph, and I would take Ruth from him too.

It would not give me control over my life – the kind of control I wanted, that I thought I once possessed, was unattainable – but it would finish this episode, the one in which I was so clearly out of control, and it would provide me with an escape.

19

The prosecutor was on his feet and he faced Benny, who was in the witness box, with the mean, pinched look of a vigilante. He had a small head and a mouth that was no more than a scar. He was a man who enjoyed his work and he postured self-righteously in front of the jury. I could see Benny only in profile and I knew him well enough to know that he loathed the man before him, whose task it was to make him look like one of life's miserable dregs.

The prosecutor said, 'Let us be certain on this point. Mr Turridge, your counsel, acting on your instructions, has put to Detective Inspector Lloyd and Detective Constable Willmott the suggestion that they fabricated a confession.' The prosecutor paused before leaning forward confidentially and saying, without looking at Benny, 'Is that right?'

'Yes.'

'Yes,' the prosecutor repeated quickly. 'What you are saying is that they made it up, are you not?'

'Yes,' Benny said, patiently.

'Detective Inspector Lloyd and Detective Constable Willmott invented, fabricated, made up a confession.'

'They verballed me, yeah.' Benny's patience was being tried. I willed him to hold on.

The prosecutor knew he was riling Benny with his repetition and to cover himself with the jury he added, 'I'm sorry to have to labour the point, but you see, Mr Morris, you are making very serious allegations against serving police officers and, in fairness to them, and in fairness to you, I have to be certain that that is what you are saying.'

'I'm saying they fitted me up and they verballed me.'

'They fitted you up and they verballed you. Very well. Now we know where we stand.' The prosecutor paused again and pretended to be momentarily at a loss for words. 'Well,' he began in a reasonable tone, 'can you perhaps explain to us why these men should want to do such a terrible thing?'

'They want to fit me up.'

'But why?'

'Because I used to be a thief.'

The prosecutor had not expected such candour. I knew this was part of Benny's plan, to shock the court with his honesty, but I could not see how it could work.

The prosecutor took time to recover. He evidently abandoned the line of questioning he had prepared, and said, 'While we are on the subject of your past, may I just clarify one or two matters.' He picked up a thick file and fished out a sheet of paper. He read to himself for a moment and then said, 'Yes. We can, I think, leave aside the miscellaneous juvenile offences, nothing overly serious there. Your criminal career, Mr Morris, that is to say, your serious criminal career, began sometime before 1966. In October of that year you were tried on charges of taking and driving away, assault and demanding money with menaces. Is that not right?'

'Like I already said, I used to be a thief.'

The prosecutor said sharply, 'I know you said that; I am now asking you if in 1966 you were tried for . . .'

'Yes, I was.'

'And found guilty?'

'I pleaded guilty.'

'And sentenced to three and a half years' imprisonment?'

'Yes.'

'In 1969 you again stood trial, in this building in fact, on charges of armed robbery?'

'Yes.'

'You received a seven-year prison term, did you not?'

'Yes.'

The prosecutor glanced at his sheet, a smirk spread over

his face. He continued, 'And in 1976 there was another trial, was there not, again here at the Old Bailey, in which you stood indicted for armed robbery and manslaughter. Is that correct?'

'Yes,' Benny said quietly.

'And you were convicted on both counts, is that not correct?'

'I put my hands up to it.'

'What did you say?'

'I pleaded guilty.'

'Tell us, Mr Morris, whom did you kill?'

Benny did not answer straight away. I imagine he was surprised by the savagery of the question. Turridge could have objected and saved Benny from having to answer, but the damage had been done and I supposed he was gambling on Benny's reply.

'I killed a security guard,' Benny said. He did not say it in a half-whisper, in the hope that the jury somehow would not hear, but out loud and with a tone of genuine regret.

'You hit him on the head with a crowbar, did you not?'

'Yes. I hit him over the head with the crowbar. I didn't mean to kill him, but I did and I pleaded guilty to that and all.'

'Would you say, Mr Morris, that you are a career criminal?'

'I used to be.'

'I put it to you that you were, and remained until the day you shot your own leg off, a career criminal, an experienced and desperate armed robber.'

In a restrained voice Benny replied, 'I was what you say I was, but I didn't go on the Birmingham robbery. I was out of it all by then.'

'So it was just a coincidence that you, a self-confessed armed robber, happened to be in the car park of a Birmingham supermarket as a security guard was attacked by a man carrying a shotgun? Is that what you're asking the jury to believe?'

'Yes, it's the truth.'

The prosecutor let go of the sheet from which he had been reading Benny's antecedents as if it was something noxious. It sailed errantly to the side and came to settle on a bench to the left, from where it was retrieved by a junior colleague who tucked it back into the file.

The prosecutor went on, 'In contrast to you, Detective Inspector Lloyd and Detective Constable Willmott are both decorated police officers, men of unblemished character.'

'If you say so.'

'And yet you allege they have invented a confession in order to convict you of a crime you did not commit.'

'This is a bollock ache.'

When the judge rose for lunch I left the gallery as quickly as I could and made my way to the main doors where I waited until Harriet and Turridge came out. Turridge shook my hand without much enthusiasm; I was a former client somewhere in his career and he had little interest in me now. He told Harriet that he had to rush to meet someone and would see her later.

I handed Harriet an envelope; it contained £200, repayment of the money she had given me the night I walked free from Lambeth Magistrates' Court. I had difficulty in getting her to take it; she insisted that I keep it and I only persuaded her by saying she could give it to Benny. I asked her how she thought it was going. She sighed. She told me the prosecutor's name was Roy Amhurst and she said she thought he must have been the school sneak. I asked her when there was likely to be a verdict in the case, and she said in a businesslike tone that Benny's cross-examination and re-examination would take up the rest of the afternoon; the closing speeches would probably be the following morning and the judge would make his summing-up to the jury in the afternoon. After that it depended on the jury. The jury in the first trial had laboured for three days before admitting defeat and trooping back into court to tell the judge they could not agree on a verdict.

'Have you heard any more about Tempest?' I asked her.

'I'm afraid not. Have you seen him?'

'No.'

'If you want to make a formal complaint to the police I can help you,' she suggested.

'I don't think that would help.'

'It might not help, but at least it would be a matter of record.'

'Thanks, but I don't think so.'

I asked Harriet to give Benny my regards, to wish him the best from me, and she said she would. She said it in the way you do when you want to bring a conversation to a close. She smiled briefly and went hurriedly on her way. I had often experienced a sense of loss when Harriet left me; this time it was more profound. I felt sad and dissatisfied with myself. I was not sure I would see her again.

I had arranged to see Ruth in a bar. She sat in a green chesterfield chair at a low table. She wanted a glass of white wine and I bought myself a beer. She wore a dark-grey suit and a silk blouse with the first two buttons open, and as I stretched into the seat opposite I was very conscious that I liked the look of her. She had a crooked bottom tooth and her skin was not too clear, with a little makeup to cover the blemishes; but there was no part of her I did not like.

She smiled and we waited; it was as if we were each waiting for the other to decide how our future would go. If I had had the nerve, if I had trusted her, I would have said more than simply, 'How are you?' But that was what I said.

'Fine. How does the trial look?'

'Not good.'

'If Benny does get out, what would he do? Where would he go?'

'I don't know. His wife left him to live with another man. He might try to get her back.'

Ruth – perhaps it was from guilt, the reminder of someone betrayed by a lover – turned away. If it was guilt I did not share it. I was past that.

I said to Ruth, 'Where did Ralph put the money?'

She pulled on her cigarette and exhaled nervously. She said, 'He never told me.'

'Why not?'

'He didn't want to involve me, I suppose.'

'In what?' I said it sharply. There was something about Ruth's voice, a certain tone, or inflexion, that always made me want to doubt her; I never knew if I could believe her. I suspected lies came easily to her, that she was the kind of woman who would lie when it was the simplest way out of an awkward situation. I hated it, the thought that she would lie to me, that for all her seriousness, for everything that was fine about her, there was another part to her: the pretty schoolgirl who double-dated and fed men lines, always convincingly.

She was a little annoyed. 'He didn't want to put me in any danger, didn't want me to be involved in his crimes.'

'He didn't mind when it came to coming to me to ask if I would get it for him. You knew all about that – you must have talked about it with him.'

She stubbed out her cigarette and raised her glass. Again I noticed the tremor in her hand. She sipped her wine and then said quietly, 'Please don't speak to me like that, as if you don't believe me. It tears me in two.'

Did I believe her? I just could not tell.

'You're so untrusting, so bitter,' she said, but it was not an accusation, not a rebuke; it was a sad observation. 'What made you so bitter?'

'I don't know. There wasn't a single event.'

'It doesn't work like that,' she said. 'Bitterness comes up from behind, slowly, and it takes you over without you knowing it.'

'You sound like a doctor. Is there a cure?'

'I will cure you, my love.'

There was to be no more bitterness in me that night. She so rarely said anything to express what she felt about me that the few words were to me like a long letterful of poems and songs of love for me. Not even later, when we were driving back to my flat and she raised the question of the money, did I feel anything other than complete trust in her. She had the power to make me happy with so little.

'Ralph won't tell me where the money is,' she said. 'But he'll have to tell you. He's out of London for another three days, seeing Natalie again. He'll be back on Friday. The two of you can meet then and go over things.'

'Does he want me to do it on Friday?'

'I don't know. What do you think?'

'I'd like to get it over with. Friday would be best.'

'I want it to be over soon too.'

'What will we do?'

'When you've got the money we can do anything we like. Have you got a passport?'

'No.'

'You can get a visitor's passport at the post office. How would you like Seville?'

'Why Seville?'

'I've been there. It is beautiful. There are orange trees and cool bars and squares to sit in.'

'Seville sounds fine.'

We drove on through the dark and as we approached the flat Ruth asked, 'How are you going to get into Joe's house?'

'It depends on what it's like.'

'What if there's trouble?' She gave me a sideways glance.

'I have a gun.'

She said, 'Please don't hurt Ralph.'

It had been a clear day with muggy heat. But the night air was cool, and rain splashed heavily on the road. When the car was parked, Ruth said, 'I love rainy nights. I like being in bed when the rain beats on the window. I like weather – weather, weather.'

I kissed her on the mouth, and when I knew she wanted me to go on I parted her jacket and put my hand on her breast. She pushed into me and kissed me harder. I undid the rest of her buttons and put my hand inside her blouse. Her breath came faster and she leaned back a little, making it easier to get to her. Her right leg came up and I put my hand on her thigh, just below her skirt. She kissed me deeply, pushing her mouth against mine until it hurt, then pulling back before renewing her kiss. I moved my hand up her leg under her skirt and held the flesh at the top of her stockings. I pulled back to look at her: she was beautifully dishevelled, her blouse open, her bra pushed over one breast, her skirt around her waist. I smiled at her, and she suddenly laughed dirtily, put a hand to her hair, and looked away. I had not intended this, but her dishevelment and her laugh made me want to go on. She kept her head turned to one side, to the driver's window, while I eased her legs apart. I put my hand between them and traced my finger across a folded, fat lip.

Ruth froze, and then screamed. I jerked back. There was a man, dressed in a long coat, a scarf covering most of his face, standing in front of the car. I thought at first he was a peeping tom, but the way he stood, making no attempt to hide the fact that he had been watching us, alerted me to something else. He held a gun in his hand. He leaned across the bonnet, raised his right arm and stretched it out towards us. He did a slow sweep with it across the windscreen, pointing the gun first at me, then at Ruth, then at me again. It was a small calibre revolver. I saw the hammer draw slowly back as the man squeezed the trigger.

The shot was like a detonation followed by a ping. I had blinked involuntarily at the moment the gun went off. After the shot I opened my eyes to look at Ruth, who had turned almost on to her side in an effort to curl up into a ball and hide.

By the time I looked back to the windscreen the gunman had vanished.

20

The sound of the shot was still in my head, like the memory of a scream from a nightmare. Ruth was pale and her voice small. She sipped some water and said, 'Do you know who it was?'

'Yes.'

'How could he have missed? – he was so close.'

'He lost his nerve.'

'What makes you so sure?'

'I know him.'

Her breathing had become more normal. She drained the glass.

'Who was it?'

'Later.'

'What are we going to do?'

'It doesn't look as if anyone heard the shot, but we can't stay here. He might get his nerve back. Do you know anywhere we can stay until Friday?'

Ruth thought about it for a moment. 'Yes. I think so. I'll have to make a phone call.'

'Good. When Ralph gets back we'll take the money and then you and I can get out of all this.'

She put her head on my shoulder. 'I have to trust you,' she said slowly, 'to take the decisions from now on. I don't know how to handle this.'

I kissed her. I liked the feeling of control her words had given me. When we separated I expected to see a softness in her eyes, but it was not there: her eyes were harsh and clear. It made me doubt the extent to which she was relying on me.

I said, 'I have to get something.'

I went to the kitchen and from a cupboard below the sink gathered a handful of rags which I stuffed into a plastic carrier bag. Further back in the cupboard was a bottle of white spirit. I took that too.

There was no sign of anything abnormal in the street. I took the car keys and left Ruth in the doorway while I approached her car from behind. There was no one around. The bullet had made a small hole in the roof, a fraction of an inch above the windscreen. I got in and checked the interior. The bullet had gone into the back seat slightly to the right of centre. I imagined the trajectory: the gunman had aimed too high, the bullet pierced the roof and had probably just whispered over my right shoulder before entering the seat behind. The gun had looked to be of a small calibre, a ·22 or a ·32. The bullet had probably lodged somewhere in the boot.

I was in too much of a hurry to check to see if it had damaged anything important, so I started the motor and pulled out into the road, turned at the junction and drew up outside the flat. I stretched across to open the passenger door for Ruth.

'Lock the door,' I told her. 'Do you know Finsbury Park?'

'Yes,' she said.

'Direct me.'

She told me to take the next right and go right again. We drove for about fifteen minutes. She said, 'Where do you want to go?'

'There's a disused railway line. I want to collect something I left there a year ago.'

She looked faintly puzzled. 'I know the line. What part of it do you want?'

I gave her the name of the street in which Dec lived and described a bridge nearby. The bridge was my landmark. She thought she knew it and gave me further directions.

We found Dec's street without any trouble and I slowed down as we passed his house. There were lights on, though by now it was almost one o'clock. The bridge was a couple of hundred yards further on. I turned left into a side-street and parked.

I said to Ruth, 'I have to go and get something. Get out, walk up the road a bit and stand by the tree, do you see it?'

'Yes. Why?'

'The man who shot at us knows this car and he may be following us.'

She looked out the back window. 'I haven't noticed anything.'

'It's safer to get out of the car. Keep out of sight behind that tree and keep your eye on the car. I don't want someone sneaking up on it and giving us a nasty surprise when we get in. I'll be ten minutes at most.'

She got out and I watched her walk to the tree. I found a tyre lever and a torch in the boot and took them with me. I climbed a muddy path beside the bridge and made my way north along the disused line to the chestnut tree I had picked more than a year before. I scraped away some earth from the shallow grave and found what I was looking for. I took it and made my way back to the car. I got in, started the engine and drove up the road to the tree.

Ruth was not there. Fear hit me and blood beat against my ears and eyes. I took the tyre lever and got out of the car. Ruth was not behind the tree. I looked around in the dark. Nothing moved; all I could hear was the hum of the car engine. I heard myself say, 'Oh Ruth,' and I began to understand what people meant when they said they were going to pieces. No part of me would work. I stood looking blankly around, not knowing what to do or think.

Ruth came hurriedly up the street and needed only one look to understand what her absence had done to me.

She said, 'I'm sorry. I noticed we had passed a phone box so I went to make that call. I'm so sorry.'

There was still the same unnerving clearness in her eyes. They had micas of light, reflections of the street lamps and the shine in the puddles on the street. I breathed out heavily and said, 'Let's go.' It's strange, but the relief felt at the return of a missing lover or brother quickly gives way to anger. I had to bite my tongue to stop myself from saying something harsh.

Ruth drove, and on the way told me that she had arranged on the telephone to stay in a flat in Barnes which belonged to a girlfriend who was now staying with her fiancé. There would be no one in the flat and we could pick up the keys from a neighbour.

It took nearly an hour to get to the flat and during that time Ruth chatted about small things, about how much she would like to give up smoking, that she wanted a new car, that the woman in Barnes, whom she had known for years, was half Turkish and had a funny-looking dog. I would have liked her to go on and on, and I began to wish I had some small thing to tell her. It reminded me of what she had said about the limitations of the life I had led. I remembered that when I had been staying in the flat in Bayswater I had gone to a bar. It had been a beautiful sunny afternoon and I was feeling thirsty. I ordered a drink and watched as a group of people came in. They sounded as if they had just finished work and were in high spirits, joking playfully with each other. A pretty young woman with auburn hair and a soft Scottish accent bumped into me and apologized. She gave me a bright smile and commented on the weather. She loved the sun, she told me, and she was going to a Greek island for her holidays. I bought her a drink and she smiled again. She was relaxed and easy. But I found myself tongue-tied; I could not think of anything to say to her.

'I work around the corner, on a magazine,' she said.

'Yes?'

'I'm the chief sub. What do you do?'

I looked blankly at her. What do I do? She was disconcerted by the obvious difficulty I had in answering so simple a question. I think she started to get nervous. I could do no more than finish my drink and hurry to leave the bar. At the door I glanced round and saw her whispering to another woman. They looked at me suspiciously over their glasses and turned away. I went home and lay on the bed. I realized I had nothing to say.

So it was with Ruth. She was happy gossiping away, but after a time it began to make me nervous. For the first time I wondered what our life together would be like once this was all over. I tried to imagine us doing ordinary things; nothing came.

She took a little time to find the street, although she had visited the flat before.

'It's a converted house. There are two front doors, side by side. One leads into the ground-floor flat, the other opens up to a stairway and the flat above – that's ours. There it is.'

I stayed out of sight while Ruth apologized to the neighbour for the lateness of her call. He was a tall young man with a professional voice and did not seem to mind. He joked good-humouredly with her before handing over the keys.

Once inside I went to the kitchen with my package and spread an old newspaper on the table. Ruth started to make some coffee.

'What is that?' she asked me.

'It's a Tupperware box.'

'What's that it's wrapped in?'

'It's called Denso Tape. Plumbers use it to keep out moisture. It's useful if you bury something in the ground that you don't want to rust.'

'Like a gun?'

I cut away the tape and opened the box. Inside was a Model 39 ·38 Smith and Wesson. Before I had buried the gun I had smeared it with grease and wrapped it in oily rags. I peeled them away and released the magazine, pulled back the slide, checked the breech then let the slide slam forward. The action was smooth. I checked the firing pin and the hammer spring; they were in good order. I thumbed the rounds out of the magazine and one by one inspected them. There was no sign of moisture or corrosion. I wiped them with a rag and, careful to leave no prints, pressed them back into the magazine. I wiped the gun over with white spirit and oiled the working parts. I put the magazine into the housing and hit it once with my palm to click it home. I checked the gun from every angle, but could not find a single rust spot.

I cleared up the rags and the newspaper and dropped them in a carrier bag, then washed my hands. Ruth sipped her coffee, observing me closely.

'What was the gun there for?'

I opened a drawer under the table and put the gun inside. I said. 'I collected it when I came to England. There was someone I was going to see. I didn't want to carry it with me, or to have it lying around the flat I was living in in case the police came, so I buried it.'

'Why there?'

'Dec. He told me he used to take a bottle of drink and sit by the old railway line and get drunk under the stars. We fixed it up that I would join him one night. He pointed the place out to me, so the next night I went along and buried the gun. The night I was due to meet him I planned to go along early, dig up the gun, clean it down, meet him, and we'd have a few drinks.'

'What happened?'

'The morning before I was due to see him the police called.'

'Would you have killed him if you hadn't been arrested?'

'Yes.'

Later that night, in bed, Ruth said, 'This is frightening me. I used to feel this way with my husband.'

'Tell me about him.'

She moved away from me and lay on her back, hands by her sides, looking up into the dark.

'I met him when I was very young. He was quite a bit older, and dangerous, like you. The men I had been going out with were so bland compared with him. I always felt I had the upper hand with them. I don't mean that to sound manipulative; it was just that they would swear they would do anything for me, and I felt, well, so what?'

She paused, looking inside her head, I supposed, at images and moments from the time she was speaking of.

She went on, 'I never knew what my husband was thinking. And I got caught up in his net. Everyone who comes in contact with him gets that feeling, as if he's using them, playing games. And they're right.'

'What do you mean?'

'That's what he does. That's his life's mission.' She stressed the last word and gave it a bitter sound. 'He has no purpose other than to manipulate.'

'But he fell in love with you?'

'I don't know that he ever did. He felt something, but I don't know what. An obsession, maybe. Passion? I don't know.'

'Why is he after Ralph?'

She turned on her side and put her arms around me and pressed her skin against mine. 'Let's not talk about it.'

'Tell me,' I said, avoiding her mouth when she came to kiss me.

She let go of me and rolled on to her back. She sighed deeply before speaking.

'Ralph needed a favour, something important. My husband did it for him and now he wants paid.'

'Money? Is that why Ralph is desperate to get to Joe Varvakis's money?'

Ruth's voice had a catch in it. 'Not money. My husband deals in souls.'

'I'm curious about something.'

'What?'

I did not want to sound like a jealous rival so I hesitated before going on, doing my best not to sound malicious. 'What are you doing with Ralph?'

She was defensive, as I had expected. 'Ralph is a very kind man.'

'I know that.'

'After I left my husband I had a few relationships. They were fairly short-lived and for the most part not very memorable. Nice enough men, but that was all. One night, it was pouring with rain, I was sitting in a restaurant by the window alone when I saw a man shuffle up outside. He didn't seem to notice anything around him. He leaned his head against the window and began to cry. It was an awful sight.'

I knew. I had seen Ralph cry in his cell in Brixton. I remembered the blind prisoner who had been attacked by the screws, and Ralph fishing through the wire to save the man's letter from the alsatian.

'He was drenched through and looked one step away from destitution. The manager of the restaurant, I suppose he thought he was a drunk or something, went out and told him to move on. When I saw his face, it just had such pain and misery on it, I don't know. He needed help. I went to him.'

'What then?'

'He was embarrassed, he insisted he was all right, he apologized for making a fool of himself, all that kind of thing. I asked him where he lived and got him a cab. I rode home with him, left him there, and a couple of days later found myself wondering about him, worrying. I went to the house.'

'Do you love him?'

'I had been living with a man who was hardly in the real world. Ralph was so sad, kind and loving. It was easy to be with him. He needed me and I couldn't say no.'

We said no more. I fell asleep and had troubled dreams. I dreamed Ruth was the auburn-haired Scottish woman in the bar. She kept asking me what I did and I had no reply. Her questions became more persistent and eventually I turned on my heels and ran away.

In the morning Ruth peered into the fridge and said, 'It's a pity there's no food here. I would have made you breakfast.'

'How long can we stay here?'

'Two weeks if we want.'

'Is anyone else likely to arrive?'

'I shouldn't think so. As far as I know this is the only set of keys apart from Sally's. Sally owns the flat.'

I checked the gun in the kitchen table. It lay in a drawer beside the knives and forks and spoons – a big, dangerous-looking, black metal block.

Ruth said something more about food. I said, 'I'll cook for you tonight.'

She looked surprised, then said, 'Okay. But I have to warn you I refuse to eat canned food. I only eat expensive food.'

'I'll get expensive cans.'

'I knew you'd be the sort to eat junk food.'

I pushed the drawer shut and said, 'I'm going to go down to the Old Bailey to see the end of Benny's trial. I'll be back about six. Will you be in?'

'Yes. I have to go out, but I'll get back for six.'

We embraced and she kissed me, an awkward, girlish kiss that touched me. I laughed and stroked her hair.

'Hey,' she shouted when I was at the door. 'I need something from you.'

'I'm interested.'

She motioned me to wait. She returned a moment later with her handbag from which she took a small notebook and a pen. 'You don't have a birth certificate, by any chance?'

'No.'

'No, I didn't think so. I'm going to get you one. We'll need it for your passport. Today, you go to one of those photo machines and get your picture taken. Now, details please. Date of birth?'

*

The spectators' gallery had three tourists, lean blond men with watery blue eyes, long faces and wispy beards. Amhurst was speaking, it was a dry summation of the prosecution case and the tourists quickly got bored and left. As they clambered noisily over the narrow benches Benny looked up at the gallery and saw me. His face broke into a broad smile and he winked.

Amhurst told the jury that the evidence would not confuse a child. The prisoner was guilty and their duty was to convict. 'The case against Morris,' he said, 'is unshakeable. It rests on two pillars: the confession and Morris's own presence

230

at the scene of the crime. These pillars are of marble, not even Samson could tear them down.' Amhurst's parting shot to the jury was that Benny was a career criminal who had been caught in the act of committing an armed robbery, and who, out of desperation, had invented a fantastic story in an effort to pull the wool over the court's eyes. Most of the jurors, I thought, looked as though they agreed with him.

When Amhurst sat down, Turridge lazily got to his feet. He was a big man, broad, with a fleshy face of the kind caricatured in prints of eighteenth-century judges. Amhurst was small and thin and had to fight to be noticed. All Turridge had to do was stand up. He began by telling the jury that his client was innocent. He said it with such force and conviction that for a moment I thought I saw the shadow of doubt cross the faces of the jurors who only moments before had seemed convinced by Amhurst.

'Members of the jury, Benjamin Morris is telling the truth,' Turridge declared. 'You know he is, because he told the truth even when it hurt him. Think back on the evidence you have heard. There were two notable occasions when the defendant told the truth when he didn't have to, when it would have been better for him to tell lies, lies that no one could have disproved. But he didn't. He told the truth even though, on the face of it, he was damaging his own case by doing so.

'You will recall that when Mr Morris gave evidence he was asked about his savings by my learned friend Mr Amhurst. The police had recovered a building society savings account passbook with £3,150 in it. Mr Morris, who, as you have heard, was signing on as unemployed since the time of his previous release from prison, was asked how he had earned the money. He gave an entirely satisfactory answer: that he had been buying and selling antique furniture. Quite wrong, of course, since he was collecting dole money. But Mr Morris is not on trial for defrauding the Department of Social Security. He was able to show that the money did not come from robbery. Mr Amhurst, you will remember, put the following question to Mr Morris.'

Here Turridge read from a notebook. 'Mr Amhurst said as follows: "Isn't that rather a large sum of money for an unemployed man to have in a savings account?" To which Mr Morris replied: "No. I told you I had been buying and selling as well. But if it helps you any more I had another account, I think it was with the Nationwide Anglia. I had another five and half grand in that one."

'Members of the jury, the police did not know about any other account. Mr Amhurst did not know about the Nationwide Anglia account. Only Mr Morris knew, and even though the prosecution was using evidence of savings against him to support its contention that he is "a career criminal", he readily told the prosecution about the other account. Members of the jury.' Turridge's voice was rising in a plea, 'That is not the answer of a man trying to hide something. It is the answer of a man putting forward the truth, relying on the truth to vindicate him.'

Turridge sipped from a glass of water and let the jury take in his point. Benny looked serious, his head slightly bowed.

'The second time,' Turridge continued, 'Mr Morris told the truth when it hurt him to do so was over the question of his previous convictions. You have already heard, several times, that defendants are under no obligation to disclose any prior convictions. Mr Morris has done so. He could have presented himself to you as though he had never been in a police station in his life. But he did not. He told you everything, running the not inconsiderable risk of frightening you, members of the jury, as Mr Amhurst no doubt hoped, into saying, "Well, he's nothing but a robber; even if he didn't do this, he probably did something else; so let's lock him up anyway." Members of the jury, from where Mr Morris stands that was a terrible risk to run, and there are many lawyers who would have strongly advised him against such a course. But he insisted, and what you got was Benjamin Morris, warts and all. It is further testimony to his honesty that he told you forthrightly about his past. Nothing was omitted.'

Turridge moved on the core of the prosecution case. 'The two pillars holding up the charge of robbery are not made of marble, as my learned friend Mr Amhurst has said, but of clay. And it wouldn't take a Samson to topple them, a child could do it.' Turridge said this with a certain weariness, the kind employed by advocates when they want to suggest that their opponent's arguments are so ridiculous as to merit nothing but scorn.

'The pillars are the alleged verbal confession and the presence of Mr Morris at the scene of the robbery. The prosecution appears to forget that of no fewer than eleven witnesses to the crime only one, Mr Keating, the security guard, has identified Mr Morris as the gunman.

'Now obviously there was a great deal of confusion at the scene, and it is only to be expected that some witnesses would get it wrong. But the question you must ask yourselves is why are ten wrong and one, Mr Keating, right?'

Turridge's voice quickened, he was driving home an easy point. 'Listen, for example, to the evidence in chief of Mrs Campbell. Mrs Campbell, you will recall, was in the car park, having left the supermarket, pushing a trolley of shopping towards her car. Mrs Campbell said, "I was about ten feet from the security van when I became aware of something going on. There were quite a few people around. I didn't realize at first what it was. Then I saw a gun. I saw two men with guns. They seemed to be pointing the guns at a man in uniform. I think he was a security guard. The first man was about thirty years old and had brownish, collar-length hair. He was over six foot tall. This man had a handgun of some sort. I do not know if it was an automatic pistol or a revolver. I do not know about guns. The second man had a bigger gun. This man had a dark coat which he had over his right shoulder. The gun seemed to be pointing up from inside the coat. He had light-coloured hair, but I can't remember what length. I think he had a fringe. I did not see his face clearly, but I seem to remember he was quite pale and I had the impression he was a little older than the other man, that is to say early to mid thirties. He was as tall as the other man, about six foot or a little more, and was of medium build."

'Let us pause there for a moment, members of the jury. Compare Mrs Campbell's description of the two gunmen with Mr Morris. Both over six feet tall. Mr Morris is five feet nine. One had "brownish, collar-length hair", the other had "light-coloured hair". Mr Morris has black hair with touches of grey. The first gunman was about thirty, the second "a little older . . . early to mid thirties". Mr Morris is forty-five.'

Turridge waited for the jury to digest the point before continuing. He read from a file before him. 'As to the events themselves, Mrs Campbell says she became very frightened. "People started to scatter. There was a lot of confusion. I heard a shot, but did not see anyone fall down. I saw the man with the pistol run off towards a car. I do not remember what kind of car but I think it was dark red or cherry-coloured."

'Members of the jury, when I asked Mrs Campbell during cross-examination if, during all the confusion, it was possible that the man carrying the shotgun could have shot an innocent passer-by, she replied, "Yes. I think it is possible." Members of the jury, that is exactly what happened. Benjamin Morris was, like Mrs Campbell, like hundreds of others that day, going about his normal everyday business, shopping in a supermarket, when he was accidentally and tragically shot during an attempted robbery. The robber dropped the gun and the dark coat which he had used to conceal the gun and made off with the other man to the getaway car.'

Turridge took the jury point by point through the rest of the evidence, citing in support of Benny's case two further eye-witnesses as well as the nurse who had treated Benny after the shot. She had originally thought the coat, which had shotgun shells in one of the pockets, had belonged to the injured man and this had appeared in one of her earlier statements. But on closer examination, Turridge emphasized, it turned out that this was merely an assumption.

She had seen the coat, which was splattered with blood, lying next to Benny, and had put it over him when he went into shock.

Forensic evidence called by the prosecution, Turridge reminded the jury, had not established one way or the other whether the wound had been self-inflicted or not: its severity – eighty per cent of the flesh on Benny's thigh had been blown away – made it impossible to pronounce on the matter with any certainty.

Although the security guard would not be convinced otherwise, Turridge conceded, ten members of the public were unable to identify Benny as the gunman, and most of their descriptions had been nothing like him. It boiled down to whether they chose to believe the security guard or the other ten people and Benny.

'Here the prosecution is outnumbered eleven to one. This pillar of the prosecution case, the presence of Mr Morris at the scene as the robber, is manifestly made of clay. It topples, members of the jury, it comes crashing down, and the police, only too aware of this, fall back on the time-honoured strategy of verballing, of inventing a confession. This is what we say happened. Two detectives, Inspector Lloyd and Detective Constable Willmott, realizing the weakness of their case, made up, invented, fabricated a confession.'

This was harder for Turridge to pursue. The officers had been good witnesses, and although Turridge had picked them up on minor discrepancies during cross-examination, they had remained adamant: Benny had made a verbal confession. When it came down to who the jury should believe on this point Benny was outnumbered, and Turridge, wanting to provide the jury with an alternative, pointed out that the interview took place five days after Benny had had his leg amputated. 'The interview took place not in a hospital, but in a police cell.' Anything Benny, still suffering the trauma of a major injury, *might* have said could not have been reliable.

At the end of his speech Turridge leaned forward to rest

on a pile of law books and files before him, and joined his hands as if in prayer. His tone changed, he became quieter, as if he was about to break bad news to a father whose son had been killed. He paused and looked away from the jury to let them know he had to find the right way of saying it. He did not want this part to sound too rehearsed.

'Sometimes, members of the jury, it takes your best friend, or your barrister, to say things about you that you would rather not have said, but which need to be said. Something happened to Benjamin Morris which has hardly been touched upon in this court. Certainly, we have not heard about it from the defendant's own lips.'

Turridge leaned forward further, pressed his palms more tightly together and breathed in deeply. 'The fact is that Benjamin Morris sustained a terrible, permanent, crippling injury. A man shot him in the leg and left him lying on the ground, where he would have bled to death had it not been for the quick thinking of a nurse, who happened to be passing. Benjamin Morris subsequently lost the leg. Members of the jury, it says something about the man on trial, here, before you, that he has not once alluded to his injury in an attempt to win your sympathy. Again, it takes your best friend or your barrister to say that his refusal to do so is the mark of a man of pride and, above all, integrity. Benjamin Morris is an honest man. He has exhibited in this court great courage and integrity. You can believe him when he says he did not do what the prosecution says he did. Benjamin Morris is an innocent man. It is your duty to acquit him.'

Turridge sat down. It was 1.10 p.m. and the judge announced that he would adjourn until 2.30 p.m. when he would begin his summing-up to the jury. We got to our feet to let the judge out. Benny waved to me from the dock before two prison officers led him down the stairs to the cells. I saw Harriet talk to Turridge but she did not look up.

Outside in the street I began to make my way towards the café when a voice from behind said, 'I wouldn't hold out much hope.'

It was Tempest. His tan had gone and the beard and pale face made me think of a man who lived behind closed curtains and only came out at night. He gave me a cracked smile that faded quickly away to reveal something harsher. His eyes were dark, anger just beneath the surface.

He said, 'I've never had hope, of any kind.'

It sounded detached and the more menacing for it. I knew hard men who used the same trick. Seanie used it. To Maxi, on the last day of his life, I had heard him say, 'We are come to ask an account of all the innocent blood that hath been shed,' his face and voice deadpan, giving nothing away. Tempest was the same, but with him it was no trick. I thought, they must have got on well, Seanie and Tempest, they were so alike in that respect. Was that why Seanie informed for Tempest? Because he recognized in him the same deadly quality?

I said nothing; I waited for whatever Tempest had planned to do or say. Eventually, in the same flat voice, he said, 'I have watched you, stalked you. I've been moving the people and things in your life. For the last six years I have been your policeman, your jailer, inside prison and out.'

'You're deluding yourself,' I said, and made to turn away. He grabbed me violently by the arm and said savagely, 'There isn't a single person close to you that I haven't touched.' His words chilled me, but I was able to stare into his face without showing what I felt. He let go of my arm and left me with the cold, sinister look of a man who believed his power was without limits.

I could not eat, and the coffee tasted only of warm milk. I sat and thought of Ruth. Tomorrow, Friday, Ralph would return. He would tell me where the money was, I would take it, and Ruth, away.

*

Ruth wore an open white shirt of mine and nothing else, and she sat before me on the floor. She drank wine from a beaker and smoked.

237

'You're late,' she smiled at me. 'I have a terrible feeling you're going to be unreliable.'

'No. Benny's jury went out this afternoon. They hadn't come to a verdict so the judge called them back at seven and sent them off to a hotel.'

She reached over to her handbag and took out an envelope. It contained a copy of my birth certificate.

I said, 'I got the passport photographs.'

'Tomorrow all you have to do is go to a post office and fill in a form. They'll issue you with a passport there and then.'

Ruth got up and went to the kitchen. She opened a cupboard above the sink and reached up for a glass. Her shirt moved up over her hips. She took a bottle of wine from the table and came back, a cigarette in the corner of her mouth, and said, 'I'm going to get you drunk.'

She poured the wine and ordered me to drink. 'Tell me what happened at the trial.'

'The prosecution and defence made their final speeches and the judge sent the jury out. It's a good sign, I suppose, that they haven't yet come to a decision. It means there must be someone on Benny's side.'

'How long will the judge give them to reach a verdict?'

'I don't know. Another day, maybe two. If they can't agree, Benny will have to be acquitted; he's already had one hung jury.'

'So he has a chance?'

'A small one.'

'Drink up.'

She filled my glass to the brim and chuckled suggestively. I lay on the floor and drank in the wine along with Ruth's sensuality. I felt happy, and told her so.

There was a knock at the door. I leapt to my feet and went to the kitchen. I took the Smith and Wesson from the table drawer and put a round into the breech, easing the slide forward to minimize the noise. I flicked the safety on and went back into the room where Ruth was pulling on a pair of trousers. I led her to a corner and whispered, 'Go to the door. Stand to one side of it, against the wall, and ask who it is. I'll be behind you, don't worry.'

Ruth nodded and started for the door. There was another knock and she stopped and turned to me. I motioned her on. When she got to the door I crouched on the floor and took aim, my sights fixed on the middle of the door about five feet up. Any shot should hit an average-sized man square in the chest.

Ruth said in a strained voice, 'Who is it?'

'A friend. I've got an important message for Kane.'

I mimed, 'Who?' and Ruth put it into words.

'He helped me bury my father,' was the reply.

21

I motioned Ruth away and waited until she was well behind me before I advanced, gun arm outstretched, to the door.

'I'm going to open this door,' I said. 'I've got a gun and if you move I will kill you.'

'You're all right. I'm not here to try anything,' the voice from the other side came back.

As quietly as I could, I turned the Yale lock and put it on the snib. I took three paces back, still aiming at the door, and said, 'Push the door slowly, it's unlocked.'

The door creaked open. A man, heavy-set with pale red hair, stood calmly on the threshold. 'I'm Seanie Smith's son,' he said earnestly. 'You don't need that.'

'Come in,' I said, lowering the gun.

He shook his head. 'You come out. What I've got to say is for you only.'

I knew he meant it. He was, I calculated, twenty years old, perhaps even younger. But he looked much older and was resolute beyond his years, a hard man like his father, used to saying no if he was asked to do something he did not want to do.

'I'll get my jacket.' I told Ruth not to worry and that I would not be long. She was anxious but not frightened.

'You're sure it's all right?' she asked.

I said yes, and she glanced at Seanie's son and nodded.

Once we were out in the street he said, 'You're keeping some funny company these days, Kane.'

The night was coming in. The air was still warm and people strolled by in shirt sleeves and summer dresses.

'What do you mean?'

'Later.'

'I didn't recognize you until yesterday,' I said, 'though I've seen you around several times. I saw you opposite my flat. You were outside the café near the Old Bailey, and I saw you on the viaduct. That was when I realized who you were.'

He said nothing and we walked on towards the river and the busy road. 'What's your interest in all this?' I asked at last.

'I'm doing what you're doing.'

'What's that?'

'Finishing something. But I need your help.'

'You'll have to tell me a little more.'

'You know who I am?'

'You're Seanie Smith's son.'

'Except my second name isn't Smith, it's Gerard Coogan. Coogan was my ma's name.'

'What help do you want from me?'

'I want Tempest. You can put him in a spot where I'll know where he'll be. I'll take care of the rest.'

'I can't do that.'

'Yes you can. With one phone call.'

'You want me to arrange a meeting, or something, with Tempest so that you can kill him?'

'Yes. Have you got something against me killing him?'

'Nothing. Why do you want to do it?'

He said, without any drama, without any emotion at all, 'He killed my father.'

It was more than a year since Seanie had been shot. It was possible that Tempest had killed him, I thought, but unlikely. The word in the jail was that it had been done by a youngster; there was a rumour that it had been his son.

Gerard continued, 'Tempest is closing in on me, and you too. He's starting to tighten the net and he's going to drag both of us in. I have to do this now.'

'I can't help you. Tempest won't come to any meeting I suggest, or if he does it will be with a dozen other cops.'

Gerard smiled and walked on. Time passed. We stopped at

a busy junction near Harmmersmith Bridge and leaned against the railings. He said, not looking at me, 'You can do it.'

'How?'

'You're keeping funny company,' he said laconically.

'So you said. What's that got to do with Tempest?'

'It's his wife you're sleeping with.'

The words made my stomach heave. The fumes of the cars and lorries tasted like poison that I wanted to retch out. I managed to fight down the feeling of sickness, but I was left feeling numb and cold.

Gerard said, 'When Tempest throws out his net he gets everything he wants. He leaves nothing to chance. He uses people. That is his gift.'

'How do you know so much about him?'

Gerard looked suddenly sad. 'I used to work for him.'

'Doing what?'

'Things that he needed done.'

'What for, money?'

'Sometimes.'

'If you worked for Tempest, why is he after you?'

'Because that's what he does when he has no more use for you. That's why he has abandoned Dec to you. Dec has been running around trying to get everyone he can think of to help him call you off, Tempest included. But Tempest doesn't care now. Dec has only one more use for him, and that is to put you where he wants you.'

'Where's that?'

'Standing over Dec's body with a gun in your hand. That's when he'll move in on you.'

'Why doesn't Tempest just shoot me down? Why waste time like this?'

'Because this is his way of doing his job and getting his kicks at the same time. It makes him think he's God.'

He turned to look straight into my eyes and said, 'You can get Tempest for me. I can get Dec for you, if you want him.'

'I can get Dec myself.'

'I'm not saying you won't. But he'll be hard to find after trying to shoot you last night.'

242

'You know about that too.'

Gerard nodded sagely. 'I advised him against it, I thought I had talked him out of it. But the stupid bastard went ahead. I could have predicted he would fuck up.'

'You're friendly with Dec?'

'I wouldn't say friendly. I was trying to get to Tempest through him, but it didn't come off. Tempest has abandoned him to his fate – you. He's waiting in the wings until you go for Dec. When you do, that's when he will have his fun. He will have seen the old unit killed one after another and he didn't have to even pull a trigger. They did it to themselves. Except for you. Then it'll be time to kill you off. After that he can go on to whatever other sick games he has set up.'

'You know where Dec is?'

'Yes. He trusts me.'

'Seanie used to say that there was no point in starting off down a road unless you go on to the end.'

'It's the kind of thing he would have said.'

'Are you carrying?' I asked Gerard.

'Yes. I've got a ·45 Colt automatic. I know you're carrying. So I think we have what it takes. Get Ruth to ring Tempest. She tells him to come and meet her at a certain place tomorrow night. You tell me. I'll arrange to bring Dec.'

'I don't know if Tempest will come.'

'If Ruth asks him he'll come. He's still in love with her. You should hear him go on about her.'

'Where?'

He gave me an address. 'Do you know Silvertown? It's in the East End. Ruth can say she's staying there, whatever, it doesn't matter. He'll come if she tells him.'

'How do I get in touch with you?'

'Tomorrow morning. You'll be going to the Old Bailey. Get the tube to St Paul's. Be there for nine o'clock. Walk up the escalator. I'll contact you.'

'Tomorrow then.'

He nodded and seemed to be about to go, but thought better of it.

243

'You know, just because I bring Dec doesn't mean you have to go through with it. Dec's a beaten docket, he's in pieces as it is. Tempest wrecked his life more than seven years ago when he turned him into a tout. Why do it?'

'Why do you want to kill Tempest?'

'I have to get out of something that happened. Killing him is the only way.'

'That's why I have to kill Dec. It's to close something down.'

Gerard nodded. He was about to go, but this time I stopped him.

'You say you want Tempest because he killed Seanie. That's not true.'

'I don't mean he pulled the trigger, but he made it happen.'

'How do you know?'

He smiled and said flatly, 'Because I pulled the trigger for him.'

As I watched him walk over the bridge I reflected on how quickly I was learning the things Ruth said I had not known. I understood how fragile is our sense of well-being, how easily undermined: better to walk around like the man fearful of the sky falling in on him than let yourself be fooled by sunshine and birdsong. Nothing good can come of life or the people in it; be suspicious, all the time, it is the only way.

I started back to the flat, slowly, with a leaden step and bitterness sliding over me like a poisonous snake. I could taste the venom on my tongue. People were looking at me strangely, I realized. I walked to the riverside and peered across into the gathering dark. My anger was giving way to self-pity, and self-pity to delusions: it wasn't true, there were explanations, it need not be the end.

I hurried back to the flat so as to hear Ruth dispel my fears. As the house came in sight my delusions suddenly vanished, and left me feeling cold and without shelter. That was when I started to think straight for the first time since Gerard had told me Ruth was Tempest's wife. The truth was that I loved her and could not give her up.

*

I knocked at the door and Ruth answered from the other side. 'Who is it?'

'It's me.'

She unlocked it and when I first caught sight of her I was struck again by the harsh clearness of her eyes. Her mouth was slightly open and I pulled her to me. I said, 'I love you with all my heart.'

She threw her arms around me. 'You were gone so long. I had no idea what was going on.'

I put a finger to her lips and said, 'No more. No more talk.' I took her hand, pressed it against my face and kissed it.

She said, 'Come with me.'

I lay on my back while she dozed beside me, on her side, her head just under the covers. Her smell was sweat-sour and smoky. I put my hand on her hips and stroked her until she came slowly awake. She blinked and put out a hand to squeeze mine, then closed her eyes.

I said, 'How do you see the future for us?'

She opened her eyes wide and said, a little startled, 'What do you mean?'

'After we get the money, how do you see the future?'

'The money won't last for ever, a couple of years. It doesn't matter, something will turn up.'

I thought about how Tempest had described his wife, a woman whose past had been spent moving from man to man, each one, for a while at least, offering her something. When that was exhausted she would move on. I thought, don't let it be true. Let Tempest be wrong. I moved on top of her. She looked so serious. I kissed her and in my kisses sought to get away to a different place. One night after the time Ruth had spent with me, when I felt completely alone, I had imagined getting into a car with her and driving and driving until all the signs of people and their things had disappeared and there was only Ruth and me. When I kissed her I dreamed of a journey to another place, where our pasts would be wiped out, where our lives would begin again, as happy lovers setting out together have a right to expect.

I heard her say softly, 'You're crying?'

'No.' I put my head in her shoulder and tried to breathe normally. 'I'm happy.'

'Kane,' she said suddenly. 'Why don't we just leave the country. I've got enough money to get us a ticket. Let's leave, forget the money. We'll drive to the airport and get the first plane we can.'

She pulled my head up and kissed my swollen eyes. 'Oh my love,' she said quickly.

She kissed me and held me, and at last she moved under me: I had never felt closer to her than I did then. I held her head in my hands and raised myself to look at her. Her eyes searched mine. Her hair was wet with my tears. She pulled herself up and kissed my eyes and licked my cheeks and nose.

I loved her asleep, watching her. She was childlike in her heavy sleep, snoring very quietly. I would have stayed awake all night to watch her like that, but tonight I had to wake her.

I kissed her and said, 'Do you like sparkling things?'

She said dreamily, 'Hmm?'

'Jewellery.'

'Hmm. I love jewellery,' she said, without opening her eyes.

'I'll buy you a wedding ring.'

She buried her head in my chest and put her arms around my waist. 'It's what I've wanted from the start.'

'When will your divorce be through?'

'Not long.'

'Are you still in touch with your husband?'

'Not really.'

'But you can get hold of him?' She did not make any answer and I prodded her. 'Can you?'

'I suppose so.'

'Good. I want you to phone him now.'

She laughed happily, but when she realized something was wrong she pulled back from me and put her hand to her hair.

'What?'

I touched her face. It felt hot and slightly puffy.

'I know who he is.'

Ruth put down the receiver. 'He'll be there,' she said in a dead voice.

'What time?'

'He can't make it before eleven.'

'Why didn't you tell me?'

She sobbed. 'I tried to. Don't you remember last night? I wanted desperately to tell you, but I was afraid of losing you.'

'What part does Ralph play in all this?'

She drew deeply on a cigarette and blew the smoke away. 'My husband, Henry, had Ralph arrested on a fraud charge. With Ralph's past – he has half a dozen convictions for fraud – it looked like he could get five years; not much to someone like you, but you can imagine how Ralph felt. Henry was ruthless. He said things like what chance did he think there was that I would wait, that he would be,' she paused, not wanting to say it, 'impotent by the time he got out, and that I would be running around screwing young men. It got to Ralph. That's not Henry's way of talking normally, but he knows how to play on people's fears.'

'Yes,' I said, 'I know that.'

'So Henry offered him a deal. He said he would arrange for Ralph to get a suspended sentence if Ralph, while he was in prison, spied on someone for him – you. He didn't expect Ralph to uncover any secrets, I don't think – Ralph's not cut out for that anyway. Henry just wanted to find out about you, keep tabs on you.'

'How much did you know about all this?'

'Henry never talked to me much about his work, what he did. It wasn't the way some men just don't talk to their wives. He did it deliberately. He adored me, you see. I don't mean he loved me a lot. He adored me, as something apart from all the sordid things he got up to. I was, I think, his lifeline to the real world, to real people and real feelings. So he had to keep it separate, and never told me much.'

'You must have known he was shot in Belfast.'

'Of course. He was away most of the time in those days. We had hardly been married, and one day I got a phone call to come down to meet a man, I forget his name, in Guildford. I went and was taken to a military hospital where they had Henry. It was after that he spoke a bit about what he was doing there. He said at least he had eliminated most of this group of men he was after. I didn't know, I swear I didn't know, that you were one of them.'

'When did you find out about that?'

'While Ralph was inside. Ralph used to tell me about it – he hated having to spy on you. He used to tell me on visits. Between us we put two and two together and it dawned on me why Henry had such an interest in you. You're the last part of a mission he feels he didn't quite complete.'

'What about the business with Joe Varvakis?'

'What about it?'

'Is that connected to any of this?'

'No. I don't think Henry knows anything about it.'

'Is the money real?'

'Yes.'

'Ruth,' I said, 'you've all been playing a game with me. Dec, Ralph, Tempest, even Seanie, and now you. I swear I have never been more confused. It makes me feel sick. I have told you what's going to happen to Tempest. I have been honest with you. Now you have to be honest with me. Do you understand?'

'Yes.'

'You have to tell me the truth.'

'Yes.'

'What do you want from me?'

Without hesitation she got to her feet and came over to me. 'Everything I've said to you about how I feel is true. If you want me, I'll do anything for you.'

I did want her. I wanted always to be with her. I had

only ever loved one other woman – Roisin, and I had let
her get away from me. I would not make the same mistake
with Ruth.

Ruth, swollen-eyed and pale, sat on the bed and watched me dress. It was half-past seven, and we had had less than two hours' sleep. I felt shaky and nauseous and was hardly able to tie my laces.

'Ralph will be back this afternoon,' Ruth said.

'Where are you meeting him?'

'I told him to come here.'

A rush of jealousy went through me and Ruth picked it up.

'There's nowhere else for him to go. It'll only be for a few hours. When you come back he'll tell you where the money is, then we can get away. You've got your birth certificate and photos?'

'Yes.'

'Have you enough money for the passport?'

'How much are they?'

'I don't know – ten pounds, maybe less.'

'Yes, I've got that.'

I fetched my leather jacket and drained the dregs of the coffee from the cup.

'I'll be back sometime this afternoon,' I said. 'You'll be here?'

'Yes.'

We had things we wanted to say to each other but were both too heavy-hearted and tear-exhausted. It was beyond me to extend even the smallest sign to her. In her face, what was there? It was so difficult to tell with Ruth; the fences she put up at times made her seem hard, too self-possessed, were it not for the passion, and the tremor in her hands I had so often seen. It made me angry that she did not trust me, that she held back some part of herself.

I said, 'I want to be the one to tell Ralph. Don't say anything until I get back.'

She nodded slowly, then said, 'You said you'd tell me who it was that tried to shoot us the other night.'

'It was Dec.'

'What are you going to do about him?'

'Don't worry. I'm going to take care of him.'

I pulled my jacket on and left. I walked to the underground station and joined a short queue at the ticket office. The woman at the top of the queue was taking a long time to write out a cheque and I searched my pockets to see if I had enough change for the machine. I held the coins in my palm and was adding them up when Ruth appeared in front of me. She wore a white raincoat and her legs were bare; people looked at her as if she had come out in her dressing-gown. I led her away from the queue.

'My love, don't leave me,' she said in a whisper. 'I sense you're going away from me, maybe that you've already gone.'

'No.' I pressed her head to my chest, but she resisted and struggled to look into my eyes.

'If you go I don't know what I'll do with this love I have for you.'

'I will never go away from you,' I said in her ear.

She hugged me tightly and we stayed like that for several minutes.

'You will love Seville and Andalucia, the orange trees and the olive groves, the sierra. There are so many things I want to show you.'

The queue had dissolved and, aware of the time, I disentangled myself and kissed her, a goodbye kiss.

'Child,' I started to say but stopped.

'What?'

I smiled, 'Nothing.'

Her arms fell hopelessly to her sides, and I went to buy my ticket. When I turned she was gone.

At nine o'clock St Paul's station was black with people

who moved on to the escalators like bottles fed along a factory conveyor belt. I could not see Gerard anywhere and I began to doubt whether he would see me.

I reached the main ticket hall and looked around, but there was no sign of him. I made my way towards the stairs to the street when I heard Gerard's voice from behind. I stopped. Commuters pushed impatiently past us.

'Did she talk to him?'

'Yes.'

'Will he be there?'

'Yes. At eleven tonight.'

Gerard considered the news for a moment. He said, 'There's no need for you to be there at that time. I'll take care of Tempest. You come at, say, half eleven. I'll keep Dec there for you. You never know, you might change your mind about what you want to do. If you're not there by midnight, I'll take it that you don't want him and I'll let him go.'

'Where is this place?' I said. 'What about noise if there are shots?'

'It's in Silvertown. You said you don't know it?'

'No. I hardly know London.'

'Ever seen pictures of Berlin after the war? That's what Silvertown looks like. The place I've picked, no one will hear anything.'

'Tempest will be suspicious.'

'I don't think so. I know him, he's fucked up about his wife. He'd go to Antarctica in his slippers if she said she would see him.'

'I'd be suspicious.'

'You're you. But don't worry. It's my problem, I'll handle it. By the time you get there Tempest will already be stiff. Goodbye.'

'Goodbye.'

'By the way, I hope your friend Benny gets a result. From what I've heard he's a good guy, one of the people.'

'Yes.'

'We don't have to see each other again,' Gerard said.

'You can disappear. Go away with Ruth. You can walk away from it.'

'I'll see you tonight.'

'So it is.'

He went in the direction of the escalators back to the platforms while I climbed the stairs to the street and made my way along Newgate Street to the Old Bailey. At the main entrance I asked what was happening in Court Fifteen and the officer, who now knew me by sight, checked through some papers on his table and told me that the jury was still out. The officer, who was friendly and helpful, added that, if I wanted, I could wait in the lobby until the jury came in.

'It could be a long wait, though,' he commiserated.

While I was deciding, Harriet came through the revolving doors. She greeted me with a smile and put her handbag and case on the officer's table. He gave it a cursory check, put it through the X-ray machine and waved her on. Harriet thanked him pleasantly and I could see the officer was warmed by her words. I had noticed before Harriet's effect on men, particularly older men. It was not exactly an unconscious charm because I was sure she was aware of it, but, I imagined, she really did not know why they responded in the way they did. She was herself, no caprice, no tricks, slightly reserved but not chilly; well dressed, fashionable in a quiet way, but making no effort to stand out. At first you hardly knew Harriet was there, but once you became aware of her presence you found yourself wondering how you could have possibly overlooked her.

She took her case from the table and asked me if I wanted a coffee in the canteen. As we walked towards the wide sweep of the staircase a thought struck me.

I said, 'I've been trying to get a visit with Benny, but I'm not an approved visitor so they won't let me in to see him. Do you know if there is anything you could do?'

Harriet nodded and said, 'Benny would love to see you. I'm sure there is someone I can talk to.' She checked her watch. 'Give them another half an hour to get settled and I'll see what I can do.'

The cafeteria contained an assortment of lawyers, young and old, breezy-looking, just another day in an office of sorts; and it contained men and women, dressed in poor people's good clothes, whose most noticeable feature was a shared distress. They were relatives, most of them, of prisoners: a few were men on bail, waiting for their cases to be called.

'Have you found another job yet?' Harriet asked.

'No.'

'I'm sorry. I can ask around if anyone knows of a job for you.'

I gave a half-laugh – she was sorry. That was just like Harriet. I liked talking to her, there was something touching and gentle about her, but also a resoluteness. I could not imagine trying to change her mind about anything.

'Have you had any trouble with the police?' she asked.

'No.'

'What about Tempest?'

'I think he's forgotten about me.'

She regarded me closely. She disbelieved me but said only, 'I doubt that.'

A voice on the tannoy summoned a defendant. I watched a lawyer gather up her things and smile encouragingly at a young man who was working hard at covering his anxiety with bravado. They exited, followed by a drawn middle-aged woman I took to be the man's mother. She lagged behind and drew furiously on a cigarette. She stubbed it into an ashtray and breathed deeply before trailing off to the court.

The tannoy buzzed again. The jury had come in in Court Fifteen, Morris.

Harriet quickly got up. 'That's us,' she said. 'I'll have to go.'

'Can I get into the gallery?'

'I think so. I have to dash.'

I had to leave the building by the main door, turn into an alley, pass a security check at a side entrance and climb several flights of stairs to get to the spectators' gallery. As usual I was the only one there. I was working my way over the narrow benches to the front when Benny emerged into the dock. He saw me and waved. I waved back and an officer behind me told me brusquely to sit down or be thrown out.

Harriet and Turridge took their places. Amhurst sat with an amused look playing on his face.

The judge entered and took his seat while the usher called in the jury. The jury box was under the spectators' gallery so I was not able to see the jurors. The judge asked them if they had come to a verdict. A voice said they had not, and that they had a question to ask.

The judge did not conceal his disappointment. The voice asked for the description of the robber given by Mrs Campbell to be read out again.

Amhurst got to his feet and offered to do so, since he had a transcript of the testimony to hand. The judge nodded and Amhurst read it out.

When he had finished, the judge turned to the jury and said, 'I hope that will assist you in your deliberations, ladies and gentlemen of the jury. It is testimony to your own thoroughness that you have returned to seek clarification on this point. If, during the course of your deliberations, you need further clarification on any matter, do not hesitate to let the usher know. I must say that it is gratifying to see you take this matter so seriously. It is proof positive of the strength of our jury system that you have spent so much time already arguing the merits and demerits of this case.

'However, some things are often simpler than they first appear. Do not be confused by smokescreens, ladies and gentlemen of the jury, for the evidence in this case is really quite straightforward. The charge against Morris is one of robbery. The prosecution has brought forward evidence of a verbal confession, contested, it is only fair to remind you, by the defence. If you accept that Morris made this confession freely it is your duty to convict. Morris denies it. Two officers of exemplary character say he confessed. The question is, whom do you believe? A man who by his own

255

admission has a long criminal past, including a conviction for manslaughter and other convictions for robbery, or two police officers. Some of you may already have come to a view on this. It is entirely a matter for you.

'If you are not satisfied as to the reliability of the confession there is the undisputed evidence of Morris's presence at the scene of the robbery. Do you believe Morris that he was the unfortunate victim of a bungled attempt by two wicked men to steal money at gunpoint from the security guard, Mr Keating? If Morris is telling the truth he deserves to be freed immediately, for he has suffered irreparable harm already. But, ladies and gentlemen of jury, you may choose to be persuaded by the evidence of Mr Keating, who identified Morris as the gunman and who withstood the most fierce questioning from Mr Turridge during cross-examination. Mr Turridge, I must emphasize, was doing no more than his duty in trying to discredit Mr Keating in the witness box. He is, after all, trying to get his client off.

'Ladies and gentlemen of the jury, the evidence, when you think about it, is really after all quite straightforward. Please retire now and continue with your deliberations.'

I had just glanced at Benny to see how he was taking the judge's remarks and turned back to the bench when I became aware of a sudden movement in the dock. Benny lunged unsteadily forward and grabbed the rail before him.

'You devious old bastard,' he shouted. 'Why don't you save time and just order them to convict me!'

The judge, with perfect grace, addressed the dock officers. 'Will you please take Morris below? If there is a doctor available, would you be so kind as to ask him to visit Morris? He's clearly overwrought.'

'I don't need a doctor, you wicked bastard!'

The judge bore the insults with dignity and was careful to let the jury see this. Benny struggled as the officers led him below.

The judge said, 'Ladies and gentlemen of the jury, you must not let this show of ill-temper in any way prejudice you against Morris. You are to consider only the evidence you have heard in this court. You must put this unfortunate display of bad manners out of your minds.'

One of the dock officers reappeared briefly, almost embarrassed, to collect Benny's crutches.

The judge smiled broadly at the jury and I heard below me the sound of people getting out of their seats and shuffling along until there was the sound of a door closing.

'How is your life?' Benny looked tired. He sat hunched forward, his puffy white face almost pressed against the glass that separated us.

'Complicated. But it's going to get straightened out tonight.'

'You think so?'

'Yes.'

'Don't you believe it. It's only in stories that lives get straightened out in one go. In real life the things that make life complicated go on for a long time, sometimes for the rest of our lives.'

'My life is made complicated by people, not things. People go away, or they die.'

'It's harder to get straightened out with people. Even if they do go away, or they die, or,' he paused, 'or you kill them, it's hard to shake them off. Unless you're some kind of mental case, you end up carrying a memory of people with you, always. You ought to know.'

'I know I can't go on like this, like my life is not my own.'

'You need your old pal out there with you, don't you?'

'I do. So why did you lose your rag and start screaming at the judge?'

Benny winked. 'I never lost my rag. That was deliberate.' He tapped the side of his head with his forefinger and said with a smart smile, 'I had it all worked out. When he started going on at me like that I thought to myself, what would an innocent man do now? This judge is telling the

257

jury to convict him, politely, but not in a very subtle way, for a crime he did not commit. An innocent man would be miffed, he would be a trifle upset, and he would say so. I had to let the jury know.'

'Well, maybe it worked.'

'Don't you worry. The reason the judge had a go at me was because of the jury's question. They wanted to hear Mrs Campbell's evidence – remember her? She was the one at the supermarket who gave descriptions of the robbers that looked nothing like me. Someone in the jury is holding out for me and the judge knows it.'

It always saddened me when Benny spoke optimistically about his chances. I changed the subject.

'Have you heard from Sheila?'

Benny waved his hand and made like it was a matter of no importance.

'She's gone. It's not a problem any more. I know the geezer she's living with. He's a good, he's a good . . .' He was having trouble getting it out.

'He's a good man?' I suggested.

He nodded. 'He's a good man – no, he's a fucking dog! When I found out who it was I couldn't believe it. But if that's what she wants . . .' He smiled, to show that everything was under control. 'How did you get down here anyway?'

'Harriet arranged it. She charmed some screw into letting me see you.'

'She's a blinder, isn't she?'

A screw tapped my shoulder and said, 'Two minutes.'

Benny said, 'Why don't you call off whatever it is you've got going tonight? Wait for me to get out. I think you need my advice.'

'I don't think so.'

'Are you going to be around this afternoon? The jury might come to their senses and give the judge the glad tidings that an innocent man is languishing in custody and should be released forthwith.'

'I can't. I've got a passport to collect and then I've got to see a man about some money.'

Benny dropped his head and sighed heavily. 'Don't do it, Kane. Wait for me.'

'It's not something that'll wait.'

'Then take care.'

'You too.'

I got back to the flat at 2 p.m., passport in hand. I rang the bell and waited for Ruth to let me in. The door opened, but it was Ralph who stood on the other side. He beamed at me and put out a hand.

He looked ill. His cheeks were too rosy for the rest of his bluish face, and his eyes were stretched as if with the effort of staying alive.

'I'm so glad to see you again, old boy.'

Ruth was not in the flat. Ralph explained, 'Ruth's had to go to get a few things. We're going to go abroad after,' he gave me a tentative look, 'after things have been settled.'

I said quickly, 'Let's get this out in the open.' I wanted to confront him now about Ruth; it was as good a time as any. Ralph eased himself into a chair, like a patient recovering from an operation.

Before I could begin, he said, his voice thick with emotion, 'I'm so ashamed.' He swallowed. He had lost weight in the year I had known him. His neck was shrinking back to the core, and his adam's apple pressed through the falling flesh. He said, 'I don't know that I could go on without you and Ruth. I'm no good any more. I have to depend on the two of you.'

He put his head in his hands and began to cry. It made me angry and I strode into the kitchen and pulled open the table drawer. The gun lay there with the cutlery. I lifted it out and pushed it into the waistband of my trousers; it fitted snugly at the small of my back. I lifted a bottle of whisky, poured a measure and brought it to Ralph.

'Take this,' I said.

He seemed to need time to recognize what I had in my hand. But he drank it down gratefully.

259

'I'm frightfully sorry, Kane. It's terribly good of you. Ruth told me on the phone that you had agreed to help us.'

'Yes. Tonight I'll get the money. All you have to do is tell me where it is.'

I flexed my shoulders; the movement made me conscious of the gun.

Ralph said, 'It's a big house in Highgate. There's a main sitting-room with two old sofas, antique. One is a three-seater, the other seats two. The three-seater is against a wall below a painting, a Gainsborough copy. Joe loves the gentry and the sporting life. The money is in a big envelope, brown. It's mostly in fifties, there are a few twenties as well, I think. The night I hid it I pulled the sofa away from the wall. It weighs a ton. God knows how I managed it. It has a cover, golden colour, very good quality, and there's a fold at the back. I stuffed the envelope into the fold and pushed the sofa back against the wall.'

'What if he's had the covers cleaned?'

'I pushed the envelope down into the join with the seating. It should still be there.'

'If the sofa's still there.'

'I don't think he'll have got rid of it.'

'If he has I can always ask him who he sold it to. That should surprise him, an armed man breaking into his house to find out who he sold his sofa to.'

Ralph managed a half-hearted laugh. 'Think of what the new owners will think when you go calling on them.'

I patted him on the shoulder and took a seat in the chair opposite him. He wiped away the last of his tears and began to collect himself. From his jacket pocket he took his wallet and picked out a photograph, which he passed across to me.

It was a black-and-white shot of Ruth in the foregound, with Ralph behind, slightly to the right. It had been taken by a professional, or by a careful amateur. Ruth was smiling; it was a genuine smile. Some strands of dark hair fell across her forehead and gave her a tousled look. Her eyes had come up pale in the half tone and the pupils were small, sharp black dots. One elbow rested on a table. It looked like a table outside a restaurant in some sunny town, and she held a hand to the side of her face. Her nails were long and painted. If I had been alone with the picture I would have wanted to drop my head, for the happiness in her face belonged to another time and place, and to another man. Ralph was a shadow in the background; he had the proud but troubled and reluctant look of a father about to relinquish his remaining hold on a beautiful daughter.

As if he had read my thoughts, Ralph said, 'People when I meet them with Ruth think she's my daughter.' He laughed sadly. 'It's an awful cliché, but it happens all the time.' He swallowed, and the adam's apple bobbed painfully in his throat. 'I can't tell you how it makes me feel. Like they're laughing at me.'

It was getting harder and harder to tell him. To change the subject I asked where the picture was taken.

'In Turkey, by a friend of Ruth's. That was the happiest time of our lives. It wasn't long after we had met. I proposed to her on the day that picture was taken. That's why I carry it with me.'

I returned the picture. I said to Ralph, 'Have you got a car?'

'Yes. It's outside.'

'It's time we took a look at Joe's house.'

'I'll leave a note for Ruth in case she comes back while we're out.'

Ralph drove. We said very little on the way. After nearly an hour, caught up in the rush-hour traffic, he told me we were in Camden and about five minutes away.

'Okay,' I said. 'Park wherever we can get a reasonable view of the house, but not too close. Does Joe know this car?'

'No. I bought this one when I got out.'

We came to a fork in the main road and turned to the left. After another minute or so Ralph made a right turn and we found ourselves in a street of houses that were large, but far from the palatial residences I had been expecting from Ralph's account. All the same, the houses had big gardens, garages and burglar alarms: this sort of area always made me nervous. It would be hard to explain what I was doing here, I thought, if I was stopped.

Ralph pulled up beside a post-box and pointed ahead.

'Do you see that house, four down on the right? That's where Joe lives.'

'Shit,' I said through my teeth.

'What's the matter?'

'I'm no burglar, and even if I was it looks like a lot of security there.'

'Only alarms. He doesn't have cameras.'

'Well, let's be thankful for small mercies.'

'How are you going to do it?'

'Assuming someone's in, I can go up to the door and knock like everyone else. They might not open up, if they're the suspicious kind. Another way is to wait until someone comes home. When they go in, I'll go in with them.'

Ralph said, 'There was a time I would have done this myself.'

'When was that?'

Ralph overlooked my sarcasm; I do not think he recognized it.

'Before the war, the Korean war.'

'Oh yes. I'd forgotten. You were an air ace, was it?'

'I was a corporal – in the catering corps. I was pretty useless. The officers frightened me, I always seemed to get into trouble, although I tried hard to please. I was always the one who stood to attention and saluted when an officer passed. All it ever got me was to be put on charges for not having my tunic buttoned right, or having a scuff on my boots. The soldiers frightened me even more than the officers, there was no pleasing them. I was no good at drill, always out of step. I lost kit, I misplaced requisition orders, I was generally hopeless with guns. I was in Korea eleven months, and I lived in terror the whole time.'

'How was it in the catering corps?'

'Safe enough – for most of the time. Until an officer from the Gloucesters, one of those immensely stupid blond young men from what they call good families, who talked about "the men" and "the men's morale", decided he needed a driver. He wanted to visit his "men", who were, in his words, "a good bunch of lads" – he wasn't even twenty-two years old; he might as well have been fourteen, it sounded such bunkum. He needed a driver to take him to our positions just below Kamak-san Hill near the Imjin River – this was April 1951. There was no one available to drive except me. I wasn't too worried because the hills south of the Imjin were supposed to be pretty impregnable, so we set off. What neither of us realized was that the Chinese were gearing up for a massive assault.'

I believed Ralph so far and I wanted to hear more. 'Go on.'

'Oh, there's not a great deal to tell. The battle started more or less as we arrived. It was complete chaos. We found a platoon of Fusiliers, Royal Northumberlands mixed in with some stray Belgians, dug in on a hillside. Everyone was in these shallow holes in the ground, hardly any cover from the Chinese machine-gun fire. We'd hear these bugles sound, the signal for the Chinese to attack. They've got a billion people in China and I think most of them were at the Imjin that day. They just swarmed across the river and over the hills.

'The fighting went on for four or five days. The Chinese didn't seem to care about casualties. They just kept coming, and there was me, expert only in the use of a potato peeler, crouching in the dirt shooting at these madmen who kept charging at us.

'At one point, I don't remember clearly, the Chinese reached a shallow trench to our right. Apparently, we organized a charge and won it back. I don't remember much about it – sometimes I think they must have made a mistake about me being on the charge. I really have no memory of it. But after it was all over, the press made a whole big thing out of it.' Ralph giggled shyly. 'I had my picture in the *Daily Express*. It wasn't just me – it was a whole group of us, all smiles, smoky black faces. But you can see me quite clearly. I got a medal.'

He stopped and said, embarrassed, 'I'm boasting.'

'No. Go on.'

He reached into a pocket and took out a small box, the size of a travelling alarm clock, and passed it to me. It contained a medal. On the back was an inscription: 'The Distinguished Service Medal, Ralph Wilson for Heroism under Fire, Imjin, Korea, April 1951.'

'The officer, by the way, survived the whole damn thing. He led the charge, of course. He was too stupid to be frightened.'

I handed the medal back and Ralph took it with a guilty smile.

'It's vanity,' he said, 'carrying this around.'

'I wonder what the officer's doing now?'

'Probably staking out a house he wants to break into.'

I managed a laugh before turning to the house. I did not like it. In the streets I was born into it was normal for people to walk up to the door and knock; often the door would not even be locked. The inhabitants of houses like these were not the kind to welcome callers. I wished Joe had settled in a council flat.

We watched the house for about an hour. I did not have a skilled burglar's imagination and I could think of no alternative to simply walking up to the door.

'Does Joe keep a dog?' I asked Ralph. 'The nasty type that bites strangers?'

'No.'

'Good. All right. We'll find you a bus stop and you can go back to the flat. I'll keep the car.'

'You don't want me to drive for you?'

'No. I'd prefer to do this alone.'

'Don't worry about a bus. I'll get a cab.'

'I'd like you to get a bus. If anything goes wrong here I don't want some cabby remembering he picked up a passenger in the area.'

Ralph nodded and started the engine. We drove about three-quarters of a mile and found a bus stop.

'Go back to the flat and wait. When I come back I'll have the money.'

'I want to thank you, Kane, for doing this.'

'I'm doing it for myself.'

'Perhaps. But you don't know how much it means to me. I have only a short time with Ruth. This will make that time special.'

'I don't think Ruth's that interested in the money, she's not that kind of woman.'

'I know. But without it I can't see a future for us. It's all I have to offer her. You see, I go empty-handed to Ruth. I'm not young, witty or very bright. I don't have anything else except this money.'

I nodded, and Ralph climbed out of the car. I moved across to the driver's seat. Ralph said, 'See you later,' and I drove off.

Love is, at bottom, a selfish act, and it leaves in its wake casualties and cripples. Ralph, already one of the walking wounded, would soon be added to their number. I drove on, feeling like a sneak-thief, but not because of anything I would do at Joe's house.

At six o'clock I tuned the car radio in to a local station, but there was no news of Benny's verdict. I drove for about two miles, parked the car in a side-street off the main road and went to look for a newsagent. I picked up the evening paper and found a coin to pay for it. I remembered that I had intended to borrow some money from Ralph but had forgotten. After paying for the paper I searched through my pockets and collected whatever change there was. Counting it in my palm I realized that all I had was £1.35p.

I went to a bar and ordered a half-pint of lager, sat down in a quiet corner and opened the paper. It had good coverage of the courts. The first report dealt with a sex attacker who preyed on single professional women and was described as a fitness fanatic. He got life with a recommendation for a minimum of fifteen years. Another story dealt with a woman who had tried unsuccessfully to murder her husband who had tormented her with stories of his many affairs. He had come home drunk and fallen asleep in an armchair. When he woke up he was 'a ball of fire'. His wife of thirty years had decided she had had enough of his ways and had emptied a can of paraffin on his lap before putting a match to him. The husband, 'a company executive', survived but with 'horrific injuries'; his wife was ordered to be detained indefinitely in a secure mental hospital.

I read the reports all the way through. I was playing a game with myself: I wanted to linger over the pages without Benny's name in the hope that all the available prison sentences would be exhausted before I got to him.

A headline read: 'Robber gets fifteen years'. A jolt went

through me. This story I could not bring myself to read. I sipped from the glass I held in a trembling hand and looked around. Two men sat on bar stools and discussed traffic congestion and share prices. The barman pored over the racing results. I looked back at my paper and to the awful headline. Even when I found the robber's name in the second paragraph I searched the rest of the text, convinced somehow it must be to do with Benny. But it was not: the robber was John Winston Douglas and he had been jailed after pleading guilty to an attempted bank robbery in Muswell Hill. I turned the page and continued to search the headlines. There was no news of Benny.

I would wait until dark before knocking on Joe's door, another three hours at least. I felt drained and dirty and would have liked a bath and a bed to sleep in. I managed to make my drink last three-quarters of an hour, and by the time I left the bar it was almost seven o'clock. I went back to check the car and, remembering my shortage of money, turned the ignition key to check the petrol. The gauge showed the tank to be less than an eighth full. I looked in the *A to Z* and found Silvertown was a long way away. I began to wonder if I would have enough petrol to get there and on to the flat in Barnes. I would just have to trust and hope for the best.

I checked for my gloves and tried them on. They were women's gloves, beige-coloured leather and tight-fitting. I had used woollen gloves in the past, but rejected them as making it difficult to keep a firm grip on the gun; driving gloves were no good either, too bulky to allow a finger into the trigger guard. The hair trigger on an automatic could easily be inadvertently activated by a glove-thickened finger. I had chosen the beige colour because they would not be noticed by most casual observers, unlike a pair of dark bulky gloves, on a summer's evening.

It was half-past seven and still light when I decided I could stand it no longer in the car. I got out, locked the door and, taking note of the street name, started to walk back in the direction of the bar.

I thought about going inside, but felt too restless. By now

I was beginning to tense, my heart was beating faster and my arms and legs ached. I decided to walk on.

The night seemed to take forever to come in. I walked and walked, occasionally looking up resentfully at the sun, as if it were a malevolent opponent dedicated to frustrating me. During the time I wandered around the streets I felt less and less that I had any choice in what I was about to do. Perhaps by convincing myself there was no alternative I was making it easier for myself to go through with it. I used to get a particular feeling just before taking part in something dangerous, an act with irrevocable consequences, and I had often heard men in jail describe something similar. It is the realization that you do not have to go through with it; there is no one forcing you; you can simply walk away.

But I had never turned back. What was it that made me go on? A belief in what I was doing? Pride, courage, cowardice? I had no such feeling that night. I felt instead a kind of desperate compulsion. It was a disease of the heart, not the kind Ralph suffered from, the kind that could only be cured by gold. It was the past, pieces of which lodged in my heart like an enemy, and could only be ripped out by violence. Roisin had said I could not shoot the past by shooting Dec. She was wrong. This was my cure, it began here, outside Joe's house, and it would end in Silvertown. Like a man determined at all costs to survive, I embraced the cure with a desperate determination.

At nine o'clock the light at last began to fade. I stopped and patted the gun wedged in my belt at the small of my back. I had first been shown a gun when I was fifteen years old by a man named Archie. He had had the softest brown eyes I had ever seen, and the cruellest mouth. He had balanced a Cold ·45 automatic in his hand and said, 'If you carry one of these make sure you're prepared to use to it. Make sure that you don't have even a moment's hesitation left in your brain. If you pull a gun on a man and you're not prepared to kill him, you'll be the one that gets stiffed.' He cocked the weapon and continued, 'If you're carrying

268

an automatic you have to have it cocked, ready to use; that's the disadvantage it has against the revolver. Remember, all it takes is a whisper on the trigger to fire it. So when you're carrying it don't put it down the front of your trousers if you want to hang on to your balls. Put it round your back.'

I had always followed Archie's advice. I touched the gun again, and its solidity gave me a feeling of confidence. Then I turned and made my way back to the car. The dark was gathering.

It took me half an hour to find the car. I got inside, turned on the radio and waited until the news summary came on. There was still no mention of Benny's case. I comforted myself with the thought that at least he had not been convicted, or so I assumed.

I started the engine, noticing the fuel gauge was hovering just above the red warning bar, and turned on to the main road. I drove slowly and irritated the drivers behind. They overtook me with angry glares and I decided to speed up to avoid attracting any further attention. I did not want someone remembering he overtook a nervous driver on the night of a shooting, should anything go wrong at Joe's house.

I found the street Ralph had shown me and drove past Joe's house. The sight of lights on inside made my pulse race. I stopped the car about a hundred yards away and cut the engine. I arranged the mirror to give me a view of the driveway to the house and settled in to watch and to let more time pass.

At ten o'clock I decided the time to move had come. I calculated that I would be in and out within ten minutes, which I hoped would leave me enough time to get to Silvertown before midnight. I turned the car in the road and drove back past the house. The street was quiet, no one in sight. The other houses were all detached, with solid-looking doors and windows. I pulled the gloves on, took out the gun, pulled back the slide to put a round in the breech, and pushed up the safety. I hoped I would not have to use it.

On the other hand, if I did, the chances were that no one would hear. I patted the gun again and got out of the car, taking the keys but leaving the door unlocked. I opened the gate to Joe's driveway.

The door was opened by a stern young man. He was quite short and thin, and I liked that. I was less happy about the snarling rottweiler that strained powerfully against the short lead the young man held in his hands. The man had dark eyes, sallow skin, curly black hair and a what-do-you-think-you-want face, but when he spoke it was softly and with a polite and friendly smile.

'Can I help you?'

I was unprepared for this openness and complete lack of suspicion. Ever since Ralph's description of the half-mad Joe and his killer henchmen I had been gearing up to the use of force and threats. I wondered if I had knocked on the right door.

'Is Joe in?' I said, with a nervous glance at the dog.

'Who's calling?'

There was just a hint of suspicion now, but there was still nothing violent or threatening in his tone. My gaze fixed on the dog. It strained on the lead and the young man's smile faded when I failed to answer.

He said, 'Yes?'

I took a half-step inside and the dog surged forward and barked just as I produced the gun. I did not check to see the young man's reaction until after the dog collapsed, its legs twitching. The young man looked at the gun, then at the dog, and said in astonishment, 'What have you done?'

I pushed into the hall and calmly closed the door behind me. 'Who else is in the house?'

'No one except me,' came a voice from further down the hall.

'Stay where you are,' I said, pointing the gun at him.

'I intend to,' he answered smoothly. 'Gary,' he said to the young man, 'are you all right?'

'Yes,' Gary replied vaguely. 'He shot the dog.'

'Which one?'

'Turandot.'

The man at the far end of the hall shook his head and said to me, 'There was really no need to do that. It's a terrible waste. The dog had a beautiful pedigree, and was really very sweet.'

I ignored him and said to Gary, 'Where's Joe Varvakis?'

Gary was pale and, I thought, possibly in shock. He did not answer, and I did not have the heart to threaten him. The other man said, 'I am Joe Varvakis. How can I help you?'

He was not at all what I had expected. He stood about five foot five or six, trim and straight. He had short, wavy dark-brown hair and fair skin. His clothes were smart casual, those of a lawyer or an accountant relaxing at home after a day in the office: grey slacks with sharp creases and a dark round-necked pullover with a blue and green pattern on the chest. His accent was regionless enough to have been that of a television newscaster.

I said, 'Let's go into the sitting-room.'

Joe shrugged. 'Which one?'

'The one with the Gainsborough copy.'

'It's not a copy.'

'Let's go.'

Gary found it hard to take his eyes off the dog so I pushed him gently towards Joe, who took hold of his arm and guided him towards a door off the hall.

We entered a large room with varnished floorboards and a dark-red Turkish rug. The Gainsborough was there, and so was the sofa Ralph had described.

Joe said, 'Do you intend to hurt us?'

'Not if I can avoid it.'

'What are you here for, then?'

'Pull the sofa out from the wall.'

'By myself?' The idea seemed to shock him.

I looked at Gary; so did Joe. We realized at once that he was unable to function.

'Sit down, Gary,' Joe said calmly. 'Nothing's going to happen.' He put a hand on Gary's shoulder and guided him to a chair. Gary, his face a blank, was oblivious of what was going on.

'This sofa?' Joe said.

'That sofa.'

Joe took hold of one end and strained. The muscles knotted in his neck. I moved round, careful to keep him at arm's length from the gun so that I would be able to kill him if he tried to lunge at me, and helped to pull.

'That's okay,' I said when the sofa was far enough out.

'Thank God for that,' said Joe, red-faced and panting.

I waved him to a chair beside Gary, and he gratefully sat down while I went to the back of the sofa.

'Do you do this often?' Joe asked.

'No.'

'I thought not. Please don't take this personally, but you don't think you might have over-reacted in the way you dealt with Turandot? I mean, since you say your primary purpose here is not to do us harm.'

I said nothing, irked by his manner. I had to bend to find the fold in the cover and it was difficult to keep the gun on Joe and Gary.

Joe said, 'What is the primary purpose of your visit?'

'You owe some money to a friend of mine.'

'I'm usually fairly prompt with my payments. To whom are you referring?'

I could not reach the fold and keep Joe covered at the same time. I said, 'Get off the chair and sit on your hands on the floor. Do it. Get Gary down there too.'

Joe grimaced. He said, 'There's really no need for this. To whom do I owe money?'

'Ralph Wilson.'

'Ralph? Ralph sent you here?' He seemed genuinely surprised. Then a look of understanding crossed his face. 'Of course.' He began to chuckle, not in a menacing way, but as if he were enjoying a joke at his own expense.

'The money from the office,' he said, still laughing.

'Get on the floor,' I told him. Instead, he got to his feet and made an expansive gesture with his arms.

'Put the gun away. Ralph can have his money. I felt really bad about what happened when Ralph got arrested. The money belongs to him.'

He seemed genuine, but I did not put the gun away. Instead, I ducked behind the sofa to get my hand into the fold. I pushed down between the seat and the high back and pulled out the envelope.

When I got to my feet Joe was standing in the same place and Gary was still looking just as blank.

'Where did you meet Ralph?' Joe asked.

'In prison.'

'And he told you about what happened?'

'Yes.'

'Why did you come in here armed, for God's sake?'

'Ralph gave me the impression you might not want to hand the money over. He thought you'd put up a fight.'

'It's Ralph's money. What did he tell you I was, some sort of gangster?'

'Yes.'

Joe rolled his eyes. I had to admit to myself that in his casual pullover and slacks he looked nothing like a gangster.

'I'm a businessman,' Joe said. It was the first word he had uttered that caused me a momentary alarm; I had heard other gangsters pleading their case with the deprecating, 'I'm only a businessman'. Instinctively, my grip tightened on the gun, but I eased it when Joe continued with a raffish smile, 'Crooked, of course. Would you care for a drink?'

'I haven't time, thanks anyway.'

'All Ralph had to do was ask. It would have saved Turandot's life.'

'I'm sorry,' I said.

'At least you didn't shoot poor Gary. You know, Ralph is not the best judge of character. He tends to panic easily. He's a little paranoid. He thinks people are after him.'

I put the gun into my belt and walked around the sofa towards the door.

'Is Gary going to be all right?'

Joe looked down at him. 'Yes. He's highly strung, but he'll be okay.'

'I thought you'd be Greek or Cypriot,' I said.

'My parents were. I went to Marlborough,' he shrugged. 'Well, for one term anyway – before I was expelled.' He smiled at the memory, and that was how I came away thinking of Joe Varvakis, as a delinquent schoolboy. I stepped over the dog and opened the door. Joe came out to the hall to see me off. As I crunched along the driveway he actually said goodbye.

A mile or so away from Joe's house I pulled over and checked the road map. It was almost half-past ten, and I had no idea how long it would take me to get to Silvertown. Gerard had said he would wait there with Dec until midnight.

I was in a good mood. I had the money and it had been no trouble to get it: more than one hundred and fifty thousand pounds. A greedy thought flashed into my mind, but I fought it down. I drove on, stopping every now and then to check the route. At a quarter past eleven I stopped again, but this time it was not to look at the map. The fuel gauge read empty, and I cursed myself for my stupidity.

I got out of the car and looked around. The street names meant nothing to me and I was not even sure what area I had reached. I walked along to a set of traffic lights at a junction and looked up and down the road. There was nothing in sight that looked like a petrol station. I plumped for taking a right turn and walked on.

After half a mile or so I spotted a yellow floodlit forecourt a little further on. I ran towards it and made my way to the cashier's cubicle. I shouted into the gap below the glass that separated us that I needed the loan of a petrol can. The man in the cubicle sighed and shrugged his shoulders.

'I can sell you one.'

'I don't have enough money.'

He was not impressed.

'It's important. Can you lend me one? I'll bring it back straight away.'

'Can't help you.' He asked me to get out of the way so he could serve the next customer.

I patted the pocket into which I had stuffed the envelope and was considering taking a note out of it when a man behind me, who had overheard the conversation, offered to lend me his can. I thanked him, he paid his bill and got me the can. I put in eighty pence-worth of petrol, all I had left, apart from the one hundred and fifty thousand, and paid the man in the cubicle. The driver offered me a lift to the car and we reached it at about ten minutes to midnight. I hurriedly poured in the petrol, using a funnel furnished by the driver.

'How far is it to Silvertown?' I asked him.

'Where exactly do you want?'

I did not want to say; another witness who might remember a man asking him directions on the night of a shooting. But, I reasoned, if I did not ask him I would never find it. I gave the name of the street I wanted. He knew it and gave me directions.

'How long will it take me to get there?'

'Quarter of an hour, maybe twenty minutes. At least there's not much traffic around this time of night.

I thanked him and he drove off. I started the engine and, as instructed, took a right at the traffic lights. The road led to a dual carriageway and I speeded up.

The area I reached was desolate. The roads had potholes and were poorly lit. There were decrepit-looking houses, some shored up at the gable end with scaffolding. But mostly the streets seemed to consist of old concrete foundations through which grasses and weeds climbed up to occupy the space vacated by the houses. There were no people around.

It was well past midnight when I found the street. On one corner there was a bricked-up bar, and opposite a corner shop that might still have been doing business, or might not; it was hard to tell. I slowed down and peered through the gloom until I found the house I was looking for. Some of its neighbours in the terrace held out forlornly against the squalor, but most had surrendered.

The house itself looked derelict, and there were no lights on. I parked the car and put the envelope under the driver's seat. I checked the gun and flicked the safety off and on. I held it against my leg as I walked to the door. The good mood I had felt coming away from Joe's house had evaporated. I was dealing with a different situation, and a different kind of men.

The door was unlocked. I opened it a fraction but could see nothing inside; I listened, but there was nothing to hear. I raised the gun and pushed the door open a fraction further: still nothing. I waited, but no noise came, no voices. I was too late. Gerard had said midnight: Tempest was already dead, and Dec and Gerard gone. I pushed the door open and stepped inside. As I did so, I felt something cold and hard at my ear, and a voice said, 'I knew you would come. Now give me the gun, slowly.'

— 24 —

Gerard sat in a high-backed armchair, hands on the rests, and even through the gloom of the half-lit room I could make out the stupid, dull look in his eyes. Dec sat on the floor in a corner, cowering, his face streaked with grime and tears.

'Take a close look at him, Kane.' Tempest's voice was brittle with excitement.

I bent before Gerard, who showed no sign of recognition. His legs were splayed at an awkward angle, lost to him. He blinked slowly and let his jaw fall. He breathed out. I took off the glove from my right hand and reached under his jacket. I was able to feel a faint heartbeat. As I took my hand away I felt something wet and sticky. I did not have to look to know it was blood.

'What age would you say Gerard Coogan was?' Tempest said, his voice high-pitched. When I turned to look at him I saw something frightening in his face, a man who knew he had gone too far, but did not care.

'I'm not interested,' I said.

Tempest raised the gun until the muzzle was level with my head. 'Fuck you, I don't care,' I said angrily.

He chuckled. Dec said, 'He's cracked. He's going to kill us both.'

Tempest sniggered like a naughty child, then smacked his head with the palm of his hand and looked around like a stage madman.

'He's fucking cracked up,' Dec half shouted.

'Humour me, Kane. Tell me what age Gerard Coogan is.' Tempest advanced a step, keeping the gun trained at my head.

'Twenty, I think.'

'He's just turned nineteen. It was his birthday three days ago.'

'So what?'

'I pride myself on knowing these things.'

I knelt in front of Gerard and felt his hands. They were cold.

'When Gerard was seventeen,' Tempest said, 'he walked up to his father in the street and shot him dead.'

'I know. I heard when I was in jail.'

'Shall I tell you how you heard in jail?' Tempest said, eager to prove a point. 'You heard because I let it be known. Do you remember a man named Seamus Crilly? I'm sure you do.'

I did remember Crilly. We had been fairly close prison friends. 'Yes,' I said.

'He was in the same block as you. He was your friend.'

'Yes.'

'He worked for me.' Tempest grinned in triumph. 'What do you think of that?'

'I don't care.'

'You don't believe me!' His tone was accusing.

'I believe you, I just don't care.'

Tempest did not like that. To seal his triumph he needed me to care. He said, 'You gave Crilly a present for his birthday. What was it?' I made no answer. He screamed, 'What was it?'

'A wallet. I made him a leather wallet with Celtic designs, a cross. I put his name on it.'

Tempest's grin widened. 'This wallet?' He tossed something at me. It landed in Gerard's lap. I picked it up and looked at the modelling. It said, 'Seamus, Long Kesh, 1988.'

'I told Crilly to spread it around that Sean Smith had been shot by his son. That's how you found out. I was the source of everything you heard and believed.'

In the corner Dec sobbed.

'You can stop playing games. Just get on with whatever you want to do,' I said. The weariness in my voice surprised me.

'Oh no! No. I like playing games, important games like this. That's what my life has been about. Of course, it wasn't easy, getting Sean Smith killed. I had to look hard to find his weak spot – Gerard. Then I had to find Gerard's weak spot. That was easy. It was his mother.'

Gerard moaned and mumbled something. I stroked his hand and looked back at Tempest. 'Don't let him die. Let me call an ambulance,' I said.

Tempest laughed, it was off-key and frightening. Gerard sighed, and I heard him whisper 'pressure' and then 'belt'. I unfastened his belt and he sighed with relief. I undid the button at the top of his trousers. Gerard pissed; the urine spread a dark patch over the inside of his right thigh.

Tempest saw it and smirked. 'That's very appropriate. Gerard knows all about piss, and shit.'

Tempest tossed something else into Gerard's lap, a colour photograph, taken with a cheap camera.

'Look at it and tell me what you see.'

I picked it up, using my gloved hand, and saw the face of a young woman, very Irish-looking, with a thin face and pointed chin, thick dark hair with glints of ginger, tied back from a high forehead. She was smiling with young, hopeful eyes.

'That's Eileen,' Tempest said, 'before Seanie knocked her up. Eileen is Gerard's mother – a sweet young thing, at least she was once.'

Tempest threw down another photograph, a Polaroid; this of a hag lying in a bed with iron steads, peeling paint on the walls behind. The old woman wore a sleeveless nylon nightie, and there were bruises on her pale skin. Her face had caved in, her eyes were sunken, all hope for the future gone.

'I took that two years ago.' The triumphant grin was back on Tempest's face. 'It's Eileen. She's still only thirty-five years old. Can you believe it? She's in an institution near Northampton. Not one of the better sort. The staff don't really bother with her that much. She smells, of piss. They don't bath her – they're not paid enough, and anyway she's too violent.'

Gerard moaned and closed his eyes. He could understand what was being said.

'Eileen started drinking heavily shortly after Gerard was born. Look at that beautiful Irish *cailin* ruined. Seanie refused to marry Eileen, who was a very devout girl, and refused to have anything to do with her or her son. Eileen came to England and brought up young Gerard here. Gerard adored his mother.'

Gerard moaned again. He tried to whisper something, but I could not make it out. I heard him try to moisten his mouth, his tongue sucked noisily.

'Poor Eileen. She became a drunk, and Gerard, almost from the time he could walk, cooked for her, cleaned for her and, when there was no money, stole for her. He picked her up when she fell down dead drunk. He wiped up her vomit and undressed her and put her to bed. And in the night, when she fouled herself, he cleaned her up.'

Tempest made his frightening laughing noise. Gerard moaned and whispered. I thought I heard it this time, he had whispered 'back'. I moved my hand around under his jacket and gently massaged the lower part of his back.

'Can you imagine that, Kane? What effect do you think that had on a twelve-year-old boy, wiping his own mother, getting her clean for another day? What do you think it does to a young man's mind? How do you think it makes him feel about his father, the man who ruined his mother?'

Tempest stretched the gun out at me. His eyes were wide and his hand trembled. I stopped rubbing Gerard's back, and that was when I felt what Gerard had wanted me to find. At first I thought it was a gun butt, and I had a sudden rush of hope. Slowly I drew it out. I felt my heart drop: it was the handle of a knife. Why couldn't it have been a gun? But I did not need much persuasion to pull it out of its sheath. I felt Gerard's eyes on me.

In the corner Dec sobbed. 'He's going to kill us, Jesus Christ, he's going to kill us.'

Tempest pointed the gun at him and Dec cringed. Tempest said, 'I'll let you kill him, Kane. That's what you came here for, wasn't it, to even things up between you and your old friend?'

'No,' I said.

Tempest frowned as if he heard something he could not quite comprehend. I could see he did not like it and I drove the point home. 'I came here to let him know that it was over. I don't want him dead.'

Tempest did not want to hear; he shook his head violently to keep the words out of his ears. He went on, changing back to something that had worked the way he had planned. 'Eileen was Gerard's weak spot. All it took was a little prompting from me.'

Tempest giggled and suddenly aimed the gun at Dec. Dec cried 'Oh no!' and buried his face in his knees, his hands clasped around the back of his neck. Tempest swung the gun away from Dec to me, then to Gerard. 'I have touched everyone close to you, Kane,' he said flatly.

There was an explosion that made my heart thump once with such force I felt I would faint. I saw the hair at the back of Gerard's head lift up, as though a blow-drier had been turned on. Gerard's head jolted to the side, forward and then back against the armchair. His right hand spasmed, closed in a tight fist, and opened slowly, like the petals of a flower. The stupid look in his eyes faded away until there was nothing there at all.

Tempest's own eyes were wide but they did not seem capable of taking anything in. He was too far from me to lunge at with the knife; all I could do was stay where I was and wait for a better chance.

Slowly Tempest came to. He said in a faint voice, almost dreamily, 'There's no one close to you that I haven't touched. Of course,' the tone suddenly changed; angry, high-pitched, 'you've touched someone close to me. Did you enjoy her?'

'Who?' I wanted to play with him; I could see it made him angry.

'Who?' he shouted. 'Ruth. My wife. Ruth Tempest. Did you enjoy her? Fucking her? What did you do to my wife?'

He stepped up and swung at me with the gun butt. The blow came unexpectedly and I was not ready to lunge with the knife. The butt struck my head and rocked me but I did not fall down. Blood began to trickle down in front of my left eye, but I was not conscious of any pain and I was able to keep my grip on the knife handle. I cursed myself for my slowness: that could prove to have been my best chance, I thought bitterly.

'He was easiest.' Tempest, pointing to Dec, continued in a voice so relaxed he might have been discussing a book he had just read. 'There he was a man faced with twenty years in prison, a man with a young wife and a family. Of course he was going to accept my offer. There was never any real challenge.' He turned to me and looked directly into my eyes, 'Kill him, Kane. Make the past right.'

I shook my head. 'Let him go. He worked for you, let him go.'

My words did not get through. 'Seanie was more interesting,' he said. 'I had Seanie arrested just on the chance that we might find out something. It wasn't intended to be anything more than a routine screening. As luck would have it he was carrying a gun, a very interesting gun. It had lots of history. I explained to Seanie some options and he accepted one, which was to go free and work for me.'

'I don't believe that,' I said. 'Seanie would never have worked for you.'

'I sent you his statement. You did read it, didn't you?'

'You faked it. All you would have needed was a typewriter. Seanie was no tout.' To me it was transparent that I was playing for time. It surprised me that Tempest took my challenge seriously and prepared to defend himself.

'But he did! Everyone has a weak spot and I can find it. Seanie was a practical man. He didn't want to go back to jail for another ten or fifteen years. I played on that practicality. I didn't try to convince him of the moral rightness of working for me – I have used that one, with results. Crilly fell for that. I didn't try to turn him against a rival or an enemy. Seanie was immune to that. What I offered him was a business deal. I would let him go if he gave me one piece of information. I knew what went through his mind when I made the offer. I knew he was at that very moment planning to pay me back.'

'What do you mean?'

'All in good time.' Tempest chuckled. 'You know what he told me, don't you? He said Kane was planning a hit and that Hugh Gallagher would be picking the weapon up from a dump. As it happened I already knew, thanks to Declan there. But it humoured me to pretend that it was useful and it meant there was no way out for Seanie: he couldn't pretend to himself later that he hadn't really told me anything I didn't already know.'

'I still don't believe it.'

Tempest's face darkened. He jabbed the gun under my nose and pressed it against my upper lip.

'Don't fool yourself. It's true. I'm not saying he was mine in the way Declan was. He wasn't weak like him.'

Suddenly from the corner Dec shouted, 'You hopeless, mad bastard. I might be weak, but at least I ain't no fucking nutcase.'

Tempest turned the gun away from me and fired. The shot went past me and I saw Dec rise and fall back against the wall before slowly slipping to the floor. The bullet had struck him in the chest and blood seeped through his shirt and jacket. He was still alive, though. I thought at first he looked surprised, but it was closer to embarrassment, as if he were saying: Excuse me, I've made this terrible mess. Tempest fired once more. Dec was thrown back again, most of the lower part of his face blown away.

I hung my head and sighed. 'Oh Christ.'

'Seanie was never mine. The minute he told me about your operation he decided to kill me. That was how he salved his conscience. And later he came very close. I still carry the scars Seanie gave me. Now do you believe me?'

'I don't care.'

'No,' he said, 'neither do I.' He dropped the gun to his side and said, 'Fuck it. I had a gift for winning people over.

I never had to try hard, it was a natural gift. I could have won you over; I nearly did. When I said I had lost my way, you knew what that meant. You have a wide streak of self-pity; you keep it carefully under wraps, but it's there and I saw it. So when I said I had lost my way, that self-pity in you rose to it like you had found a kindred lost soul. You haven't shaken off the past, you wallow in it still.'

He took a step back and I knew now that this would be my last chance. I pulled the knife clear from Gerard's jacket and lunged at Tempest. He stepped back swiftly and I lost my balance and fell heavily to the floor.

'That was my last little joke,' he said. 'I knew the knife was there and was hoping you'd go for it. You haven't disappointed me, Kane.'

He stared at me in silence. I watched as he raised the pistol. I saw his lips move and was aware of the sound of speech but it did not make any connection with my brain. His lips moved again. They said, 'You can go now.' He handed me my gun and covered me until I left the house.

I got into the car and shivered, but not from cold. With a last look at the house I started the engine, released the handbrake and let out the clutch. As I passed the bricked-up bar on the corner I heard a dull thud, more like the sound of a man falling heavily to the floor than a shot. I assumed it was both. Tempest's game had come to an end, and in his own mind he had been the winner.

As I drove away my thoughts turned with sadness to Ruth. I loved her with a passion that made me sick. Images of her, soft and vulnerable, hard and angry, yielding, self-possessed, laughing and crying, crowded in on me. From the day Ralph had shown me the holiday photograph of her in the sleeveless dark-red dress she had crept into a corner of my heart and lodged there. I thought of her when I woke up in the mornings and when I went to bed at night. I had dreams of her. I had conversations with her when she was not there, and when she was there I kissed her and laid her down beneath me and loved her. She had a magic for me.

But when I looked into the future I could see nothing for us, just my own passion for her slowly turning inwards on itself. At first it had not seemed to matter; Ruth's magic was there to dispel such fears. The last twenty-four hours had done nothing to destroy her magic, or my love for her, but they had brought me back to a place Roisin had tried to make me leave, the prison of the past. Roisin was right, again: you cannot shoot your way out of the past. The past, too, is a disease of the heart, and has no cure.

The petrol lasted, to my surprise, and I reached the flat in Barnes. It was half-past one and the night was still and warm. I found a place to park the car near the flat. I took the envelope, ripped it open and pulled out a packet of banknotes. They meant nothing to me. That was a disease I did not have. I dropped the packet back among its companions. I checked the ·38, flipping the safety off and on, then pushed it into my belt.

There were lights on in the flat. Ralph would be waiting, and Ruth. I walked quietly to the door, careful to make no noise. When I reached it I checked the inside pocket of my jacket and found what I wanted. Ruth looked beautiful. The hint of suspicion in her eyes fascinated me. She would have to look out for herself; she had had it too easy in some ways, with men who adored her. The future turns against people like that. I took a last look at the photograph and dropped into the envelope, and, as quietly as I could, pushed it through the letterbox.

I had always felt sorry for Ralph, but that did not stop me wanting to rob him of Ruth, or stealing away his memories of her. Once before, in prison, I had returned the photograph to him, and it had been as if I were giving Ruth back to him. Then I had felt vaguely guilty because I had coveted her. This time I should have felt relief, or a sense of redemption, but I didn't. I felt ten times worse.

The car did not take me far. I left it at the side of the road, it was near the river, and started walking. I crossed Hammersmith Bridge and, after checking there was no one in sight, tossed the gun into the river. A little further on I came across two young men about to get into a car.

'Which way is it to Kentish Town?' I asked them.

I could tell from their expression that the directions would be complicated. They suggested I carry on to Shepherd's Bush and ask again. One of the men noticed the bruising on my head and shifted warily, as though I were an unpredictable drunk.

'Is it far?'

'Shepherd's Bush? No.'

'Kentish Town?'

'Don't expect to arrive before morning.'

I checked my watch and saw it was a little after three. The night sky was already beginning to dissolve. The prospect of a long walk as the day was breaking did not bother me. I stopped more or less everyone I passed to check on my progress. One or two sent me off in the wrong direction; either that or I had misunderstood them. I found myself at Oxford Circus tube station just as the gates were being unlocked.

'How do I get to Kentish Town?' I asked the man at the gate.

'Central Line to Tottenham Court Road and get the Northern Line from there.'

'I mean on foot.'

He cursed at me and disappeared down some stairs.

It was shortly after eight o'clock by the time I reached Harriet's house. It was a big, ramshackle building with large windows and a small, untidy lawn. The people inside were having breakfast and the smell of coffee, eggs and toast made my stomach rumble.

Harriet was alarmed at my appearance and said she would call a doctor. I managed to dissuade her, so she sent her husband, a good-humoured, softly spoken man who gave every appearance of treating the sudden arrival at his house of a man with a badly cut forehead as nothing out of the ordinary, to search for a dressing. A lanky teenaged boy with curly red hair collected a school bag and said goodbye to Harriet. He gave me a look of mild curiosity that lasted a mere instant and was gone.

'There's someone you should meet,' Harriet said.

'I don't think so,' I said.

'I always said you were an unsociable bastard!'

Benny stood in the kitchen doorway. I got up and hugged him.

'Careful, you soppy git, you're nearly knocking me over.'

'You got a not guilty?' I said.

'Not quite,' Harriet corrected me. 'The jury came back at about four o'clock yesterday and said they couldn't agree on a verdict. The judge asked them to have one last try and sent them out again. They eventually returned at about half six and told the judge flatly that they wouldn't be able to agree. He had no choice but to enter a verdict of not guilty by virtue of Benny's earlier hung jury.'

'Truth will out! I always say that. It was my honesty that made the jury see right, or at least some of them.'

I had the impression this was an area Harriet did not want to hear too much about. Her husband, his name was Will, came in with a box of Band-aid and some cotton wool. He directed me to a cluttered bathroom and I wiped away the dried blood. The cut was more superficial than I had at first suspected and I covered it with the largest-sized plaster.

When I got back to the kitchen Harriet said she had to

get to work and that I could stay as long as I wanted. When she had gone Benny and I sat in silence for a time.

'Let's get some air,' I said.

We walked slowly along the streets around Harriet's house.

'We ain't been out on exercise for a long time,' Benny said.

'Any news about Sheila?'

'No!' he said emphaticially. 'It's all over. It's in the past, I can't waste no more time over it.'

'Sometimes you can't help yourself. It just seems to drive you on.'

Benny stopped and said in his most serious voice, 'Only if you let it. You and me have got our chance now to get free, properly free.'

'I don't know.'

'You better tell me about that cut. Has it got anything to do with what you were telling me about last night?'

I told him everything, beginning with Roisin's visit to my flat. I told him about Ruth and Ralph, about Joe and the money. I told him about Turandot the dog, and about Gerard and Dec.

He frowned in concentration.

'Do you think Tempest did himself in?'

'I heard a shot as I was driving away.'

'Why did he let you go?'

'You don't ask sane questions about insane men.'

'All the same, he was after you. I mean he spent years tracking you down.'

'I don't think he ever wanted to kill me. Roisin thought he did, but he didn't. What he wanted was to have control, except that meant nothing unless he could display it to someone, someone who had a delusion of control himself.'

Benny nodded.

'Whatever way you look at it, he won,' I said.

'No. You're still alive, and now you have a chance.'

I did not answer and we walked on until we found a bench by a corner on the main road. It was made of metal and painted red.

'What the fuck is wrong with wood?' Benny complained. 'I mean, I've been parking my arse on wood all my natural life, plastic sometimes when there was no choice – but this is outrageous. I'm going to write a letter.'

We sat and watched the traffic go by. After a while Benny said, 'I think what you did about the money was right. I owe you an apology. There was a time when I thought you might be tempted.'

'Don't apologize. I was tempted.'

'Money ain't the way out. It traps people worse than what they already are, just in different ways.'

He was quiet for a time and then asked, 'Is there anything to tie you to the house?'

'I had to take my gloves off but the only thing I touched that I could have left a print on was the knife.'

'It's not the best thing in the world to leave a print on, specially with three corpses in the room.'

'It had one of those handles like rope. I don't think they'll be able to lift anything off it.'

'What about door handles, things like that?'

'Nothing. I was very careful. I took the gloves with me when I left and I'll burn these clothes as soon as I can get a change. I'm pretty sure no one saw me entering or leaving.'

'What about the car?'

'It was a fairly ordinary car, a dark saloon. It's possible someone noticed it, but there's no reason for them to have noted down the number or anything like that. Even if they did, it wasn't my car and there will be no prints of mine on it.'

'They could trace it to you through Ralph, if he talks.'

'Ralph's leaving the country. He may already be at the airport.'

Benny lapsed back into silence, still looking worried. At last he said, 'There ain't been anything on the news about it yet. Maybe they ain't found the bodies. Well, I suppose you didn't actually do anything illegal in the house. So even if they somehow link you to it they wouldn't be able to make any charges stick.'

'I'm clear of it.'

'What are we going to do now?'

I nudged Benny in the ribs and he giggled.

'What?'

I said, 'You've been holding out on me.'

'What do you mean?'

'You're loaded. Two building society accounts.'

'A man has got to put a little away for a rainy day.'

After a bath and a shave I decided I looked respectable enough to travel. Benny was on the phone arranging train and ferry tickets while Will made toast and coffee. When Benny hung up he said gleefully, 'We got to be at Victoria at five.'

'How long does it take?'

'Altogether about eight hours. You going to be all right?'

'No problem.'

We watched the television news at one o'clock. An airliner had crashed somewhere, killing a couple of hundred people, and most of the bulletin was taken up with footage of the disaster. A politician's speech was briefly mentioned, but there was nothing about a shooting in Silvertown. Benny gave me a quizzical look. Will left the room. I said, 'I don't like staying here any longer than we have to. I know I'm not wanted by the police, but all the same I don't want to land Harriet in anything.'

'You're right. I've got everything I need, building society passbooks included. Let's get going.'

We said goodbye to Will and he wished us well. We caught a taxi. Benny gave our destination as Victoria, but asked the cabby to look out for a branch of the Nationwide Anglia or the Woolwich.

'We got to find one, or you won't get your fare,' Benny said a few minutes later, after deciding the driver was not putting sufficient effort into it. The cabby grinned unpleasantly.

'There are some really stupid dogs in the world, ain't there?' Benny said.

Near Holborn the cabby pulled up and said gruffly, 'There's one.'

Benny clambered out. 'Stay here, my man, I won't be a minute.'

He was gone at least half an hour and by the time he returned the driver was beside himself. I doubted if Benny noticed. 'Victoria,' he said brusquely. To me, he said in a voice filled with outrage, 'The cozzers had been on to them. That was the reason I took so long. You'd think it wasn't my money, the way they was going on. In the end I practically had to threaten them to let me have me own money. What is this sodding country coming to?'

We passed a newspaper stand and Benny ordered the cabby to stop. 'Hop out and let's see what sort of shape the world finds itself in today.'

I bought a paper and jumped back into the taxi. Three-quarters of the front page was taken up with the wrecked fuselage of a jumbo jet, and inside there were more pictures of wreckage and blanket-covered bodies. We searched the paper, but there was still no mention of any shooting.

At Victoria we paid off the taxi and I joined a queue to buy our tickets. We made for a bar and killed time.

On the train to the coast Benny said, 'What do you think?'

'About what?'

'What we're doing.'

'What are we doing?'

'Escaping.'

'No,' I shook my head, 'we're just running.'

'It's more than that, you'll see.'

The train got in twenty minutes late and it was a long walk to the embarkation point. I took what little luggage we carried, but Benny could only move so fast. We were the last passengers to get through customs and by the time we were on board Benny was exhausted. He found a seat and told me he hoped with all his heart he had misread the timetable and that the journey would only last ten minutes.

Kids screamed, old ladies complained about the price and quality of the sandwiches, young men spilled beer from plastic cups. There were long queues outside the toilets. I left Benny and went on deck.

The sky was darkening and there was a strong wind. The cold made my ears ache, but it cleared the deck of the holidaymakers. I looked out to sea and tried to think of Ruth. Somehow now the only image that would come into my mind was that of her standing beside Ralph the night they called at my door. I tried to remove Ralph from the picture, but he was too stubborn to go. Like me, Ruth had a past that still had hold of part of her heart. Perhaps that hold would slip as time went by. Then maybe we could try again. But then, perhaps the past would tighten its hold and strangle us both.

Benny's optimism, his childlike exuberance, touched me; it always had. Here we were on a boat with no destination in mind. For him it was a planned escape to begin a new and better life. For me it still amounted to no more than running away.

A man at the other end of the deck battled against the wind. It was Benny. In one hand he held a crutch, in the other a rolled-up newspaper. When he was ten yards away I caught the look of alarm in his face. He came on and extended the hand with the paper.

'Read.'

It was folded on page four. There was a portrait-shaped photograph of a semi-derelict house. The caption gave the address, a street in Silvertown, 'where the killings took place in the early hours of the morning'.

I read the first paragraph and looked up at Benny, who simply stared. I re-read it, but nothing had changed. I read on. The report said the bodies of two men were found in a deserted house in Silvertown. The men had both been shot sometime within the previous twenty-four hours, but no one in the area recalled having heard anything suspicious. Police went to the address after a telephone tip-off. The dead men were named as Gerard Sean Coogan, aged nineteen, and Declan Patrick Mulholland, aged thirty-four.

There was no mention of Henry Tempest.